To Plough Van Dieman's Land

Kev Richardson

A Wings ePress, Inc.
Historical Novel

Wings ePress, Inc.

Edited by: Karen Babcock
Copy Edited by: Jeanne R. Smith
Senior Editor: Leslie Hodges
Executive Editor: Marilyn Kapp

All rights reserved

Wings ePress Books
www.wingsepress.com

ISBN-13: 978-1-59705-700-4

Published In the United States Of America

Wings ePress Inc.
3000 N. Rock Road
Newton, KS 67114

What They Are Saying About
To Plough Van Dieman's Land

Acclaimed historical writer Kev Richardson, continues his personal introduction to Australia's famed Letitia Munro, her eleven children, and their extensive families during their convict beginnings in Van Diemen's Land. In her strength and foresight Titia wondered, "Does it really matter that we all came as convict stock?" ... but to some of them, it did.

Kev Richardson has a way of introducing the reader to each of Letitia Munro's family members, making the history in the late 1700s and early 1800s come alive.

Eventually the names of England's uncompromising penal colonies in *"New South Wales"*... and *"Van Diemen's Land"* were changed in an effort to hide the social guilt of inhumane suffering, starvation, deliberate brutalities, and unpardonable cruelties dealt against the prisoners, whose misdeeds were often only 'crimes of desperation,' simply to survive the hard times. However, it was these beginning years that established the convicts' loyal code against their captors, formulating the heritage of 'bonded relationships' of today's population.

Men were paired with eleven- and twelve-year-old girls, to populate this new land under devastating conditions, often being uprooted and moved to new locations when England was at war with the French. Because owning property became a step toward respectability, many convicts became docile in order to receive these granted farm lands. Even then, they fought to make ends meet. They struggled to grow crops, and raise stock... hogs and sheep, while surviving draught, range fires, taxes, bigotry, and illiteracy.

Still others were continually in trouble with the law because they couldn't give up their scallywag ways. Adam Newitt, a cobbler by trade, was such a man. So, throughout the years, each generation faced its own hardships, yet was determined to be known as trustworthy and respectable.

I highly recommend Kev Richardson's historical tales. He brings history to life.

JoEllen Conger
Conger Book Reviews, USA

This fiction was inspired by the roles played in the founding of Australia by

Sarah Goodwin, daughter of First Fleet convicts
William Woolley, convict (*Calcutta* 1803)
Benjamin Briscoe, convict (*Calcutta* 1803)
Mary Rohan, convict (*Canada* 1817)
Mark Ashby Bunker, convict (*Lady Castlereagh* 1818)
Adam Newitt, convict (*Asia 5* 1827)

Preface

Dear Readers,

An historian writing about real people of the past finds, recorded in archives, some dates and places pointing the directions of his characters' lives.. Yet when the characters were illiterate, as were the majority when talking of Australian history prior to the nineteenth century, they wrote no diaries, no correspondence to give insight into what sort of people they really were—were on the 'insides,' that is. We can only cogitate, hypothesise, on how they thought about what was happening in their world, about the how and why they were drawn into the situations in their lives, recorded as 'events.'

All we in fact know about them are these 'events,' because prison records were maintained on every convict as well as many once emancipated, and many such records survive; so to now write a tale honouring them and their achievements, the parts they played in creating true history, we must suffer the guilt of making assumptions on their personalities, loves, hates and goals.

We know only some of the things they *did*, yet realise that there were many emotions attached to the little, unrecorded things, minor events that never reached the record books.

History affirms that the white Australian civilization was spawned as the world's biggest prison, created to relieve the pressure of overcrowded gaols in Britain. The authorities of the day despatched in chains pickpockets, thieves, forgers, and other petty criminals over a period of eighty years. Such was the beginning of the history of the white Australian civilisation.

Letitia Munro, first in this trilogy of an Australian family's heritage, told the true story of pioneers casting off shackles, fear and insecurity to develop a unique culture, pioneers who were, in the main, illiterate and penniless; yet each made indisputable contribution to the Australian ethos. Titia was typical of those whose genes created over several generations in Sydney Cove, Norfolk Island and Van Diemen's Land a family inheriting the intrinsic peculiarities born of the convict desperation to claw their ways out of hopelessness, grasp chance and create opportunity.

Convicts were accompanied to the shore at Botany Bay by only military guards and prison administrators, and all struggled to survive with their very lives as they quickly ran out of food as well as finding themselves at war with the displaced Aborigines.

None realised that their efforts to cope were laying the foundations of a unique ethos inherited by the Australians of today.

Australia's convict forebear was essentially British in culture, staunchly British in allegiance, yet the axiomatic sense of freedom in his descendants was inherited not from British freedom but from British oppression. It was the very ignominy of servitude that cast his blood-and-guts dignity and bred in him his irrefragable support for the underdog. The very essence of the convict system developed his flippant attitude to the conventions of class distinction, so he learned early to derisively snap fingers at those standards—in fact to all forms of authority. And the 'stick up for your mates' syndrome was obvious from the start, for when the founding colony at Sydney Cove was but six months old, Governor Phillip on 24th July 1788 wrote in dispatches:

> *I note most of our Thiefs (sic) escape detection. The*
> *Convicts stand by one another, and even the offer of*

a really tempting Reward—a bag of flour or even a Pardon—will not induce them to give a fellow away.

Convicts were generally illiterate vagabonds who even once arrived in the colony were denied formal education through several generations. In 1810 Governor Macquarie, reporting on the combined colonies, wrote:

....not only are nine tenths of the population either convicts, those who have been convicts, or are the offspring of convicts, but illiteracy among all is practicaly (sic) universal.

Yet these 'vagabonds' became leaders by example in establishing the cultural trends of Australian society. Convicts emerged from their world of oppression and intimidation establishing traits of self-reliance, doggedness, and obstinacy of purpose, essential ingredients in creating a culture of initiative and stubborn resolve. In fostering friendships, pursuing ambition, rearing children, they unwittingly established social standards suited to their unique circumstance.

Convict attitudes and demeanour, influenced more by whips and chains than by examples set for them, were perforce overt, their opinions forthright and even blunt, traits adopted by their children.

In *To Plough Van Diemen's Land* and *The Terrible Truths*, second and third works in the series, you are led through the following generations, the children of convicts—'the Currency' as they were called—who found that, as society values changed, the sins of parents became beholden on them.

Having grown up in the shadow of the gibbet, within sight of triangle, the lash, treadwheel and chain gangs, none escaped the realisation that they were of a convict colony. The impact of convictism in a world jaundiced by prejudice had marked influence on their upbringing; yet each remained unaware that his world was unique.

The day arrived, however, when a different dawn greeted their attitude to daily life. When the greater world made a change, about-faced, declared the convict system a mistake, that it be scrapped, that the world of children in turn would no longer be a prison of punishment around which their lives revolve, they found themselves exposed to argument decrying the system that for all their lives had been savagely forced upon them.

Parents realised that their children's world would be one of different attitudes, that the 'normality' of society would henceforth cloud their forebears in stigma, that people must emerge from the convict world of confinement, class consciousness and total subjugation into one of liberty, equality and free expression to face the challenge of preparing the next generation to cope.

A challenge indeed.

~ * ~

License has been used in respect of assigning personalities to the characters... yet, even so, these have been assessed relative to recorded incidents in their lives. There is nothing to suggest that the sum total of the fortunes and misfortunes of the convicts and their children presented in these tales were unique. Their stories are broadly typical of the 162,000 convicts transported to Australian shores 1788 through 1868 to found a nation, a culture and a unique heritage.

~ * ~

There are many I would like to thank for their significant help in filling the gaps in archival records, but in particular, were Olwen Bignell, Margaret Broadby, Yvonne Englert, Valerie Greenhalgh, Barbara Kolle, Allan Newitt, Barbara Roulston, Cheryl Timbury, June Tobin FGSV, and Peter Woolley who shared knowledge won from dedicated research.

There are also published authors of Australian histories, Dr. Portia Robinson, Marjorie Tipping, and Reg Wright, who gave not only help but personal encouragement.

Early research assistance was readily forthcoming from Les Brown (local historian, Norfolk Island), Ian Pearce (State Archivist, Tasmania) and Frances Brown (Latrobe Librarian, Melbourne).

And last, but certainly not least, was the contribution of *The First Fleet Fellowship* and *Descendants of Convicts Inc.* members who gave freely of their wealth of knowledge.

~ * ~

Following, let me lead you along the paths travelled by Titia Munro's children and other convicts they met in the course of their lives, those who joined them to further develop Titia's long line of family. You will discover how each, in turn, contributes to earning for today's Australians those unique characteristics of sticking up for their mates, always rooting for the underdog and ever ensuring a hospitable welcome—all the while illustrating unabashed brashness and basic forthrightness.

Sincerely, *Kev Richardson*

To Plough Van Diemen's Land

BOOK 1

The Men and Their Women

> *The very day we landed*
> *Upon the fatal shore,*
> *The planters stood around us,*
> *Full twenty score or more;*
> *They ranked us up like horses*
> *And sold us out of hand,*
> *They roped us to the plough, brave boys,*
> *To plough Van Diemen's Land*

—convict ballad c1825

One

For William Woolley (c1781-1844):

> *Myself when young did eagerly frequent*
> *Doctor and Saint, and heard great Argument*
> *About it and about; but evermore*
> *Came out by the same Door as in I went.*

Rubáiyát of Omar Khayyam — XXVII

Salisbury, England, 11 March 1802
"Stop, thief!"
Oh, can I make that door before someone stops me?
His eyes swept across what stood between him and freedom, his mind calculating his chance of making it before the trap sprung.
It all depends on those two burly ones. But might they, too, be shavers? Themselves out of work and on the nick? Oh, why has it all gone so terribly wrong?
Will Woolley had rehearsed it over and over. For three days he and Gus had practised on each other. They had sworn, despite more hungry each day, that they wouldn't take to the streets until having it

perfect. Too many mates had gone off half-cocked, made a botch of picking a pocket deftly enough to then clear out before it was realised.

Every shaver knew that these days getting caught meant transportation, but Will reckoned he'd by now become adept enough to 'give it a go.'

Hunger had forced it on him.

Mastering such an art had become the life of many a lad tossed into the gutter to starve once the truce was struck, the army shedding numbers to save costs until a proper peace with France was secured. All too quickly they discovered there weren't enough jobs to go around. The Salisbury barracks were flushed out with no more consideration given the men than the military hardware jettisoned or mothballed.

"A man might as well have got himself blown to bits by artillery as fighting to bloody stay alive," they now reckoned.

Lifting that purse looked so bloody easy, a job practised over and over until three times in a row, I got it from Gus's pocket without him feeling it.

But the burly ones sitting over their ales by the door proved both unlucky for Will as well as quick. They saw him making his dash, grasping the purse as if it were full of gold, guessing in the instant what had happened—and that a reward would be in the offing.

It was not a full purse, Will realised even as he hurtled for the door, but heavy enough to promise food and ale for a time.

He was strong, healthy and twenty-two, but neither agile enough nor strong enough to best two burly ones. They had him on the floor in a trice and held him while others called the watch. And it came quickly, to clap irons to his wrists and ankles. They let him up then, just in time to see the gent he had robbed, his purse regained, untie it and count out a shilling for each hero.

At the 1802 Wiltshire Lent Assizes, Will was charged with, at St. Thomas' Inn, Salisbury, stealing a purse, value sixpence, containing seven guineas in coin, property of John Charles Esquire.

He was found guilty and sentenced to seven years transportation.

~ * ~

Having to wait on the hulks had him worried far more than being sent across the seas.

Life on the hulks, hearsay has it, is hard labour indeed.

Army life had conditioned him to being sent here, there, or wherever others decided, and as he had no firm roots, transportation didn't loom too big a penalty. It was the seven years and the hard labour that promised worse prospects than location.

Will was literate to a degree, had had access to learning as a youth in Shropshire's Crunbury, enough to enable him to read a work order, understand specifications, and measure up lumber for ramparts, bridges and such. The corps had partnered him with Gus Morris, with whom a strong friendship developed, one to continue after demobilisation.

Will had heard tales of lags sent to Botany Bay, who, once having served their sentences, were given grants of land to start farming. So if a man had the stamina to suffer seven years of servitude, he had more of a chance to make a go of a life in the antipodes than, without connections, a hope of finding such in England.

The hulks, however, where a lag was held until his turn for being shipped arrived, were known as 'Gomorrahs' of torture.

Prison hulks were ships too old for journeying, stripped of masts and rigging, with cabins erected on deck for cooking or laundry or barracks for guards, the entire below-decks slung with hammocks for prisoners. Every day the convicts were rowed ashore in chains, to work as government labourers, usually to build wharves or dredge waterways.

Will wasn't afraid of hard work, but the living conditions were not only degrading but dangerous, with typhus and cholera regularly cutting swathes through convict numbers. Even the healthiest man, in such situations, was as much at risk as the most sickly.

"One man in every four in the Langston Hulks dies, they reckon, Will, but that's still better'n on the Thames where it's one in three. I'm as worried as you, mate, about this stretch of our bloody journey."

That had been the summation of his new mate, Davie Gibson, as they stood in the supper queue on their first day.

Davie was a stonemason who worked with Will on repairs to Fort Cumberland. It had been built some fifty years ago to protect Portsmouth harbour, and much of its timbers were rotting.

Result of bad workmanship in the first place, Will quickly realised.

Davie was a broad-tongued Scot with a riot of hair atop his head, the reddest shade of ginger Will had ever seen.

"Told 'em I was a stonemason, Will. I'd had the word dropped that life on the *Portland* Hulk is better than on any other. And hopefully, mate, by the time they realise I don't know which hand to hold the bloody chisel in, it'll be time to ship out."

Davie was a tad older than Will, but whilst Will's inclination was to talk little, 'think much but say little' having been his motto for years, Davie was a talker, full of bombast on how he believed in doing everything on a grand scale.

"Never think in halves, mate," he boasted on their first meeting.

And indeed on a grand scale was the robbery to land him in chains. He bailed up a jewellery salesman to steal his entire portmanteau with several gold watches, coin and banknotes, all to the value of sixty pounds—enough to win Davie a life sentence.

"The Red-haired Rascal is what they call me," the Scot proudly insisted.

And maybe for reason of the oft-quoted adage that opposites attract, Will and Davie struck up, if not a friendship, at least an understanding. Each realised the necessity of such in the life allowed prisoners on the hulks. Sharing light-heartedness, however defensive, was far better than commiserating one's plight alone. Both were army discards, conscious of the value of friendship in ranks.

And after a month of hulk life, just when Will was beginning to wonder how long he could keep up his brave face in respect of not only the unwholesome and insufficient food, but victimisation from guards, no matter how servile one was prepared to be...

...and I am bloody prepared to be servile, having seen how mates illustrating foolish bravado, are treated...

...an addition to their present ranks arrived. It was one to surprise Will no end, yet one to offer both amusement and pleasure. It was his very own partner in crime, Gus Morris.

"Didn't take you bloody long to slip up once parted from my good influence, mate," Will greeted him.

And Gus, it was quickly clear to see, had been having little better of food and treatment, despite free, than had Will.

"Wondering if I might meet up with you here, Will. And I'm glad I have. Better that I've got a mate again, than finding you'd already been shipped. I made the same slip as you, mate, not careful enough. Nicked clobber from the guv wot had given me a day's work. Seven years they give me mate, same as you."

"Well, welcome you are, Gus. And this is my mate, Davie. Another sawyer they've made him since he proved so hopeless a mason. The three of us will likely be working together."

"But not for long, Will m'boy. You know me. Can't abide chains, mate, so they'll not confine Augustus Morris for long. Turn their eyes off me for a minute, and I'll be off."

"The army took your age into account for that bolt, Gus. If you'd been more than your tender eighteen years, they'd have cashiered you instead of just chaining you for three months. But you won't find bolting as easy here. Always chained when ashore, we are, and the guards here aren't like the army—they'll shoot to kill if you try a bolt."

"Well, if you are to bolt, mate, let me know, and I'll go with yer. They'll not hold the Red-haired Rascal either."

Fearless, both my mates are, fearless but bloody foolish!

In one sense he envied men their determination to test the system, yet could see that earning extra punishment was only foolhardy. Gus had really suffered, Will knew, during his three months in army chains. There had never been much flesh on Gus; he was tall, of gangly build, and exceedingly lean at the best of times, let alone having been on a starvation diet as well as in chains. Before even the first month was up, the irons had cut deeply, near into the bone...

...Yet here he is, determined to again try a bolt.

However, the system on the Hulk *Portland,* perfected over years in preventing escapes, kept Gus and Davie, during the next month, ever alert for a chance.

But finding no opportunity, Gus decided on a sudden inspiration to create one.

"There wasn't a chance to get you in on it, Davie," he later apologised.

Only an hour later it was, after his bolt, that he was apologising, because it had been a foolish decision that had had no chance of succeeding. He had been taken by his guard away from the work party ashore, into the scrub where he could let down his breeches to poop. As soon as Gus saw the guard turn his back to light a smoke, he hastened to finish what he was about and, instead of letting the guard know he was finished, pulled up his breeches and hightailed it into the scrub, the noise of him lumbering through the bracken alerting the guard.

"A bolt!" shouted the guard, a signal to always bring other guards running, each and every one pulling his ready-primed pistol from his belt, calling to Gus to 'stand to' or be shot.

And a mild Gus surrendered meekly.

"Realised straight off, mates, that the direction I ran in led only to water's edge and that I had nowhere to go except back towards them."

"To bolt proper," admonished Davie, "it's got to be planned proper."

So Gus found himself in chains again, day and night. He was sentenced to wear them for a year.

And it was only a handful of days later, in the supper queue for their ox-head soup with a scoop of dried beans and fistful of bread, that Gus whispered:

"My guard said there's a ship in 'arbour waitin' to take us off to Botany Bay."

"Be more than one ship, then," Davie asserted. "I heard that no ship can depart alone for Botany Bay. Should the truce collapse, a lone ship on the high seas is in mortal danger."

"Well, maybe there's more, Davie, but he said 'a ship.'"

"If we have to board ship, Gus, you'll maybe get your chains off."

"If not, Will, then I'll wear 'em with pride. You just see if I don't."

Will wagged his head.

But one has to admit that the crazy Gus faces his burdens full on. Even pride, there is, in the way he wears his bloody irons. Important to Gus, it is, that every lag and every guard admires his spirit even if not his lack of common bloody sense!

Will had long ago vowed to avoid being sucked into Gus's bravado, and particularly now with him under extra punishment.

Will would ever remain careful to refrain from submitting to foolhardiness, no matter what his mates did.

Two

For Sarah Goodwin (1791-1871):

> *There was a Door to which I found no Key:*
> *There was a Veil past which I could not see:*
> *Some little Talk awhile of Me and Thee*
> *There seemed—and then no more of Thee and Me.*

> *Rubáiyát of Omar Khayyam — XXXII*

Ten is the perfect age, I reckon, between being a child and being a Miss.

Right now she was full of excitement because of the coming party.

And with Christmas quickly following her birthday, it was her favourite time of year.

She was in her tree, trying to ignore her ma calling her.

Sarah hated housework and was glad she wasn't the oldest.

It would then be my chore to fetch water—and carrying heavy pails is the hardest of all work on the farm. Not as if Ma's calling because a friend arrived—I can see every-which-way from here, and no one has come. So it's a chore of some sort. Maybe to mind the littlies?

Watching over the toddlers often fell to Sarah when her ma was bulging.

And this time, Pa is again hoping it will be another boy. But Mary's in the house; she can help out.

Sarah could see the boys across the creek cleaning troughs. Uncle Willie and Pa were thatching new sties. Her pa had the biggest piggery on all Norfolk Island.

It's good getting past the stage of no longer being a littlie, except when second in the family. Mary's twelve now, but we both get the worst of things, especially since moving.

"That lot is a bargain," her pa had told Uncle Ed Garth, "too good not to take advantage of."

Sarah hadn't been sure what that had all been about, only that they left the big farm where she grew up and moved here when Ma was big with Meg.

"The bigger house is necessary," Ma told them, "with the family soon to be nine."

Ma seems always in the family way. "You keep havin' girls, Letty," Pa had said after Meg was born—*always calls her Letty, he does, when everyone else calls her Titia. Letitia is her name really. And Pa was only joking, just letting Ma know that boys grow up to be more help.*

Her Uncle Willie lived with them, though slept in the barn. He wasn't her real uncle. She had come to realise that many of her parents' friends who she called Aunty and Uncle weren't really related.

"It's simply that these are such close and dear friends, they seem like family," she'd been told. And Uncle Willy had worked for her pa since before Sarah was even born—and living on the farm with them, she reckoned, certainly made him part of the family.

She liked Uncle Willie. He found time to sit with her as she'd grown, telling stories. Pa and Ma, with the growing farm on the one hand and the growing family on the other, seemed always with too many other things on their minds.

"Worked for yer pa since he got his first grant, lassie. Mostly rock it was, that Creswell Point lot. Awful hard work me and yer pa put in on it. Weren't sorry when he quit that one, you can be sure."

Pa calls him 'an old rogue of a lag,' but always said with a laugh. He's one who always makes convict stories sound funny when most people shake heads and close up about that part of their lives.

"Seven years for eight penny-worth," Uncle Willie had said. "More than a penny a year is wot I paid back."

And I remember, when little, wondering who it was that collected his penny every year.

"Come on a big ship, I did. You remember when your pa took yer on a ship to Sydney Town? Sydney Town on the mainland?"

Sarah had vague memories of billowing sails reaching into the sky. Her ma often talked about Aunt Ann, who came with her from England. They once journeyed back to the mainland on a visit. She had always been vague about the details, remembering only a big town with many people, certainly more than lived on Norfolk. And she certainly remembered kookaburras. Never would she forget their happy laugh echoing through the forests.

Ma called again, so Sarah folded up the mental pictures of those early days, tucking them into a cranny of her mind so she knew where to find them later. Conscience had begun to niggle, and Mary had already gone to the creek with the pails.

"Coming, Ma!" she yelled.

It was a pannikin of hot tea waiting.

"Take this to the men, Sarah. Then there's a treat if you hurry back."

A strong smell of syrup and Ma's apron smeared with flour meant a batch of honey snaps was due from the oven, so she resolved to be back in a flash.

Come evening, her ma served up pork stew with bread that she'd baked fresh so it was fluffy the way Sarah liked it. And after the stew came honey snaps and suet pudding.

The kids were usually sent off after meals, that the downstairs was free for the grown-ups to eat in peace, talk on topics that Sarah found boring.

The upcoming party was the excitement on all childish lips, however. Many would come Sunday: the Lucas, Garth and Tucker tribes. Aunt Liz was a Tucker now after two previous husbands. Sarah's best friend was Susan Garth, who Sarah always felt sorry for, with five brothers. And the Lucas tribe was too many to count. Sarah was unsure about numbers past ten.

Uncle Willie had promised to lead them in games, and although she wasn't supposed to, she'd sneaked into the barn where she knew he was making something—to find a cut-out donkey for pinning the tail.

When evening mosquitos began to whine, however, they returned indoors. Sarah was anxious to remind Ma of her promise to again tell the Uncle Bill story. Her ma had a way of telling yarns from the past to make most of the funny sides. Tragic it really was, Ma always explained, the sinking of *Sirius*, and Sarah often wondered how it could have been a tragedy when so many funny things happened.

When the kids were abed, Titia blew out the lamp, heaved her bulging frame into a chair, and began the tale that Mary and Sarah could recount word for word. Uncle Billy she met when in Sydney Town, though the memory was hazy. He was Aunty Ann's man. Titia Goodwin didn't mind repeating the story, for she liked it herself, remembered well how she'd seen the funny side of it once the shock had waned.

"*Sirius* was the frigate leading the fleet bringing me and your pa to Botany Bay. When half us were to come live here, *Supply* and *Sirius* brought us. Me and Pa and you, Mary, a babe in arms, were on *Sirius*.. It was raining something dreadful when we arrived, and we all were drenched getting from Cascade Bay to Kingston. Aunty Ann was along, too, and Aunt Liz. There weren't a road then, just a muddy track through jungle..."

Titia told the story as she had a dozen times. It was already the island's tale of legend. But she paused every now and again to tend the babes when they stirred, yet Mary, John, Jamie, and Sarah were as intent on the story as ever.

"...So when *Sirius* was breaking up after going aground on the reef, they asked who could swim. Your Uncle Billy and another come forward. Lines were put about them so that once aboard they could drag out hawsers, and they made the heroic swim. All us ashore had hearts in mouths. Cheers went up, of course, when through the rain we see them clamber aboard, thinking that any minute the hawsers would start moving. But nowt happened…"

The boys giggled, knowing the farce was about to start.

"…After a time we was amazed to see the flicker of flames. The *Sirius* wreck was afire. So others made the swim. And when they arrived, there were the two in a merry state. Not only had they found a broken cask of rum but had lit a fire to warm themselves while they settled into getting drunk."

All four now guffawed loudly. They never failed to picture the consternation ashore while the heroes abandoned dedication to get tippled.

"But they paid dearly," continued Titia, "paraded before all the colony afterwards for people to make mockery of, locked in chains that they wore for many a month. But their gallant effort of braving the churning sea nevertheless led to saving much of the cargo before the wreck broke up."

"Is that when Aunty Ann married him, when the chains come off?"

"She had another man then. When they parted she took up with Uncle Billy. When he got his pardon, she wedded him."

"Tell us about his next trouble, Ma, with the redcoats."

But Titia called it a night, told them to tuck up.

"Another time. You boys got chores for Pa come morning, and you girls must help with baking for the party."

Sarah, satisfied with her favourite tale having been told again, snuggled up to Mary, with whom she shared a bed, to let her mind dwell on what presents would be brought for her, come Sunday.

"Ah, I look forward to seeing my old friend again. It is fortuitous that he is now governor in Sydney. Philip Gidley King and I will have much to reminisce on."

"Mrs. Collins will travel with you?"

"My wife, M'lord, cares neither for travel nor colonial hardship. She remains in Kent. A soldier's wife is as used to life alone as is her husband, I'm afraid."

Hobart smiled. Maybe the rapport between Collins and King stemmed from the similarity of their marital situations. Each had taken a 'colony wife' during the First Fleet settlement, each being presented with children.

Yet when he continued, it was not touching such sensitive matter.

His smile faded into a sigh. "Ah, to stay in England—sometimes I wonder should we expect this can remain as happy a fair isle. War seems to have become a way of life, leaving unhappiness in its wake. I sometimes think the emigrant might have a better time of it in the long term, shaping a new domicile to suit his needs."

"Yet war provides employment," replied the soldier. "Since the treaty, our tents have emptied occupants into city gutters where they beg and pillage in order to eat. I wager that many I take to Port Phillip found his way into chains by such a route. War may be harder on the taxpayer, M'lord, than on the soldier. At least on active service, the fighting man eats."

"That is cynical support indeed as reason for war. Yet I agree many farmers find the quartermaster a lucrative customer. Better than having livestock poached that unemployed Britons may eat. Such disillusioned farmers as the latter, my friend, make up the migrants you take. Settler families seek better opportunities in New South Wales than they have confidence of finding at home, it would seem."

"I have assigned the free families to *Ocean*. Accommo-dation aboard a convict transport is confined enough without the difficulty of policing division between classes."

"What difficulty?"

"Many convicts have heard of the 'good fortune' of predecessors benefiting by land grants to achieve some worldly value in life.

However, methinks they ignore news of the many who failed. Every man pictures himself, on expiration of his term, in landed comfort. It will not sit easily to first labour hard and long for free settlers on free land before he can turn to labour on his own behalf. Difficulties will arise between convict and free, I am sure."

"This is a different circumstance from '88, Colonel. Settling a free community presents different problems from establishing a prison. You just said you expect higher convict morale, and surely that will lessen difficulties?"

"Similarities remain, M'lord. Whether free community or prison, I still must extract from them the effort to build storehouses, barracks, hospitals, churches, all the public habitation a new settlement requires."

"I have no doubt you have given much consideration to all factors and that you are equipped to deal with them. But speaking of churches, Colonel, what think you of Robert Knopwood's appointment?"

Now it was Davie Collins' turn to smile.

"He may well add savoury sauce to an otherwise dry pudding, M'lord."

And both smiled.

Hobart's shoulders then straightened, a gesture to finalise the interview.

"I have written King, instructing him to be diligent in hearing your requests for assistance if in need. It will be a matter of liaison, exchanging artisans as you each require them; it is unproductive leaving quality wanting in one settlement if skills are idle in the other. I have perused your list of stores to be purchased in Cape Town and have every confidence your planning is thorough."

He picked up a paper. "You have five hundred and forty-seven persons. Provisions give you the four pounds of pork and seven of beef a week for each man, six ounces of sugar and twelve and a half pounds of wheat or an appropriate quantity of biscuit or flour for two years, as requested. Wine and spirits are approved for the free and tea for all. At your discretion, wine and spirits may be dispensed to convicts on medical grounds, or as an indulgence when pertinent. And you have your medicines and vinegar for the sick."

Collins bore in mind the frustrations Arthur Phillip had suffered.

"I am more than conscious, M'lord, of the readiness displayed in acceding to my requests. Would I be so sure the task ahead will prove as rewarding."

"I repeat, my friend, that you have my confidence. God speed."

~ * ~

"Biggest ship I ever did see, Gus."

Will Woolley had one eye to the rigging while trying to also keep both on his feet. The plank was narrow, and the shuffling, clanking queue was an hour long.

Yet every man negotiated his boarding without mishap, even Gus in his chains.

"If it's as far as they reckon, Will, then better a big ship."

It was indeed a big ship, later to be realised that HMS *Calcutta* was the tallest of all the nine hundred tall ships to bring convicts to Australian colonies; yet at the time, they could but marvel, stare into the far rigging, pleased it was the call of others to risk life and limb in a tossing ocean.

Quarters below were less grand, however, cramped and airless. Yet, weather permitting, they were told, deck visits would be regular.

"More than a tad better than the hulk, Gus."

"Well I'm glad it's bunks we got, Will. Chains and hammocks don't make a happy marriage."

The three had had their ten minutes with the ship's surgeon when he visited over the last week, pushing and prodding, inspecting eyes and teeth and having them do stretching and bending exercises.

"Glad it's you and not me, mate," Will challenged Gus, "in chains for the entire journey. Keeping your feet will be more difficult at sea, I'll wager. But it's the devil in yer what did it."

However, they were to find that, once aboard, they must wait for *Ocean*, their store-ship, to arrive from London.

"And more lags are coming from the Thames hulks," they were told.

The weeks of waiting proved tedious, with every man, for the nonce, in chains.

"Shackles will be off once at sea," had been the message for every man except Gus. It was feared that unless in chains, the shore so close would be too tempting an attraction for lags.

Daily deck visits helped ease the boredom, however, and twice weekly they stripped to the waist to wash, a routine not to the liking of all. And wagons arrived daily with more prisoners, some surprisingly young. Two nine-year-olds were youngest: Willie Steel, who nicked from a draper, and Will Appleton, who won his seven years for a milkman's apron.

"What you in for?" Will asked a fair-haired lag settling into the bunk above.

"Nickin' a wallet."

Will laughed. Picking pockets was the most common crime.

"Me too, mate. What's yer name?"

"Ben Briscoe." Ben was also twenty-two and had arrived in rags.

"They'll give yer new slops," Will told him, "and put some flesh back on yer bones. The food here is like a banquet after what they gave us on the hulks."

Ben had been on the notorious Thames hulks, even more renowned for poor fare than any other.

So when *Ocean* arrived, they departed. The cold weather had begun to wane by mid April, although the wind and sea held wild. Most aboard were laid low, wanting nowt but that the vile vomiting stop. Will took no food for days, for even the smell of stew made him retch. But he progressed to eventual health, and with chains off at the end of the first week, he could rub the sore flesh of his ankles. For near a year on the hulk he'd worn fetters during every day, and in the near two months since boarding Calcutta, the wounds had had little chance to heal before the unyielding iron broke the skin again.

Gus, however, had become a master at the art of stuffing rags into ankle-irons, and he dispensed advice and help with good-natured gusto.

Conversation aboard naturally concentrated on things familiar, left behind, and things unknown, drawing closer. Will was one content enough at leaving England. He believed that what had gone before in life was now of little consequence.

"The past," he told his mates, when bunked down one night, "should be abandoned. It's what lies on the shore of life ahead that takes on meaty significance, in my book—and on the shore ahead is where we're to found a settlement in a wilderness. The only thing we have any real expectation of, is that all will be hard work."

He then scratched his head. *It'll be like beginning life over...*

The thought sounded like his voice, yet from some misty distance. So he lay back, then, hands tucked under his neck, listening to the ocean rushing past beneath...

...now taking even the present with it!

Many lags were unused to hard labour, so for Will at least, there was the consolation that he and it were no strangers. He had good health, and compared to the state Ben and his mates arrived in, his stamina had held.

It's those never exposed to toil, who have spent life expending no more energy than lifting pockets or fleeing a chase, that will find the work hard.

Ben was an umbrella maker, so he and all with trades of the fingers or the mind, when set to breaking rock, felling trees, and toting logs, would tire quickly.

And they'll realise that anew, no doubt, at the end of each and every day.

Will had letters enough to make a little sense of reading, yet found writing tedious, his fingers too clumsy to easily form the letters...

...so they'll likely put me to physical work before anything scholarly. But I'll be enough at home on the end of a pit saw—if on the top end more often than the bottom, that is.

Savages though, mounted a new dimension. At home every man knew his environment, lived in no dilemma of such danger, but knowing cannibals were watching and waiting would indeed be a fear, especially for bolters. And to fail would earn the lash, a thought to make his inside tremor like the tinkle of shattering glass.

Not for me will there be the suffering that the lash must cause, let alone the alternate risks of being cooked or eaten alive. There'll be no bolting for William Woolley, that's for sure!

The free settlers aboard *Ocean* would be most at risk, he reckoned, setting up farms on native land.

But all will unfold, in time.

Shipboard gossip occupied much time, in that lags were ever eager to whisper around, especially if aimed at 'wigs,' as they nicknamed all officials, and an obvious butt was their prospective governor. Often on deck in his smart scarlet uniform, Lt-Colonel Collins, via snide asides from rumour-hungry lags, earned backhanded respect even so early in the voyage. Clear detail seldom reached the convict deck, yet rumours needed but a hint of substance for stories to mushroom.

Forger Matt Power, an Irish lag, was being cuckolded.

Lads on their second trip, those who'd served time and come home to be caught again, recalled that Davie Collins had been quite a one for Botany Bay ladies, actually taken a she-lag in colony 'marriage' and fathered children by her. Only thing Will had to date considered of him was that New South Wales couldn't be too bad a place if a gentleman, with choice, was returning.

And but three weeks out, he had taken a mistress in full view of all, including the loose woman's husband. The governor's reputation was done no harm as far as the lags were concerned, however, and they roundly applauded not only his luck, but his audacity; it appealed to their sense of bravado. If anyone received the brunt of ridicule, it was Matt Power.

"Wot yer reckon Robbie Knopwood makes of it?"

"He's jealous. Seems ter have a spark in the eye for the ladies himself."

Robert Knopwood was expedition chaplain with a well-earned reputation as playboy, socialiser, and womaniser with a strong partiality to tippling—all in all a most unlikely candidate for the cloth. Despite he was officially aboard *Ocean*, he spent much time on *Calcutta* for the social scene with military officers and formed a close friendship with the governor. To all outward appearances, the lag's observations were correct in that the reverend adopted no adverse attitude in respect of the illicit relationship between the governor and Mrs. Power.

During the crossing from Rio to Cape Town, those with trades were assigned tasks. Tailors made blouses, smocks and breeches; wives spun wool, made buttons and knitted shawls; cabinet-makers built furniture while carpenters and sawyers, Will and Gus among them, built pens and hutches on deck for livestock to be purchased at the Cape.

Convicts even helped work the ship, standing watch with the crew at times.

However, beyond Cape Town lay only the mysteries of an uncertain future. Few mariners had ever ventured into that little-known corner of the world, they were told. And during the forty-five-day crossing, they came to believe they were really in a savage world. Practically every day they were battered by the renowned gales and storms of the Indian Ocean.

Once inside the difficult narrow entrance to Port Phillip Bay, however, conditions were kind. From the beach by which the two ships anchored, which Collins named Sorrento, Will could see the huge bay was surrounded by sandy beaches stretching as far as the eye could see, narrowing into a pencil stroke on the northern horizon. The western shore fronted a stand of hills now violet in the dusking light, the setting sun behind them leaving a golden halo as if tempting evening closer.

After their six-month journey, *Calcutta*'s three hundred convicts had arrived to found a colony.

~ * ~

"Can't see no cannibals."

"Maybe they're back in the trees, boilin' up cauldrons."

Will, Gus, Davie and Ben hung over the poop rail, limp fishing lines to hand.

"If we're gonna turn this desert into land fit for man, we're wizards."

"A week, they've searched, and still no fresh water."

A jerk at Ben's wrist made them all start. Then the line fell slack.

"Glad it ain't rainin', mate—your umbrella would leak enough to let a man drown."

While his friends fell about laughing, Ben's chin rose an inch, fair hair flopping in his eyes as he wound in the line.

"If you was to jump over the side, Gus Morris, you could strangle the fish with your bleedin' chains."

Next day they formed into work parties to start unloading *Ocean*. Fresh water was still not found, but shore parties reported that the few natives encountered had quickly retreated, no doubt filled with fear at their first sight of ships and white men. And whilst the terrain comprised but sandy tracts of tee-tree scrub, unsuitable for aught but fuel, stands of fine forest timbers could be seen on hills to the north. So there would be hardwood for *Calcutta*'s cargo home.

For weeks they unloaded stores, pitched tents, built fireplaces, cooked, ate and slept on the beach. *Ocean* was moored as close to shore as low tide allowed, and the men, stripped to the waist in the early summer heat, ported stores through the shallows. It was exhausting work, and from time to time a token ration of rum was dispensed to aid morale.

No one was idle; boys scoured headlands for shellfish, and women laundered and cooked while redcoats supervised camp perimeters around the clock. Many lags, Gus and Davie among them, watched and whispered, studying routines, assessing probabilities against a chance to bolt.

The near hinterland provided an abundance of bird life, and both bush and waterfowl made dainty treats for officers and wigs. The bay yielded fish aplenty, so the seine was dragged from daylight to dusk that they build up a store of dried fish.

Surgeons fighting scurvy breathed sighs of relief.

~ * ~

The governor was in haste to begin planting, however, so seeds, plants and livestock purchased at the Cape, and garden tools brought from England, were priorities.

"Why spades and shovels, hoes and axes, barrows and ploughs, when we've yet to find soil? There's only sand in this God-forsaken place."

"And what will the creatures eat?"

"Precious little for us either. Both ports along the way had good tucker, yet they bring us here."

"Where we must build a town, lads, to offer vittles to visitin' ships."

"No wonder the savages are cannibals, ain't nothin' in the forest."

"Won't get meat off us, neither, lest they're quick."

Davie Collins pushed back his wig and scratched his head…

Is this to be another Sydney Cove experience?

And the longer fruitless explorations took, morale fell.

From the forested headland where Will and Gus felled lumber, they had panoramic views of the huge bay north to the skyline where it seemed to narrow, west to the distant shore, and south, beyond the two ships lying at anchor, to the narrow neck where they had entered.

"'Tis a fine view all right, Gus. And what a huge bay it is. A thousand ships could take refuge here and still leave room for more."

"Aye, Will, it's a grand scene, despite hard on the eyes with the sun glistening off it so. The sea right across the bay is as gentle as I've ever seen. A sheltered harbour, indeed."

"Yet that will serve our cause little, Gus, if fresh water can't be found. And apart from this knoll we're on, I can see no other land carrying timber, which could mean there's no fresh stream in all those miles."

"Wonder what the guv will do now?"

And back on the beach, that very gentleman was again scratching his head.

"There are few natives about, Robbie," he was saying to Robbie Knopwood, "far less than lived at Sydney Cove, a fact in itself lending weight to my fears that water and food will not be found. I am beginning to feel somewhat desperate. Several hundred souls are depending on us, including many wives and children."

"We buried eight at sea, Davie," the reverend reminded his leader, "but I fear that if we stay here much longer, more will die."

"Yet what can we do but continue exploring?"

"That is an answer I cannot help with, Davie. The good Lord has not endowed me with intelligence that can offer aught but the exploration you are engaged in. Maybe I should hold a service come Sunday and have every soul pray for luck in finding at least one of those things."

"If one were found Robbie, the other would be alongside it, for they come in pairs. And as for you holding a service, you have held none since we arrived, and you held precious few aboard ship."

"The Lord points out the difficulties of holding services where no facilities exist, Davie. With no forest cover, do you suggest we force five hundred souls to squat on the sand in the summer sun while I preach a sermon of hope, when you yourself, Davie, see no glimmer of it? Or ask them to give thanks for having been delivered safely to a desert? I am at sixes and sevens in exasperation at my own predicament."

"Yes, I suppose you have a point there, Robbie. But a miracle would help, if you thought you could conjure one up?"

"Before leaving England, Davie, were you privy to the information that Lord Hobart had of this place, the information on which the decision was made to come here?"

"Coastal surveys had it marked a safe anchorage with fresh water and arable soil. We have sortied to the western shore"—and he pointed to where the setting sun was now turning the landscape purple—"and so far for twenty miles northwards, and found nowt but brackish streams with no real greenery other than this useless tee-tree scrub. It is a huge bay, Robbie, with still some hundred miles of shoreline to search. It is a matter of waiting until our boats have sortied further."

And the Aborigines too, it seemed, had been playing a waiting game, but in their case it had been for the visitors to depart. However, now they illustrated that they had tired of the waiting. They turned aggressive, threatening scouting parties with spears and clubs, forcing them back to the beach each time they attempted to go ashore in their search.

Welcome had worn thin. Blacks even began creeping into camp at night to steal cooking utensils, tools, clothing, and even livestock. The uneasy peace that had reigned from the outset soon turned to hostility with blood spilled on both sides.

Yes. It is certainly Sydney Cove revisited.

Calcutta was cleared and ready to begin loading timber, so it moved north to where the sawyers had, for a month, been felling and trimming. Convicts could now fill her emptiness with the results of their labour, because getting her quickly on her return journey was one of Collins' urgent priorities. And unless he could, by the time she was loaded, find arable land, he must have her first call at Sydney to advise Governor King that the settlement could not proceed, that another site must be found.

The unloading of *Ocean* continued, the summer heat that December delivered in the land burning bodies unused to extremes as temperatures touched the century. No rain fell, and flies, mosquitoes and giant ants made life a misery. Livestock became visibly skeletal, and several convicts deserted, despite knowing there was no fresh water in the forest.

Ocean discharged the last of her stores before *Calcutta* was fully loaded, so Collins, desperate because of their situation, despatched her to Sydney. And immediately after it departed, three men bolted. And within a week, encouraged by the fact that none of the three had been found, five followed.

Since arriving, despite rigid supervision, twenty men had decamped. Will and Gus were still at Arthur's Seat, but on the beach, Davie Gibson watched and counted. After several more days, five miscreants returned hungry and fearful of the natives. A search party seeking the others apprehended five more at an incredible sixty miles distant, bringing them back in chains.

Yet in all the sixty miles, they reported, no pasture was sighted.

Reverend Knopwood, wearing his alternate hat of magistrate, put aside principles of Christian forgiveness to order the bolters a hundred lashes each. Davie Gibson was diligent in learning from every man, however, each detail of his experience. Ten convicts remained at large.

"Escapin' is easy," Davie confided to Ben. "It's survivin' what is difficult."

But suddenly, unexpectedly, *Ocean* returned.

There was considerable excitement as she beat her way through the heads. The timber cutters were granted a holiday and returned to the main camp, surprise awaiting Will and Gus when Ben quickly sought them out.

"Davie's gone, mates."

Amidst the distraction of *Ocean*'s return, Davie and a Langston mate broke into a redcoat tent, nicked a musket, powder and shot, and decamped.

"Well, he finally did it, Will."

"Aye, Gus. Sorry you weren't here to go with him?"

"Might have gone, had I been, now with the chains off, but they'll not have an easy time of it—yet with the musket, they'll at least eat."

"The others each got a hundred," Ben told them, relating events of note during their absence, "which Davie knows, of course."

They smiled wryly and turned their attention to the dramatic news that *Ocean* brought... England was again at war with France.

But of even greater significance, they being now so far from that sphere of activity and more concerned with things local, was that the 'promised land' denied them at Port Phillip, had been discovered.

Governor King in Sydney sent instruction to Collins to lift camp and move to Van Diemen's Land, where a site offered the advantages of fresh water in abundance, protected harbours and arable soil. *Ocean* was at their disposal for the move.

"You mean all we done here is for naught, we're to up and leave it?"

"Did the same at Botany Bay, sent a whole fleet full of lags only to discover there was nowt but arid soil and no drinking water."

"They reckon this Derwent River is the place all right, though."

Will Woolley settled down to sleep that night, giving thought, apart from the fact that tomorrow they must begin the tedious task of getting stores back aboard ship, on how Davie was faring. If he were to give up and return, he would find them gone. He would be marooned.

HMS *Calcutta*'s role, however, was clear; she was again a fighting unit that must return to England in haste. She was quickly prepared and decided to sail with the timber to date loaded.

She was given a rousing farewell.

Collins rued losing the use of *Calcutta*'s marines that had been on loan to him, supplementing his own meagre force of fifty, particularly with the extra supervision now required in breaking camp.

And his concern was proven when on Christmas Day, with work suspended for observance, several lags decamped, among them Will Buckley, not to be seen for thirty years.

Watching natives were no doubt bemused as every man began reloading all they had so painstakingly brought ashore.

"They'll think they've scared us off," Will joked.

"No change for the reverend," declared Ben as they sucked on pipes before curfew. "Robbie Knopwood lives the gentle life even here. When his boat beached yesterday," he told them, "I had to help tote his catch, and it included not only a crayfish but a pelican."

"Every meal's a feast for Robbie. He takes sharin' his fancy repasts in turn, governor one day, officers the next."

"And his pint of fine wine a day seems more a quart."

"Eats better than ever he did in England, I reckon, spends more time eatin' and tipplin' than writin' sermons. No service in many weeks now, except for Chrissy Day."

"And only purpose that served was to give Will Buckley his chance."

The reverend made no attempt to hide that his role in the expedition came second to satisfying hedonistic pleasures. Bringing the gospel to lags was well down his list. He disliked lag company.

"And he certainly ain't inclined to play missionary to the niggers."

"Governor still waltzes his Sarah Power," noted Will. "Would I had a woman to offer him when I see Matt Power set up in his comfortable hut with double rations and no work detail."

"And him a fourteen-year man at that, mate."

And come late January, within but a week of sailing, who should scramble into camp but Davie Gibson, emaciated almost beyond recognition after four entire weeks in the bush. He was rushed to the hospital tent, but even before treatment, he demanded to see the governor.

"I got news," he declared, "news Colonel Collins will want to hear."

And when taken before the astounded governor, Davie informed that at the far north of Port Phillip Bay was not only a huge freshwater river the blacks called Yarra-Yarra, but that its valley was lush with verdant growth and its soil appeared in every respect ideal for agriculture.

"With the broad river as port for shipping, guv, and the valley to feed people, Yarra-Yarra is perfect for settlement. I left George still runnin', but come back to give yer the news, guv."

Yet Davie was the one amazed. The governor was unimpressed.

"Didn't care a jot," Davie exclaimed to his friends. "Told me such news comes too late, that we're movin' to this Van Diemen's Land."

Davie was devastated that his return with such news had fallen on deaf ears. He had expected to be proclaimed a hero, granted a pardon.

"You wasn't to know about the Derwent, Davie."

"Yer can't know how difficult a decision it was, to come back."

"By the look of you, you weren't doin' too well."

"Anyway, I'm not to be punished, seein' I did bring the news."

And was it the slightest glimmer of a smile that Will discerned behind Davie's eyes?

By month's end the settlement was dismantled; the ninety men *Ocean* couldn't fit aboard remained camped on the beach with supplies and arms. *Ocean* would return for them once unloaded in the Derwent. Of the three hundred and eight convicts shipped, eight had died on the voyage, fifteen lay in graves at Port Phillip, and six bolters had failed to return.

Port Phillip had not been a happy three months, and none mourned departure. And once the beach party was taken off, the only visible remains of the Sorrento settlement would be the fifteen graves on the rise behind the beach, home of those who succumbed to the hardships of the brief colony.

As *Ocean* sailed off, the beachhead was lost in a shimmer of haze, all aboard wondering about the lags still missing.

"Maybe dead by now, of snakebite or starvation, or eaten by blacks."

"But if alive, they are forsaken. No chance for them once the beach party is gone."

To Will Woolley, it merely illustrated the futility of placing hope in escape from chains, in such wilderness.

<h1 style="text-align:center">*Four*</h1>

The babe her ma had been expecting not too long after Sarah's birthday was another girl. The Goodwins named her Maria. Her pa had said he was happy about it, but Sarah knew that was only sop to her ma, for he had been saying all along, as she got bigger, that he wanted it to be a boy.

"If I keep telling her that," he used to insist, "she will. The spirits inside her can hear me, and they might just do what I ask."

Sarah wondered if he might have been joking. She talked it over with Mary, and they decided to wait, see if it might happen that way next time. But when another year later little Lizzie followed, despite Pa had kept talking to Ma's inner spirits, Sarah had to accept that it probably had been a joke.

Mary, however, by then thirteen, had been told there was never any knowing whether a woman would have girl or boy. It always would remain a matter of surprise, either a good one or a bad one, and that it had nothing whatever to do with inner spirits.

"Ma talked to me about womanly things, Sarah. And soon she'll likely talk to you about them, too."

"Is this something to do with you bleeding as if you'd cut yourself?"

"How you know about that?"

"Susan Garth told me it happens. It happened to her, and her ma told her it happens to all girls our age."

"Well, it was after it happened to me that ma gave me the 'Woman's Talk.'"

"You didn't tell me."

"Because Ma asked me not to until it happens to you. Then I have to tell her."

"Why does it happen?"

"That's what she will tell you, silly."

So Sarah didn't pursue it.

Maybe it mightn't happen to me anyway.

It did, of course, when her ma was big with little Ann.

~ * ~

The Derwent River was indeed a magnificent waterway.

Will Woolley was mesmerised at how Storm Bay stretched a dozen miles across, and they could see as they headed into the river mouth that it maintained its imposing breadth for many a mile. A towering, flat-topped mountain reminiscent of that behind Cape Town dominated the river's western shore, and as far as the eye could see in that direction, wave upon rolling wave of wooded mountains promised ample fresh water and abundant timber.

The advance party Governor King had sent from Sydney was camped on the eastern shore. They hadn't explored because, having roused native ire by firing on first sight, they'd been kept pinned on the beach.

Ocean quickly took in sail as clouds rolled like surf on seashore, gathering blackness every minute. Soon, lightning pierced the gloom in jagged slivers of flame, and the very ship trembled with the vibrations of booming thunder. They arrived at the campsite during a torrential deluge.

Collins expressed reservations about the cove's exposure, so immediately the weather relented, he sent parties in search of better, deciding on a bay on the western shore under the lee of the towering mountain. He had the ship anchor as close to shore as depth would allow, by a small rock island onto which they could unload, the island affording easy wading to the beach.

He named the mountain Mount Wellington and the site of the new settlement Hobart.

Aboard ship, Will surveyed his new home, thickly wooded hillsides rising gradually at first from the sheltered cove, then in a dramatic sweep up the dominant mountain.

Will Woolley, Ben Briscoe, Gus Morris and Davie Gibson, with their three hundred mates, bent backs under stores and equipment to establish the new colony of Van Diemen's Land.

~ * ~

When beginning his new life at Hobart Town, Will Woolley was two years older in age than when arrested, and ten years older in worldly experience.

During his months on Hulk *Portland*, the near six at sea aboard *Calcutta*, and the three on the beach at Sorrento, his eyes had been witness to men dying of scurvy and of seeing them flayed to within an inch of death, it seemed, strung up to a triangle on the sand, strips of flesh torn from them with stroke after sickening stroke, their blood running thick to drench the sand where they stood.

Davie Gibson returned from his bolt, when after only four weeks his body was reduced to skin and bone from eating nowt but grass and bark of trees. Nothing Will had seen in his years in the army could equate with the suffering the convicts endured.

In war, a man either dies in seconds or pretty damned quickly after being wounded from loss of blood or gangrene, but here in peacetime when neither fighting the nation's foes or murdering fellow man in fits of rage, but rather Englishmen guilty of nowt but petty theft, perjury or forgery, a man's mind gets frazzled simply trying to understand what is called British justice.

He was incensed!

If it be merely to determinedly torture the poor wretches, surely then it is more deserving than having to call on God for help, to rather challenge God to bring down his wrath on the floggers. Ceding years of forced labour to pay for petty sins is surely punishment enough, in repaying society, without being tortured as well.

So sleep didn't come easily to Will Woolley. He couldn't erase the sights his eyes had beheld. Even when his entire body was exhausted from each day's work, the pace set being so frantic, he could not easily fall asleep.

The governor was paranoid about getting stores built to lock-up stage, not only to quickly empty *Ocean* of stores so it could return to pick up those left on the beach at Sorrento, but because at that latitude there could be snow within three or four months. Anything not covered against the weather or locked up against pilfering would spoil. And no plantings could then be made even if land were cleared, until after the long winter.

So with his body short of sleep from reliving the daily horrors, it began tiring, pressured during the day by the threat of the whip if he didn't keep up, and pressured by night revisiting the day's events.

And I'm not alone in this. There's not a lag here who doesn't suffer the same as me, yet none wants to lumber his problems on others. So we bottle them up. And the reverend makes it clear with the severity of his sentences when wearing his magistrate cap that no succour will be forthcoming, even if anyone were gullible enough to approach him, praying for mercy.

"Knopwood hands out the heaviest penalties of any magistrate," was a common complaint. "Reverend or not," all agreed, "when he's in the chair, lags shudder. How any God can be so unkind as to pick him for the bench the very day a man is seeking succour, ain't Christian."

With five years still to serve, it's a daunting bloody prospect, having to realise that this pace of work can only persist!

"There's but two horses in the entire land," Gus pointed out one day, "so that makes us lags the only beasts of bloody burden. We don't just have to fell the trees, mate, we got to bloody tote them, too, and after grubbin' out rocks because there's no oxen to pull heavy loads, a man must first break them where they lay, even if it's snowin'."

Collins brooked no slacking, and all were under threat of punishment if they lagged or malingered, so most rose early each morning still aching from yesterday's hardships.

By the end of the second frenzied month, the free farmers were being settled a mile north of the main camp, the governor granting holdings to not only widows of men who had died since leaving England, but to wives of convicts, their husbands then assigned to them as labourers. The objective was that whilst it was not yet time to plant, the clearing of farming land, the grubbing out of rocks and ploughing the fields with nowt but lags themselves to pull the ploughs, could all be done during the winter.

"And the food, mates, ain't enough to hold a man together to see him through a bloody day. We ate better on the bloody hulks."

Surviving another five years of it loomed a daunting prospect, so convicts resorted to natural instincts, nicking what they lacked.

So even heavier punishments ensued. And morale deteriorated even further.

Yet whilst Collins in some ways illustrated a keen sense of what contributed to convict morale, in others he was dreadfully, in convict eyes, remiss. Typical was the instance of his paradoxical blindness to malcontent caused by his persistent concessions of blatant favouritism.

"Hear about his latest handout?"

"To Matt Power?"

"Aye, given the bugger a free pardon, payment for use of his woman."

"But you gotta admire the man's bloody spunk, mate."

And then there was the persistent problem of natives, which accelerated at an alarming rate. The initial skirmishes at Risdon Cove had sparked the flame, natives illustrating an aggressive attitude from day one, to be exacerbated with each extra acre of land cleared. The newcomers took what game they wanted, and marines answered native anger with deadly fire. Many Aborigines died. And floggings of horrendous brutality became commonplace for not only bolters who returned, but for even minor insurrections.

Will could only look on the miseries of all involved, aghast.

~ * ~

Uppermost in Collins' mind was the coming winter.

"Securing stores ashore is our most urgent priority," he insisted to Geil.

Major Andrew Geil was commanding officer of the colony's marines, so vitally involved in all that was being achieved by convicts.

"Then surely, Davie, with good soil under our feet, gardens must show results more quickly than could be achieved in Sydney. Furthermore, apart from our convicts having been selected for fitness, they've had the benefit of those months ashore at Port Phillip to recover from the voyage. Nor do they suffer from the fear of having been abandoned by England as you found at Botany Bay. So all other things being equal, we have far better opportunity for success in the long term."

Collins had, from early in their relationship, come to admire Geil's considerable foresight and common sense. He was a worthy confidant.

"Failing unseen calamities, yes, my friend. And regular supplies will arrive, if not directly for sometime, at least via Sydney."

He then looked pensive.

"The other side of the coin, however, is that we have the responsibility of looking to the needs of free settlers. And now that this site is decided upon, they are impatient to have their grants established. Yet we have call on only a hundred and fifty convicts and their few wives for labour. And I don't need to explain to you, of all people, how short of marine protection we are."

Apart from the convicts lost during the voyage, those buried at Port Phillip and the bolters never seen again, a score were currently hospitalised.

"Certainly the ninety on the beach at Port Phillip, and your men guarding them, can be put to good use once we can get them here. But we cannot send *Ocean* back until cleared of stores. So from what other essential area do we transfer convict labour?"

It was a no-win situation, and both smiled as they faced each other with upturned palms, both conscious of already being halfway through the two years of stores brought.

It was essential that they move quickly. Time was running out.

"The convicts have also benefited from experience, Davie. At Port Phillip they were taught to be cautious in respect of bolting. Few refrained from surrendering ideas of freedom once faced with lack of sustenance in the forests, and it became increasingly obvious how the realisation struck home that they must return to suffer the consequences."

"True enough. And, likely, all who failed to return were set upon and killed. Here there is abundant fresh water in the forests and therefore more game, so it is essential that we assign more of your men, Andrew, to guarding against bolting, than watching over settlers."

"Every day I notice how many more wisps of smoke are in these forests than we ever saw at Port Phillip. The convicts, too, must notice that, Davie. Each will realise that they cannot get far undetected. The majority must therefore choose to err on the side of caution. And I am sure, especially as we appropriate more land, the more warlike the natives will become."

Collins wagged his finger.

"Keep pressing that point out there, Andrew. It's not me that you have to convince. Meanwhile, I shall keep applying heavier penalties on bolters who return. Tell them that also!"

Within weeks, some wattle and daub huts were constructed and a start made on a stone warehouse, a hospital and a wharf. Busiest were the tree fellers and sawyers, urged to provide as much timber as possible before the chills and slush of winter arrived.

Then as winter frosts began, building increased with frantic haste.

~ * ~

Most survived their first winter, despite a little snow. Land was cleared for spring planting and building continued. Yet when summer warmth made the forests seem more inviting, a resurgence of escapes began. The settlement began to show even more earmarks of a penal colony. Collins responded by resorting to the common use of chains, the more unruly finding themselves fettered both at work and in bed.

And after ten months, Will and his mates were summing up their prospects:

"Not only have thirty-one been buried since we arrived, mates, but the rate of deaths, as food supplies dwindle, is increasing. Despite there's plenty of kangaroos in the forests, fewer shooting parties can be mounted with the natives so fierce. The only good sign on the food front is that with summer coming, there'll be more fish..."

"And the river will have more black swans come summer, Will—"

"...If the reverend don't get in to grab them first," interrupted Gus. "He's even got his own boat built now that he sends out fishing every bloody night."

"At least on the river, Gus, we have an advantage over the blacks. Our cutters are more efficient than their fragile coracles—and our seines a hundred times more efficient than their bark lines."

"So surely we'll have more to eat come summer," summed up Ben.

And there was, for Christmas—their first, just ten months after arriving—church muster, followed by, for free and convict, a sumptuous dinner of waterfowl.

"But," Collins insisted, remembering the meagre rations they'd been reduced to by the first Christmas at Sydney, "be warned—all should savour the present plenty. Should Sydney be unable to assist us during the autumn, we may well feel the pangs of hunger again, come winter."

~ * ~

On Norfolk Island there were many contrasts...

By now there were but occasional floggings. And there was plenty to eat. Nor was there pressure on time, nor natives to instil fear in every settler soul. Already it was obvious that the young were less exposed to the brutalities persisting in the mainland settlements. More prisoners arrived only as accommodation became available, and lags having served their time were granted free land to begin farming. Exposed to the carrot of such good fortune, advantages unavailable to anyone back in Britain, convicts coming up to completion of sentences toed the line in anticipation. Nor did any bolt, because the island was so small there was nowhere to hide.

So with the majority of convicts keen to maintain a good-behaviour record, punishments were rare. The island's young were reminded less and less that they lived in a prison colony. They enjoyed a developing social atmosphere.

And one Sunday, Sarah was ecstatic. The entire Goodwin family attended a function at the Lucas farm, the Lucas family not only being the island's most populous, but one of the closest of Goodwin friends.

Nat Lucas, a carpenter and builder by trade, had been a friend of Sarah's pa since the First Fleet, so they had been 'bosom buddies' for twenty years.

Sarah and young Ed Garth, son of the third of those 'bosom buddies', had crept off together, far enough to be now quite unseen from where people were gathered.

"In here, quick," said young Ed.

"My pa'll skin me if he finds out."

"Mine'll whop me til I can't stand."

"What if there's rats, Ed?"

"Ain't a rat on all Norfolk Island got spunk enough to live in Aunt Olivia's barn."

Young Ed had, of late, watched Sarah Goodwin blossom, become goggle-eyed whenever she minced a shoulder in passing or fluttered eyelashes when parents weren't looking, or tugged her bodice lower as her breasts developed, when she knew he was watching, every time knowing it made him horny.

Now they were about to do something about it, get 'a score on the board.'

Sarah had watch young Ed outgrow the gormlessness she had always seen in him, to even acquire a visage near to suavity. And she knew that if she didn't jump in and claim him, Mary might also see him anew, and home in.

So it was touch and giggle in the hayloft, prelude, they each privately hoped, to more substantial intimacy whenever they could next wangle credible excuses for absence from respective parents.

Sarah worried that at thirteen, soon to be fourteen, youth could pass her by before she could take advantage of it.

Five

David Collins' predictions proved valid.

By autumn, pangs of hunger gripped all those in Van Diemen's Land, with the exception of only the reverend.

Collins appealed to Governor King in Sydney, who replied that Vandemonians must depend on stores brought with them and from local fauna. Collins awarded King no points for arithmetic; he had now been away from England more than the two years the provisions were designed to cater. Remaining stores were meagre, now providing little by way of nourishment.

"To subsidise provisions with game," Collins mused, "King is either unconscious of, or unwilling to recognise, how great a problem are our island's natives. The settlement is so limited in military that it is out of the question that control of work can be relaxed just so marksmen can be freed to guard huntsmen."

So in April, food was rationed yet again. With winter looming, he was as desperately concerned at their by now shortage of blankets and clothing.

And because of the added hardships, escapes increased, the failure rate monitored by Gus and Davie.

And come early winter, as Will and Ben stitched kangaroo skins into jackets because their clothes were threadbare, Will whispered:

"Gus is goin'."

"When? How?"

"In the reverend's boat. With Adam. To take the *Governor Hunter*."

"Take a ship, Will? Are they daft?"

"There's five or six. Gus asked me in, but it's too risky. They'll take the ship, put the crew ashore down river, then sail to South America."

Adam Carmichael was Robbie Knopwood's trusted servant, a Scot who, when in the military, nicked cheeses and grog when on guard duty to earn fourteen years. He was regularly out on hunting parties with the reverend and often sent fishing alone at night. No one would think it amiss him taking out the skiff. But it was not fish he sought on the night of the bolt; he would row around the point and pick up waiting colleagues.

But the bolt backfired. The six were seen rowing off.

What astounded everybody was that the governor, unpredictable as ever of late, quashed the sentences. The bolters, chased and caught by marines even before reaching the ship, got off with chaining and short rations.

"The dilemma I have," Collins explained to Geil, "is that every lashing takes men off the work detail. Even if only a week, it puts us that much further behind."

But the same were to go again.

Men were becoming truly desperate as food ran out. Even grog ran out, and the little colony was reduced to starvation level even before winter arrived, the remaining salted meat now inedible and the grain infested with vermin. Sickness was soon so rife that both workloads and severity of punishment were reduced, bodies unable to tolerate either.

But come spring, Gus and two mates decamped with not only a cache of stolen food, but dogs to initially provide protection against natives, and eventually meat against starvation. But again Gus's freedom was short lived—they surrendered after but three days, having been continually harassed by natives.

And again the governor forgave them, every man needed able-bodied.

It was on their next break that Will Woolley forsook his good intentions of avoiding a bolt, to be drawn into Gus's risky scheme. His desperation was enough to tip the scale.

"Even conscious of your dismal record, Gus, m'boy, I have to believe that we should go while we've strength enough. We die of starvation if we stay."

It was the December of the colony's second Christmas, with everybody starving. The summer crops had failed and people were eating grass and seaweed to suffer inevitable gut-wrench and gripe.

And the red-haired rascal joined them.

Of the friends, only Ben Briscoe was strong enough, or afraid enough, or sensible enough, to hold back. But he wished them luck.

The bolters numbered five—Adam Carmichael, he who had earlier nicked the reverend's boat, Will Woolley, Gus Morris, Davie Gibson and Liam Cocksworth, who had been on Gus's previous bolt. Davie and Liam were lifers, Adam five years into his fourteen, and Will and Gus three years into their seven. Starvation was their deciding factor.

"Bein' so many, the guv won't be hard on us if we return. He needs us workin' fit," Gus declared.

So they bolted.

~ * ~

A month later...

"Three hundred lashes and wear chains for a year!"

Will Woolley was stunned, but Gus crossed arms and smiled.

"Don't worry, me darlin's. The governor will remit it. Just wait."

Four long, gruelling, decimating weeks after their bolt, they had been led into court to find a stern-faced Robbie Knopwood in the chair. That his Adam had now twice betrayed his trust would alone have been sufficient to sour his temper, yet that Adam alone had failed to return left the reverend uncompromising. Will lacked confidence in Gus's prophecy that the governor would be lenient, for much would have happened during the month they were absent.

"The pardons he issued in order to keep men at work rather than have lacerated bodies idle may no longer be relevant."

Their four weeks in the wilds had seemed a lifetime. Even now they created shudders through Will every time his mind harked back. He had no need to finger his by now skeletal body to recall the rigours...

...the gnawing pains of persistent hunger, I will never forget. All will remain vivid in memory; the desperate chewing of raw grubs and beetles, grasses and ferns, all to bring on bouts of retching and bellyache enough to make a man want to die; the forever starting, heart in mouth, at every strange sound, fearful it be natives intent on murder; the agonising over whether to admit failure and the likely terrible consequence if deciding to return...

Eventually, after the third week, starvation and fear decided them to fight their way back, suffer the consequences if only for the satisfaction of having something regular in the belly, no matter how little.

Will had enough numbers to work out that three hundred with the cat was more than three thousand bites, slices, cuts to the bone, each casting chunks of Woolley flesh about the forest floor. Images of the worst flogging he'd seen had ever stuck in his mind, a poor wretch lashed at Port Phillip, slobbering and vomiting, his body shuddering each time the cat bit, blood streaming down his legs to quickly become a flood, staining the beach crimson.

He was petrified at what was to come.

And they were flogged.

Will found every fear devastatingly fulfilled. Over and over he suffered agony as each bite bit. He quickly lost count, his senses dulled by pain that he realised it less, even, than the rhythm of the torturing strokes that each time shook his body so much that the ropes about his wrists, criss-crossed to the triangle's apex, cut deeper and deeper.

He survived the ordeal, the last two hundred strokes hardly consigned to memory because his senses had, by then, entirely deserted him.

The pain came later when no matter which way he tried to position his body, only one realisation was clear...

These scars I know I must carry in my mind as well as on my body until the day I die.

~ * ~

Queenboro had to be the most beautiful part of Norfolk Island, Sarah reckoned.

Their house was in a quiet valley, a stream running through it, either side of which was a gentle hillside, not so steep that the hogs couldn't be penned on the Mount Pitt side, while on the other was the house. By it, Pa had built an arbour from old tree trunks, over which grew masses of purple bougainvillea that each year, she noted, covered more of the arbour to not only provide shade inside but gave the whole appearance of the house being draped in a cape of deepest carmine.

Ma had spent her time digging into the Mount Pitt slope that from the house she could now look out on trees—a rainbow of hibiscus interspersed with the brilliant scarlet of poinsettias. She had won from her Andy a promise that, each day, the boys were given time to carry pails of water to feed every tree.

"If we are to live in a sub-tropical paradise, we should make the most of it," she insisted.

In the arbour were benches enough that the entire family could sit, although each night after supper while the older girls cleaned pots and dishes, the younger were made help, the quicker all was done. Sarah hated the pot-scrubbing chore on which she and Mary took turns, yet worked with a will that all could the quicker move out to the arbour.

Pa would by then have lit his pipe, and he and Ma would talk on grown-up things that Sarah for so long had thought boring; topics that she now realised helped her understand some of what she had ever seen as simply silly rules that the governor kept insisting on, rules that she felt touched unkindly on every family.

"What we've learned, Letty," Sarah's pa was that night expounding, "is that laws made to keep prisons running smoothly and ensuring convicts don't get too many leniencies are not the best laws for settlers. We need a voice where the bloody decisions are made; but no matter how often we ask, they keep sayin' how the laws are made in England;

and of course over there they have no bloody idea what problems we face here. Whatever we grow, be it beef or pork or corn or wheat, we can sell only to the government store, and it decides where and how it will be distributed. And with fixed prices, where do we find extra coin for bigger plantings? They complain we don't produce enough, but what do they do…?"

And if Sarah cared to notice her ma's reaction, it was usually a shrug of shoulders…

Ma knows Pa is going to carry on and tell it anyway…

"…They just release more bloody lags to start farming new ground now that more are being shipped in. But they're lags what know nowt of how to bloody go about it, Letty. We old blokes who have done the trial and bloody error work can yield twice as much as newcomers in half the bloody time if given the extra land ourselves—and more bloody convicts to work it."

Sarah knew he had no more letters and numbers than did Sarah herself, or even Ma who seemed to have answers for just about everything else, but her pa had learned values all right. She had one time heard her ma talk about things with Aunt Liz. They had come on the same ship…

Ma had then told Aunt Liz how much her Andy had learned about business since being put on the land.

But because it was usual that when Pa was on a fist-pounding subject he never liked being interrupted, Sarah had come to realise how her ma would always wait until he'd let off his steam. She knew she could then have her say. And it now seemed, she reckoned her time had come…

"When you dropped me off at Dr. John's the other day, Andy, he told me about a new settlement on the mainland—a place called Van Diemen's Land, a week of sailing south from Sydney. About two years old it is now."

"Yes. I heard the same. But why have another settlement? There's land enough around Sydney for as far as one can ride horseback in a month."

"It's to do with hunting seals, Dr. John said. And Mr. Collins has come back as governor there."

"I hadn't heard that part of it."

"That's what Dr. John said."

Sarah knew her pa would be happy about that. Ma had told the kids as a bedside story one time, how when Pa was in trouble with some bad redcoats, Mr. Collins took Andy's side, rescued him from a hanging.

So there obviously were some nice things happened for convicts. For the worthy ones at any rate.

~ * ~

A year later Will Woolley was to find that good fortune could sometimes befall a man as well as bad. And good fortune could come about in strange ways...

Major Geil was in need of carpenters-come-sawyers. He was building the colony's first impressive residence. On his spread across the river at Risdon Cove, he'd already erected a sign declaring the property Geilston. The major was also the settlement's largest grazier, not only shipping wool to England's mills, but providing much needed mutton for settlement tables; he now needed men to build many miles of fences.

Will Woolley was one assigned, and a great side benefit, Will found, was that domiciled on Geilston, he ate considerably better than in hungry Hobart Town.

Convict gossip travelled quickly on Hobart's airwaves, and it wasn't long after starting his new job that he heard of Davie Gibson's latest caper. Lady luck had also looked kindly on the Red-haired Rascal too, it seemed, for despite his three hundred lashes, he had bolted again, to that time be successful. Always 'doing things big,' he joined a large contingent to steal a vessel and sail away. It was to be a long time before his friends could learn the details of his adventures.

As for Adam Carmichael of the previous bolt, he was never heard of again.

Will also got to hear that Ben Briscoe, who had for so long resisted the temptation of bolting from the horrors of hunger, eventually fell victim to the lure of the bush, and he too, in desperation, took the risk with but a year of his sentence to serve. Yet he wasn't as lucky as Davie; he was as unlucky as Will, returning to give himself up, a starving shadow of his normal self, to suffer the same fate as his friend—the agony of three hundred lashes by courtesy of the Reverend.

Distressing news of what was happening over the river in the town continued to seep through to lags on Geilston, and each was getting sadder than the last. The storehouse to which all grain and produce must be sold was now bereft of meat, tea, sugar, soap, candles, oil, butter and wine. Work had staggered to a standstill because every man lacked the stamina to rise each day. Governor Collins had appealed to Governor King for help, but Sydney was also in a situation of desperate want. The combined colonies' largest food basket, the Hawkesbury River basin west of Sydney, had again been inundated by floodwaters that destroyed the entire season's crop.

Visiting ships seeking provisioning at either of the only two ports in several thousand miles were being sent away with hungry crews.

David Collins' situation was desperate.

He couldn't but believe that the very future of his Van Diemen's Land venture was in doubt.

~ * ~

Another year later...

"But I thought it was my brother Ed you were interested in," exclaimed Susan Garth.

"I was, but you, too, have grown up a lot since you were thirteen, I've noticed."

"Do you reckon, Sarah, that it's womanhood we've reached?"

"Well at fifteen, Susan, I've reached it anyway. Maybe you are just maturing more slowly, what with having all brothers and no sisters."

"You are so lucky having sisters, especially Mary being older. She must have so much to tell you about men."

"She has her Will Fletcher. She's even told me she wants to live with him. But she's frightened of what Pa will say."

"And do they do anything?"

Sarah looked about in case anyone could hear.

"Of course!"

"Oh, Sarah! Do tell!"

"He got very hard. She could feel it pressing against her."

"Ah!"

"But when I asked what happened then, Mary went all pink and didn't want to tell."

"But didn't you insist?"

"Of course! And it took a long while before she would tell me."

"And what did she tell you?"

Susan was all a-tingle.

Sarah looked about again, then nodded.

"He took her hand..."

Susan grabbed Sarah's hand, eyes pleading.

"...and slowly put it on his hardness..."

Susan's spare hand flew to her mouth ... "Oh!"

Then in the silence that followed, Susan summoned up more breath.

"What? He was still fully dressed?"

Sarah leaped back, hands ahip.

"Susan Garth! Are you suggesting my sister might have actually had a sexual thing with him when they are not even married?"

Susan simply nodded, frantically.

"Yes," she said. "Did she touch it?"

"I am not going to tell you. Do you think I would betray my sister's confidences?"

Oh, how superior it makes one feel to desert one's best friend in what is so obviously her moment of desperate need!

~ * ~

"I want you as foreman on the fencing, Will. I need Gabriel full time on the house now. Can you handle it?"

Will shuffled.

Of course I bloody want it! But it could mean problems.

"I wouldn't want to set myself apart from the men, Squire. Been in this situation long enough to know that a man loses friends if he's seen as favoured."

"I'm not granting favours, Will. I need the best man on the job. Gabriel recommended you, and I'll have him make that clear to the others."

Gabriel was a free man, and Andrew Geil obviously had trust in him. He left him in charge during his many absences.

Will had confidence in his own organising abilities, all right; it was simply that in the dog-eat-dog world of convictism, the fine line of mateship was an issue that must be considered.

"Well, I'll give it a try, Squire, and I'd like it explained that way to the lads, if that's all right. I've some ideas for getting more done each day without extra effort; it just needs organising, I reckon."

"Then ring the change, and we'll see how it goes. You report to me now, and not to Gabriel. Understood?"

"Aye, sir."

"Then I'll have Gabriel talk to the men at end of shift today. I'll be there to show that you have my support."

~ * ~

"Isn't it wonderful, Sarah, my dear, when one hears her own parents saying how girls in their mid-teens are years older than boys of the same age?"

"Are you saying you've never noticed it for yourself, Susan?"

"Well, I no doubt had, but it's not easy to recognise when you have only brothers. One never stops to think about which one you leave behind your own intelligence."

"All my brothers are younger, quite juvenile in fact."

"How do they see you?"

"Do you think I would dare ask? I have only disdain for their sense of values anyway. At sixteen, Susan, I am of marriageable age. But them? It's laughable that in two years they could even approach me in maturity, let alone consider themselves marriageable."

"I agree we have both reached an age, Sarah dear, that we can look further ahead. What think you of this dreadful talk of having to quit the island?"

"Oh, yes. My folk are in such a state over it. Mary has already said she will go with her Will to Sydney. Pa reckons the wigs are bluffing, that they will retract."

"But the new governor in Sydney has said it must happen. And quickly. They are going to move all of us to Sydney or this Hobart place, then burn everything here."

"They said it before, Susan, and nothing happened."

"When Mr. King was governor, yes. My pa said Mr. King kept telling England that we should not be shut down. But now he's retired, Governor Bligh insists the island must close."

"Well my pa says we should do nowt, just wait until they change their minds. Ma doesn't want to go, either; she keeps on about what a paradise this is, all our flowering trees and things."

"Well they won't be flowering once the torch is set."

"Why would they burn everything?"

"So there's nothing here for the French or Spanish should they then take over the island."

"Well, my pa won't go to Sydney. He says the blacks are firing the corn and spearing settlers. And nobody knows aught of this Van Diemen's Land except that it snows in winter."

"My pa says we will go to Hobart."

"My pa's going to sit it out, see what happens."

It was a case all over again that the wants of little people could not be heard in England. With now the Hobart settlement established, ample safe harbours with arable soil and fresh water in abundance were available on the mainland. The cost of now bearing such a small settlement as Norfolk Island that didn't even have a harbour for the safe mooring of ships had reduced its value to nowt but a fiscal burden.

~ * ~

"But why now, Robbie, why now?"

"My dear Davie, I am but a humble parson. Surely you are more privy to such intelligence than I?"

Collins, in a rage, stomped across his little sitting room that doubled as his office. He threw Bligh's despatch so angrily on the desk that other papers scattered to the floor.

"Bligh must be mad, Robbie. He knows our situation. King would never have allowed this. I cannot feed the people I have! Where in God's name do I find food and shelter for thrice the number?"

"The good Lord, Davie, will no doubt be shielding his ears against the oaths and curses I fear are on the tip of your tongue."

"And damned right you are, you shameful man of the cloth. If you were worth your salt you'd be on your knees praying for a retraction."

William Bligh of *Bounty* fame was renowned for sparing no man, exercising no compassion when duty called. He brooked no sympathy for the rearguard action King had fought. He cared not a whit that King had been delaying until Collins was more ready to receive such an influx of people. Whitehall had instructed Bligh to proceed with the closure forthwith. He considered it a duty to proceed without question. His instruction to Collins was to be ready within a month to receive twice as many people as already comprised his settlement, to provide them with succour in the form of food and shelter, give them land grants, livestock, tools and equipment on arrival, and to supply provisions to every man, woman and child for a year.

"Damn the man, Robbie. He tells me to give them food I don't have, shelter I don't have, land that cannot be surveyed until the native problem is solved, give them more tools than the colony possesses, livestock that doesn't exist and a house equivalent to the one they leave when my own people are domiciled at best in wicker huts. And I am to provide them convict labour from a force already extended on essential works. How am I to quickly open up land? Where am I to quickly get marines to safeguard expansion? If we thought we had the rumblings of riot before this, Robbie, I fear we now face the prospect of civil war when these people arrive."

"My dear Davie, we've learned to suffer the heartache of having no wine and porter, the crutches that preserve sanity in this place. Surely the Norfolkers can ride out this hurdle. Take heart, Davie; if there were a drachm left in our cupboards, I would happily drink to the success of your challenge."

"Would that you offer supplication that our orchards would suddenly flourish, the cornfields yield double, nay, treble, that our livestock erupt with multiple births... We need a miracle, a series of miracles."

He knew the Norfolkers would carry more in their fob than he could give them.

When they discover how unable I am to fulfil Bligh's promises, they will lynch me!

And on the frontiers of his tiny settlement, the Aborigines, as if on some perverse cue, began attacking farms, plundering stock and burning houses.

Six

Once the first contingent of Norfolkers had arrived with sixteen settler families, Collins' palpable good sense began making some order out of desperation, to realise that on the other side of the penny once the chaotic beginning was behind them all, were advantages.

He had shown those families land at an upriver site they promptly named New Norfolk, to then return them to billets in town while getting the site prepared. He could clearly see that if only the timing were not so wrong, additional numbers were a good thing. The Norfolkers were not only successful farmers to quickly turn newly ploughed earth into vegetable gardens and growing mutton and pork on the hoof, but many were millers, builders and other tradesmen. All livestock left on Norfolk was being quickly cured and salted and shared between the Sydney and Hobart settlements, so hopefully that should quickly begin supplementing existing stores of food. There was also the fact that many *Calcutta* lags approached their pardons and could also be settled as soon as additional land was opened up.

It is all simply a matter of timing, his clearing mind kept repeating.

Attempting to go further inland would only exacerbate the native problem, so he concentrated on clearing along both sides of the river.

But how to house so many so quickly, while land is cleared?

He rose, called his aide and arranged for all senior officers to meet first thing tomorrow.

Somehow, he told his saddened spirit, *I must find a way to further spread our limited numbers of convicts and redcoats to, in the interim, get more work done by fewer hands.*

Poor, frustrated Collins wagged his head as he now began planning the arrival of the next, larger shipment of near two hundred expectant, demanding settlers, due aboard HMS *Porpoise.*

~ * ~

It was indeed a miserable Christmas Day for the Goodwins.

Tomorrow they must board *Porpoise,* leaving their all to the flames.

Mary was already gone. She and her man had left for Sydney, so Sarah, at sixteen, was oldest in the family as *Porpoise* set sail.

She carried '...*55 settlers, 11 delinquents, 37 women and 78 children.*'

All the children were delighted because what lay before them was adventure.

Whilst saddened parents assembled on the poop to grudgingly let their eyes see the last of their beloved Norfolk Island, the children assembled in the bow.

To them, they weren't leaving somewhere—they were going somewhere. What lay ahead was where they were to spend the rest of their lives.

"Just think, Susan," Sarah whispered, "how many more eligible men than any we knew on Norfolk, await us on the mainland!"

~ * ~

Ben Briscoe and Gus Morris stretched their backs. They were part of a group of some twenty convicts bivouacked at a new site across the river from Hobart Town, to which Governor Collins had given the name Clarence Plains. Its major advantages were firstly that it had excellent soil and secondly that it had a broad frontage to a protected bay, part of the same broad waterway into which the Derwent flowed, giving the area also access to the town, all the way by water.

"What you going to do after all this, Ben?"

Sharing options on what a man was to do when his pardon came was high on every seven-year man's mind at the time. All, in fact, looked forward to the following twelve to eighteen months during which each would see his particular date arrive.

"Well, I don't reckon a man could make enough to live on from making umbrellas in a land of a thousand people, Gus. And I know nowt else. So I reckon I have to try farming. With the guv offering help to every man while he learns, I reckon that's the way to go."

"This all looks good land."

"Even some of the redcoats reckon they'll not go back once they've served their three years—they will stay here and take a grant. And they, too, reckon this particular area looks good."

"Well, it's likely they know no more about farmin' than you or me. That's what I reckon."

Ben rested his shovel.

"Who ever knows what you got in your mind, Gus Morris, unless it's another chance to bolt?"

"No more bolting, mate. Three hundred lashes makes a man think twice."

"Aye, except for Davie. Likely we'll never know if he made it away or if they might've sunk as soon as they got to sea. None knew about working a ship. I recall Davie telling me when he said they were going, that it all would be a great risk."

"Who knows? He might be on some magic island makin' love to dusky maids."

They smiled.

"Always talkin' on doing things big, our Davie. Maybe he has found himself an island. Might be its king by now, knowin' him?"

"But this land we're right now workin' on, Gus—I hear rumours it's all for Norfolk Islanders, farmers who've been promised convict labour."

"I heard tell us older lags are getting assigned. You know anything on that?"

"Yes, like Will. He's assigned to the major until his time is up."

"Maybe we'll get assigned to Norfolkers?"

"I reckon. And that's a sure way of learning how to get a farm going."

~ * ~

Aboard HMS *Porpoise*, Sarah Goodwin didn't join the excited throng at the rail; she instead clambered up rigging enough that she could see over their heads. The Van Diemen's Land shoreline was taking the shape of beaches and bays, so it was hand to forehead to shade her eyes. Her gaze followed the line of clouds smudging the western horizon, clouds to gently billow, violet now with the sun behind them, leaking flashes of burnt orange and amber through cracks, colouring the hillsides that tumbled to the sea.

She was captivated as each new image merged into focus as they plied north.

She was bemused by the alien vegetation.

Friends joined her to share the excitement, for all about was bustle.

People chatted, pointed, proclaiming; children shrieked as they played tag amongst the clutter as crewmen decried the difficulty of working the ship with people clambering in rigging.

Sarah's mind raced months, even years ahead of the moment, picturing the delights awaiting her. In all her sixteen years she knew nowt but the Norfolk Island she could never return to...

...But here will be new people. I knew every soul on Norfolk, but here will be the challenge of strangers, and that will be only one of new things to enjoy.

Her mind flashed back to early childhood, vague memories of visiting Sydney Town. From deep in childish recall she thrilled again at the wonder of finding herself in a large town with big stone buildings, busy shops, and oh, so many people.

Hobart will be like that.

She was suddenly freed from the limitations of youth, a bubble about to burst, excited at the prospect of grasping new life with ambitious arms. Her impatience to be ashore was paramount, trying to push behind her the pessimisms her parents expressed. She had little patience with their attitudes.

They are but trying to prepare me when pointing out 'disadvantages,' insisting that because I know nowt but a sub-tropical climate I can't envisage cold and sleet; warning of savages, the risks of living beyond a town, of living amongst cruel convictism, floggings and hangings. Oldies live with bitter memories, I know, but I'm of a modern generation. Their outlook will ever be clouded by consciousness of their past. Hobart is a new world waiting to embrace us all, if only they could realise it.

She would accept cold and sleet despite she knew neither. And there would be redcoats to guard against natives...

...Besides, I am no longer the child wanting to romp in the woods, explore the unknown.

She even looked forward to seeing the maligned native, assessing the threat for herself. Nothing would deter her from believing everything in life was changing for the better.

She chatted with Susan on such matters until the sun dipped below the folds of mountain to leave the skyline trimmed in gold. Then she quietly marvelled, as the ship slowly reached into the Derwent mouth, land either side closing in, at the silhouette of Mount Wellington—rugged, wooded, and momentous...

It is simply so much taller, bigger and grander in all respects than Mount Pitt.

Everything here boded nowt but promise of an exciting future.

She bubbled, impatient that the ship was being hove to overnight.

~ * ~

Collins had been right on the ball, predicting that once enough time had elapsed, things would be better for having the Norfolkers.

The arrival was ugly. The *Porpoise* people arrived to find that many from the first shipment were still billeted in other's houses while their granted lots were being readied; they saw the rude huts that were being erected as 'housing' for them; they saw that soldiers had been turfed into tents so their barracks could become accommodation for the new arrivals. There was indeed, a near riot.

And when it was realised that there was little food available, Major Geil assembled redcoats with bayonets attached, should riot develop.

But time mellowed much of the discontent despite the emancipists really did have to start again from scratch, having to satisfy themselves that there was no option but to forget all the gains they had made since receiving their pardons, to start again with no more comforts than when they'd been convicts.

But they quickly had the corn up, gardens and orchards producing increasing quantities of goodies that little by little began appeasing the hunger pains of all.

~ * ~

Nine months after arrival...

"Six years ago, it was, Sarah, in London's Aldgate. I saw the man slide his pocketbook into a side pocket of his greatcoat, and followed him until he stopped where many people clustered about a spruiker. Got it out, I did; but he looked around right then, to see me with it. Never forget his face, I won't, as he in the instant recognised it. He grabbed at me...

"'Thief,' he yelled. I dropped his pocketbook because suddenly it was burnin' my hand. I could only think that if I got caught I shouldn't have it on me. I run up the Whitechapel High Street, but I was soon grabbed. Always on London streets are those who on hearing the 'Thief' shout, will stop a bolter, knowin' there'll be sixpence or a shilling reward. Then I was tried and sent to the hulks. That's as I remember it, at any rate."

"Seems you remember it like yesterday, Ben."

"A man don't forget. It's with yer always."

They were sharing tales of their lives.

Sarah had told Ben of Norfolk Island, the weather, the lush vegetation.

"Like a garden of rainbow flowers, my ma always called it."

And she had told him of her bitter disappointment on arriving in Hobart.

"It but goes to prove what I said, Sarah, if a person's not gentry they tell nowt o' the true matter o' things."

Sarah Goodwin and Ben Briscoe were working out marriage plans.

"I wonder if the reverend will recall? It's only six months since me lashin'."

"One hears many stories. Is he really a playboy? Difficult to believe, with him bein' the vicar and all."

"Believe it, Sarah."

Ben began ticking off fingers…

"Robbie Knopwood loves women, his bottle, food, religion. In that order, I reckon. And some say he is even a dab at cards. Or does he love his bottle more than women? And he dines on crayfish and black swan. Playboy is a good label. Yet without him, Sarah, the early days would've been worse. As well as lashin's, he gave us things to laugh at."

Ben had been assigned to Andy Goodwin as labourer when the Goodwins eventually got their Clarence Plains grant, so it didn't take him and Sarah long to form an attachment. Apart from the physical attractions, there were many other aspects that either consciously or subconsciously influenced their decision to marry.

She had never asked him about the whipping. The scars were witness to its horror, and this was his first mention of it. He was sensitive to the memory though, she reckoned, in that he brushed over it so lightly. His pardon was due soon, and he expected a grant among new Clarence Plains lots. There they would be but a mile upstream from the Goodwins, on the Hobart Town road.

"Glad we'll be near them. Pa can be a big help to us."

She had quickly discovered that the little community had no bachelors other than either convicts or those she had known all her life on Norfolk, and no familiars appealed as prospective husband.

Van Diemen's Land was in the unique situation of having seven men to every woman, and a sixteen-year-old free woman, she found, had suitors flocking around her like bees around a hive. Whilst she could have felt flattered, however, she had rather felt intimidated….

…most are brash and uncouth men starved of women's company all their adult lives, or older men not having been with a woman since before their transportation—and most are after nowt more than sexual relief.

"And how many of them can be believed," Susan Garth had asked on one of the many occasions they discussed the subject, "when they assure you they don't have a wife and family back in England?"

And in Ben, Sarah found, was a gentleness. He was a man not only quite handsome, she reckoned, his fair hair tied back in a ponytail and with the brightest of blue eyes...

...but one who pays me respect along with just about the right hints of lust!

From Ben's point of view, here was a young woman with her parents seemingly well enough off—and her pa also of importance enough to be on friendly terms with the governor, enough anyway, that when lots were up for distribution, Andy Goodwin got the best lot going.

"When I saw that lot risin' so gently from the mouth of that little river, its hills and dales ideal for growin' any sort of crop a man would want to plant," Andy had said, "I knew I'd not find another as promising; and with Letty lovin' the view across the bay to the forested hills in the east, a man felt he must bloody have it."

"He was a real mastiff, Sarah, the way he gripped on to what he wanted. I was there with Gus, workin' on the land when your pa grabbed the governor's arm. I saw it. And I knew all the lots were up for bidding, but your pa got the best one. He's a good man, your pa, Sarah. Lags here take note o' First Fleeters. Achievers they are."

Sarah didn't know the business side of a farm, had always shied off projects to do with numbers, yet now with Ben as unskilled, she reckoned on trying to learn the pitfalls, why so many lags foundered. She hoped Ben, when his pardon came, would get the Clarence Plain lot he'd applied for. It would be good to live so close to her ma and pa...

...Pa could keep an eye on Ben, and I can keep an eye on Ma.

"When troubles reach their worst, they start to mend," was a saying her ma often quoted, and it many times sparked each in the family to take a more positive view of problems at hand. Titia had a good knack of pulling people out of mental doldrums, setting them on a more purposeful path, Sarah had come to realise.

She's done it often enough with me, all right. And with Pa.

Sarah had also come to realise, since arriving there, how her ma didn't seem so young any more. Maybe it was that Sarah herself had developed to the stage of looking on her ma with more realistic eyes, or maybe again, it could have been the sadness of giving up Norfolk.

And she had a hard time with little Titia, still a sickly babe. Yet right now, of course, she's happy about my wedding so close, and that Aunt Liz has finally arrived.

Liz's second 'colony husband' had also recently died, and later arrivals said she had taken up with Corny Burrows, who adopted her family. They crossed on the last settler ship, left a sad little community, Aunt Liz had told Sarah's ma, the island empty save the team slaughtering and curing flesh before setting the torch.

But whatever happened to it now, Sarah had set her mind to accepting, didn't alter the fact that her future was Van Diemen's Land.

Norfolk is gone. This is where Ben and I must cement our minds.

And come marriage day people assembled on the Goodwin farm, bare and barren of flowers and blossoming trees, but with a start already made. The ferry made many trips to Kangaroo Point after the service at St. Davids, and Andy arranged a wagon shuttle from the Derwent's eastern shore.

Ben missed his mates. Will Woolley was assigned over the river, Gus Morris was upcountry, and of course Davie Gibson had sailed off to never-never land. So none could come. Sarah's friends arrived in numbers—the Burrows, the Garths and their several young'uns. Guests would bed down on the Goodwin farm or with neighbours because no ferry braved the Derwent after dark.

Titia and Sarah had baked for a week, and the girls ladled out ginger beer and lemonade while Andy instructed the boys in the art of tapping a keg without blowing the beer. He set up planks on upturned pails in the shade of a stand of gums where bush-flies fought with people for the food.

Sarah left Ben to sit with the menfolk and took Susan Garth aside to catch up on what had been happening in their respective lives.

When they were sure they were far enough from prying ears, Susan asked, "Have you and Ben done it?"

"Almost."

"What you mean by 'almost'? Did you or didn't you? Because, Sarah Briscoe, I want to know what it's like."

"Well we played around a bit, but we didn't actually do it."

"Well, what was the playing? You can be very teasing at times, you know?"

"Well, he showed me his, and I showed him mine."

Susan nearly had a convulsion.

"Was it big?"

"Very big and very hard."

Susan's eyes bulged. "How you know it was hard?"

"Because I held it, silly. It was also very hot."

"Ahhh!"

"You held it all? Put your hand right around it?"

Sarah nodded.

"And did he touch you?"

"No! I wouldn't let him. Told him he'd have to wait until after the marriage, I did."

"Well, what about tonight, then?"

Sarah just shrugged her shoulders and giggled again.

"Will you go all the way tonight?"

Sarah nodded again. "I reckon so. He's been waiting a long time."

Sarah was, of course, at the trembling stage herself over her 'First-Night-Fears' as her ma called it when explaining to Sarah what would likely happen.

But there's no way I'm going to share that with Susan.

Well, not yet anyway.

Seven

Will Woolley breathed deeply, holding his breath until his lungs near burst.

It was good air, free air.

"You don't have to go, Will. Grants take time, and I can use you here."

Pardon automatically terminated a lag's assignment, and Squire Geil had found Will a good worker.

"There are pitfalls in farming. You can only find along the way just how much there is to learn. So don't rush off half-cocked. You've a job at Geilston for as long as it takes you to learn all you need. I'll pay a wage."

"You're a good master, Squire. Many a lag's not been so lucky. And yes, I've seen many crack up for havin' gone off half-cocked. Only got to look at the Norfolkers to see the difference in a man knowin' what he's about."

"True indeed. While we struggled, those old lags came bursting like firecrackers in getting the corn up, and the wheat, and pasture enough to get our grazing on the go. And all learned by trial and error."

"Right, Squire. Only a daft man would knock back such a chance."

"I know you want to graze sheep, and I can help. You've seen how my flocks flourished."

Squire Geil then told Will of his plan to breed racehorses.

"There'll be good business for the first man to set up a breeding stable. Its very presence will foster the sport to the colony, especially with free settlers starting to arrive in numbers, including gentlemen."

And to concentrate on his new venture, he needed Will to run Geilston's grazing. He admired Will's approach to work as much as Will admired the squire's approach to lags joining the work force. The major was held in high esteem by all in the colony, in fact, for apart from being a respected soldier, he was an astute businessman, highly regarded in even government circles.

"No doubt about it, Squire, you don't miss a trick. Reckon Robbie Knopwood will be keen when your racing carnivals are on."

They laughed like friends rather than master and servant. The reverend was a regular visitor at Geilston, he and the squire moving in the same circle. Yet the major had never hidden from his trusted men how he knew the reverend was a target for lag jokes. Quite often he had made his own little joke.

Another thing he liked about Will Woolley was that he could joke in confidence about his master's friends without letting respect slip. Such trait of familiarity was beginning to emerge amongst emancipists, he'd noticed, one that none would have had the courage to exercise in England. But after what the lads had been through, it was expected they should ridicule gentry's pomp. Whilst they retained a respect, he admired the honesty of them not deferring to a man's social position. It was but another obvious element emerging in the colony's developing culture.

"Quite so, Will. In fact it was Robbie Knopwood sparked the idea in my mind, bemoaning the fact over a porter. By the time I set up, there will be many wanting a good stable, and I intend to have the bloodstock for them."

Will offered a wry smile.

"You know, Squire, I read in the news last week that a good mate from *Calcutta*, Ben Briscoe, got himself married to a Norfolker. He was another who bolted when the hungry days were on us, and he too got three hundred lashes with the compliments of the reverend. If yer don't mind me saying."

"They are days happily past for you and all those friends. The reverend was but doing what he was told, same as we all were."

~ * ~

Andrew Geil was to prove his word.

A year later when Will's grant came through, he saw to it that the price of the thirty head of livestock Will bought would not over-extend a man embarking on his first venture.

"But don't depend on just one product, man, have a second string to your bow. Take my advice and plant wheat. When weathering a rough time with one, the other can help you over the stile."

Will's thirty acres was good land both for grazing and growing grain, but Green Hills was frontier country, thirty miles from Hobart as the crow flies. Yet by the difficult bullock track winding through steep hills and gullies, it was twice as far, and that only after having ferried a man's all across the Derwent. Yet it was magnificent soil in beautiful country if one could ignore the getting to it—and the problem of blacks once there. In the heartland of Aboriginal territory it was, since the natives were pushed back from Risdon Cove and Clarence Plains.

"But there's redcoat patrols keeping watch," he was told.

The thrill of being a settler, however, surpassed all worries for Will. *Problems will be dealt with if and as they emerge.*

His land was something of his very own, which made it more than merely precious of itself; it was earth to sow and reap, earth never before tilled by man so had a smell of special vitality. It was a tangible thing. And with the land came labour, his own lag on assignment, as Irish as the blarney stone itself.

"Why don't yer talk English, Dannyboy? I can't understand a word yer say to me."

"'Tis the blarney in me, begorrah, and I'll no be changin' the way o' me words ter satisfy the English. If they be unhappy about leavin' God's blessed land of Erin to the Lord's most blessed people, then

Dannyboy'll cherish the little of it what's left, now his heart's there and his body's here."

Dannyboy was a political prisoner, one the English call 'insurgent.'

"Any who speaks against them is a rabble-rouser, William, a reactionary against England's bid to subdue the blessed Irish people."

"Are you telling me that you hold a grudge against me when we're to work together, when it's me who'll decide if you're doin' your bit?"

"No begorrah, William laddy. They cast you from your home same as me, disowned all who they tore from wives and mothers, husbands and fathers, lovers and bairns. You be as outcast in this land as me, laddy."

And it was later when Dannyboy saw the gnarled welts, the mangled flesh of William's back, that his mind became further confirmed in the belief that England disowned even its own, that the British arrogance he suffered was directed as much against its own serfs as against the Irish.

And when Will thought on Dannyboy's references to it being British arrogance that his countrymen suffered under, he smiled wryly.

And he will one day see that arrogance vent its spite against the natives of this land also, if I've got my predictions right.

Will's priorities were to first erect a shelter while he built a substantial hut before winter, then clear six of his thirty acres low-rise by the creek for grazing, three to be kept in fallow and three in pasture. Soon as the first were ready he would bring his flock from agistment at Geilston, then take the squire's advice and plant wheat. But the flatland acres for wheat would take another season. Logs from clearing he would split for the cabin and barn. At least he had the expertise for making best use of the property's ample timber.

But brushwork between stumps will have to suffice until we can start on fences.

The expense of horse and wagon was beyond him yet, but he and Dannyboy were fit enough, he reckoned, to trim and port the timber and pull the plough...

We'll simply have to be bloody fit enough!

In Hobart Town he had not only acquired Dannyboy but had tucked around them in the bullock cart supplies for two months: tools for clearing, sawing and building; sacks for storage and bedding; roo-skins for blankets, drawers and breeches for each; and at least as important as any of the stores, he believed, a reliable old Brown-Bess with powder and shot. The word in town was that Aborigines were on the warpath around the Pitt Water, in which district his property lay, so to protect his all from thieving, he bought several stout trunks with chains and padlocks.

They spent as much of the journey walking as riding, for there had been several days of fine weather and the track was firm. It was no joy travelling bullocky in mud, for when heavy wagons couldn't grip, beasts couldn't keep their feet on slopes, and every man, teamster or passenger, was kept busy toting rocks to pack behind wheels on up-slopes and in front on down-slopes when the brakes couldn't hold. On the flats, Will and Dannyboy walked alongside getting to know each other, flicking at flies with switches.

He made it clear to Dannyboy that he would respect the Irishman's politics and his devout religious faith, yet wouldn't be preached to on either.

"There'll be no Godbothering at Green Hills," he declared bluntly. He told Dannyboy straight that such cut little sway with William Woolley.

"When a man's seen what he's seen, suffered what man metes out to man as we've both seen, Dannyboy, each has the right to decide on the likes of right and wrong respecting God and man. Yours is as may be for you and I'll not try to convince you otherwise, and I'll thank you to do so for me."

"May Mother Mary bless yer, William, I couldn't ask yer ter make it more clear. I'll not be botherin' yer. And if yer be the man I think, yer'll soon be makin' it clear if I do it in the unconscious."

"We'll be working too hard, Dannyboy, to be doing much of anything in the unconscious. Hand ploughing ten acres will leave scant time for banter in the sleeping hours, I'll wager. And yes, I'm interested to learn about the problems in Ireland, it's just that I've no wish to be drawn into taking sides."

"The essence o' discretion I'll be, William me boy, you'll see if I'm not."

They worked hard. Will toiled with a determination he never realised man could conceive, building something to his own end that others would so look upon that he could smile. Dannyboy worked hard because he ate well and was treated well, advantages to be lost if Will were displeased.

At night in their rude hut, little better than a lean-to with a roof of bark, Will slept with Brown-Bess his constant companion. Only twice did natives appear during the days, and neither time did they come close enough to cause concern, simply seemed content to observe. The sight of man felling trees, which the black never did, digging up ground for planting, which the black never did, and fencing off areas to isolate some land from other, which he never did, always provided them with bewildered amusement. To destroy the feed of ground-game, the home of birds, to disturb ground that harboured such essential diet as lizards and grubs, to build barriers that hamper the stalking of game, were all negative things.

A platoon of redcoat troopers patrolled often enough to ensure the blacks were conscious of its presence.

Aborigines had a great respect for the white man's fire-stick; its magic of striking a man down simply by pointing in his direction was cause for respect in itself. Such a power sat easily with people with belief in the spirit world, who themselves had power to bring on a fatal malady to he who had the ceremonial bone pointed at him. Yet bones didn't leave a bloody hole from one side of the body to the other as big as you could fit several fingers into. And such was Brown-Bess's spiritual power.

So work on the property progressed at a rapid pace, despite the black presence.

"But yer'll not be satisfied without havin' taters, William laddy. And a man needs more o' the staple diet than will keep in good quality in a barrel until yer next journey ter the town. And the tater grows by itself if it has the magic touch o' Blarney. When an Irishman buries one in the ground, William, it yields up the biggest and sweetest crop you ever did see. Let me take a few from the store, and I'll show yer magic."

He selected not only the best potatoes but seeds for onions and carrots. Will's planned ten acres as stage one became twelve. What they couldn't eat, he would barter with neighbours. And they dug irrigation channels to sluice water to the crops come summer. Will applied his learning experiences to his future, complemented by many tried and proven practices from the green swards of Ireland.

It was time to replenish stores, and Will decided to make a trip to town before winter rains closed the track.

To wait will mean going all the way by sea, a journey taking wasteful extra days. And I need to see the squire about getting my sheep to Green Hills.

"I'll leave Brown-Bess with yer, Dannyboy. Blacks will not be so cautious if they see me leave with it, you'd then be fair game, like kangaroos."

"And it's heedin' yer trust I am, laddy."

"If you want, yer can swear yer trust in God's name," Will challenged, putting his lag right on the spot, but the response was spontaneous.

"In the name of Holy Mother Mary, I swear, laddy, that I'll be waitin' for yer. I've no desire to be testin' me Irish luck with the heathen savages."

Will laughed. "And I'll leave you a note should the troopers come by and wonder if you might have done me in and buried the evidence."

"Bring the porter yer promised, laddy, and all the saints will bless yer."

Will smiled again. Giving liquor to lags was forbidden, but the practice was widespread. A problem arose only if the lag were caught abroad with grog on his breath or if he decamped under the influence. In frontier land it was part of the camaraderie, that essential ingredient to survival, to blink one's eyes at officialdom—another convict trait for Andrew Geil's list.

This trip was also for building materials. Will planned a two-roomed cabin with separate cookhouse. He would make a table and stools but must buy pails and water barrels, cooking utensils, nails, lime for mortar in the chimney, and pins for thatch.

He smiled in retrospect at the planning, the lying awake nights adding each inspiration to his list.

It's like the days spent with Gus, Davie, and Ben working on our bolt, the secret planning, plotting, and hoping while awaiting the opportunity.

His current planning however stemmed from higher ideals, purposeful rather than simply hopeful.

But by mid-winter I want an indoors with a real fireplace for cooking as well as the luxury of warmth—and a flagon or two of porter—and a dog so I can close both eyes at night. A good dog around sheep can be as productive as another man, I reckon.

~ * ~

"A free man, a father, me own farm, and corn about to yield. It all makes a man feel extra proud, Sarah, love."

Will Woolley's mate was not far behind Will in tasting his freedom.

"Careful, Ben. Free you may be, but it doesn't mean everything will just fall into place. You reckoned our first tot would be a son, remember? And you was wrong. Now you're saying the fields are about to yield corn. The spring's not finished yet, Ben, so don't go counting the corn until the ears is growed."

Sarah pulling on the reins of his bolting mind was becoming habit. Too often Ben raced off into a world of dreams. He was a good man that she was more than happy with. She loved him dearly, and even with the babe now, she still looked forward to him making nightly love. Yet his inclination to dash headlong into fantasy worried her.

"Yer head is full of bright lights before you've lit the wick, Ben," she would tell him, an expression learned at her pa's knee. "We're all happy at your pardon coming through, but it doesn't mean everything will simply happen right. Let's take things in their turn, Ben, wait for the eggs to hatch before counting the chickens."

The farm struggled. Bushfires had swept the country to devastate yet young growth, so Ben borrowed more money to hire labour that more corn could be planted, as if to make up for the lost time.

"The corn doesn't know you've spent more money getting it planted Ben, and grow twice as quick," she cautioned.

But the farm was coming on well despite there were yet no comforts. The government had built the regulation two-roomed cottage and a cookhouse for them, and Ma and Pa had given them some furniture to get them started. Pa Goodwin gave Ben a loan to hire extra labour to get the scrubbing done that the soil was quickly cleared and ready for ploughing, yet it was a loan that Sarah saw little hope of Ben paying back with still so much owing on other essentials. And it was likely the crop, when it did arrive, wouldn't bring more than needed to pay new bills.

Ben was no money manager, both had discovered. He saw money simply as a means of getting the things he was impatient for, with little idea of how to repay it.

"Things we need won't be just handed to us like before you was pardoned," she kept telling him. "We got to plan, pay back what we borrow before we buy more."

Many men were anxious to quickly erase the hardship years, capitalise on casting off shackles, impatient to build on years of dreams. The colony was beginning to burgeon with activity, for apart from the Norfolkers, all *Calcutta*'s seven-year men were settling into new lives, many planting, some with tethered ewes until they could build fences, sharing a ram between neighbours that one day they might have flocks to count. Most had a cow or two for milk, butter, and cheese. All were starting to contribute to easing the people's hunger and the governor's dilemmas.

Clarence Plains was not as troubled by blacks now. Sarah's Pa had been right when predicting that with so many redcoats settling in it, the area would be safer the quicker. Sarah, like her ma had done for years, hitched up skirts between feeding the baby to plant seeds, wield the hoe, swing the axe, help her man labour in the field before returning indoors to stitch and mend, cook and launder, all the time making the best of living in little better than humpy conditions. Yet most found time to help out if neighbours were in crisis. Sickness and death remained part of life so most had also to find time for helping others in emergencies. It was a real community spirit that Sarah began to recognise, one she slowly realised had ever been part of emancipist life like her parents discovered on Norfolk.

Children of course were selfishly hobbled to youthful desires, but as adult mantles were shouldered and as convict men emerged into the world of self-sufficiency, they together began learning their ways along the new paths. These daughters of the more experienced came to realise they had a role to play in helping their men in the transition.

Yet none realised all of that was part of a new culture emerging.

~ * ~

"Transportation makes it easy for England to rid darlin' Erin o' misfits, William. Many an Irish Defender who's arrested disappears, whisked off by a will-o-the-wisp. We know he's been shipped. That's how I came here, laddy."

"You guilty of no crime, then, but speakin' out?"

"Sedition they calls it. I spoke up to protest a new law aimed especial like, against none but of Roman faith. They called it sedition. Never was a trial, William m'boy, I swear it."

"The English always did have different laws for the poor."

"Another porter, William? Aid me memory it will."

Will obliged. Dannyboy was slurring his speech, but it made the accent easier to understand. Will waved him to continue.

"It's the same laws for all, just that the poor hain't the money ter buy compassion."

Will knew of many trials in England testimony to that. There was always a way out for those with influential friends.

"People all over Ireland are starvin', William laddy. Tenant farmers who've been able to at least feed families are now taxed so high they can't pay rent, let alone buy clothes and meat. And yer can't raise family on only taters. So they're evicted, and when they sit pat cos they've nowhere to go, the bailiffs set dogs on 'em, hunt 'em out like foxes. The houses are then given to families of the very soldiers wot evict the tenants."

Tears sprang to Dannyboy's eyes as memories returned.

"A yeoman of Erin I am, William." He straightened shoulders. "'cept my arrows are but verbal barbs enough to land me in Van Diemen's Land. Erin is a beautiful land bein' raped, devastated by fire and bayonet. In many a village every tree is a gallows, men bobbin' about on branches like apples..."

Will started, distracted by the dog. Its ears pricked, alert.

"What is it, boy?"

The answer was a growl, jowls parting, fangs clenched in a snarl. Will snuffed the candle as he crept to the door to ease it so the mutt could scamper through. Then he felt his way along the wall to where Brown-Bess hung. But a shot startled them. The dog barked again and again, racing into the night as the doorpost splintered, the ball thudding into planking, inches from Dannyboy.

"Holy Mother of God, what's that?"

"Shhh." Will strained for sounds as he fumbled to fill the powder horn.

They heard savage snarls, sounds of battle between dog and man, barks, curses, growls, oaths. Then silence.

Will drew back the sacking that served as both window-sash and curtain and searched the night. In the dim moonlight two men ran through the potato field towards the trees.

They buried the dog next morning. It had bled to death from a six-inch slit in the throat. Blood was clotted in his claws to prove his attack had not been half hearted. And in the storehouse, spilled flour was evidence that saddlebags had been filled. The teabag was gone, and potatoes were tumbled across the floor. Will and Dannyboy had been just through the wall yet heard nothing. Even the dog had heard nothing until the thieves were leaving.

"Next dog will sleep in the storehouse," declared Will, "and its mate will be on a runnin' cable from the porch."

Troopers came by next day. Bushrangers had bailed up a farm on the Pitt Water, killed the dog and relieved the settler of money, a brace of pistols and several chickens. And left the man senseless.

Eight

For Mary Rohan (c1788-1848):

> *Alas, that Spring should vanish with the Rose!*
> *That Youth's sweet-scented Manuscript should close!*
> *The Nightingale that in the Branches sang,*
> *Ah, whence, and whither flown again, who knows?*

> *Rubáiyát of Omar Khayyam — LXXII*

Liffy Hollow, County Kildare, September 1816

Mary Rohan waggled an admonishing finger at her brother as she washed his bloody forehead.

"It's a foolish man yer bein', Connor. Anyone might think yer can outrun a racehorse instead o' bein' the first man they're likely to catch. Stick to bein' their lookout; then yer safer than puttin' yerself in the front line when a skirmish is on. They'll ship yer off if yer caught again, yer know."

Her brother had been known as Crooked Connor ever since as a lad, he jumped off the roof to show his pa how brave he had grown.

Her ma had been alive then, but Mary could still remember Connor's screams as her ma and pa held him down on the table while

Ma tried setting the fractured leg and fastening splints to it. Badly broken it was, but there were not enough pennies in the cookie jar to pay a physician. They never got it properly reset of course, so it had remained crooked. For the rest of his life he would not so much walk as limp in long, loping strides, dragging the damaged leg behind with each step.

He had learned to live with it although ever hated the helplessness of having to be driven if any distance were involved, or carried down any stairs. He could laboriously manage an upstairs climb, but coming down was beyond him. Sometimes he would even, out of what Mary called sheer stubbornness, walk his laborious and surely painful way all the way to the inn if Paddy couldn't drive him, but it being the best part of a mile from their cottage, such occasions were rare.

Life under British overlords was ever fraught with the risk of being arrested on an insurgency charge. Once upon a time it had been a matter of being formerly charged if caught at any sort of meeting not approved by the local constable—and 'any sort of meeting' even included a gathering of friends or neighbours in anyone's own cottage. Troopers had the right to burst in at any time and arraign everybody present, even if on a trumped up charge. And it was not only if the cottager himself had a reputation for speaking out against the system, but even if the particular troopers on the raid were in a bad mood or had a grudge for any reason, against any person present.

If a formal charge were laid, it invariably meant a trial, and no villager had the coin to hire a lawyer, so the verdict was always 'guilty' and the man would be shipped off to Botany Bay. And in ninety-nine cases out of every hundred, no man charged could afford to buy any sort of concession. Of late there was never even a trial; villagers would be shipped off to Botany Bay with false papers, no one, not even his family, knowing of it. All that was ever known was that their husband, son, or brother never came home, and neither the local troopers nor wardens of the prisons would know aught of the matter.

The other major worry for every villager was having enough coin come rent day.

All but the local squire and his hired help rented their acre of land, which would yield little more than enough to keep family bellies full enough to work gardens, dairies and sties. Life for all was one of subsistence farming at its most basic. Every soul lived in a rude stone cottage of one or two rooms, with earth floor and thatched roof, the only coin they could raise being from the little surplus they had to sell come market day in Maynooth, some eight miles distant.

And being frequently late in paying could well mean eviction.

Mary's contribution, apart from physical help in tending their vegetable garden, feeding the hog and cow, doing the milking and cooking for her pa, Crooked Connor, and herself, was to spend each morning at the manor milking its cows. That earned enough to pay the rent, so that the little surplus of vegetables they could send with their neighbour Paddy to market each Wednesday could pay for Pa's medication. He suffered severely from consumption and needed constant rest, hot food and expensive medication that Paddy would each week bring back from Maynooth.

Three nights after Crooked Connor had had his head broken by the constable in the confrontation outside the village inn, when he and his mates objected to being told to move off the street, he had gone off with Paddy to a meeting at the inn. Mary didn't know what the meeting was about, for no member of the meeting would ever divulge, to anyone not involved, its purpose. Not knowing kept all other than the participants safer.

Mary reckoned it was likely half-nine or ten by the time she had tucked her pa abed in the large cot he shared with Connor in the cottage's tiny second room. She had finished scrubbing the cook-pots and supper dishes and was just about to turn in to her single cot behind the hanging blanket, when there was a thunderous banging on the door.

"Mary, Mary," Danny's voice called.

She quickly opened it to let him in, conscious that her pa had sat up, rubbing his eyes.

Paddy was in a state, having, he gasped, "run from the bloody inn."

"The buggers raided us, Mary. Connor was by an upstairs window on lookout, but they must have crept up to the back door ready to burst in, even before the wagon come into view out front. They had broke a wheel of every buggy or wagon parked in back, the buggers, and—"

Mary shook him by the shoulders.

"But what of Connor, Paddy? For the love of Mother Mary, what of Connor?"

"They've got him, Mary. Poor Connor o' course was trapped upstairs. First we knew of it was Connor yellin'. 'Troopers, mates,' he called, 'the wagon's just come into view.'

"We all scrambled, Mary. They got Nick. I seen that before I dived through a bleedin' window, glass and all."

"What've they done with Connor?"

"When I found the wagon wheel broke, I hid behind the smithy's shed lookin' to see if others might be comin', but none did. Maybe they were just satisfied to get Connor and Nick for out the front door they come with both of 'em manacled. Christ knows how they got Connor down the stairs, Mary, but there was only Connor and Nick. They bundled them into the wagon and took off on the Maynooth road. So it's home I run, to tell yer."

Next day Mary said to her pa before leaving for the dairy, "I'm goin' to Maynooth after work. Paddy can't take me because he needs to still hide. I've enough from the cookie jar to hire a gig from the inn. For your dinner I've left a slow fire under the pot, and there's a suet pudding in the kettle for supper if it's late back I am. And there's bread in the crock."

She walked the mile to the inn from where, having rented a gig from the stable, she drove to the Maynooth police station. She hadn't worn her bonnet, because there was no sun this time of year anyway and she was always proud of her fire-red hair that fell halfway to her waist. For all her twenty-eight years she had believed the time spent grooming it had been worthwhile. As a child she would happily sit while her mother brushed it, and since old enough, had always engineered the time to do it herself. At the dairy she wound it up into a bundle under a mop-cap, but on occasions such as today, she had made it into a bun to sit right atop her head with enough wisps escaping to creep across her forehead. Her ma had always told her how well her hair and bright green eyes set each other off and that she should always make a feature of that.

So whilst driving the gig, she tied a scarf over it so the bun wouldn't break.

"How do you spell that name?" she was asked, so she awkwardly wrote his name. She could never remember whether Connor should have one or two Ns, so told him not to spend too much time over that because she knew she had the name Rohan spelled right.

"Me name is all I know how to write," she told him, "so I know well enough how to do it right."

He drew out a large ledger.

"I weren't on duty last night, ma'am, and I've only just come on duty today, so don't yet know who we got that might be new. But it'll be in here if the Liffy Hollow constable brought him here."

But his name wasn't there.

"Surely it's not direct to Belfast they would take him?"

"Well, I don't know. We got only this one day-book, and there's no record in it."

"Well, what about his friend, Nicholas Leary? Both were taken from the Liffy Hollow ale house last night."

He looked again.

"No, ma'am, but I'll go look in the lock-up."

With a flick of his hand and a waspish smile as his eyes flickered up and down her proudly tall body, he left her wait while he went through a door marked 'Private.' But he was quickly back, to raise both hands, palm up.

"Just like the book says it should be, ma'am, the lock-up is empty. I reckon you should try police headquarters in Dublin."

She drooped her shoulders. It was a long day's journey to Dublin and back by stage. At least they ran regularly, for it was on the main route from both Galway and Sligo. And she would have to go.

Hopefully I can get Sybil or someone to do my dairy stint tomorrow.

She rued having to lose a day's pay, but find Connor she must. She would arrange with the stable at the village to keep the gig overnight.

It will save me walkin' that mile again tomorrow, so I can likely then catch an earlier post.

The man at the stable had a ready eye for Mary, she knew, so he might not even charge her for those overnight hours seeing she would be renting again tomorrow.

And on the morrow she kissed his cheek for that extra service.

She was able to get her friend Sybil to do her dairy stint, so again left dinner and supper for her pa. She was up early enough to feed the chickens and hogs, milk the cow and again raid the cookie jar. She hoped against hope that not only would she find Connor but that he would be able to come back home with her. Not only did she not want on-going trouble with the authorities, but knew how impossible it would be for her to manage all that had to be done daily at home, without him.

That he might be already whisked away for despatch to Botany Bay was simply too dreadful a prospect to think about, so she forced herself to keep that firmly out of all the possible things that could be happening in Connor's life right now.

She said several voiceless Hail Marys as the laden post jolted its way east.

At least my most winning smile won me an inside seat in the post.

And she smiled at how the young man selling the tickets had been so easily won. Approaching thirty, she reckoned, made her far too old to expect flattering responses to a little coquetry, but it had worked well enough to not only save her from having to sit atop, but considerably lightened her heavy mood.

~ * ~

Sarah's pa harnessed up Dobbin to the buggy while Ben attended to things in the barn. Ben had got his Clarence Plains grant, although it was yet far from being productive.

Andy and Ben were joining one of the dray-loads of neighbours making an early start for Hobart. News of the governor suddenly dying had spread quickly, and his funeral was to be the biggest formal occasion the colony had witnessed. Her pa told her that her ma didn't feel well enough to go along so was staying home for the day. Sarah decided to take the baby and spend her day with her ma. She thought it highly likely Titia was pregnant again, and she'd had severe problems with baby Titia.

"Wished Ma would soon get beyond the falling pregnant stage," she had told Ben. "It's clear to see that pregnancy no longer puts a bloom in her cheeks. So I'll take MaryAnn over there and do whatever cooking or laundry Ma wants done."

"You need house-help, Ma," she told Titia once arrived. "Lucy and Meg still aren't up to doing heavy work around the house. You had Edith back on Norfolk, so why don't you get a woman to either live in or come in daily? Pa can afford it these days, and you've got to take more care of yourself. You're no chicken any more."

"Listen to you, Sarah, with your sounding off! You get more like your pa every day."

"It's common sense, I'm talking."

Sarah then cast about to be sure none of her sisters was within hearing. The boys were already in the field, she knew.

"Are you in the family way again? Because, Ma, if you are and you won't ask Pa to get a woman to help you, then I'll ask him."

Titia shrugged rather than smiled. And nodded.

"I think so. And little Titia's still such a handful. I don't know what it is that constantly ails her. None of the rest of you was ever the trouble she is. Last thing I want right now is to go through carrying another, but it seems that's the way of things."

"Does Pa know?"

"No, and I'm not telling him until I'm sure."

Sarah made a mental note to tell Ben when he got home, that Ben could slip the hint to her pa. That way everyone's nose was kept clean, but Pa would then approach Ma on it and the fact could all come out. Then Sarah could insist that Ma needed an 'Edith.'

Titia sat plying a needle into a canvas patch she was putting in Andy's breeches.

"Just look at that skyline now, Sarah. Every day I wish I had the time to just sit and watch the changes as the sun moves higher. And in each season it is different, I've noticed, particularly in the colours."

Sarah knew her ma enjoyed the vista from her veranda. And it was indeed a delightful view across Ralph's Bay to the forested shoreline and hills beyond.

"I love it best when dusk is falling," Titia continued, "when the sun's rays peek over the roof to draw a pencil line of gold along that eastern crest. It narrows so quickly as night shadows hasten up the hillsides. Then come each morning the sun announces its new day with a bursting brilliance from behind those same hills, to chase the shadows back into the bay."

The hours passed in chat, sisters Lucy and Meg doing lunch. And in late afternoon the men returned.

"Just collapsed across his desk, he did, Letty, no warnin', they reckon. Just sittin' over his books and things he was, when a seizure took him."

"I can picture him now with the governor and Mr. King in the longboat, the gold on their uniforms aglitter under the sun. And holdin' the peace for so long between the governor and Major Ross."

"And outsmartin' that Luke Haynes bugger," added Andy.

"It were the days at Port Phillip that I remember him most," said Ben, "tipplin' with the reverend on the beach, waltzin' his Sarah Powers."

"Wonder what will become of things now?"

"Only time will tell. Be a while before they get word to England to send a new man."

Sarah pushed the long folds of her skirts aside and struggled to her feet.

"And on our plan for the morrow, Ben Briscoe, yours and mine, is yet another early start. So down yer cuppa and let's be gettin' home."

Sarah and Ben's farm was a mile upstream from the Goodwin river-mouth, served by a well-beaten track already locally known as Goodwin's Road.

~ * ~

Out on the frontiers, however, news of the governor's passing passed with considerably less notice. News to outlying districts, of course, could take anything from several days to a month to reach the people, so quite often even the news being so late, tended to lessen its impact.

Will Woolley had had no personal contact with David Collins, but on hearing the news, he too found his memories of the man, those aboard *Calcutta* during their six months at sea, parading his Sarah Powers around the deck, her cuckolded husband sitting in his comfortable chair, watching.

But life will go on without him, I reckon. A new man will eventually come.

~ * ~

"Sorry, ma'am, but no one of that name was admitted here. Maybe they took him direct to the prison?"

In the busy city, Mary felt like the stranger she was. She had been to Dublin only once and had then been escorted wherever it was that her father needed to go. Now she felt utterly lost, with everything and everyone unfamiliar. Police Headquarters, she had found to her relief, was close to the post-house, and the directions given her had been easy to follow, but the prison was not going to be so simple.

"It's well out, ma'am." And he drew the map for her, but she had to remember all the names he wrote because other than her name if written in big, bold letters, reading was beyond her. His 'running-writing' was, to her, nowt but a meaningless scribble.

Several times she stopped to show people her map and to ask if she were going the right way, but while all were helpful, she nevertheless was becoming more stressed the further she went. It was indeed a long walk, and she hadn't the price of a hired cab; and every time she tried crossing a street, the persistent traffic had her intimidated. But she eventually made it, and what a cold, dank place it was—all of sinister, blackened stone...

Like a shiver seeking some passer-by's spine to run up...

Whilst she dearly wanted to discover that he was there, that she had at last found him, she at the same time hated the thought of him being incarcerated in such a place.

Having three times been asked to explain her mission since arriving before the daunting façade, she was eventually directed to a door beyond which was a long counter with several signs designating, she assumed, the type of business the clerk behind it was conducting. So again she was asking who might be able to tell her where poor Crooked Connor might be being held.

And again, having found the appropriate clerk, she waited while he consulted a large tome, running his fingers down the page.

She sighed deeply, feeling already physically and mentally drained despite not yet having learned anything from her search other than that Connor was not at Dublin's Police Headquarters.

But in seconds from now I may know!

"Sorry, ma'am, we've no man of that name here. Twenty-three admissions in the last three days, we've had, but no Connor Rohan. Are you sure it was to here they were bringin' him?"

She shook her head.

"I know only that he was taken in a police wagon from the inn at Liffy Hollow, off along the Maynooth road—and the constable at Maynooth tells me Connor was never admitted there."

"Well, we can't help yer, because he certainly ain't here. I reckon it's the Dublin Police, ma'am, that you should try."

Mary sighed deeply. She had heard talk of tales exactly like this, where a man is taken from a village but simply disappears, no one having any knowledge of who it was who took him, let alone where he might have been taken. It was sometimes later heard that he had turned up in Botany Bay. And New South Wales was on the far side of the world, a journey of many months.

"I've already been there, but they say the same as at Maynooth. Are there any other prisons?"

"No, only lock-ups where men are held until brought here."

"Is it that you're sayin' I must travel all over Ireland to ask at every lock-up in every village if they're holdin' my brother?"

"Every lock-up is supposed to put in paperwork of every prisoner and send it here. But they don't always do it. In fact, they seldom do it. In some towns, ma'am, they simply hold 'em for the next assizes, then delivers them up to the courts."

Mary, tired and exhausted, walked the long way back to the post-house, to then leave for home. She had eaten nowt, for the prices people wanted there in the city for even a single bowl of soup was more than it would cost her at home to make broth enough to last the family a week. And that night she sat consoling her father, the stress of his worries over the last two days having brought on a severe attack of wheezing.

Nine

Edward Lord, who by public agreement, being a prominent and popular citizen in the society, had sat for a time in David Collins' chair of office, awaiting decision on his request to be appointed Lieutenant Governor, was so distressed when word came from England that a new governor would be sent that he resigned on the spot.

Major Geil then took the chair until the arrival of the newly appointed governor, Colonel Sir Thomas Davey.

After his arrival, however, law and order began to fall apart.

'Mad Tom' Davey was the nickname dubbed on him, for he quickly became renowned for not only his unguarded attitude to people's sensitivities, but for his many ill-considered decisions—or, as most accorded them, his 'absolute bloody gaffes.'

He believed radical approaches to problems would solve them, yet it was soon realised to all but the governor himself that most succeeded only in turning them from problems into chaos. One of the most serious had been granting, despite warnings from experienced subordinates, leniencies to convicts. He insisted that convicts would respond positively if granted concessions, envisaging himself being hailed a hero by appealing to their better natures. But when placed on trust rather than in chains, most lags bolted, the forests quickly filling with escaped lags who fed and clothed themselves at the expense of travellers and farmers. Bushranging flourished.

Less than a week after Will's farm was again attacked, with fortunately no severe loss or damage, thanks to well-trained dogs, other settlers at Green Hills and everywhere else, he was to discover, called a meeting at Hobart, which the governor agreed to attend.

So Will journeyed to Hobart, to be pleasantly surprised when crossing a Hobart street...

"Yer lookin' grand, William m'boy."

It was Gussie Morris.

"And grand to see you, old friend."

They embraced like brothers and turned into *The Bricklayers Arms.*

Over ales they caught up on what had occurred in their respective lives and exchanged news of other friends.

"No Gus Morris anymore, m'boy, Augustus Morris Esquire I be, and sometimes 'The Don.'"

Gus sat, waiting for Will to enquire details.

Will obliged, knowing his swaggering friend would proffer no more until promised eager interest.

"Why 'The Don,' then, Gus?"

"A term of respect, m'boy, for bein' the most successful of enterprisin' men in Macquarie district."

"I've always admired your modesty, Gus, but surely you're understating achievements. I hear you've become one of the richest men in the colony."

Will had heard no such thing, but Gus had always responded to ego inflation. The trait only added gloss to his colourful character.

"Not quite, William m'boy, but on the way, yes, on the way. 'Tis Davie wot's the one really landed on his feet; see quite a bit o' the Red-haired Rascal I do. He's really makin' a name for 'imself in the north."

"Always angling to do things big, was Davie. But I gather he's back, eh? I hadn't heard about that."

"After eight o' the lags commandeered a vessel off North Bruny and made off, as yer might remember, they was captured as was usual for our Davie, and taken to Sydney on a charge of piracy. The ship's owner spoke up, tellin' how they treated the crew well and that the lags didn't deserve bein' branded pirates. So a death sentence was commuted to life."

"Davie now has two life sentences, then?"

Gus nodded and proceeded to explain how, whilst in Sydney, Davie was assigned to Mr. Robert Campbell, an influential man there.

"Well, William, yer know how our Davie always was able to talk his way out of an iron stew-pot with the lid tight on—" Will nodded. "—well, Mr. Campbell gives Davie a letter of introduction and a recommendation as an upright and honest feller..." Will sneezed into his ale. "...to none other than Ensign Piper, head of the New South Wales Corps in Van Diemen's Land's north, who has massive land holdin's as do all the NSW Corps officers thanks to years of havin' fingers in the money-box in Sydney and who plonks our Davie plumb in the middle of the colony's biggest sheep run as manager. Then Davie wangles himself a pardon—"

"From two life sentences?"

"—from his two sentences, yes mate, same old Davie, and a land grant direct from Governor Macquarie himself, of no less than a thousand acres."

It was incredible news, highlighting the magnitude of Davie's ability to not only get out of the troubles he continually brought on himself, but to bounce all the way to the top of the hill of fortune.

"And that's not all," continued Gus after pausing for breath.

Should I be really wondering if by some chance I was wrong in remembering Davie hailed from bonnie Scotland rather than from the land of Dannyboy's leprechaun magic?

"I can't believe there's more."

"Davie's a family man now with his own property and sheep run."

"How come all this? Maybe the truth is stretched in the telling?"

"Not at all, William. Davie tells me this himself, for I see him regular. He runs his own property while still boss of Piper's run, so that's two incomes. He treks a bullock team up and down the north-south road, a third income, and oft rides the team himself to save payin' wages. So passin' through Macquarie River he stays over, and we chat over an ale just as you and me are doin' now."

"With so much to tell, they must be all-night sessions."

Gus laughed. "But tell me about yerself. Got yerself a wife yet, Will?"

"No, but I got a farm. Not like Davie's by a long shot, but it's mine."

Will told Gus of his time with the major and of his thirty acres and what he had achieved so far. And that like Davie, he was holding down several jobs, making time to ply his building skills erecting stockyards and barns for neighbours.

"What about the blacks?"

"No blacks, but I had some lucky escapes from bushrangers..."

After hearing Will's news, Gus went on at length explaining how he was married with two littlies and that he'd had several scrapes with the blacks, actually getting speared one time. And that he had a ferry across the Derwent by the Black Snake.

"...You remember Will Stocker, mate?"

Will did, a *Calcutta* lag, nabbed for counterfeiting and who brought his wife, who died on the voyage. He now had the butchery in Hobart supplying not only the town, but visiting whalers and sealers.

"In partnership with Will Stocker, I am, mate, grazin'. Got a cattle run. We together supply prime beef to his butchery here in Hobart Town. I built a slaughterhouse as part of me own business, so money comes in from both directions. And I run sheep."

Will grinned again. All over the colony there were stories of convicts become profitable traders.

"Who'd have thought, Gus, when we bolted all that time ago, that we would come out of it so well. Reckoned there wasn't a future worth having, we did."

Both were in town for the settlers meeting, and they expected to see many old friends.

The Derwent Hotel was the popular drinking spot for *Calcutta* lags when in town, so they repaired there to continue their camaraderie in broader numbers. Will wondered if Ben might be there.

"Maybe not. Not in the bushranger belt, he's not. Clarence Plains is clear of forest now."

Will hadn't known Ben was at Clarence Plains.

"How'd he get there? Thought all that district was taken early."

"Married a Norfolk girl, her pa a First Fleeter who cut up rough with Davie Collins over gettin' his grant. Probably put in a word for Ben."

"Well how's he doing then?"

"Got himself littlies already I hear, didn't waste no time."

They arrived at The Derwent as the meeting started,

"All right, lads," a voice called over the hum of conversation, "let's set about decidin' what we want to come away with, from our meetin' with the governor."

~ * ~

Mary arrived at the dairy next morning, to sight Mr. Higgins, the master's butler, arriving from the house.

"Good morning to you, Mary. I heard yesterday that Sybil was doing the milking. Were you sick, girl?"

"No, Mr. Higgins. Brother Connor got himself into a spot of bother, and I had to go to Dublin."

"Ah, the rumpus at the pub the other night, eh? I heard the coppers made some arrests. Was that your brother's bother?"

"Aye, sir. Paddy saw Connor and Nick Leary bein' taken off in a police wagon, but I cannot find where he's been taken. Me and pa are greatly stressed, sir, at not knowin'."

"Well I hope it all soon sorts itself out, lass. Do you know aught of the butter churn having the squeaks? Cook tells me it has a creak and might need repair."

"I know nowt of that, sir, not being here yesterday."

"I'll check it out then."

He went one way once inside the door, and Mary went the other to don her mop-cap and tie on her apron.

Each day there were four cows to milk. She had already milked the cow at home and while working here she continued to fret over Connor.

If he has been whisked away for transportation, there is no way of knowing about it unless Paddy knows someone who might know where to ask questions. The alternative is to wait until the unlikely chance of a rumour reaching us that he has turned up in New South Wales.

Yet she then shook her head...

Such would take some six months for the journey each way. It would be more than a year, then, before we could ever hear something, if ever.

When Mary brought the first of the two pails of milk to the kitchen, Mrs. Flaherty, the master's housekeeper, was there.

"Ah, Mary. Will you come with me, please?"

Oh bother. What can she want now of all days, with so much waiting at home to be done?

In Connor's absence, her workload at home was doubled, but she had little time to cogitate on that, for Mrs. Flaherty had turned on her heel and stridden off, her bunch of keys on the chain about her waist jangling annoyingly. Mary had little time for the woman. She carried airs as if her position entitled her to consider herself gentry when she in fact was as much a peasant as any not born in one of the manor's grand beds. She seemed to enjoy the jangling of her keys, Mary had always reckoned, as if they illustrated a symbol of class as much as if she were bearing some jewel-studded sceptre.

And only when turning yet another corner in yet another hallway, as she followed the jangle, to find herself in what could only be the main entrance hall with its grand staircase, Mary suddenly realised that it was likely to the master's study she was being led. She had already removed her mop-cap but still wore her apron, but subconsciously raised a hand to finger-comb her hair that it look at least a little tidier than it otherwise might.

She waited as Mrs. Flaherty stopped at a doorway and knocked.

She didn't then wait for a signal but immediately turned the knob and marched in.

Mary followed.

The master and a strange gentleman stood beside the huge mahogany desk covered untidily, Mary thought, with papers. Mr. Higgins was standing a little to one side.

"Ah, Mary," said the master.

Mary stopped by the desk, dropping the hint of a curtsy, conscious of Mrs. Flaherty now moving behind her. She must have then simply stood to attention because there was no sound of jangling keys to suggest she had taken her leave.

"This gentleman, Mary," the master said, indicating the stranger, "is the police inspector from Maynooth. Did you happen to see Mr. Higgins in the dairy this morning?"

A little shiver ran up Mary's spine.

"Aye, sir, we arrived at the same time and exchanged greetings, sir."

The master nodded but did not look towards Mr. Higgins. It seemed to Mary, therefore, that the master was already aware of the meeting.

"Did you see him again during the morning?"

"Yes, sir, he returned when I was milking my second cow, sir. He went briefly into the workshop, then left again."

Now the policeman asked, "Did anyone else enter the workshop during the morning?"

Mary thought back.

"No, sir, I found it very lonely this morning, sir."

"Did you go into that room, Mary?"

"Only to get my milking pails, sir, two of them."

"So you went twice?"

"No, sir, only once."

"Did you see a timepiece sitting on a butter churn?"

Now she felt a considerable chill shudder up her spine. And she was sure it showed, because suddenly her composure felt pricked like a balloon.

"No, sir."

She glanced again at Mr. Higgins, who seemed uncomfortable.

Now the master resumed the exchange.

"Mr. Higgins went there this morning because cook had reported one of the butter churns needed attention—" He broke off in mid-sentence and turned to the butler. "—what on earth were you doing there anyway, Higgins? Surely we've odd-job men enough without you getting into that sort of thing?"

"I looked to see if it might have been something simply fixed sir, before calling in O'Hara."

Then the policeman addressed him.

"And you put your fob-watch on one churner while you fiddled with the other, eh?"

The butler again looked at Mary as if by way of apology.

"Yes, sir."

"And you later returned when you realised you'd left it behind, only to find it missing, eh?"

"Er—yes, sir."

Mary now began visibly trembling. Her mouth dropped open, and her legs began violent trembles. She was conscious of raising her hands, palms upwards, her expression obviously illustrating surprise and innocence.

Several seconds passed with now every eye, Mrs. Flaherty's excepted for she was still behind Mary, glaring into her very soul.

The master then broke the silence.

"Mrs. Flaherty, please."

There was a jangle of keys, and Mary felt Mrs. Flaherty's hands touch her hips, both sides, feeling upwards, and then inspecting the pocket of her apron. Mary knew she was noticeably trembling, her very expression showing not only her shock but the very repugnance of being so handled.

If only they can see how unfair this all is! Oh, Mother Mary, help them see how dreadfully mistaken they are!

Through her mind flashed images of her being dragged to a police-wagon much as Connor must have been, cast into the misery of Dublin Gaol, the sight of which only yesterday had sent such shivers through her, of her father left not only without Connor but now with the only other help and succour so essential to his staying alive...

Mrs. Flaherty found no watch, of course, but even Mary realised that the circumstantial evidence was damning.

The policeman took her by the elbow, not roughly but nevertheless firmly and walked her out to where a constable waited by a gig—well, almost walking, for her knees trembled so much that she was amazed they still supported her. She felt in a nightmare, as if this were not all really happening, that soon she would awake to the euphoria of utter relief.

But there was no awakening, no relief.

They drove directly to Maynooth and confined her in its lock-up.

~ * ~

Sarah rued the fact that Susan Garth lived way over the river, through the town and then some, where her father had the town's dairy. She missed having someone to chat through her worries with, and she didn't want to burden her ma.

Ma had confirmed the suspected pregnancy but had seen through it as bravely as she had her first ten, although now with the house-help her Andy had hired for her, things had become somewhat easier. It was another boy at last; Andy so thrilled about it that they gave him his own name.

Sarah had often thought on the fact that it had taken them so long to getting around to calling any of their children after themselves. Little Titia and now young Andy.

However, Sarah's major current worry was Ben. He was illustrating stress, but she couldn't get the reason out of him.

He had pressing worries, in fact so pressing that he was stressed over how to tell Sarah. But it had to come out. He had failed at hiring labour to harvest the wheat.

"So, Sarah, if I cannot find someone to work for the promise of later payment, you'll again have to ask a neighbour to sit the babes while you do the threshing."

"Ben Briscoe," she responded, hands ahip, "you know how I hate the threshing. It has me forever sneezing. You never have money put aside for when needed. You know by now when the hiring is due, whether it be for planting, reaping, threshing, or shearing, or any other chore, but you never do it Ben, you never look ahead, Ben."

He'd learned his seasons well enough, she realised, and achieved his fair share of sales shillings from the stores, but by the time he paid interest to the usurers for loans taken out to pay earlier loans, there was never enough left. And Sarah had made him swear on the bible that he wouldn't again ask her pa.

"How can I ask help from neighbours when every family's got its own reapin' on? MaryAnn might be six and tough for her age, but the twins are still a toddlin' handful, Ben—too much for her. And I can't feed little Benjie and thresh at the same time. I turn me back for a minute, and you let money slide through yer fingers. Others manage, Ben, why can't you? Not as if we don't get good yields with the help Pa gives us. There's many a farm around don't yield what we do, yet they manage."

Ben bit his tongue. Six years had taught him he couldn't best Sarah in argument. She had her pa's doggedness when it came to gripping teeth into things. And never making excuses for things that didn't turn out right.

"If it's proper planned, Ben, it'll happen proper."

And her pa's forthrightness!

Ben knew his shortcomings, didn't make excuses for having no letters, no numbers, for few lags had. Yet many were successful, despite it.

As she said.

Half the people in the colony were old Norfolkers and most with no letters or numbers, but they'd learned, come through it. He envied Sarah's pa. Never talked about his convict life, old Andy didn't, which Ben knew must have been at least as tough as his own, yet Andy just kept getting on with the job. And he'd come through, could now sit back nights with his pipe, having paid his bills, could buy his Letty the odd comfort to make her life easier.

Maybe Corny's got the right idea with a ferry instead of a farm. Risky job though, with the river so touchy. But at least it's regular money a man can count each day so he knows where he's at.

He thought, too, of all the convict transports now arriving from England.

All that extra labour for hire if only one has the shillings put aside.

~ * ~

After the two longest days in Mary's life, she was taken to Dublin gaol to await trial. The same young man who so recently seemed in sympathy with her in her search for her brother was the admitting clerk. He showed surprise although said nothing other than to ask the correct spelling of her name.

Later she wondered if it might be prison policy to refrain from unsolicited information on prisoners being admitted.

But maybe it's in case he might, by some mischance, complicate matters for me if such conversation were overheard?

Prison was neither better nor worse an experience than she had pondered on when wondering what Connor might be experiencing. Women were held separately from men, she was pleased to discover, although it would seem conditions were no better; absolutely everything about the place was basic. They handed her a well-used blanket, which at least smelled reasonably clean.

Almost threadbare it is, so how lucky can one be, it bein' the height of summer.

She still hoped that Mr. Higgins' watch would turn up, that they'd realise at the manor that she'd been wrongly accused and would come for her.

She hadn't yet considered, however, that the whole thing might have been a trumped-up charge based on the fact that with Connor already gone, and her father terminally ill, only she stood in the way of them acquiring their cottage for a larger family, one to provide more cheap labour in the manor workforce.

There were no separate cells. All inmates were together in a huge room, biggest she'd ever seen, needing stone columns here and there to hold up the roof. There were no cots, only palliasses laid atop straw that covered most of the stone floor as if the place were intended for cattle rather than people. But the straw likely gave some protection from the cold. The walls were surprisingly high with the only windows so high off the floor that even the tallest person couldn't see through them; and with no furniture, there was nothing to stand on. Iron grills barred the windows, and the rays of daylight beaming down were peppered with fine, swirling dust.

Oh, how thankful am I that I don't have breathing troubles. Else I'd be coughing and sneezing a treat. But with so much of it about I wouldn't be surprised if even the healthiest of bodies, here for a time, wouldn't develop some kind of problem.

Her pa's complaint kept her conscious of the need to keep the lungs clear.

At the far end of the room where no palliasses lay because of the telltale stench of it, was a room with washtubs and latrines. She didn't need to use one now so would leave that unsavoury experience until the urge arrived. She wondered that there weren't a door for it, so it could be closed against the smell.

Nor were there as many women here as she would have expected, especially considering the size of the chamber. The palliasses strewed about would have been a hundred or more, she guessed, yet less than a score of women stood about chatting, and only a half dozen were either sleeping or too ill to be afoot.

She didn't want company anyway. She had too much to think about, what with worrying over her pa no doubt fretting that she hadn't come home from work. He would likely walk over to Paddy's place, or to Sybil's and ask them to go check at the manor.

And oh! The fretting for him when they come back to tell what happened to me. I know he'll not believe me guilty, but that won't make a difference, only leave him with more questions than answers.

The question of there being so few women in the gaol was answered when dusk began to fall, a situation only as telling as the amount of light beaming through the dirty windows allowed. The sound of the lock in the big iron door through which she'd been ushered signalled it opening, and what must have been several score of women entered, most in considerable dishabille to illustrate that they'd been in the prison for some time. All seemed to know each other and obviously knew what to expect this side of the door, for each made directly for a palliasse to flop down as if physically exhausted.

On the mattress closest to Mary arrived a lass maybe three or four years younger, a pretty girl, Mary thought, given opportunity to dress her hair and her body better than conditions there allowed.

The girl smiled.

"New, aren't you?"

Mary nodded.

"Maybe an hour ago, I came. I wondered at there being so few here. Is it out to work you go?"

"In a different building we make army uniforms. Work in teams we do, cuttin' from patterns, stitchin', needle-workin' motifs and fixin' buttons. There also be a laundry where hard-labour women from a different part of the prison work."

"My name is Mary, from County Kildare."

"I'm Bridget, County Mayo."

"Can we send messages out of here?"

"Oh Lordy, no! They're not wantin' people out there knowin' how things is in here."

Mary's hopes slumped. Anyone looking for her here would likely get the same run-around that she'd had last week.

"You've been here how long, Bridget?"

"Six weeks. Waitin' for the Summer Assizes I am. Next week they start, so they tell us."

"I'm for them, too, I'm told, so my stay will be short."

"What you do?"

"What do you mean? What I do?"

"Your crime, what are you charged with?"

"Stealing a watch. But I didn't do it."

"No, deary. Course not!"

Mary didn't answer. She'd have her say at the trial. At the courts she could tell the truth of it all; she would rehearse each evening while feigning sleep, so she'd have logical answers ready to combat every charge. But she would like to get a message to Sybil so she could round up friends to come speak for Mary's honesty. But with messages not allowed, she would have to go it alone.

Although I reckon I could get a message out if I had coin!

But she had no coin. The little change she had from her excursion seeking Connor she had returned to the cookie-jar, the sacred honour-box on its kitchen shelf. She lapsed into regrets again at the thought of how her pa would now survive the week until she could get home again. But would the manor take her back?

Surely, once they've realised their mistake...

~ * ~

"Michael Howe, Your Excellency."

"Oh please desist, Colonel Geil. We dispense with formality when not on show. 'Your Excellency' is exceeding misplaced in this backwater. 'Colonel Davey' is satisfactory. Colonel to colonel since your promotion, eh? Now this Michael Howe fellow, calls himself 'Governor,' eh?"

"'Governor of the Ranges,' Colonel. A saucy fellow. With his band of brigands he wreaks havoc on frontier properties, burning and looting. Quite the cavalier with the ladies, however, doffs his hat and showers compliments aplenty before robbing them. Then as often as not, fires their outbuildings."

"Maybe he and I should talk. Governor to governor as it were, eh?"

Andrew Geil ignored the scampish gleam in Mad Tom's eyes.

"Within ten minutes, Colonel Davey, you face the delegation of angry settlers the other side of that door. Many have travelled more than a day to bring their complaints to you. They are desperate, Colonel. They not only want help, they need help in order to continue their very lives. And we need it to ensure progress of the colony. They expect decisions from you that have a credible expectation of success, not further attempts at negotiation."

He avoided adding that Mad Tom's half-hearted efforts to date already had him such a figure of ridicule.

"Then what do you suggest we do, Colonel?"

Andrew Geil withdrew several documents from his satchel.

"Quickly scan these, sir—or better still, call on me during the meeting, to present these, your recommendations, for the meeting to ratify?"

"Admirable, Colonel. We make a great team, eh? Let's go."

~ * ~

Mary's trial, when it came, was a farce.

She wished she had better opportunity to present herself in something more presentable. The work-frock she habitually wore to the dairy, by now, having been slept in every night, looked pretty much the dishabille that graced all the prison women. At least each morning in the 'wet' area by the latrines they could wash; and there were brushes and combs to give at least cursory grooming so she could face each day feeling and looking the best possible.

Mrs. Flaherty appeared and gave evidence that was as biased as it was inaccurate. Mr. Higgins stuttered and stammered his way through his side of her story, and Mary found it significant that he avoided looking at her the whole time. And when the master's foreman took the stand, he who always led the strong-armed men on rent-collection day, took the dock, he pointed an accusing finger at Mary declaring that her entire family comprised worthless wretches, her father a lazy good-for-nothing, and that even her brother was a convicted criminal against the crown—news to surprise Mary no end.

And when those people had given their evidence, Mary waited to be called to answer the charges—but no invitation came. The magistrate simply picked up his gavel, looked over the top of his pince-nez to declare in his bored tone, "Guilty as charged. Transported for seven years. Take her down."

He banged his gavel, and Mary was destined for Botany Bay.

~ * ~

"It ain't Botany Bay no more," the shocked Mary was told on return to the prison. "Yer off to Van Diemen's Land."

And that was all Mary Rohan knew of her prospects in life, on which to contemplate, until arriving there.

Ten

For Mark Ashby Bunker (1789-1868):

> *Come, fill the Cup, and in the Fire of Spring*
> *The Winter Garment of Repentance fling:*
> *The Bird of Time has but a little way*
> *To fly—and lo! the Bird is on the Wing.*
>
> *Rubáiyát of Omar Khayyam — VII*

Cranfield, Bedfordshire, March 1817

"Yer a daft man, Mark. I wouldna be keepin' it in t'house."

Mark Ashby Bunker rolled up the skin while Bill Peacock stuffed a joint of mutton into his sack, left threepence on the table, took his leave of Bess and let himself out. Other joints hung from a rafter, still dripping blood into basins. The stench of the freshly killed sheep pervaded the cottage.

"In the barn," said Bess. "I'll clean it come daylight."

There he lit a lantern and spread the skin over a barrel, a twist to his lips.

Not too damned good, is it?

Skinning a sheep was not one of Mark's skills. He would have liked to stretch it with weights as the tanner did, rather than leave it show every sign of amateur ignorance...

...but the clumsy slashes would then only widen. But it might fetch a bob or two.

Bedfordshire was Bunker country, his father had ever boasted.

"Nary a Bedfordshire village," he would say, "without a Bunker brand."

And Cranfield had two Mark Ashby Bunkers. Bess had presented him with a son but three months since, and he named the boy after himself.

The elder Mark was the only son given his mother's name. She was of the Ampthill Ashbys, a worthy family, and he liked the ring of the name Mark Ashby Bunker. It carried a tone of quality that appealed to his innate, even if misplaced, many would say, sense of eminence.

"Tom will come tomorrow," he told Bess when back in the house. "He'll take most of the mutton."

"Yer a trustin' man, Mark Bunker. Village butcher he may be, but he's also the law."

"Tom's all right—he knows the price of a bargain."

Tom Osborn doubled as village constable, but Mark knew he was safe.

"He'll know how to sell it quiet."

But Mark was too trusting. He hadn't allowed for the conflict of interest his ill-gotten sheep would pose for Tom, who arrived wearing not his butcher's cap, but his constable hat. He arrested Mark on suspicion of poaching and, ten days later in Bedford court, Mark was charged with stealing the sheep, to then languish in gaol for four tortuous months awaiting the summer assizes.

"You were a fool," Bess scolded, having travelled the seven long miles from Cranfield to visit. "They'll send yer off for good, y'know, and what'll happen to me and the bairn, eh? What'll become o' me and the boy?"

"Don't fret, woman. I'll get but a year, maybe less."

He wrote notes for her to take to friends he could depend on, for character references, those who, once aware of his plight, would come to court and speak for him. He couldn't afford a wig so he would plead his own defence. It would be a guilty verdict, he knew, but with good pleading, he should get away with no more than a year.

If only Father were still alive. As a wool classer, he knew the squire well.

Yet the trial, when it came, was quick.

The squire's son, Wil Robinson, called his shepherd Bywaters and hands Fascut and Barrington as witnesses. The three obviously considered security of employment ahead of Mark's friendship, for they each identified the markings on the skin and the coarse lock of the wool, unique to their master's flock. Then Tom Osborn told how he bought the skin when Mark offered it, to then show it to Squire's son.

Mark expected the mandatory death penalty for stealing livestock, which was always, by then, commuted to a gaol sentence. He pinned his hope on the magistrate being sufficiently swayed by his character reports to treat him kindly.

Yet despite some friends came and vouched for him as an honest man, the magistrate was unimpressed. He commuted the penalty to transportation for life.

"Life?"

Mark's composure, self-assurance assembled over waiting weeks, collapsed in the instant. He glared in disbelief, gagged in impotent rage.

Bess shrieked in shock and fear, startling all in court, yet heard by Mark only as if from a distance, through a fog.

His mind was in a stupor.

Admittedly several of the friends I asked to come speak for me failed to show, but those who came gave glowing reports—surely sufficient to get me a light sentence.. So how could I have been so wrong about the leniency of the magistrate? And wrong about Tom turning me in? And wrong about the allegiance of Bywaters, Fascut, and Barrington?

And the more he pondered on it, the more despondent he became...

They sided against me, opted in favour of the man with the shillings in his pocket.

Mark was indeed bitter, badly let down.

I've learned a lot this day, seeing so-called friends deny allegiance for mercenary gain.

His torment was that it was now too late for recriminations. Hindsight was no help, because there was no second chance. He must now pay for his oversights for the rest of his life.

Had Mark a mirror to look into, however, to see how others saw him, he would have suffered another shock. Many erstwhile friends saw Mark Ashby Bunker akin to a ship in a bottle, sails in full rig, flags aflutter, yet going nowhere. He would surely have believed them mistaken, for he took pride in being a loner, shrewd, careful to weigh odds, calculate probabilities...

And I have not been wrong too often. Of course the problem with Hannah was simply bad luck, nowt but a prank, no more than innocent philandering. It was unreasonable of her, taking me to court.

Happily he didn't concede to her demands as he later did with Bess.

Bess proved a far better proposition, despite her failings. Yet those two experiences taught me caution in reading values in a friendship. Or so I'd thought!

It's simply not fair now, though, to be so let down again.

The more he thought about Tom Osborn, Bywaters, and Rob Fascut, the more his heart hardened. He realised too late that he had never been calculating enough in assessing with whom to align and who and what to ignore.

But from now on, by God, I will see things differently. When in future I am drawn one way or another in any situation, I will take exceptional care to come down on the side of calculated security—no matter how moral or loose might seem the ethics!

Mark had but two weeks to fathom his new philosophy of life, embrace its principles, before journeying in chains to London and the infamous *Justitia* hulk. *Justitia* and *Censor* were the original river prisons with more than a thirty-year history of filth, vermin, disease, and death. Mark had never shirked work, always attacked it with a will knowing that at the end of the day he would receive his wages without scruple or diffidence, as his father and others had taught him. Yet he knew from hearsay that work on the hulks was gruelling, that man invariably longed for the day transportation would deliver him from their horror.

And there will certainly be no wages.

The thought of his infant son again brought a jagged lump to his throat.

Each time he thought of his boy he suffered horrors anew in the realisation that he could never see him grow, help him find his way in the world. Being sent away forever merely served to increase his new resolve to be selfish, shut emotion out of decisions.

I have to somehow assure myself that there can be no room for sentiment in a convict heart—especially when under sentence for life.

Mark Ashby Bunker tried to measure what was really in his heart in respect of what he was leaving. His parents had departed their present life, so the only family he would miss, apart from the boy, was Bess—and theirs was not a marriage born out of love. When she'd found she was pregnant, she was keen to marry, yet he had no desire to tie himself up. But like Hannah, Bess took the hard line, refused to make it easy for him to walk away; she too charged him, took out a summons, and he again found himself in court on a bastardy charge that would cost him dearly. And without a father to help, the second time he couldn't raise the money, so gave in.

He married Bess to avoid prison.

No, I won't fret too much over leaving Bess.

~ * ~

"Well, what happened?"

Dannyboy was more than anxious.

Will found him waiting in frenzied fear after five days alone. Will had wanted to arrive back yesterday, eager to settle the new dogs into their role, but the wind had risen on the river, and ferrymen suspended services. Several passenger drownings had sobered their daring in respect of braving the sudden squalls that frequented the Derwent. And once across, there'd been no bullock train departing and only a man more foolhardy than Will would take to the track alone.

If the natives didn't attack a lone traveller, bushrangers would.

"It's martial law, Dannyboy."

"Been martial law since I was born, laddy."

"All tickets of leave are revoked, and there's a curfew as if you or me are fool enough to go abroad at night. What it means most, Danny, is the governor can now hang bushrangers instead of sending them to trial in Sydney. He's raising extra troops to seek them out, back to their lairs. Colonel Geil reckons they will soon have so many swinging from gibbets that bolters will think twice about taking up the sport."

"Well, until then, William m'boy, maybe we should keep watch, take turns like. We can't keep losin' sheep at the rate they're bein' nicked."

Will was sure Dannyboy's main concern was not the sheep.

"Stand watch? Over a man's own bloody castle?"

It was fear glinting in Dannyboy's eyes as if hoping Will had said a redcoat watch would be stationed on the farm.

"It's all right for you and me, Dannyboy—we're grown men. It's settlers with families I feel for, littlies who can't defend themselves. And widder farmers with bairns, no men about other than their lags, who might not be as prepared to help in the situation as you."

Many lags aided bushrangers, stealing from masters to provide handouts to the brigands.

"And they'll be setting up provincial bases for companies of troopers, one here in Pitt Water. Meanwhile, Dannyboy, we got these new pups to train."

He tossed one into the Irishman's lap.

"Here boy, get to know your other master."

~ * ~

Sarah and Susan Garth were together again.

Susan was now married and had long since satisfied herself on the intricacies of the marriage bed, yet on the few occasions they now had to get together, they still shared the intimacy of topics personal, especially now, those of others.

"But it's not gossip," they reassured each other, "unless it's unkind things we're saying."

"And it's not unkind to talk about someone finally marrying the father of her children, surely," said Sarah, as if believing the analogy a legitimate excuse.

"Well, I remember that on Norfolk Island, she never married Tom's father."

"Nor then, the father of both girls."

"And how many has she now, then, given Corny Burrows?"

"Three…" answered Sarah, drawing the word out to emphasize that it was even more than the number she'd given either of her previous colony 'husbands'."

"Then why has she decided to now marry for the first time?"

"She says, according to Ma, it's to set an example for the girls."

"Example for the girls?"

They talked of Sarah's Aunt Liz, who had been Titia's dearest friend since First Fleet days. She was not a real aunt, but one who had always seemed part of the family.

The colony had ever suffered under the imbalance of sexes, and the burgeoning influx of free settlers arriving was swinging the pendulum even further in the wrong direction. All maturing girls were in great demand, and Liz's Maria had only last year married at fourteen; now her Ann, at twelve, was to marry a middle-aged *Calcutta* lag, still without a wife after fourteen years in the colony.

Many hundreds of older lags still waited in the queue.

But little did Sarah realise the tragedies about to strike not only Aunt Liz's family, but also her own—similar tragedies indeed.

In fact it was only a matter of weeks after the Aunt Liz and Corny Burrows marriage that the first struck.

"Ferries is always a risk, Sarah," Ben said, "and Corny knew it better'n most. The Derwent is treacherous. A man flirts with death tryin' to cross in a squall. Takin' to that water when the wind is up is like jumpin' into a pit with slippery sides."

"It's Aunt Liz, Ben, left yet again. She seems ever to draw the short straw with her men."

"People been callin' for a long time now for ferries to be made of pine instead of stringy-bark. Pine floats. People have something to grip on to for a time."

Corny's ferry had left the western bank with twelve passengers, a cart and horses, and other cargo, to be blown upriver by a squall. It was upset when trying to turn about, all aboard being tipped into the water and drowned.

~ * ~

During the following week, Will and Dannyboy instituted the precautions Will had planned during his journey, to protect Green Hills against further attacks.

"I bought a half-dozen stout barrels, Dannyboy. We can station them at strategic points. It'll take days of cartin' creek water to fill the buggers, but wherever fire might start, if by accident, bushranger, or native, there'll now be water handy to douse it. And this new brace of pistols, I'll be tuckin' in the thatch within ready reach, one in the cookhouse and one over my cot."

For the next year they lived with one eye on the job in hand and the other casting about for sliding shadows, sunlight glinting on shiny black skin or bushranger gun barrel. Some natives showed themselves, but each time disappeared as stealthily as they emerged, fading into trees, when Will and Dannyboy would breathe sighs of relief.

Yet came the day Dannyboy's pardon arrived. And he straightway told Will he would move back to town.

"I'm not the world's hero, William. I'll be a happier man out o' the forest. You've been a good master, and I thank yer and we'll meet again if the Lord be kind."

And Will, ever conscious of the assistance Andrew Geil had given him on reaching his own milestone, presented Danny with a modest purse to help him start his life's career.

"Hobart has grown since you saw it, Dannyboy, emerged from a wattle and daub village to the makings of a town with some fine stone buildings, many more people and businesses, workshops, retailers, and agents. Many opportunities for yer."

Then Will laboured over a letter of recommendation to assist Dannyboy find work in his safer environment. It was a sad time for Will, who hadn't realised how attached he'd become to the verbose Irishman. He hired a free man who happened along as was common in the districts, seeking work. Hiring a free man was more costly than taking a lag on assignment, yet Will felt he might get better allegiance this way in that he shouldn't expect to be so lucky with another lag. Many a lag aided the bushrangers at their master's expense, or even bolted to join their ranks.

And John Gould fitted in well enough.

One night as chill winds whipped through every crack in the cabin walls, Will sat in the cookhouse poring over his ledger; not a proper ledger, rather an untidy jumble of words and figures scribbled in every tiny space on the by now dog-eared pages. There were holes in the paper where he'd pressed too hard, and there were smudges galore where a spittled finger had erased his many mistakes. No accountant could ever understand the jumble, but it told Will how much he would need to sell for bills of exchange in lieu of money that the colony had about run out of, as against what he could barter, to still buy more pregnant ewes or plant more acres or pay labour to reap and thresh.

Biggest problem was that as weeks and months went by, there was more to do, more work than he and John could handle. For some time he had realised that with one man and from time to time hiring casuals, and the two dogs that more than earned their keep with the now three hundred strong flock, there was woman's work undone.

John rightly complained about the food Will served. It was good food, wholesome and copious, but monotonous. And when he thought about it, Will realised there should be more to eating than having mutton and potatoes every meal every day with only occasionally things like bread, cheese and cake bought from neighbours. A woman, if one were there, could serve up such things regularly, and sew garments, and maybe smarten up the cabin, all giving him more time to concentrate on the real work. And she might even add a chicken run.

Mmmm... his tastebuds twitched at the thought.

His conversation with Gus in *The Bricklayers Arms* had driven home the fact that all his friends had wives and children. Marriage was something Will had always pushed from his mind because the dangers of the times made Green Hills no place to bring a woman. But he was getting no younger, and if he wanted family, he shouldn't be looking too far beyond his thirty-five years. He had never felt easy around women. Some worked in one fashion or another for neighbours, and young widows often fluttered an eye, popped an over-zealous courtesy, flashed unmistakable encouragement, but he had stood by his resolve.

But his body had been used hard since long before the hulks, and he couldn't expect it would forever provide the extra effort he wanted from it. Before many more years, he would need sons to shoulder some burden.

Yet it's not a wife I'm lookin' for now. The need is simply an assigned woman, not too young or so comely she'd be a coquette that every man in the district might covet, but one whose attention is undivided—strictly on providing the domestic needs of Will Woolley's household.

Eleven

"I swear, Bridie, the people in this Sydney Cove hail from every county in Britain."

Their languages jangled in Mary Rohan's ears like discordant music.

"Lilting Irish, roupy Scots and throaty Welsh, apart from English in its countless accents. Just listen, will yer?"

But Bridie pointed to a particular spot on the wharves.

"'Tis glad I am, Mary, it's not here we're stayin'. Look at them poor wretches, so many chains that they weigh more'n their bodies, I reckon."

"Hobart will be no different."

The good ship *Canada* was moored in Sydney Cove by a cluster of rocks a tar called the improbable name of Pinchgut. The town was bigger than Mary expected, yet had no idea what had given her a measure in the first place.

Half the women off *Canada* were being unloaded in this town. The rest were for Hobart.

Many ships rode at anchor in the huge harbour of white, sandy beaches and the strangest forest ever, green in a fashion, yet not the verdant green of sacred Erin.

'Drab' is a fit word for it, no life to it; it's a tired, lazy green. And forests of it stretch as far as a body can see in every direction. Oh, how I'd love to climb the rigging, see the view from there. I don't fancy the climb, o' course, but to be so high would be exciting— watching the gulls screeching in their incessant swoops illustrates such an enviable sense of freedom. And they have a good view, of course.

She felt inspired by all she could see about her.

"But so many redcoats, Mary, everywhere one looks!"

Mary was far happier watching the freedom of the gulls and the sunlight glistening on the water, but the mention of redcoats brought her mind back to the other reality of her being there. There was always a catch in every breath back home, of course, when a redcoat platoon rode into an Irish village. *Who this time?* would flash through every frightened mind. Troopers seemed always presage to wailing and screaming as husbands and sons were marched off.

Which thought brought her mind back to Crooked Connor.

During the voyage she had thought much on both the likelihood and the unlikelihood of coming across him in this land. 'Botany Bay,' she had learned since starting the voyage, during which there were many occasions for chatting with the crew when on deck for exercise each day, was a general term applied to the entire land. It was the particular place where the First Fleet with the first white people to ever settle came, just south of Sydney Town, only to find there was no arable soil or fresh water. So two other sites were chosen, Sydney Harbour being one and Norfolk Island the other. Then some years later, Van Diemen's Land.

The Sydney settlement has already been fragmented into several districts, so the likelihood of finding Connor, even if he indeed was shipped here, is already remote.

But Bridie again interrupted Mary's meandering mind...

"Happy I'll be when ashore, to feel solid ground under me feet."

"Not happy am I though, Bridie, that we've more sailin' first. Havin' got this far, I'm anxious to have it done with. I'm no sailor."

"They say 'tis but a week to Hobart and all the way is close to shore."

Mary had made close friends with none of the women aboard, not for want of being unsociable, but because for all her years, she'd found no comfort in others' problems.

Scant satisfaction helping them find solutions, for in the main none are to be found. There's simply no way out of the Irish problem. and it will ever be so while people let politics rule emotions, people like Connor.

It was not that she didn't share the fear all the Irish people lived in; it was that she realised there was nowt she could do about it. She had vision enough to realise there could be no change during her lifetime, so why not accept the way of things?

She harboured no ambition of martyrdom.

And without book learning, how can any woman, in a country oppressed, expect aught but be somebody's drudge?

So she had kept to herself since leaving, rather than be dragged into the politics that brought to most families only more miseries to heap on old.

Every woman aboard, comely or shrew, had wailed and sobbed during the journey as if lamentations might change their situation. Mary regretted finding herself seven years a prisoner yet had no more wish to burden her disappointment on others than she cared to shoulder theirs. Bridie had been a good substitute for company, however, a woman aware that Mary wouldn't let her too close. So it had proved a safe friendship, because neither could know the chance of staying close...

...and that's been good enough reason for not getting close now!

"I wonder the prospects for findin' husbands," had been a question persistently asked aboard, one to always prompt a plethora of answers.

"They say there's several men to every woman. Maybe it'll be a choice that we're given."

"More likely they'll herd us straight to church to take the next in line."

"They got no church. No real church. These people is all English and Scots."

"Well, I won't be marryin' in one o' their churches, to live the rest o' me life in sin."

Mary wondered how many of those voicing such opinions already had a husband. She felt beyond the age, or stage, in life, of being agog about romance, so had little time for the topic. Those more deserving of sympathy, in her book, were those leaving bairns behind, likely never to see them again.

There are many, I know, who can't seem to live without a man, hold a fundamental need to be both bedded and protected. But I'm happily past the dreaming stage, content now to leave being wooed to coquettes. Protection isn't something so easily dismissed, however— simply the inequality of numbers in this land lends emphasis to that. Yet I'd like to have children, so can't afford to wait my seven years of sentence before following that road—which adds up to getting married, I guess—which certainly means a husband. But I'll simply wait and see.

She smiled.

"At least, Bridie, we won't be in the situation of every peasant wife in Ireland, in danger of a husband being overnight whisked away. Given the chance to choose, however, I'm ready to settle for a man not too radical and not too political. If Botany Bay has such, he'll suit me well enough."

"But he still won't be proper Christian."

"Mmm. The prison padre kept sayin' how marriage to any man not received into the Papal bosom will mean our children will be bastards. But what can we do if there is only one church?"

"I reckon this is why we hear so many sobs at night."

"Yet there bein' no real church, Bridie, nor any priest to marry us, will be but only one of our problems in this land. I'm not going to let that one bother me too much."

A tar touched her elbow. It was the chippy, his face engraved deeper with lines of living than any etching he carved in the call of duty, she'd often thought, who had for whatever reason, taken a fatherly interest in her. He pointed out *Elizabeth Henrietta* furling the last of her sails.

"She plies Sydney, Launceston, Hobart regular, lassie. Just back from Hobart she is, and she'll need but a day to provision. Then yer'll be off."

A tiny ship, thought Mary, her mind again on the tossing and pitching.

Yet while she didn't look forward to the journey, she was thankful it would be short. Not so for her chippy friend, returning to Ireland. She would never understand how a man could choose risking the dreadful dangers of a life at sea.

Yet at least he knows his future better than any of us can perceive.

~ * ~

Mark Ashby Bunker's prospect of a lifetime of deprivation and penance continued a heavy pressure during his three months on *Justitia*, a thundercloud threatening to burst with unimaginable horrors to engulf him in timeless purgatory. He could never but believe he was ill done by, unjustly dealt terrible retribution for so trivial a slip.

And whilst the horrors of hulk life proved a sentence in itself, he survived the conditions by clutching the only straw of hope he had, the challenge that he would somehow, someday, not only be recognised, but even envied, for rising above the ignominy of his present sorry state.

So maybe Mark Ashby Bunker was beginning his life of servitude with a more positive attitude than contemporaries?

He at least recognised his challenge. It was the only straw he had.

And he was lucky to be assigned to *Lady Castlereagh*. She was not only a new ship but the first especially fitted out for transportation. She had no walls below decks, only cells of iron grill for maximum ventilation, and separate cells provided opportunity for convicts to be graded, ruly from unruly, boys from lechers.

On her maiden voyage, she brought Mark and three hundred fellow lags non-stop to Sydney in half the time of the First Fleet's journey. Four months after setting course down-channel, she unloaded some in Sydney Harbour before sailing south to Hobart.

And by the time Mark arrived in Van Diemen's Land, his strength of purpose was fortified by the belief that he could achieve his challenge by cultivating a shrewdness based on truer values than held in his hapless past. With a life sentence, he could not look forward to again being a free man, so resolved to work towards a day when he could at least command respect—a challenge indeed for a lag, as everyone already in the colonies realised.

During the journey, he and fellow convicts were instructed in the assignment system. Whilst many variations depended on circumstance, it was basically that on arrival they were parcelled out as labourers, rather than be a cost on government stores. Prospective employers had access to ship surgeon's records before opting for eyeball assessment and undertook to feed and clothe their lags with the right to inflict punishment if they failed to perform.

Unlike early convicts who worked for the government, now most were employed by settlers. Charles Cox of Clarence Plains was a came-free settler, and Mark found him not too demanding a taskmaster, tough but fair.

And in the course of neighbourly fraternisation he met Ben and Sarah Briscoe.

During his first year in the district, he came to know them passably well.

~ * ~

Mary's further week at sea proved less fearful than expected, and the approach to Hobart was as impressive as she'd found Sydney Harbour.

She wondered if all ports in this vast continent were as magnificent. The dominance of Mount Wellington impacted like a bastion on a castle wall; and broad vistas on every side, as they plied upriver, aroused a hypnotic mood. All was scenically beautiful. There was chill in the air, the mountain capped with snow, despite the sun shone brightly, shimmering on the water, glistening on the sandy beaches, glancing off the mountaintop.

Seagulls screeched, wheeling in circle after circle, inspecting the intruders before darting off to resume fishing. She could not but feel more positive about the fears that had dogged her since setting sail.

Van Diemen's Land will be no Utopia. What prison could? Yet surely there is no more delightful part of the world outside Ireland, if this first sight is a sample. At least if I'm in prison for any length of time, and if that prison is like Belfast as prisons everywhere likely are, I'll know that just beyond the bolted doors, beauty beckons—and that will give heart and hope to those inside.

Hobart was a tiny town, hunched on the river inside a cove. Behind it, tentacles of habitation stretched along ridges. Yet as *Elizabeth Henrietta* furled sail, approaching the jetty, Mary could see the docks were as busy as Sydney Town's.

A line was rowed out and the little ship hauled in with practised efficiency.

The women were not manacled for disembarking, and she felt herself tingling as she crossed the plank. For the first time in months she was to stand on solid ground, no longer having to concentrate on tired muscles struggling to keep her body balanced. Women already ashore were standing feet apart, flexing knees, enjoying the sensation.

A smile parted her lips as she followed, conscious of a tingling on the querulous nature of what fate, now arrived, would be meted out to them. Was it dare-devilment to feel she was facing life as a 'thing' rather than a person, felon rather than free?

Maybe coping with such a situation is like rolling with life as the ship had to roll with the ocean?

And so pondering, she followed up a stack of boxes into a cart, where a redcoat quickly brought her to felon reality by pushing her into a squat, admonishing all to keep backsides on the floor or risk chains for a week.

At the prison they were quickly behind the bolted doors she'd pictured, in conditions no better than the poorest she'd expected.

"It's dry and warm," she chided those who complained. "It's here I'd rather be than still shivering in the musty stench o' Dublin Gaol."

Clerks asked names, ages, acquired skills, and informed there would be no delay contracting them out on assignment.

"Prospective masters are already in town to make selections," they were told.

"Tomorrer you'll do well to present yerselves comely," they were also told.

Basins to bathe, clean slops, combs and brushes for all, would also be provided.

"Puttin' us on display like cabbages at market."

"Like gentry paradin' horses for the gallery to gawk at."

"Want to see our teeth, too, no doubt."

"Hope the new slops have a low bodice, I do."

Another knelt in quiet prayer, at which Mary smiled. Neither was she sure what to expect, but certainly nothing worth praying over, in search either of hope or fear.

But on the morrow she washed and dressed, watching many pinch cheeks, bite lips to bring up colour, generally preen for display.

She dispensed with her mop-cap. Her blaze of ginger hair flowing down her back made her feel considerably more comfortable, as well as confident.

"Mary Rohan."

She moved to the front to be led to a table and shown a stool opposite from which sat a middle-aged man.

There was little about him to arrest attention unless that of all the men seated along the table an arm's length apart, it was he who illustrated the least discomfort. He had a strong face, suntanned and weathered, his whole demeanour depicting him a man of outdoors. The hands clasped on the table were large, rough hands carrying scars she recognised, the same scars that adorned the hands of her father and brother, scars of a myriad small, but hurtful farm accidents.

They rested on the written document that her interviewing clerk had written yesterday.

William Woolley didn't realise that to her he seemed composed, for his nerves were as taught as a drawn bowstring. He just hoped it didn't show. Nor did he rise as some did as their woman approached. But he noticed that she bobbed the hint of a curtsy anyway.

His eyes roved her so briefly she almost missed the movement; but he smiled, a reassuring smile, she felt, neither patronising nor superior, albeit awkward.

How will he open? Will he first ask about my crime, work, religion, comment on my age?

"You've recovered from your frightenin' journey?"

She, too, was more nervous than she hoped showed, and flustered.

"Thank you, yes," she mumbled, so muffled that she didn't hear.

But he would have seen the lips move.

"Can you cook, make cheese and butter?"

Words wouldn't come, so she nodded.

"And bake bread?"

Another nod.

"And sew?"

A nod.

"You'll live on a farm with another man and me and have your own room, is that satisfactory?"

This time she felt a need for more emphasis, and the words came sharply. "Yes, sir."

He smiled, and she was conscious of a faint parting of her own lips.

He picked up the form and folded it to pocket size. And stood.

"You'll do very well. I'll call in the morning."

Then he walked off to where the clerk sat.

She was totally flabbergasted.

He is the first of the men to have finished and asked nowt about me. All the form contains as far as my crime is concerned is the word 'stealing,' I know, so surely an employer would want to know stealing what? What were the circumstances? Yet he asked nowt, nor comment on the fact of me being twenty-eight but unmarried, nor about religion. And I don't even know his name, what type of farm he has, if there are other women in his village. Nothing. All I know is that I'm now assigned, that he is my master, will feed and clothe me, expect work in return and dispense punishment if he feels I'm not doing it well.

It had been the strangest of interviews.

Yet there was strength and a welcome aura of right and wrong about the man.

Other voices about, she now realised, were raised, some women crying, intimidated.

She'd been given no reason to doubt her safety or wellbeing other than the unknowns in the brevity of the interview. And his opening statement, nay, question, "You've recovered from your frightenin' journey?"

He asked as if he knows the fears. Has he too, made it? A convict out of his time who chose to stay? His voice is not an educated one, which I'm thankful for. I'd have felt intimidated if he'd presented himself above my class as some others in the room are obviously doing. But I felt nothing in that respect.

On leaving the room, she looked back to see him pointing her out to the clerk. She watched the clerk nod, reach his quill towards the inkwell.

Mary Rohan had much to ponder that night as she waited for sleep.

And tomorrow she would be ready early in case it was early he called.

~ * ~

"It's pleasing news, Will, to hear things are going well for you."

"Thank'ee, Squire. It's not come easy, but I was lucky to have a good man assigned. I lost him, but, when his pardon came through he was so scared of bushrangers and blacks that he moved into town. I'd even told him I could afford a wage."

"Ah, the wretched bushrangers. Yes, Will, Mad Tom has a lot to feel guilty about. It's incredible how a simple change of governor can bring about so much chaos. But this Sorell man seems the sort we need. He seems to have summed up the problems of a frontier society quickly. His values seem further in the right direction than were Mad Tom's."

Will had called at Geilston in the hope of purchasing thirty more ewes and a young stud ram. The colonel had a huge run by now, and agreed without hesitation.

"Go see Gabriel. Tell him what you want and that I said I would leave you two to agree the particular stock. Same price as last, if that's all right with you?"

"It's a pleasure to do business with yer, Squire, on those terms."

And as he wandered off to find Gabriel, he ruminated on the fact of how much trust the colonel must have in not only his Gabriel, but in Will himself.

He arrived to greet Gabriel with a slightly more expanded chest than that with which he had departed the squire.

But I've yet to see how this William Sorrell fellow works out. But if he's the sort who will listen carefully to the squire's advice, then he won't go far wrong.

~ * ~

The Cornelius Burrows tragedy was followed a year later by an even greater catastrophe for Sarah, emphasising Ben's concern about the ferries, in prophetic, devastating irony.

It was reported in the press:

> *HOBART TOWN GAZETTE & SOUTHERN REPORTER*
>
> *September 25, 1819*
>
> *Yesterday about one o'clock in the Afternoon, a most melancholy Accident occurred on the Derwent. A Ferryboat the Property of U.Allender was returning from Hobart Town to Kangaroo Point, with the two Boatsmen, George Hatton and John Ambridge, and a Passenger named BENJAMIN BRISCOE, a Settler at Clarence Plains; owing to the boisterous and stormy Weather which prevailed the whole Day, when near the Point the Boat became unmanageable, and suddenly went down; when the Whole were unfortunately drowned.*
>
> *The sad Disaster was seen by Persons in another Boat; but from the instantaneous manner in which it took place, they could render them no assistance. We have the distressing task to add, that BENJAMIN BRISCOE has left a Wife and a large infant family to deplore the loss of their Parent.*
>
> *The Body of Ambridge, and the Boat, shattered to pieces, were picked up this afternoon, as far up the River as New Town.*

And another, two months later:

> *HOBART TOWN GAZETTE & SOUTHERN REPORTER*
> *November 13, 1819*
> *Last week, Joseph Bennett, an elderly Man, was committed to Gaol, charged with embezzling Money entrusted to his Care. It appears, that the Prisoner was employed to solicit Subscriptions for the Widow and Family of the late BENJAMIN BRISCOE, who was unfortunately drowned some time ago in the Derwent; for whose Benefit he collected several Sums from benevolent Persons, but destitute of all the Feelings of Humanity, he appropriated them to his own use; thus converting the best of Intentions to the worst of Purposes.*

Nov 20, 1819

A CASE OF REAL DISTRESS

> *The Widow and Five Children of Benjamin Briscoe, who was unfortunately drowned in the River Derwent a few weeks ago, are by that unhappy accident deprived of their only Source of Support. She, therefore, most humbly submits her melancholy Case to the Humanity of the Public, in the hope that she may be enabled by its Assistance to provide for her infant Family. The smallest Donation will be thankfully received by Mr. Richardson at the Derwent Hotel; and Persons in the Country wishing to lend their generous Aid by sending Orders on their Agents in Town, by addressing them as above, may be assured they will be delivered to the disconsolate Widow. She has to acknowledge her most sincere Gratitude for the generous Donations of £17.7.6.*

Dec 11, 1819

The Widow of the late BENJAMIN BRISCOE, who is left with Five Children by the unfortunate Accident of her Husband being lately drowned in the River Derwent, at a Time when he was their Support; but most unhappily for the Widow his Affairs were rather in disorder. With a View to put his Debts in a train of Settlement she looks with confidence to the kind Assistance of the Humane and Charitable, to whom her appeal she is confidant [sic] will not be made in vain. Whatever Sums she may receive from Friends of Humanity will be faithfully applied to the Purpose before stated; and the Donars [sic] will have the consolation of having the little Property (her all) from being sold. She wants words to express her Gratitude for the kindness already experienced. Gratuities total £5.15.0

The clippings lay strewn over the table, unintelligible to either.

"Mr. Cox cut them from his newspapers, Pa."

"Well I thought the second would bring more than five pounds, Sarah, but we shouldn't look gift horses in the mouth. At least it topped up monies enough to save the farm. The bailiffs won't snatch it now."

"But debts took every last farthing. Biggest trouble is, Pa, there'll be no income for many a day, to pay labour. I can't put in the hours with three still toddling. MaryAnn's proving her worth, poor little pet, but a ten-year-old can't cope with laundry and cooking as well as minding the littlies."

"I tried hard, Sarah, to stop Ben takin' on more than he could pay for, but he was impatient. Yet tears don't undo what's done. The pasture paddocks are at their best, so that's one thing on the good side. We can't sacrifice wheat because those acres are the bulk of yer income, girl, so we leave that alone. Maybe come autumn we might look at quittin' some sheep. Keep enough for eatin' or barterin'."

"But I need labour now. I can't be a man short all summer."

"I can do without your brother. Jamie is footloose, waitin' to take up his own spread, and I can get by without him."

Sarah hugged him.

"Bless you, Pa."

There followed a long silence, both deep in thought, before she broke it...

"Do you know Mr. Cox's man, his assigned man?"

"The Bunker lag? You got an interest in the Bunker lag, girl?"

"Well, I wouldn't say that when he looks at me that my skies are more blue nor the river more glistenin' nor the trees more pretty, any more than I reckon he sees me as cream on his cake. But a woman alone in need of a man's support, one happy to care for her fatherless children, a widder who can't carve out her own living with six littlies, then I could do worse than set my cap at Mark Ashby Bunker. I reckon he's a man practical enough in a land so short of women that he would see one with property and stock, a reasonable catch."

"You got good sense tucked up in that head, Sarah, same as you got good in your heart. But the Bunker lad's got a reputation. Many say he wears big boots, sees himself a leader when he's but a lag."

"Yes, he's a tad high, when he's really as close to the ground as all lags. But he has letters and numbers. And plans things. And he is not cowed like many—he stands his ground when he reckons he's right— like you, Pa. And his heart seems on a straight path. There's many good points in all that."

She sighed, then waited before continuing...

"To someone who's had a man as well meaning and loving as Ben, yet without experience, hurrying along a path without really knowing the way, getting his fingers burnt because he couldn't see how short was the taper, Mark Bunker's faults look real attractive. Ben was a good man, but he's gone. And I need someone more practical."

Andy laid a finger on her knee, as much of reassurance as caution.

"The Bunker lad is a lifer. You'd ever be married to a lag with a chip on his shoulder, openly illustratin' shame at bein' a lag. Mark Bunker would not only be your husband but your assigned man for the rest o' your lives. Think careful, girl. You got common sense as well as that stout heart. Just don't rush into something without care."

She looped her arms about him to kiss his brow, lips conscious of the ruts and ridges left by his years of sun, sadness, and pain.

She let the kiss linger a little on the ruts, as if to soften them.

Twelve

Mary would remember her journey to Green Hills for the rest of her life.

All was in such contrast to what, to her, was normal. She quickly realised how such an entirely different world must change her life.

She had followed this man, whose name she learned was Mr. Woolley—or rather run after him, for he walked quickly as he shopped through Hobart Town—around every corner of which were strange sights: convicts in chains making roads, labouring on building sites, mending broken-down traps and gigs. Then it was by ferry with his wagonload of purchases, across the Derwent, that most magnificent of rivers—and the strange accents of people he spoke to, the boatman, other passengers, all of whom seemed at home amidst the strangeness. She would also remember that packed in his luggage were iron fetters the prison gave him, should he consider them needed...

....or even at his whim, I guess, once having me captive on his farm—and last night at the inn once across the river, expecting that at any moment he might burst through my door wanting favours as if his chattel—but I was rather not spoken a word to until coming down to peck at what was an absolute mountainous breakfast.

Then after the shopping, she was confronted with a bullock train memorable in itself, on realising it was their post, and every strange sight the forest and land itself presented. A muddy track wound up inclines one after another, to each time wend down through rocky outcrops. And she couldn't avoid, every few miles, looking back at the snow-tipped peak of the mountain behind the town, still sentinel, bastion standing proud, glistening against its backdrop of ever brightening blue sky. Overhead, for much of the time, brilliantly coloured parrots screeched enough to burst eardrums, temporarily drowing out the chortle of what he explained were kookaburras as they watched from hiding places high in the trees. Then there was the near pandemonium when all the men snatched pistols from belts as two black savages with spears, naked as the day they were born, ran across the track, thankfully to disappear as quickly into forest beyond, and the seemingly forever wonder of how far it might yet be to his farm.

And will his cottage be as rude as those we called at along the way, made all from lumber as if there is no stone?

It was indeed a journey of discovery.

And when arrived, what a strange farm for a woman used to green swards and peat bogs shrouded in morning mists...

The colours are more grey and yellow than green, and the little green there is, is certainly not what I've ever called green—it's a mere drabness, the only trees being grey-leafed gums. And the grass the sheep roam is more the colour of the barley in the far paddock, and the crop I didn't recognise, but which he told me is wheat. And the sheep are all white, not black and white like real sheep. The only thing familiar is the barking of dogs—their language seems much as Irish dogs bark.

The cottage was indeed rustic, and of lumber—and obviously reorganised during her master's absence, for John Gould hastily enquired if the re-arrangements were 'OK'? There were two rooms, both bedrooms, one of which she was shown to, its doorway off the lean-to veranda newly built, and iron rests for the bar on the inside freshly forged. Her room was simply furnished: a stool, a rude table with tin basin and ewer, and what they described a 'bush bed,' stretched canvas suspended in a frame of saplings. And rough shelves hung from the thatched roof on knotted ropes.

She smiled that the connecting door to the other room had been freshly nailed up. And there was no floor but earth, trodden hard.

The cookhouse had two rooms, a kitchen come parlour and a storehouse with John Gould's cot in a corner. The cookhouse, her cookhouse now, she assumed, although it would be sitting room for all, at least was timber floored.

Will told her to take time getting used to things.

"Can you make a list of what you need? No?"

She shook her head.

"...No matter," he then added with a smile. "When we sit in the evening, you tell me what I should order from town, and I'll write it down. In a fashion."

During the journey he had said, "I'll call you Mary. You call me William."

"Oh, that wouldn't be proper, sir. I'll call you 'sir' if that be all right."

"Then call me William when you feel ready to."

John Gould is a surly one. He and Mr. Woolley seem to have little to say, seeming content to communicate by nods and grunts. Affable grunts, though, so I'll not let that bother me.

But Mary was astounded to discover their eating habits, of the whole country, she was later to realise. It came as a shock when asking what they liked to eat for breakfast they gave what she considered an order for meal of the day. And for dinner the same. And for supper the same again.

"Then 'tis three dinners a day you'll be gettin'. It's obviously a land of plenty they've brought me to."

But I know I can give them more variety than it seems they've been getting from mutton and potatoes.

When they completed the list of what her cookhouse lacked, with quite some prompting from William, who obviously had plans in mind for things he expected, it included pullets and laying hens, the fittest cock the agent could find, geese for breeding and ducklings for the dam. She was pleased when he nodded and smiled as he laboriously made notes. He questioned nothing of her contribution.

Surely it's a land of great riches that I've come to, where, despite the rude abodes, the frugal nature of everything in sight, there are obviously pounds and shillings available to supply whatever someone's whim dictates.

And the ensuing weeks brought such surprises to Mary every day.

Most were mild, however, like when one evening over tea William gave her sketchy details of his convict life, to learn he was on the first ship to settle the colony, that this man first broke the soil of this farm, turned the first stone—a historic event indeed. She had seen the dreadful state of his back when she one time took lemonade to them in the field. He cut a fine figure, she reckoned, other than for his back. He told her how the colony grew from those first days, and then with some pride, of how several lag friends, as he called them, had achieved success at turning their hands to business. And this 'small' farm as he referred to it, though huge by her standards, was already more than paying its way. She was amazed that in this land, men without the advantage of a worthy birth could own their own farm and make a good living.

Oh the sadness of Irish serfdom!

Then came the day the quiet of the farm exploded into terror, when panic seized her, when after it she was in such a state the men had to comfort her. She was plucking a chicken once the poultry had been delivered, for the first change in diet she would serve up, when both men came running, shouting at her to bring Brown-Bess. And she had no idea who was Brown-Bess.

Then she saw the naked blacks, fiery spears raised. Panic consumed her. She could later remember only screaming and covering her face with her hands.

"They weren't goin' away because you couldn't see 'em, Mary," she was told later.

"When there's trouble like that, you gotta face up to it, and quick."

The blacks had not run away, of course. They came on behind the men to throw their flaming spears at the house, high so they landed in the thatch. From a window, William had let fire to then drop the musket and fire off a pistol that he snatched from under the thatch. That ball found a mark, for a savage screamed as they ran off. John Gould was already throwing pails of water on the flames, and Mary was called on to help. She remembered the trembling of her knees, the ringing in her ears from the gunfire, and the blood-curdling scream. And the tears in her eyes from impulsive crying from sheer terror.

"They somehow don't understand the advantage of attackin' with force of numbers, John. They only ever attack a farm three or four at a time."

"I rue the day, Will, when they realise numbers would crush our resources mighty bloody quick."

"Is it that yer sayin' this happens often?"

"Nay, Mary. But even seldom is too often. What you will do right now, my lady, is sit down and listen. I'll show you how to reload Brown-Bess after I've fired it, then I'm goin' to show you how to reload the pistols."

She shuddered, frightened.

"Then I'm goin' to teach you how to use them."

After that he talked much about the natives and bushrangers.

"After the previous governor, Mad Tom, took office, lawlessness grew in stampede proportions. The stupid man was forever introducing great schemes to fix problems, but few ever got off the ground. They foundered on the great sea of inefficiency that seemed to wash over everything he did. But a year ago now, the new Governor Sorell set about turnin' things around. He even set up bases for troopers to keep watch over frontier farms like this one..."

Oh, and just look at the neglect of poor farmers in Ireland!

"One was just a few miles away, and already it's takin' the shape of a town. He named it Sorell, after himself. So we're not so isolated now. The day will come when we've beaten the buggers, when we can sleep easy and not expect a spear to come flyin' at us as we work."

"But surely it's sympathy you should have for them, William. It's their homeland you're taking over, just like in Ireland. Surely you don't expect they'll lay down their spears to let you take their homes?"

Will had no sympathy for her argument. He'd earned his land.

"There was nothing here when I came, and there's hundreds of miles out there with not enough niggers to fill quarter of it. They can have all that. I want only this."

In his heart, Will did feel some sympathy for the blacks. The forests were their livelihood and were being destroyed, but there was plenty left and he saw no reason why they shouldn't move over, share it. It suited him not to see otherwise.

And she felt it prudent not to argue yet vowed that in future she would walk around the property with eyes seeing backwards as well as forwards.

"If you're goin' near the tree-line, Mary, take one of the dogs. They're trained to smell porridge ears and blighted eyes from fifty yards."

~ * ~

"If any man knows just cause why these two should not be wed, let him speak now or forever hold his peace."

The Reverend Knopwood waited while the children giggled.

Mark Ashby Bunker didn't expect to hear a response, yet his heart pumped faster. He hoped only that it wasn't audible or that anyone would notice his agitation. In his mind's eye was Bess, waving and screaming, trying to attract attention, but no one could hear. She held forth his child, the world's other Mark Ashby Bunker, but no one could see.

The moment passed, the ceremony proceeded, and he married Sarah with her by now *'seventy acres of prime Clarence Plains land of which ten were in wheat and sixty in pasture, two head of cattle and sixty sheep, a modest dwelling, outhouses and equipment.'*

But in all good conscience he would honour his obligation. His feelings for Sarah went beyond mercenary. He was indeed fond of her, and she was a fine mother, her children ever recognizable abroad by clean faces and neat attire, despite that at home they were dirty and grubby like children everywhere. And she had a sensible head and infectious wit...

...All in all, qualities any man could be happy to fall in love with.

He felt quite achieved, fully satisfied to now be legal husband to a woman of property with prospects. He was entirely content in taking on the responsibility as stepfather to her six Briscoe children.

Also all in all, Sarah Goodwin-Briscoe is entirely satisfactory as a prospective mother of Mark Ashby Bunker's children!

He liked to think he was now cleansed, that sin, if denial of Bess were such, was back in that other world from which he was now finally and cleanly severed.

Here is penned the start of a new chapter in life, the first step on a righteous path on which to negotiate the future with aforethought, with care to be seen upright and respected—a path no longer traversable back in that other world.

Sarah made immediate application for Mark to be assigned to her, and Charles Cox was happy, in the circumstance, to release him.

~ * ~

Meanwhile, at Green Hills…

Oh, how life has changed.

Last thing a man would've reckoned he wanted was somethin' else to keep his mind from the jobs at hand—and what's it been now? A year? Well, at least six months. No, it'd be a year because the reapin' was all done and it was comin' up shearin' time—yes, that was the way of it when Mary arrived. It's not so much the farm that's different, except that I've more sheep and all the planted trees are a year bigger—even the willows along the creek. But the startlin' thing is that a man feels different. There's more purpose in getting things organised now. And all because of Mary. Her influence is everywhere. The way she got the bloody pens built for the chickens and ducks and geese when a man was already stretched for enough bloody hours to get more fencing and a new bloody barn built—necessary with all the extra sheep a man ends up with after every lambing season. But it wasn't until after I got the bloody henhouse and rabbit hutches and things bloody built that a man realised how he must'a been all but bloody conned without realising it, to have changed his bloody priorities like that? But a man can't go bloody crook. Mary's got that knack of gettin' what she wants out of a man in such a nice sort of way—makes me feel it's me gettin' the bloody favours. But maybe that's woman's guile? Pat Conlan over the creek's always sayin' how his Mrs is like that. Almost bloody deceitful it is, Pat reckons. Another thing different is that John's not as bloody surly as he used to be—but that couldn't be because of Mary, I don't reckon. Or could it? A man'll have to think about that.

We certainly eat better since Mary come, o' course, with her fancy recipes in her head. Certainly a change from boiled mutton and spuds that John and me would eat meal after bloody meal for months on end. And cakes and puddings! And roast duckling! Ahhh! And with gravy! And a man don't feel as strange with a woman about the place as I'd reckoned, but maybe that's because she lived so long with her father and brother. And she never complains like the Conlan woman. Mary just gets on with things. Well, she never complains to me, and there's no one else to complain to when she doesn't know anyone else. And she never complains about that either. And she seems to understand how I feel about things, doesn't go off about all the things she must find unfamiliar—she just accepts that she must find a way around strangeness, around things and people, too, I guess. And I'm lucky, I reckon, that she grew up roughing it, so doesn't miss comforts. At least she seems content enough with everything that's so bloody Spartan around here. How bloody lucky was I that I didn't chance on a woman with fancy notions, eh? Only thing that seems to flummox her is that the farm brings in ready-enough cash that I can lash out a bit sometimes to buy a touch of luxury. So much of what she tells seems to only add support for what Dannyboy used to reckon about life in Ireland. I sometimes thought he must be exaggerating, but Mary's stories back his up. So maybe a man finding himself in bloody chains for a few years might have to start realisin' it was worth it in the long run.

All in bloody all, though, I feel easy with her around the house; and she's a stunner too o' course with all that fiery hair and bright green eyes...

But on that other point, if maybe it just might be Mary that is makin' John bloody Gould a mite less grumpy about life these days—I might just have to shove a spoke or two into his bloody wheels if I see him taking more than just casual bloody interest in her.

~ * ~

A year after their marriage, Sarah presented Mark with their first child.

They named her Elizabeth, and one might wonder if this were Sarah's choice in honour of sister Lizzie or Mark's choice by way of compensating another Elizabeth for having being so discarded—and for thankfully being so far distant.

Sarah and Mark saw the occasion as a double celebration, in fact, it coinciding with Mark being granted his Ticket of Leave. The laws in respect of convictism were forever being changed, subject to circumstance, and with firstly free settlers now arriving in greater numbers and wanting labour to help establish farms to produce food for the colony at large, and secondly, with new convicts now arriving from Britain in their thousands, good-behaviour lags were beginning to have sentences reduced. It was important that as many farms as possible were servicing the needs of the growing community. Incoming lags could be used for the hard labour.

The Ticket of Leave ceded Mark certain privileges, the main being that whilst still a serving convict, he was free to at least hire himself out at his own discretion.

"There is a significant indication, my dear, that I am at last on the path of achieving social respectability."

Sarah couldn't help but wonder at that goal being so important in Mark's endeavours. Nine out of every ten men she knew, as well as many women, either were or had been convicts. She simply could not see why it bothered Mark so much.

Mark's mind in the moment, however, travelled not Sarah's path, but that which turned on to the wider path leading to his Conditional Pardon. Provided he continued being careful of avoiding any adverse note on his record, that next goal was now in sight...

The ultimate goal, of course, will be my Absolute Pardon.

Sarah being beneficiary of Ben's property, Mark encouraged her to have it formerly registered in her own name. With the distant milestone of life sentences now being pardoned in progressive stages, the ownership of property was a significant point. A convict's Absolute Pardon designated him, in the eyes of the law, a man as free as any who had never been convict; and the law also read that a wife's property automatically transferred to her husband on his being declared free. He wanted clear title in her name that such a happy event would automatically come to pass.

"Do you know Will Hardy's crime, Sarah?"

Mark was ever interested in others with life sentences.

"No, but it's by the way, Mark. All I know is he arrived about the time we married. Ann is taking the baby to the church but still won't say if he's the father as well as groom. And Lucy is having another, have you noticed?"

"I don't keep up with all your sisters' births. It seems nine out of ten women in this colony are content to conceive, married or not."

He was subtly illustrating disapproval of the colony's many births out of wedlock and would like to make particular issue in respect of Lucy and Meg Goodwin. Yet he put it on hold. If the future were to see him happily pardoned, however, he would then more strongly emphasize the need for a socially clean Bunker image. Yet there wasn't waiting time in the case of Sarah's first-born, young MaryAnn, now twelve.

"I hope MaryAnn is prepared for the dangers to be faced in that direction?"

"Of course, Mark. There'll be no swain catching her off guard."

Mark of course chose to ignore his own wayward past in that respect, of which Sarah was safely unmindful, in any event.

Thirteen

"Well, I don't care for them, Mary, but if it's church you want, then we'll wed in church."

"For sure it's not a real church by my reckoning, William. But if it's the only church, then it's where I would like to wed."

So she and Will would go to Hobart, site of the colony's only church, leaving John to hold the frontier reins.

"We'll be but four days, John. As I pass, I'll ask the troopers to leave a man with yer until I'm back."

And in Hobart, as his friend Ben had done eight years before, William stood before the tippler parson, not on that occasion to be ordered three hundred lashes, but to wed. Feeling fiercely proud, he married his fire-haired Mary, who he decided looked prettier in the moment than ever, face radiant under the carrot top, her green eyes wide, sparkling, a contented smile lurking on her lips.

He'd tried to show her how to sign her name to the marriage, but 'running writing' as she called it, was beyond her.

"I can write it in big capital letters, but my mark is the signature I've used all my life, and after this I'll never be using the name Rohan again. So why go to the bother?"

"Then I'll teach you to write Mary Woolley."

Mary never learned to sign her name.

~ * ~

Eighteen happy months after her first Bunker child, Sarah sat one evening with their second babe, Meg, at breast, all the other children being abed.

"You know, Mark, how you were reading the other day about the death rate?"

She waited until he nodded.

"Well, only today Ma told me that Aunt Liz suddenly died. We don't know from what. Ma is distressed, of course, especially with those littlies now both motherless and fatherless. It's as well the older ones can take them in. Do you reckon it could be those diseases?"

Sarah referred to a newspaper article Mark had read to her, on the colony's high death rate.

'Rampant diseases,' it had reported, 'are by-products of hygiene ignorance.'

Many souls succumbed to sicknesses such as typhus, cholera, dysentery, and countless ailments for which diagnosis was unknown, let alone cures. Some doctors laid the onus on poor hygiene while others claimed that transported convicts brought the diseases from English prisons.

"The problem is a many-edged sword, Sarah. Increased transportation on the one hand is a consequence of increasing crime and unemployment there, and on the other, honest jobless there are emigrating. Our population explodes, and our economy booms with cheap labour abounding. So diseases may well be being imported along with the increased welfare."

Mark was indeed conscious of the prosperity, for he kept careful vigil of emancipist progress. It was not only financial security that careful time-expired lags were acquiring, but more importantly, increasing dignity through achieving success.

Mark saw himself in the forefront of convicts manoeuvring family aspirations towards such a goal and tried never to miss opportunity of raising social attitudes in Sarah, she who had ever been content to wear her convict breeding with a stout and loyal heart. And he recalled that Aunt Liz had married Corny Burrows, third father to her several children, only after having borne several out of wedlock.

"At least Aunt Liz could be buried with the honour ascribed those who had not lived all of their lives outside the sanctity of marriage."

Then, emboldened by her seeming indifference, he felt the time opportune to bring into the open his feeling in respect of her family.

A sad misjudgement…

"Which is more than can be said of so many in the colony, Sarah. Even sisters Lucy and Meg seem content to bear children out of wedlock, particularly Lucy with her three fatherless daughters, maybe—"

"Mark!"

Sarah stamped her foot, startling the suckling Meg.

"You are my husband, and I give you the respect a wife should. But I cannot listen to my family being talked down as if you were the Lord himself. How my sisters live their lives is not our business. One person's measure is not another's."

She moved the namesake Meg from left breast to right.

"And the children, Mark—what you tell them outside my hearing, I can do nowt about. But you'll find me unable to stand by if I hear you tell them their own flesh and blood is wanting in virtue."

"Then I suggest we change the subject, my dear. It ill behoves us squabbling should they overhear."

He recognised the need to quickly douse the fire so incautiously sparked, so allowed a minute to pass.

"I read that Clarence Plains is being renamed. It is to become Rokeby. And exciting things are to happen in this new Rokeby."

He waited.

"And what are they?"

At which he breathed more easily.

"A church is to be built, no doubt at the instigation of Reverend Knopwood, for the third piece of news is that he is to retire and take up residence here—a coup for the district, indeed."

Sarah's reaction lacked Mark's enthusiasm.

"He'll miss Hobart's bright lights then, if what I hear of his social philandering is right. Him being a parson, his amours with the ladies would stand to question in your book, I would reckon, Mark?"

He had been about to impart the fourth of the day's newsworthy items but decided that in the circumstance, its content could be seen as needling: that the governor had decreed all settlers and military officers must marry their 'convict wives' or deliver them to the women's prison.

It was an edict to prove highly inflammatory behind many colony doors, yet one highly applauded by the aspiring Mark Ashby Bunker, Esquire.

~ * ~

Life during the 1820s was good for the Woolleys.

Early in the decade Will would sit in his rocker of an evening, bouncing little George on a knee, love for Mary oozing from his heart as he ogled her naked breast where baby Liam snuggled. Roses bloomed in her cheeks now, proof of her happiness too, he reckoned, traumas of past life forgotten, blown away like wrinkled autumn leaves, that buds of new blossoms form.

A year after the marriage that each saw as more an act of convenience in their lives than anything more but which turned out to be the dawning of a love to envelop both in anxious want of each other, she gave him little George.

"George was my father's name, Mary, and I'd like to honour him with that. I left home early to join the army and never got home again before they shipped me out. And with our second son named William after me, girl, I'll be happy for you to choose the names of all our future sons."

She had cuddled him then, realising that as she moved into her thirties, and after the problems she'd had carrying her second, perhaps she might never see through another pregnancy.

George kept his name as his familiar name, but to save the confusion of two Williams in the family, little William the second's name was shortened to Liam.

"...as is the custom in Ireland, William."

And it was on one of those evenings as they sat in their rockers on the veranda Will had built on to the cottage, the time of day they gave to each other when the men, after dinner, for Will had taken on a convict assignee to offside John Gould, had repaired to their bunkhouse, that Will read an article in newspaper that had come wrapped around china plates Mary bought from an itinerant salesman. It was an article on Ben Briscoe's death and the plight of his widow.

"Sad it is," he said, "when life is plucked from a man before he can see his little ones flourish. And so soon after all he'd been through. Drowned in a ferry accident on the river he was. Ben was a good mate during the difficult days. Many times it was friendship with Ben, Davie, and Gus that kept me sane. You'd think if there were a God, Mary, he'd give a man a few more years before snuffin' him out. But it's not for me to say, I guess."

Mary blessed herself.

"A promise it is I made you, that I'd not be 'Godbotherin' as you call it. But I'll say as much as, that on this matter, I agree it's not for you to say."

They didn't pursue it. They valued the harmony grown between them and happily put differences aside.

Will hadn't wanted George baptised, and Mary didn't mind because in a country with no Catholic church, it wouldn't have been a proper baptism anyway. If both emotions could be felt together, it left her both disappointed but satisfied. And Will never regretted not having the child christened. In fact it was with some perverse pleasure that he was able to acknowledge that the lad was growing a healthy child anyway.

And like his land, his farm, his darling wife 'so luckily won in the draw' as he liked to jibe, his boys were added possessions to his pride. It was important for lags to aspire to ownership, so there was no dissatisfaction for Will Woolley. He simply felt thoroughly satisfied with the way his life was going.

As the colony prospered, the Woolley farm grew to yield more than could be bartered with neighbours, so Will now shipped to town for market day. His hired help grew to two lags and two free men, and every time a wagonload of onions, potatoes, carrots, or radishes trundled away, he smiled over the earlier Irish influence in his life, insisting he plant vegetables.

And Mary had a proper house now. Will had extended the timber cabin with two mud-brick rooms. Rammed earth sods, sun-dried and cemented with mud, made a warm and durable dwelling. Four rooms for a family of four was luxury indeed.

"Absolute elegance," she said of it.

When devouring the weekly news that was now available, Will would often read of his other lag mates, and relate it to her. Davie Gibson's holdings were on their way to becoming the largest spread in all Van Diemen's Land.

"Not bad, Mary, for a lag who survived two life sentences and was forever boltin'. The Red-haired Rascal ever was one to do things big."

Yet such happy news was followed by sad when he read that Gus had been widowed with four still little tots. Then but a year later, to read that Gus himself died.

"Like Ben, Mary, sad he couldn't enjoy a tad more freedom to watch his littlies grow."

Will then vowed to share every possible minute with his own sons.

But there was one tinge of disappointment in Will Woolley's marriage, one that kept niggling, so he had to keep a tight rein on it. Mary had upheld her promise on 'Godbothering,' so he was honour-bound in the second matter, despite the importance of wanting to take the opposite tack. He had agreed not to take part in the new governor's push against the natives, to drive them off the land once and for all. Mary ever equated the plight of the Aborigines with her beloved Irish, ever seeing the English as invading tyrants, stealing land and culture.

So Will must sit and watch.

"But not regardin' the outlaws, Mary," he gave firm notice. "I've made no promise about makin' war on bushrangers. If I'm called on for that, you'll find me takin' sides."

"And on that, my dear William, I will be siding with you."

The new governor George Arthur had heard the people's clamour for protection against the blacks. His taking office coincided with the colony winning independence from New South Wales. Van Diemen's Land became a colony able to institute laws and establish courts to rule on its own problems. Arthur was all-powerful and, by nature, was a despot, a tyrant to brook no counsel, who believed he'd been born to rule by decree and dictate. So his influence was to have marked effect not only on social disorders, but also on the very nature of convictism.

He inherited a colony of fourteen thousand souls of whom six thousand were convicts and six thousand emancipated lags and their children, a statistic to illustrate that first-generation convict blood flowed in eighty-six percent of its people's veins. Few, if any, in the entire colony, were perforce left untouched by the system's influence, especially as, every year, England despatched more convicts than the year before.

And under George Arthur, the horrors of convictism took on terrible proportions.

Under his administration, the prison for second offenders at Macquarie Harbour on the west coast became a Gomorrah of imaginative torture, human degradation and agonising yet thankful death. It was the first of the institutions to earn Van Diemen's Land's unenviable reputation of a convict-hell-on-earth.

The Williams and Marys across the land winced at tales filtering through.

With that prison unable to cope with the numbers despatched to it, Arthur built the dreaded Maria Island on the east coast; both were later to have their heinous reputations eclipsed by the governor's infamous Port Arthur prison. In his twelve-year leadership, Arthur earned himself the hatred of the convicts, the distrust of the settlers and the nickname *Butcher*.

Yet he attacked social disorders with an energy as ruthless as that against convicts, placing a bounty on the heads of bushrangers and declaring open war on Aborigines.

He introduced martial law in respect of these and proclaimed:

> '....*and I do hereby strictly command and order all*
> *Aborigines immediately to retire and depart from, and*

> *for no reason, and on no pretence, save as hereinafter provided, to re-enter such settled districts, or any portion of land cultivated and occupied by any person whomsoever, on pain of forcible expulsion therefrom, and such consequence as may be necessarily attendant on it...'*

Mary laughed aloud when Will read it to her, a brittle, accusing laugh.

"It's mad the man is, William, besotted by his own arrogance. This can mean nowt to the natives. All it can do is give settlers the right to murder on sight, not only every Aboriginal man, but his women and babies."

And so it came to pass.

Will, forced by his promise to Mary that he would not get involved, watched as neighbours read into the proclamation what they wanted, to ride off with troopers and dogs into native camps, slaughtering with wanton abandon with shot, cutlass, and hatchet. It was genocidal carnage in the name of justice.

"And listen to this—," he read soon after, faltering and stumbling in the reading, "—the governor's grand plan is to round up the remaining Aborigines for settlement on Flinders Island, up in Bass Strait."

The military was directed into the biggest field manoeuvre that that quarter of the world had witnessed. Towns and farms yielded up men to form a human chain moving south through the entire colony. Natives would have no recourse but to surrender as it approached, or retreat until the net closed in the south's narrowest isthmus.

During the exercise, there was excitement on every farm and in every village as the line passed through, people lending support to this humane way of ridding their lives of the black menace. Yet when the net eventually closed at the pinch of Eagle Hawk Neck near Port Arthur, it was empty. The tactical military exercise had proved a debacle.

Mary was delighted. She recognised the irony of white superiority with all its sophistication, challenging the ignorant savage to no avail.

In the arrogance she considered so readily epitomised the English, they had pitted skills against the savage at his own game of bushcraft and stealth, to be beaten hands down.

However, the natives conceded a tacit victory. The manoeuvre proved that the white man would not retract, waver in wanting more land.

To a man, the sad, defeated Aborigine laid down his spear and submitted to exile.

And having finally delivered his people from that long-lasting problem, Arthur turned his attention to bushrangers. Before settler blood could cool, every resource was directed to a systematic hunt for brigands. And in that instance, because of Will Woolley's participation, Will smilingly chose to insist to Mary, it became a resounding success.

Van Diemen's Land bushrangers were hunted down in military operations and either shot or hanged.

The people at last breathed freely, slept comfortably.

~ * ~

"Your pa tells me, Sarah, that brother James has received an additional land grant. This new carrot dangling before all with a proven farming record could apply to us, I reckon."

"I heard about that, but thought it only for large properties."

"It would seem not. Rather than depend solely on lags being emancipated or free immigrants arriving, to qualify for grants, each of whom are risks in the success stakes, the government is offering additional land to those whose success is already illustrated."

"Do you reckon then, that with our wheat, a hundred sheep and the poultry and tools and things, it's enough for them to look kindly on?"

"No doubt it should. But to help the application along, I'll ask Mr. Cox to give me a reference. A good word from him, being of the gentle class, cannot go astray."

"And we can tell them about all the children, the twins and all?"

"Maybe the governor is not interested in how many children bless the farm, Sarah, but by all means, include them if you wish."

So Sarah had a scribe complete her application, and within only a month, received her grant. She now had one hundred acres.

The late 1820s was a time proving itself of considerable plenty, and Clarence Plains, now Rokeby, enjoyed its share of the prosperity. In fact Van Diemen's Land, since Governor Arthur had so successfully rid the colony of both the bushranger and Aboriginal menaces, had become everywhere, it seemed, fertile fields and sheltered glades.

Towns had sprung up throughout the countryside, and with the roads now safe, travelling hawkers with imported luxuries, genteel clothing, bonnets and ribbons, soaps and perfumes, trundled their wagons to every market day in every town. And modern farming tools from the industrial revolution in Europe began appearing at festivals and markets.

In many respects, life for the Bunker family was beginning to blossom.

Her father too, took advantage of the boom to retire, to begin taking things easy after his hard life. Her ma, Sarah was pleased to see, was now content that her family was grown and off her hands. She, too, could sit back for the first time in her life.

Fourteen

For Adam Newitt (1794-1874):

> *Ah, fill the Cup—what boots it to repeat*
> *How Time is slipping underneath our Feet:*
> *Unborn To-morrow and dead Yesterday,*
> *Why fret about them if To-day be sweet?*
> > *Rubáiyát of Omar Khayyam — XXXVII*

Many convicts, from their first day in chains resolved to toe the line, earned no added discomfort in a traumatic life, like those of Mary Rohan's ilk. Some began with such resolve, yet the lure of release from horrors triumphed over caution: the William Woolleys, Benjamin Briscoes. Some from the first day, resolved only to defy all risks, challenge Lady Luck over and over: the Augustus Morrises, David Gibsons.

Then came he who lacked the resolve, or simply the common sense to avoid even minor risks, to be in trouble time after time through foolish bravado.

Adam Newitt.

A larrikin? Or was he, last of the core of convicts to Botany Bay and Van Diemen's Land who forged the founding paths of those forming the family of this trio of convict histories, simply folly-prone?

When it came to persistently falling foul of authority, truly deserving of the term 'lag' in the vernacular sense, he who refused to be intimidated by the system, Adam Newitt's careless misdemeanours dogged him and maintained him true to his reputation even unto death—when the coroner found Justifiable Homicide at the grand old age of eighty.

In the same year First Fleeters were starving at Sydney Cove, Adam was born in the Northamptonshire village of Long Buckby, to follow in its tradition of cobbling; shoe leather to prove his nemesis. He was caught stealing it a second time, earning transportation for fourteen years when thirty-three years old, twice married and father of six.

Son William was Adam's first mistake, born two years before his marriage at seventeen. Having then sixteen years later arrived in Van Diemen's Land, he continued adding mistake to mistake—or was it simply acts of folly to acts of folly in Governor Arthur's unyielding system?

He arrived as Governor Arthur was mopping up the colony's native and bushranger problems, when the economy was turning Van Diemen's Land into a land of plenty. There was no hunger or hopelessness when Adam arrived, and he never experienced fears attached to native or bushranger; yet he engineered his own sequence of problems beginning soon after assignment at Sorell.

The safety and comfort of the day's assigned men were vastly improved from frontier days when every man took life in his hands each hour. Adam, spared those stresses, merely found himself in a raw, dusty, uncouth land where for the first time in his life he slaved at menial tasks, hard physical work in impossible heat with flies, mosquitos, spiders and snakes adding to all other discomforts. And his diet of mutton stew with the odd potato or onion quickly lost flavour when served up day after day, week after week.

When questioned by redcoats in Sorell village, there was little doubt but that he had a number of reasons why he was in town without a pass from his assigned master, yet each fell on unforgiving ears. He had broken a rule of the governor's unforgiving system. And the penalty?

...Forfeiting assignment and sent to prison.

Maybe for a short time, during the surprise of having been so treated, he rued the heroics, yet his spirit remained undented, his confidence undaunted.

Adam Newitt was quickly assigned again, however, for shoe-making craftsmen were in great demand. A week later he sat in conversation with fellow lags at Government House buffing the leather patch he'd just applied to the coachman's boot. Sharing the chat were other lags polishing silver cutlery, cruets and napkin rings that the imperious governor might see his facial features gleaming back at him over each meal.

"Always bounce back, I do. Who would've thought as I clutched me empty belly in the lock-up yesterday, that today I'd be here in this lap o' luxury?"

Government House Hobart was a far cry from even the most humble of England's stately homes, hardly one to be termed 'lap of luxury,' yet surely in the wilderness of Van Diemen's Land it was the best a man could hope for. However, he quickly discovered that the governor expected it to run with the same precision as a military exercise, quite in contrast to Adam's idea of privilege.

His entire karma seemed based on impetuous risk, and he was, as well, instinctively careless, so the lure of freedom all too quickly, again, beckoned.

It was with some shock when the governor's butler used the term 'bolting' in his report, for Adam had simply been 'taking a break.'

He found the consequence far beyond a reasonable expectation.

Absconding from assignment from such a worthy master was looked on most unkindly by the magistrate who consigned Adam to the quarry where the treadwheel was harsh punishment indeed... a massive grindstone in diameter twice his height and in width twice his girth, a dead weight requiring Herculean effort to keep rolling for endless shifts in the October sun. He suffered blisters on blisters and cuts on cuts as bare feet continually slipped under the strain. Collapse brought no respite, for he was simply revived and chained closer to the wheel.

Adam learned that hard way to survive, even when his throat was constricted hour after thirsty hour. It was torture enough to chasten any man.

Well, maybe any other man.

Back in Hobart gaol recovering from his several wounds and more than dented pride, and again rueing the loss of such a comfortable job, he wrestled with the disappointment of how little satisfaction had been his moment of liberty.

Yet within a month of release, he was again before the magistrate.

Not content with exposing himself to the penalty incurred for yet again being absent from assignment, he earned a charge of disobeying orders and another of neglect of duty, which together earned him twenty-five lashes.

Once lashed, he was again sent back to prison, where he lingered some time. He couldn't be assigned out again until his back had healed sufficiently to be fit for hard labour.

By the end of his first year in the colony, Adam appeared to have learned a lesson, the realisation perhaps dawning within him as each stroke of the lash flayed his flesh to bloody pulp. And he had near thirteen years to yet suffer...

An unlikely prospect at this rate of punishment!

"You ain't gonna convince 'em, Adam, m'lad. They'll not go easier on yer because yer've taken so much already."

"But it's not in me nature, Jack, to be confined. I can't stay penned."

"Yer not behind bars day and night, week in, week out, like if you was in prison back 'ome, mate. This whole land is an open prison, but yer still can't just take off when yer want. They'll keep hurtin' yer until the message is through into yer thick, bloody skull."

Jack Norton was another regular miscreant who had finally learned that refusal to submit gained nowt but pain. A plasterer was Jack, been Adam's shipmate on *Asia V*.. Their paths still crossed, however— usually in gaol.

"It's a rum life, Jack, kept like a bunny in its hutch."

"You break the rules, Adam, you pay. If yer don't stop, they'll pack yer off to the island. Or Macquarie 'Arbour, and no one comes back from there."

Whether or not it was the lashing that eventually curbed Adam's perverse nature, or if it were the fear of being sent to a hard labour prison to die of madness, he never bothered to consider. But Adam behaved himself for a time.

And a third factor was yet of abstract influence.

Governor Arthur had established seven classes of convict servitude, top of the scale being the lag submissive enough to be trustworthy, permitted to sleep out of barracks and work for a wage on Saturdays.

At the nether end were those whom neither chains nor lash could tame and who were sent to one of the hard labour prisons, which very few survived.

Midway on the scale was to be badly behaved enough to warrant working permanently in irons, with no privileges.

"Best I reckon I could score, Jack, with a touch o' luck, is number three—sleep in barracks, do public work, with half Saturdays workin' for coin."

"What good is coin when a lag mayn't spend money? And to keep it in a tin, it'll get nicked."

"I'll keep it safe, mate. An' I been listenin' around. I got a missus and littlies back home, and if they come here, Ann can get a land grant with me her assigned man. That's the way to go, I reckon, to get off this roundabout."

"They won't bring yer family if they're gonna be callin' on stores for vittles. You gotta support 'em from the day they arrive."

"If I work on it, it can happen. I'm a reliable bloke, Jack—just trust me."

~ * ~

As the 1820s came to a close, there was further good news for Mark and Sarah.

Mark received his Conditional Pardon, a sure indication that, provided his conduct continued exemplary, it would lead to an Absolute Pardon, the goal Mark remained ever-determined to see fulfilled.

"Yet in other areas, Sarah, I don't like the look of things."

"What things, Mark?"

"The state of our world. Everything seems to be turning sour all of a sudden. I'm at a loss to know why the governor doesn't do something to halt this burgeoning immigration; it's beginning to work against us now, creating unemployment. We'll soon see petty crime on the increase if I'm a judge."

"Well, I'm sure you know best."

She had been happy to surrender reins of family finances after the Ben experience. The country's economy was a mystery far beyond her comprehension, so she found it a relief that Mark had a feel for it. Yet if he were right, it seemed the family well-being might be at risk.

"Tax increases are killing the farmers, Sarah. England continues to send more free emigrants, five hundred a month now, according to *The Gazette*, all with empty pockets, with no job prospects on arrival. I am indeed concerned for our future."

She clutched the babe she was feeding a little closer.

"Thank heaven I planted hops when I did. At least with the populace drinking more to console itself, it is our best hope for the future."

But the subtlety of Mark's humour ballooned loftily over Sarah. She had other things on her mind, and domestic issues were, to her, far more worthy of attention than the ills of areas beyond her sphere of influence. Her pa hadn't been well, and she was concerned. Tomorrow she would dig up some potatoes and make him the broth that he kept telling her was his favourite.

So on the morrow she had one of the hands harness up the buggy and loaded several of the girls, along with the pannikin of soup, and set out for the mile along Goodwin's Road to their farm.

MaryAnn had called in with her littlies, and Sarah felt it prudent to make the visit.

The Briscoe children were passionately fond of Mark, for despite she had given him seven of his own, to date he had proved an excellent father to all six Briscoes. But a strain had entered his relationship with MaryAnn. She had married at sixteen to be quickly widowed, a testing time for all. Yet MaryAnn had inherited her mother's pragmatism, Sarah reckoned, to as quickly bounce back to the reality of still having a life to live: she took up with another, to straightway fall pregnant.

Then she gave him a second before quickly falling with a third. To Mark's aggravation she did not remarry. This sat happily enough with Sarah, for MaryAnn had a smart head on her shoulders.

Isn't she my first, enjoyed the longest benefit of my counselling?

But Mark had an unyielding will and did not hide that he thought the example MaryAnn illustrated was contrary to what he chose for the other children.

But Sarah put those thoughts aside for the nonce, for they were crossing the little bridge over the Clarence, the buggy groaning under its scrum-weight of girls, Dobbin snorting in disgust, and she could see her pa sitting in his rocker on the veranda.

He rose at not so much the noise of the buggy rattling over the rickety bridge disturbing foraging pelicans that now clamoured ungainly into flight, but by the clamour of every voice aboard the buggy in impromptu disharmony on a tune he failed to recognise.

Titia also came to the cottage door, bemused.

Both grandparents, to Sarah's girls that is, and great-grandparents to MaryAnn's littlies, were quite some time surrounded until kisses and hugs were done. Andy then eased the exhausted Dobbin from his shafts and led him to water.

"Things still not happy between MaryAnn and Mark?"

"Mark is so stubborn at times, Ma. Like a wheel bogged in a deep rut."

"There's many a lag wants to forget his past. It's natural, and some become stubborn about what they believe in."

"Oh Mark's got strong views about forgetting he's a lag all right. The day will come when he'll look us straight in the eye and deny he ever was. It's like he's trying to undo it when we all know he can't."

"Maybe it's not that he's convict, Sarah. Maybe something else is the cause. I've ever believed that it's always better to let the past sleep."

"Yes I know, Ma, and there's sense in that. But when you live with a man, give him child after child, and in every other way he is straight and perfect, it just keeps raising that one niggling question."

"Take care, dear. When you reach out at something, be sure it is the matter of it you touch and not the shadow."

"I know that. First thing on me list is to hang on to his strengths. He's a good husband in most things, just a mite haughty at times, and I can live with that. And he's not just a good husband, Ma, he's a good father. So I'll take care."

Titia leaned over to pull the rug from the baby's face.

"She's the image of you when brand new, same smudge of a nose, same hairline, same eyes."

"You can remember all your babes so clear?"

"I was so surprised when you were different from Mary. Somehow I expected you'd look the same. When you were born your hair was so thick and black and seemed simply glued to your shiny scalp in lots of tiny curls. So you being different, I've remembered. And Hannah is just like you were. She a happy babe?'

"Healthy is happy. All babes are happy if they got full little bellies."

She handed the baby to its grandma. Hannah's tiny hands grasped at Titia's lips to cling fast.

"I'm your nana, little Hannah," struggled Titia when her lips were free.

Andy walked in and smiled mischief.

"You feelin' clucky again, Letty?"

~ * ~

"Of course I will miss Green Hills. But I can learn to love Longbottom. Its house is a step up from what you could build here back then, my love. And with only sheep and no wheat, it will be easier to work, as you say."

"This was a fine house then, Mary, when a man had no choice but to hew every plank from forest. Longbottom was built to a plan, and you'll no more have a string of rooms hooked together with wire."

"Or roofed with leaky bark."

She was happy to be moving. The Longbottom house was more substantial, no mansion, yet with stone walls and proper shingles.

"Won't know how to fill my time when it rains, Will. It won't seem like home without basins spread about the floor catching drips. And boarded floors to every room, with proper rugs won't make life near so exciting as the boys digging holes in the floor for their frogs."

"Gives you spare time, Mary, to see they learn to scrape their boots at the door instead of charging in with half the bloody paddock stuck to them."

Longbottom's main advantage was being solely grazing. Will was not a well man. His body was tired, and he'd lately been in some haste to have the boys take on extra chores. At fourteen and ten, they could cope. Something was awry inside Will, for he was often in pain despite quit of ploughing and sowing, reaping and threshing acres of wheat.

Wattle Hill was eight miles as the crow flies from Green Hills, yet no further from Sorell, albeit in a different direction. The governor was building his new master prison of Port Arthur in order to close the smaller old ones, and the road to it opened up new country. Iron Creek's ample water ran through Longbottom, so good pasture was assured.

The boys were ecstatic over the move. It promised adventure. Shearing had always fascinated young Liam, and now they would have a proper shearing shed. And a large stable.

"Can I have a horse, Pa? My own pony?"

Liam was the serious one of the two, not so inclined as George to take off on whims of fancy, rushing into adventure without too much plan. Liam would think on a project, plot it, approach with caution. He had more the characteristics of his pa.

"That's something we can think on, boy," Will answered. "There'll be many things in the move to cost money, but along the way we'll see if there's enough left for a pony, eh? Maybe when we get to buyin' the mare for the trap I promised Ma, we can look for one in foal?"

Liam knew his pa enough to know that this was as good as a promise.

~ * ~

"It were a fearful time for all aboard, Adam. Two lassies died. The master let the surgeon have his way, and he kept me and the little ones isolated."

"Cholera aboard ship, Ann, lucky anyone survived."

Adam Newitt had lodged application for his family to migrate, and it was accepted on the basis of his two eldest sons, by the time they could arrive, would be of a working age; with himself an assigned labourer to his Ann, it meant the family could support itself after a two-year establishment period.

And now, after a three-year delay, all had arrived on the convict transport *Hydery*, albeit as free immigrants.

When his letter had arrived in Long Buckby, it cast Ann's mind into considerable confusion, for she was a woman greatly stressed. When Adam was despatched, only her sixteen-year old stepson Billy was of working age, while the youngest of her own five was still toddling. She was in a desperate plight because authorities brooked no consideration that a family might be destitute without its breadwinner.

Ann knew that if she did not go to Adam, it would still be more than yet ten years before he could return, and she despaired that the children would have to suffer the aches of cold and hunger so long.

But the thought of going in itself created a different dilemma.

Billy had been little more than a toddler when Adam's first Ann died, and for Ann number two, the years providing Adam his next five children had been difficult enough to cope with. Then had come his transportation for fourteen years, and the little work young Billy could scrounge fell far short of sustaining them. She applied for parish charity. Long Buckby's Independent Church agreed to a stipend of three pounds a year each for her and Billy, on condition that they laboured in the parish workhouse.

She accepted, of course, having to find time both before leaving home at dawn each day, and arriving back after dark, to tend the rest of the family.

Then after three such years came this bolt from the blue, the letter someone had written for Adam, heralding hope for an end to the helplessness. Her first inclination had been that whatever the circumstance, welfare of her littlies at the nether end of the world must be better than the wretchedness smothering her here. And there she would have Adam to share the burdens.

Yet as realisations began to meld, that in going to live with the monsters that held her man in chains, who had caused her these years of hunger, shivering and terror, she would be torn from her wider family and must cast off everything familiar. Inevitable doubts engulfed her. To embrace, without option to retract, life in a primitive land governed by gaolers was a daunting risk. There was little doubt that in accepting the risk, the load on her shoulders and stress of mind would ease, yet risking so many unknowns on behalf of the children was the dilemma. What sort of future they could expect when growing up in a prison filled her mind with nowt but further doubt.

She woke from stressful sleep that night, her cobweb mind groping for answers. Taking the bairns from the present hopelessness would in itself be the mercy she had longed for since Adam went, yet to wrench them away from all familiar, to maybe discover later that going was an irrecoverable mistake, was an even more daunting prospect than staying. The alternative remained, however: continuing to watch her babes cry from hunger and shiver in their rags every winter.

No, that is too dreadful a prospect to face every year. A future in the frightening unknown could not be worse than the terrible present.

So she journeyed to Northampton Town to advise the authorities, and near a year later when the call came saying 'Now,' she packed their miserably few possessions and the family took post for London.

Aboard *Hydery*, she found, were a hundred and fifty she-lags to serve their time in Van Diemen's Land.

~ * ~

"Five pounds? Oh, Mark!"

He flustered, his face turning red, but Sarah couldn't work out whether the red was embarrassment or his utter rage.

"I'm sorry, Sarah. But how many times have I done that without a problem? Many indeed. It was simply bad luck. But it is not only the money—it's such a backward step for me."

He slammed the summons down on the table in a pique of temper, a display quite beyond the self-control he could usually discipline.

She simmered down, seeing how much it had shattered him.

"Maybe they won't penalise you on time as well, Mark. Surely they'll take your past perfect record into account?"

He shrugged his shoulders.

"But five whole pounds! Where do I quickly find that? Six months whole wages for one of our workers, that is. And not budgeted for?"

Only a year after receiving his Conditional Pardon, the final step before Absolute Pardon that he had, before this, expected within a twelve-month, he purchased a flagon of whisky and tucked it under a sack of horsehair in his dray. The horsehair was for re-stuffing a mattress, and the whisky for quaffing as appetiser before supper each evening as had become his wont. But he was seen by a trooper who was obviously in a bad mood.

The rule was that convicts were not allowed access to liquor, and whilst it was seldom enforced, it remained part of the law. So maybe he had been unlucky. But he was nevertheless guilty and had been issued a summons on the spot. He had a month to find the five-pounds or he would go to prison until it was paid.

Sarah knew that the fact it was the first and only blemish on his record sheet was a severe dampener to Mark's considerable pride.

"As if the wretched man did not have enough on his plate coping with serious dissidents, Sarah?"

He asked the observation as a question, obviously still labouring under what he considered injustice.

Governor Arthur had indeed been pressured with the problem of housing second offender convicts. So many convicts were now arriving, and so many of them earning further punishment for such heinous misdemeanours, for instance, as disobeying orders, feigning sickness in order to avoid hard labour, or being too regularly absent without leave from their assignor, that the existing prisons were inadequate. Macquarie Harbour on the west coast and Maria Island on the east coast could no longer do the job, so Arthur was obliged to build a new, extremely large prison. He designed it himself, and it was certainly huge, occupying an entire isthmus of land in the south. The sea surrounding it was an area renowned for its infestation of sharks, so the only part of the whole prison that must be guarded against escapes was the narrow neck of the isthmus. Two fences were erected with a no-man's land between, in which savage guard dogs roamed free. And when his Port Arthur prison was completed, he would close the smaller ones.

"At least," Mark added, his temper over being fined obviously returning his mind to that matter, "the wretched trooper showed a spark of humour that by now I guess I can smile at..."

"Yes, Mark?"

"He didn't confiscate the whisky. The blighter handed me the summons, then walked off only after shoving the flagon back under the stuffing sack."

Sarah smiled.

"Then go pour yourself a nip now, Mark, and maybe toast him for so doing."

Fifteen

The timing of the move to Longbottom was lucky. The downturn in the economy saw the price of wheat tumble, so the new farm was not affected.

However, the exertion of the move left Will exhausted.

The boys had thrown themselves into it with verve as Mary's quiet efficiency ensured Will was spared the heavy work. Right now she was arching her back after scrubbing breeches, and wisps of still radiantly red hair straggled across her face.

"Now where did the boys go? They were here a minute ago."

"George is likely poking into holes terrifying wildlife and Liam measuring up the pasture to ensure there's winter feed enough."

Will was entirely happy to have only boys. He understood them. Girls and women had ever been a mystery. And not only were the boys now taking pressures off him physically, young Liam in particular was ever planning over whether this or that should wait another season. George was the impulsive doer, charging into a chore without forethought.

Nor did Mary have regrets. She loved Longbottom, where Will had built many comforts to make her living easier. She gloried in the canvas annexe he attached to her cookhouse, a proper bathhouse with piped water from a tank fed from the cookhouse roof.

"Absolute luxury," she declared to all.

"Have you noticed, Will, how dawn doesn't burst on this valley like at Green Hills? It creeps in, threads its way carefully through those hills beyond the cookhouse window. It did it again this morning."

It was unseasonably hot for May. The naked trees by the creek, already bared for winter, in today's hot sunlight looked almost stunned. There was a languor to things at that time of year, and one felt that all over Longbottom, waiting under the poplar bark, spring buds, unsure what to do, were hesitating.

"Why don't you sit, Will? I'll make a cuppa."

"Maybe old age creepin' on. I seem to wake up tired, and it bugs me when there's work to be done. Wish I could store up energy like we used to store wheat at Green Hills."

She was becoming practised at hiding concern.

"It's the heat, Will. And a long time since either of us was a blossom in the flower of youth. I feel it, too. Go sit on the porch, and I'll bring tea."

For several seasons, Longbottom had weathered the economic crisis enough that the Woolleys could eat when banks crashed, some investors losing all. And when the floods devastated much of the area, Iron Creek flooded only the low paddocks.

"Advantage of havin' sheep rather than wheat in a flood, boy," he had joked to young Liam, "is that sheep can walk to higher ground easier than wheat."

The winter proved mild, and come end of it, when news arrived that the far distant Macquarie Harbour and the nearby Maria Island hard labour prisons were closing, it passed by them with but a whiff of interest. The convict world of Hobart and news of the developing north they pushed aside from their lives now.

Will read a newspaper less and less because it was lately all negative, the economy on a downward path and unemployment and crime increasing. Governor Arthur became so unpopular that the people petitioned England for his recall; when he was finally sacked, there was jubilation. People were so glad to see the last of him that he was hissed and booed aboard ship.

"Glad we're in the country, Will. Hobart would not be a happy place."

"Ten years, Mary, since blacks and brigands raided. Yet it's started again with bushrangin' turning a better penny than farming these days. Maybe I should dig Brown-Bess out, eh? Clean the old girl up?"

Mary smiled, remembering her introduction to Brown-Bess. And Will smiled at the memory of Dannyboy when he had brought Brown-Bess home.

"Come a long way since then, we have, my love."

Once finished their tea, they wandered towards the creek. It was spring, and by Mary's favourite path, cherry and apple trees erupted in blossom, their fragrance adding allure to their beauty. Across the creek on the flat, a horse flashed by, young Liam astride, bareback, at full gallop. Will watched in silence at how the boy sat the horse so easily. Riding was something Will had never properly mastered, but to the lad it seemed natural.

He and Mary held hands as they walked.

And come moonlight, Will sat on the porch eyeing the vista, all testimony to a man not accomplished at just one thing but many, who raised sheep and a few head of dairy, built fences, cut planking and shingles, grew hops, potatoes and onions. He was content with his life now.

And after dinner, Mary quickly finished the last of her chores, pulled the curtains closed, and picked up her lamp to take to the bedroom.

Once the tedious side of her day was done, she never failed to realise her luck, escaping to loving arms each night.

No boring marriage, mine.

~ * ~

"Hard to credit you're the ones I left, especially you, little man."

Adam Newitt lifted his namesake son high, hands clasped tight around the boy's waist.

"You was but a babe in arms when I last saw yer."

The family was detained where *Hydery* had docked, waiting on the relevant paperwork that some clerk had neglected to have ready.

But the little man struggled. Scarlet uniforms and redcoat muskets were dramatic contrasts to Long Buckby sights, holding far more drama for a five-year-old than meeting a stranger, albeit told it was his pa.

"I had a birthday on the ship," little Ann exclaimed, stretching to the full height of her eight years.

At which Adam set down little Adam, to fondle the child's hair.

Then when the several reunions were done, the redcoat assigned as guard over Adam and guide to all, led them to the arrivals hut.

There, Ann was told that Adam could not stay with the family that night:

"He must return to the prison, ma'am, until your land grant papers are arranged, and then he'll be assigned to you. That should only take a day or so, ma'am."

Ann and the children were meanwhile lodged in a rooming house in the town.

Then when the paperwork was done, Ann found that 'the monsters' who had held her Adam captive were not so sinister as expected; even affable was the clerk who rubber-stamped her formal application for Adam's assignment to her as labourer. As he pinned her copy of the record to her papers, he fixed her with a scampish gleam as he then handed her the customary ankle-fetters.

"He's a bolter, ma'am," he said. "You'll be quite within your rights, should you want to chain him down."

~ * ~

Sarah sat on the ferry on her way to see her ma, picturing again in her mind's eye, as she did every time crossing the river, the frightening chaos aboard the ferry when her Ben died. A few times she had witnessed light boats with sails flapping wildly when hit by one of the Derwent's sudden squalls, each time reminding her of that significant episode in her life.

She never failed to think it could happen to her. Such a fate took not only her Ben, but Aunt Liz's Corny within a year of each other. She had heard of many like instances since, yet realized, as all in the colony had to accept, that it was a quirk of the terrain around the town and there was nothing anybody could do about it other than to exercise care once the squall struck..

But her senses of that now were heightened in particular with the devastating news that had set her out to again make the crossing. A letter had arrived informing that her pa had died.

She and Mark with only their latest babe, Caroline, were on their way to The Red Lion, one of the Hobart hotels her sister Maria owned, where her parents had been living in retirement.

And when reaching the town, Mark suggested it might be better if Sarah saw her ma alone for a short time.

"Yes, that might be best. Give me an hour, Mark, then you come?"

He nodded. He had shopping to do, so walked her to the hotel before turning about to leave her enter alone.

She found Titia sitting erect in her bentwood rocker on the rear porch, half watching a squabble of magpies in the herb garden, sitting even straighter than ever in the moment, dried tears on her cheeks, her entire body clad in black other than for a hint of white lace at the collar. They held each other in quiet embrace for several moments, before Sarah placed baby Caroline in her ma's lap while she pulled a chair close.

Titia was in a reminiscing mood, her mind reliving some events at Sydney Cove after she and her Andy met.

"...then it seemed no time before I told him I thought I was going to have his baby."

"How difficult was it, carryin' Mary without there being enough food?"

"That was another fear we lived with every day, Sarah. More than half all babes were born dead, a painful birth. And many others died because there was no goodness in the milk. Terrible it was to see the mothers so helpless. Buried so many tots, we did, before they was a week old."

Sarah took baby Caroline to put to her breast.

"Lucky I never had one stillborn. But this one made sure I'll have no more."

"Fifteen is enough, Sarah. Your pa said that when I told him about this one."

"Same age as when you had your last, forty-two. You did well through the troubled times then, to go on to have eleven. Pa didn't draw a line there," she added with a smile.

Which Titia returned.

"I'm holdin' nothin' against him. Andy Goodwin was a fine man. And considerate. I was a lot luckier than many Botany Bay women. And lucky I've been to have him till such an age. Seventy-nine's a grand age for a man who lived through all he did."

Titia went on with stories about the early days. So many times Sarah had heard tales of Will Butler, Danny Gordon, BlackJack, Nat Lucas and young Matt Everingham. She knew Uncle Ed Garth, of course. He would be at the funeral tomorrow. He and her pa had stayed friends through all the years.

"He weren't seventy-nine, Ma. Pa was sixty-nine. Mark worked it out."

"Well, we weren't good at numbers. He thought seventy-nine."

"Not if he was seventeen, as he reckoned, when he went to the hulks."

"Well, Mark would know. But it's a good age for a man, even so, when he went through so much. I'm glad he lived to see young Andy marry. Always wanted lots of sons, and I only gave him three. And he was the saddest man when John went so young, then Jamie. So Andy was happy when young Andrew wed, to raise more sons."

"She's a worry, Ma, that Lydia."

Titia straightened, sounding terse. "You didn't say that when Ann married a convict, or when you did, both times."

"You know what I mean, Ma. It's not that she's convict—she's just trouble. Going to bring trouble on our Andy, I know it. But we'll leave it at that. If Pa was happy to see it before he went, then that was the good thing."

"Always seem to be questions, Sarah, on why people choose free or convict. They don't seem to realise people is people either way. Some just get caught doing but a scant mite more than them who don't. I don't like hearing people say there's a difference, especially one of our own."

Young Andy had married a fourteen-year she-lag, who, it had later come out, had a record 'as long as her arm.' She had been in constant trouble with the authorities, and had she been a man, Mark reckoned, she would have by now been sent to Port Arthur. Since married, she had been getting persistently drunk and in Sarah's eyes was a bad mother as well. But Sarah wanted to change the subject.

"At least, Ma, here with all the staff to help cheer you up, you are better off than if back on the farm. And you can come stay with me and Mark whenever you feel like a change."

"Maybe I will. Right now, though, I'll be happier here where I can visit the churchyard. I've got my health still, and you've got your family to raise without me around your neck."

Sarah realised her ma would find life alone more interesting in Hobart than at Clarence Plains. There was ever need for guarded conversation when she and Mark were together too long.

But I'll miss you dreadfully, Pa. You were ever such a present part of my life.

Her growing up years on Norfolk had her constantly aware of him learning to adjust to freedom, how to make decisions after so many years of being pushed and pulled. And she had his dogged determination, she knew, his need to win. And when Ben died with his finances in such a mess, her pa had been the strength that helped her pull through as well as she did.

Ben had ever said Pa was like a mastiff who gripped on to what he reckoned were his dues.

"They taught me three things," she remembered her pa saying to his kids on the few occasions he would talk about his convict days. "They taught me to be cautious in trustin' people, they taught me contempt for the system, and they taught me to fight for me rights. And by God, those things together taught me to never buckle under, give in for less than a man's dues."

She remembered how sad he was and even more contemptuous than ever of the wigs on hearing Norfolk had opened up again, this time solely as a maximum-security prison like the hell Macquarie Harbour had been.

"Fancy desecratin' that place with the blood o' the damned," he'd said.

"He was a good man, Ma."

"A worthy man, Sarah."

And when Mark arrived, Sarah told him the funeral was to be on the morrow.

"Well, let's hurry home now, Sarah, and prepare for an early start back in the morning. All the children will want come for that, I am sure."

And on the morrow, it was a large contingent of Briscoe-Bunkers that journeyed to Hobart, for Mark had been right in believing every one of the children wanted to say final farewells to their grandpa.

The six surviving Briscoe children, including MaryAnn, who if even in a perverse way enjoyed the break of getting away without a string of littlies clustered around her skirts, all came along. When her husband had left her after such a short time, Will Cockerell threw his hat into the ring for MaryAnn. He had come as a child with his free parents aboard *Calcutta*, one of the six free families migrating on that historic voyage, and the Cockerells had known Ben since the first day of the settlement. So their Will was a popular choice with the family.

And with the babe-in-arms Caroline, the Bunker children numbered eight, so it was a full dray-load getting to the eastern pier, then the ferry across the river from where they could walk.

It was a bright sunny day, spring arriving early for the occasion, Sarah liked to think, and Andrew Goodwin was paid due respects by the Reverend Knopwood, as one of the colony's earliest settlers.

There were few dry eyes, even amongst the men, as Letitia's Andy, ever popular with everyone, was lowered into the grave where, once all had had the chance to throw flowers after him, the gravediggers began shovelling sods.

Andy was now reposed in a domicile from which he would never be further transported.

~ * ~

Ann Newitt's grant was east of the Pitt Water, a frontier given the name Bream Creek, a picturesque landscape with folds of green hills falling in steps to the sea, the dales a canvas of wildflowers. The fine view of the distant ocean was an instant favourite with the entire family.

It was a new community, every settler starting out with nothing, to convert virgin forest into farmland; so neighbours proved helpful all around as everyone at some time needed extra hands to 'chip in.' So camaraderie developed out of sharing.

The rude Newitt shack built by the government was no better or worse than other frontier cabins, and Adam, his wry sense of devilment ever to the fore, christened it Nun-Such after the garish Tudor manor on London Bridge.

The independence Ann had acquired during her difficult years back in Long Buckby was to now begin proving its value. Adapting to rigours of isolation demanded a more disciplined hold on things than sheltered village life prepared one for. She was also to find the forces that render survival on a frontier a hardship—hardship to highlight sinews of courage and grit, qualities she hadn't realised she possessed. Each would become more apparent as time went on, however, as she learned to cope with drought and fire and flood as each regressed the path of hard-won gains, to say nowt of coping with a husband intent, it seemed, on bucking the convict system.

Adam, however, to do him credit, applied himself with vigour, for not only did growing familiarity with local conditions occasion him more perseverance and less frustration than Ann, but his cavalier spirit, to some extent, shielded him from the weights of misfortunes. In respect of his servitude, there was now at least peace of mind for him. No longer was he the outcast miscreant without purpose; he was again a family man, this time with property.

Yet his new sense of purpose could not entirely change his errant ways.

Six months after the excitement of the family reunion, he was charged with being absent without leave from a church muster, to be let off with a reprimand.

"Yer can't expect to be so lucky again, Adam," Ann had chided.

"A man should be able to please himself if he goes to church. Not as if I'm boltin' or somethin' serious."

Yet ever prone to heroic folly, Adam failed to distinguish between fair and reasonable in his estimation and what the obdurate system demanded. He did it again, to be reprimanded again.

"They won't grant yer pardon while yer keep breakin' rules, Adam."

A short time later he was arrested in Hobart without a pass.

"Two days solitary confinement on bread and water, just for not havin' a bloody note from me own missus? What's a man to bloody do? If yer a 'yes man' yer their dupe. If yer stand up to 'em, yer their target."

"Maybe you should try keeping somewhere in the middle. It's the sheep in the centre of the flock that the wolf can't see, you know."

Yet Adam's world continued unfair.

A curse on a man they are, a neck yoke, a pothole in a man's path of life.

Next he was fined five shillings for being drunk.

And four months later, in Sorell, was drunk again.

By now Nun-Such was beginning to make a name for itself, and Adam was as well known as head of a settler family as by his scallywag reputation.

"You know better, Adam Newitt," the magistrate told him, "so you have an option. You are hereby fined five pounds for being drunk, or, you leave the town forthwith and hie home to your good wife."

Adam Newitt was uncrushable. If he thought he couldn't best a man he would simply agree with all he said. But in this case there was the fact that five pounds was a fortune, so it took but a scant second to consider. He bolted home.

A year later, two days before Christmas and twelve years into his fourteen-year sentence, Adam proudly waved his Conditional Pardon before the family.

"Look," he declared, "all I need now, to get me free pardon, is stay out of trouble."

Sixteen

Van Diemen's Land had undergone great changes. The aftermath of Governor Arthur's poor performance in respect of the economy, however, remained sustained.

Despite Sorell introduced many procedures conducive to providing the people a more modern lifestyle, burgeoning immigration meant an accelerating depression in the colony. The industrial revolution in Britain cast thousands of men on the unemployed heap, as many turning to crime to be transported as convicts, as who applied for free immigration to escape the hungers of home. At the same time, Britain put an end to the assignment system. Whilst this saved Britain some costs, it took away free labour in the colonies, a burden to exact a huge expense on colony settlers.

"What consumer has coin enough in his pocket to repay me the fifteen quid a year I must now pay employees?" complained the colonial wholesaler.

So he cut his purchasing in half.

The farmers responded next season by planting only half their fields.

The economy was quickly in tatters.

"Unemployment Becomes Our Major Import," the *Mercury* ran as its headline.

Sir John Franklin, the next governor, arrived to not only find banks failing, bankruptcies increasing and town people going hungry, but under instruction to wind down the granting of free land.

~ * ~

On their way to George's wedding, Will and Mary Woolley drove their buggy further than they had yet travelled in the land. Alongside, Liam rode astride.

The track as far as the village of Forcett was reasonably familiar, but from there to Bream Creek, some twelve miles Will reckoned, the country was new. They had not yet met Harriet Newitt, George's intended.

When rumours had become rife that the granting of land to new settlers was to be discontinued, George Woolley prevailed on his pa to apply for an additional grant before the embargo came into force. Will did so, and thirty acres was granted in a new area called Kellevie, several miles to the south. In family discussion it was agreed that Longbottom would go to Liam in the long term, Liam being he of the two boys with a flair for grazing rather than agriculture, and that George would take up the Kellevie grant.

When the time then came, he moved south to oversee the government's building of the modest regulation cabin that came with new grants, and during the period, met at the local fair she who was to become his bride.

"Harriet Newitt, her name is," he told his family. "Her parents farm at Bream Creek, further south.

The wedding was decided on in a hurry because Hobart's then Reverend Bedford, appointed when Robbie Knopwood retired, made tours into frontier districts from time to time to marry couples, baptise babes, and say prayers over gravesites. He advised the Bream Creek district that he would visit for those purposes during a particular week.

"He won't be back this way for another year," George explained, "so the wedding must be now. He will perform three marriages that day."

So en-route to Bream Creek, directions clearly sketched out for them, the Woolleys detoured at the new Kellevie site, to check progress on George's cabin.

"Oh, it's exceeding small, Will," Mary observed.

"Well, it will be up to George to add to it as he goes, same as we did at Green Hills, Mary. God knows how the boy will fare, though. You know what he's bloody like. He'll rush into doing this or that without thinking things through. I'll bet that even now he's got so many half-cocked things in his mind that he'll not be sure where to start."

"Maybe Harriet's father can help him? Or maybe Liam should stay with him for a week to sift through his needs?"

"Let's wait and see what we make of things, Mary, once meeting the Newitts."

And Mary was worried about meeting them. When asking George about them, he didn't seem to know much.

"They're from Northampton. Her pa's a fourteen-year man, nearly through his time. He brought the family out after he was four or five years here. Her ma was given the grant."

Mary otherwise knew only that Harriet had 'several' brothers and sisters.

Her mind flew back to her own situation, never having since heard anything of the family she was forced to leave behind, of her father and Crooked Connor.

At least though, it seems this Harriet's pa is a planner. Not many convicts brought their families out.

So she would wait, make up her mind once meeting them.

And on arrival they marvelled at the view, the distant ocean bringing Mary's mind back to her voyage on *Canada*, of Bridie and the old chippy.

All of which seem a thousand years ago!

At the site, a tarpaulin large enough to shelter all three wedding parties was strung between trees. The Woolleys owned no timepiece, for with never a reason to be punctual anywhere, why should they? Routines around Longbottom existed only so far as when people satisfied compunctions to do things. George had told them the ceremony would be about noon but on a cloudy day, who could tell exactly where the sun was?

So ceremonies were already under way when they arrived; luckily, though, George and Harriet's marriage hadn't begun. And when all ceremonies were complete, they were introduced to their now extended family. And the meeting was rushed. Harriet's pa, it seemed, was anxious to get quickly away to Nun-Such, where the wedding breakfast was to be held.

Harriet seems a nice lass, as does her mother seem a nice woman, Mary opined as they followed in the dust of the Newitt dray. And once there, Adam opened a flagon of what Will was to compliment him on being a 'respectable' home-brewed ale. And Ann Newitt's ginger beer was as welcomed by the ladies and children.

Mary was further impressed by not only young Harriet, but again, her mother, once having opportunity to sum them up at length.

"Ann Newitt seems a woman of considerable common sense," she told Will.

He noted that neither did Mary make any such comment on Adam Newitt.

The women had sat for quite a time, getting to know each other while Maggie, Harriet's older sister, attended the catering chores.

Ann seems to have adapted to frontier hardships pretty well. And it's interesting how similar are her experiences and mine.

"It's happy I am, Ann, to find Harriet a lass with common sense in her pretty head. She'll not find George the easiest person to live with, but she seems of a disposition to cope."

George and Liam had taken off with Harriet's brothers to inspect the property, and on the porch, Will and Adam sat with long-stemmed pipes, getting acquainted.

"They should make a good go of Kellevie, Will; it's all good land up there."

"Being so close to ocean, Adam, limits them. Sheep don't take kindly to salty air. But George insists he is for agriculture, at any rate."

"I know nowt of grazing, Will—nor much more of farming, for that matter. Been cobblin' all me life, I have. But I've had good assigned men. They taught my boys. Billy and young Ephraim are the farmers here."

"Larry, your Maggie's husband? He's one of those?"

"Aye. A good lad. Got himself a life sentence for nickin' a horse. Farmed back in the old country, he did, so has a feel for it. Maggie gave him a son after he was assigned here, and when the parson next come around, they wed."

"Bein' a lifer means he can get no grant. That'll make things hard for them."

Adam threw up his hands. "A bloody hopeless situation. They're startin' to pardon lifers now, of course, but only after twenty years— and by then, it seems, land grants will be things of history. So yes, the poor bugger can only look forward to labourin' for the rest of life."

"I've told George, Adam, that he should plant hops. With the Hobart Brewery openin' there'll always be a market for hops."

"Jesus, mate, don't the young'uns these days get it bloody easy? They can bloody choose what they want. There was no fatherly advice in our days, mate, it had to be stuff the family could eat. And all learned by bloody trial and error. Lads now get help. In our day it was a case of bend ya bloody back or get a bloody lashin'."

Will smiled. Adam had already told him that he arrived in the Governor Arthur days, so had never known real hunger or lived with the fear of blacks coming at a man with spears, or had bushrangers killing his dogs, threatening his family.

And the best Dannyboy and me had to sleep in was a bark hut we had to bloody build ourselves at the same time as grubbing stumps, tilling virgin earth without a horse, and fightin' off bloody blacks and bushrangers with nowt but dogs and Brown-Bess.

"The new generation, Adam, all the George and Harriets, mightn't have the problems of old but they still won't find things easy. New problems ever arise. Colonial life can never be aught but pioneering."

~ * ~

Sarah's fiftieth birthday was an event she would remember for the rest of her life.

Nothing dramatic happened, but her entire family, now widely dispersed on their several domestic fronts, had assembled to honour the occasion. All her sisters, her only brother, and all her own children with their children in turn, were present.

"Your remarkable ma," Mark addressed the younger generations, "provided my predecessor with as fine an assemblage of offspring as she has happily provided me; and with the exception of only little Benjie, who unfortunately died before I came on the scene, all are present today to illustrate what a fine contribution she made to Van Diemen's Land."

He went on to comment on not only the number of grandchildren in turn but on how many more, it was obvious, there would be within a foreseeable future...

All Sarah's Briscoe children had 'borne fruit,' and even Lizzie Bunker, Mark's eldest, it was already clear to see, would be very soon presenting Mark with his first grandchild.

Sarah, in responding, reminded all how she had been born not only in the previous century, but on the historic Norfolk Island. Several noticed, however, that she avoided mention of the fact that her parents were sent there as convicts. Mark had made it a strict policy within family that Sarah's convict heritage should never be mentioned. It was ever to remain a subject of taboo despite her personal belief that hiding that Terrible Truth was tantamount to telling lies.

However, it is a wife's duty to illustrate support for whatever her husband proposes, she had had to keep telling herself.

Sarah waxed long on Norfolk Island and on the family disappointment when having to abandon it...

"...But after my Ben unhappily drowned, your excellent Pa came on my scene, and we must all be proud of how he has built for us a wonderful standard of life to make us proud to be either Briscoe or Bunker."

From the corner of her eye, Sarah glanced at her ma as she made her closing statement, to note that old Titia remained stoically inexpressive other than to tilt her chin a fraction higher as if in contempt of Sarah's deference to what Titia called, in private conversation, Mark's bigotry.

Sarah well realised how much her ma held to proudly lauding her convict past rather than, like Mark, making every attempt to hide it.

But no intimation either that Sarah was being anything but totally honest in her claim, or that Mark so highly acclaimed his wife's dutiful support, or that Titia was so adamantly averse to it, was evident.

So propriety ruled.

~ * ~

Three years on...

Liam rode Irish the fifteen miles from Longbottom to discover George had raised a signpost at the foot of the Kellevie hill—Woolleys Rd.

"It's a long ride, George. I got Irish water, but he snorts for oats."

"Ain't got oats, Liam, but there's chaff. There's nosebags in the barn."

Liam fed the horse, then left him to meditate in a nosebag.

In the house, George's toddler, William the Third, reached to be lifted up.

"You stay over, Liam? The boy hopes so."

"Irish will act up if I don't, Harriet. Too far back same day."

Clouds frowned in the creases of hills as the five looked down the valley where George had begun clearing scrub for sheep...

"Enough sheep to put mutton on our table, at any rate," George explained.

Harriet's sister Maggie, her Larry and littlies also lived there now. Pardons were being rushed through for lifers so that all convicts would be free to work where they wished, for wages.

"Which is all bloody well if there were paying jobs to be had. But with the so many farmers going bankrupt...?" complained Larry.

"Pa read in the paper a week back, George, that they're closing Norfolk Island to save costs—despatching all its lags here."

"Bloody hell. They closed it once before. I remember Pa saying how it was then a good thing because Norfolk's old lags had the experience to get things up and going here the quicker. Then twenty years later they re-open it as Sydney's hard-labour prison. Now they're to bloody close it again?"

"Another English decision for the same bloody reason, to save costs. But those lags have still got their time to serve out, and with

New South Wales abandoning convictism, we now have the only hard-labour prison."

"But with assignment finished, they won't let them help the poor bloody farmers, Liam. They'll put 'em to bridges and roads where they can be kept under guard."

"And get fed, while we free ones, with no work, must starve," added Larry.

Liam looked closely at Larry.

Poor bugger really is in a hapless situation. Bringing in additional convicts merely moves him further down the list of those needing work.

Assignment was by now finally abandoned in Van Diemen's Land. George had lost his free labour, so Larry, Maggie and their three boys had moved in to help George work his farm.

"Not a penny between us," said Maggie with more than a hint of sarcasm, "but we'll at least grow enough to feed ourselves."

"With only sheep, me and Pa can manage Longbottom alone. We get by with dogs."

Then he added with a twist to his smile, "How's your pa keeping, Maggie?"

She laughed. She knew it was Liam's way of asking if Adam were staying out of trouble.

"His pardon arrived, and he danced a jig, waving it about. It doesn't dawn on him that it comes now only because his fourteen years coincides with all lags getting pardons."

Liam liked Maggie. She'd had Ephraim, a real scamp, to Larry when sixteen. After marriage came Tom, and she now nursed Harry.

The Woolley brothers discussed their pa's ailments, his failure to cast them off.

"Me and Ma do more for him every day, George. It's like his muscles are slack. He wakes up tired. And just to stand up it's like each joint needs oilin'. Days are long gone when we'd say how he launched himself at each day like a catapult."

They had to accept that 'William the First' was terminally ill with some creeping malady.

~ * ~

Sarah was nostalgic over moving from Clarence Plains.

"Not easy trying to sort one's mind around leaving somewhere that's been home for thirty years, Mark. But I agree Coal River seems to the thing to do. Jamie liked it there, called it good grazing country."

"And it's getting more of the conveniences of here, Sarah. The only downside is that it's a long way from Hobart."

Jerusalem was not a town, simply a district on the main north-south road. And surveys were already made for a railroad north from the Derwent where a bridge was planned.

Mark had seen that, with the depression Governor Arthur left behind ten years ago starting to dissipate, converting prime land into cash and buying in a new area made sense.

The Bunker family still at home comprised but six children. All the Briscoes were married, as were their own Lizzy and Meg. And Meg was already at Jerusalem, her farm but a couple of miles from the new Bunker property. Still at home were Ed at seventeen, Ruth, twins Maria and Lucy, and the still small Hannah and Caroline. Mark had been a free man two years, his Unconditional Pardon received, which he insisted should be let pass without mention despite he and Sarah privately toasted the event with gusto.

"Twenty-two years I've served, Sarah," he whispered, "but I'm at last as free as any 'came-free' man in the colony—provided, that is, my convict status is not realised in the community at large."

He was now, of course, master of the Rokeby property, having, on that auspicious occasion, automatically under the law inherited Sarah's worldly goods. And with the end of assignment upon them, and with unemployment so severe, immigration had at last dwindled to a trickle—so he had made the momentous decision...

"It will be a time yet before they cease sending convicts. Yet with assignment finished and free labour asking fifteen pounds a year, there is every reason to run a smaller farm. There'll be more profit, producing less, than paying labour at that rate."

And for Sarah, with her pa gone and her ma in Hobart, all that now beckoned for her at Rokeby, although she found it more natural to still think of it as Clarence Plains, was sentiment.

"Even old Robbie Knopwood's six feet under," she said irreverently, to which Mark made no response.

"Being near young Andy, maybe I can help out with the dance his Lydia leads him. He's my only remaining brother, Mark, and his lot isn't easy."

"What's the latest with her?"

Which surprised her. It was more usual for Mark to shy clear of family convicts.

"Well, you know they put her back in prison for bolting again..."

"Breaking assignment from her own husband is a fool thing to do once, let alone make a habit of it."

"I reckon it's because she's such a tippler, doesn't realise she's doing it. Even when they put the iron collar on her it didn't make her think twice. Now with six littlies and another due, poor Andy's got his hands full."

"See him by all means, Sarah, but on no account get involved. Andy made his bed, so he must sleep in it, uncomfortable though it must be."

Mark had further reason for wanting a fresh start, of course, which he knew Sarah would never understand. Born into her convict world she had no other measure, yet with the colony moving towards a conventional society, like that that he grew up in, not only was there talk of ending convictism, there was even agitation to change the colony name that the stigma would the more quickly dissipate.

When called Clarence Plains, for instance, the area was steeped in the background of convictism, my own history living proof of that; but already the name Rokeby doesn't conjure up the same image in people's minds. Even I am surprised at how quickly that image has waned.

Jerusalem was a new area, opportunity for young Bunkers to grow up in an atmosphere more of the free than the tainted. And unlike Goodwin daughters, his would not marry convicts unless they, like him, were of those wishing to hide the fact. So if, once newly domiciled in Jerusalem, Sarah were seen to be too close to the Lydias of the world, his aspirations would face a serious hurdle.

I am now in a situation of ensuring my family can live at a standard acceptable to the new community. And once arrived in it, is opportunity to establish a more appropriate Bunker image than that that we leave behind.

His eighty-six acres on the Wallaby Rivulet, in fact bisecting the Mud Walls Road, the main traffic route to the north, was a property of note with a respectably large stone house that would be considered a proud home even back in England. Its owner would not be recognised as an emancipated lag with twenty-two years' servitude behind him; Mark Ashby Bunker Esquire would be taking his place in a wider world where dignity reigned.

He smiled smugly at having already gained a measure of comfort that his family back in England could never have hoped to achieve, nor himself had he not, in hindsight, suffered the perverse misfortune of being despatched in chains.

Mark Ashby Bunker was about to embark on the future to which he had aspired since arriving in this land of opportunity.

~ * ~

Eighteen months after the Woolley and Newitt families celebrated the first Woolley grandchild, William Woolley the First succumbed to the creeping sickness that had been plaguing him.

Mary assured all that... "Will lived long enough to welcome his namesake grandson, an event to thoroughly excite him. It was a bright spot in his waning months," she ended with a sigh, her fiery head uncharacteristically bowed.

All realised how vital a door had closed on her life, despite his passing had long been expected.

"I was ever thankful for my luck in the assignment lottery," she told them, "and it was so sad to see so vital a man suffer such pain, particularly after all he suffered in his early years. He'd surely had enough then, to last a lifetime. And you know how thin he'd got."

"Death is ever saddest, Mary dear, when it is life's mate," said Ann. The Newitts had come as soon as they heard the news. "But it's you I'm worried for now, left alone with no daughters."

"Liam has no thoughts of marriage, Ann. Twenty he is now and will stay on. His pa made it clear Liam should keep Longbottom."

Mary Rohan-Woolley was a widow at fifty-six, and not only had she experienced the hardships of convict life but had lived under redcoat law since the day she was born. She had never known freedom as had Will. He had had the taste of it planted in his outlook for twenty years before the hulks... *So what a shock that must have been!*

Like I feel now—worldless. And his seven years, unlike mine, were hard labour. The only consolation for him in those times was having mates to share his troubles.

"It seems only yesterday, Ann, he was reading the news of Port Phillip being settled at last.

"They're callin' it Melbourne," he had told her, "but a stone's throw from where we spent them three months tryin' to find water and grow food in the sand. Right where Davie told Governor Collins it was."

"And he was so amazed, Ann, that his shipmate Will Buckley was found living there with the blacks, when for thirty years everyone had believed him dead at their hands. The expression 'Buckley's Chance' always sprang to Will's lips after that, whenever some situation with an unlikely solution arose."

"What a life sentence for a man," Will had summed up at the time.

Ann Newitt eyed her friend wistfully. More than simply friend, of course, now that they shared a grandchild. Leaving her homeland had been a bigger wrench for Mary than had her own.

And I could bring family, to arrive among my own countrymen.

Ann was conscious of Mary having found no Irish women on her frontier and had for all her life been surrounded by those she felt 'enemy.' Nor had she ever lost her vocal cant. She still trilled the Irish brogue as if singing, Ann reckoned.

"Just thinking, I was, Ann, how Will was proud for his friend Davie Gibson. Bolted together, they did, the bolt that earned Will his lashing. And that month they spent in the wilds together must have bound those men, five of them I think it was, so close. 'Loveable rogue,' he called Davie with his bright red hair like mine. He always admired Davie's gusto. 'Good mates,' he called Davie, Gus and Ben. And the last two died young. There's a comradeship among lags, Ann, that bound them tight."

"It's what they suffered together. I see it in couples, too. You and Will for instance. A deep understanding you had, from having the same heartaches, having lived the same fears. Convict women worked twice as hard, I reckon, seemed to make a far better stick of hardships than those who came free."

"That's hardly fair on yourself, Ann. You found the same stick."

"But I always saw myself convict. Might as well've nicked me way here. 'A convict's wife gets a convict life' I always reckoned."

"It goes further, Ann. Look at our young'uns, Harriett, George, your Maggie. Nothing is easier for them because they're not convict. Their babes die because there's no help, their frontier life is as primitive as we found ours. And there'll be more generations of frontier families yet, as the colony spreads. Only thing different is that they no longer fear blacks bursting from the forest."

"Yet we found it got easier. As littlies grew they change from being extra work to extra help. Even before his pardon, Adam could take it easier with Billy and Ephraim pitching in."

Mary smiled in her sadness. Since meeting the Newitts, bits and pieces of Adam's past had come out. He was typical of the many who for years simply staggered on a twisting path of confused life. And there was no early pardon for him; he served all his fourteen years, them reckoning he still hadn't illustrated responsibility.

Will had remarked at the time, with a smile, how that had seemed justice.

Dear Will, I still don't feel easy about you being in the churchyard. All through our life you were adamant about wanting no 'Godbothering.' I know the reason you kept religion at such arm's length was to do with the horror years, events that lags never want to talk about, but I also know you understand my love enough to realise my dilemma. I had to either risk you holding a Christian burial against me or deny us both when my time comes, being able to lie together, forever.

To Plough Van Diemen's Land

BOOK 2

The Women and Their

Men

Snakes, spiders, dust and flies,
fire, flood and drought,
yet women of the bushland
learned to fret and worry nowt.
Hitching skirts above the knees,
arching backs in pain —
And knowing help was far away,
just bent their backs again.

Days started early
on dusty bushland tracks,
stumps and faggots to be found
for splitting with the axe,
then poking at a blazing fire,
smoke billowing thick,
ever cook, baker, nursemaid, char,
with no time to be sick.

And big with child for many months
most of every year,
knitting, mending, rubbing, scrubbing,
wiping back a tear,
washing, ironing, weeding, ageing —
long forgotten bride,
teacher, helpmate, slave to all —
simply mistress of her pride.

—"Bush Women" by Kev Richardson

Seventeen

For Maggie Newitt (1819-1879):

> *How long, how long, in infinite Pursuit*
> *Of This and That endeavour and dispute?*
> *Better be merry with the fruitful Grape*
> *Than sadden after none, or bitter Fruit.*
> *Rubáiyát of Omar Khayyam — XXXIX*

The good thing about being near twelve is I'm old enough to know the why of things that worry children.

When little, I would wonder why, when it was snowing, we didn't have warm coats and bonnets like other kids. Or why they had boots when we got hand-me-downs only when someone gave Ma old boots big enough for Billy.

"We must always be thankful for such mercies, Maggie," Ma would say.

My name is really 'Maria,' but I've ever been called 'Maggie.' Never been sure why. And only as I got older did I know what Ma meant by not having money for other things once food was bought. Before Pa went to Botany Bay, wherever that is, we always had shoes. Making shoes was what he was clever at, same as Ma must now be clever at doing laundry at the poorhouse. Most grownups are clever at something. Billy might be old, nineteen he reckons, but he isn't yet clever at much, Ma tells him. She wishes he would hurry up and get some sense so he could earn more money. She cries at night when she thinks we're asleep, but it's hard to sleep with three in a little bed. Harriet and Ann share with me, and either this or that one is forever kicking out in a dream or something. Ma keeps saying "sorry" about us shivering when hunting for mushrooms because there's not enough clothes for all to keep warm at once. Got a letter, she did, from a place called Van Diemen's Land. From Pa. I had thought it was Botany Bay where he'd gone, but he must have moved though Ma says it's the same place—which is pretty confusing. But then Long Buckby has two names because sometimes Ma says our home is Long Buckby and other times says it's Northampton, so I'm not sure. Maybe when I get as old as Billy it will make sense. The letter said we can go live with Pa again if we want, but Ma worries about it being a place full of bad men. If we go it will be in a ship on a big ocean. I've never seen a ship. Nor ocean, so maybe it would be a good thing if we go, so I can see these things.

~ * ~

11th April 1831…

Maggie Newitt knew the churning in her tummy as the good ship *Hydery* was towed from Deptford pier into the Thames was prelude to the experience of a lifetime.

While waiting to board, a man showed her what he called a map of the world, a ball of many colours that he could turn around in its clever frame.

"All the blue is ocean, lass."

He showed her the course their ship would take to what seemed exactly the opposite side of the ball from England.

"If you was going further than Van Diemen's Land, lassie, you would be on your way home again." And she could see for herself how that would be so.

And the ship was great excitement, of course. Men were clambering about way up the masts, crawling out along the spars setting the sails even as their hackney arrived. Below decks the family had its own cabin, as small as had been the tiny bedroom the girls shared at home.

The first several days saw the weather quite foul, and Maggie certainly didn't find the sea-sickness exciting. Everyone in the family was laid low with it. Yet when the day came for her to be adeck with Billy and Ma to watch as the ship came into Portsmouth harbour, a place with the strange-sounding name of Spithead, Maggie was astonished at the ocean being so large.

Oh, so much larger than any river a person ever saw! One can't even see the other side!

At Spithead, she watched from the rail as a seemingly endless line of older girls they called she-lags was led aboard. She was startled and even frightened on realising many were chained by the wrists. She knew Van Diemen's Land was a prison, but hadn't at all associated this with people being in chains. She wondered if her father was chained. It was indeed a frightening prospect for all in the family to now ponder on, adding concern about what the future would offer each.

"It is a place where, according to the captain," her mother told them over dinner one night, "winter is less severe than in Long Buckby, and the summers warmer. And there is food aplenty to keep our stomachs full."

And every day for week after fruitless week, Maggie scanned the horizon for her first sight of the coloured ball the man had shown her...

But we never did find it.

~ * ~

Their first few years in the colony were to have countless new experiences broaden their scopes—give all three sisters, Maggie, Harriet and little Ann, many topics to ponder on.

With only two years separating each, we're luckier than the boys, Ma reckons. With Billy twenty-two, Ephraim fifteen, and Adam seven, they have too many years between each for any two to have like interests. And that makes sense, I guess.

The boys, however, took excited interest in the farm Pa had named Nun-Such, a name beyond any sort of reason any of the girls could bring to mind, yet which none cared to ask about.

"Whatever Pa says, goes," was another thing Ma kept telling the girls. "It doesn't have to have a reason, it's simply the way families work. If he thinks Nun-Such should be the name, then that's it."

So it was accepted.

Pa hadn't known much of farming. In England it had been a side of life he was happy to ignore. Now he had no choice. The boys, however, Maggie noticed, approached it as adventure...

"Far more exciting," Billy reckoned, "than making sheets of leather into shoes."

The girls lent their interests to the creatures, making pets of the cow, the old mare that doubled as plough-horse and hack for the dray, the goat and their half-dozen sheep. Rabbits they also bred, each one waiting its day in the cook-pot. Colourful parrots the boys caught in nets were confined in wicker cages, the girls spending countless hours trying to teach them to talk.

"It makes us like the Squire back in Long Buckby," Adam posed one night over supper, and Maggie couldn't help but note the half smile on her ma's face as she replied:

"Yet I should imagine the Long Buckby squire knows more about how his farm should be run, rather than having to depend on convict assignees he employs."

"Your pa likes to play the lord on occasions," she later told the girls. "But it's only a game."

"If pa were really a lord, of course," Maggie whispered to Harriet, "we certainly wouldn't be living in this little cottage—just think if we were instead living in a grand house, or even a castle....

"But then," she added, having given that more thought, "isn't it strange that Pa would play such mind-games? So maybe it's not so silly, as we've always reckoned, pretending impossible things. Not when grown-ups do it. Or is it only Pa? Ma seems to be always telling him that he goes about things like a 'big-bloody-kid when he's really a grown man.'"

Maggie would then privately ponder on the question of when a girl begins putting dreams aside to start thinking like her ma—never dreaming, but simply getting on with the hard chores, making difficult decisions.

She began noticing, of course, that dreams achieved nowt...

The hard chores really go away only once you've set about completing them.

So such became rote for Maggie Newitt. Her role as eldest daughter saw her increasingly laden with the chores a frontier cottage was ever in need of, not just now and again, but which must be done every day, and some many times over.

And each extra year added not only more responsibilities but more awareness of what life demanded of one. Nor could people be categorised, she discovered. She began realising that no longer was it easy grouping people in separate bundles: clever, haughty, meek— even lucky or unlucky. Every person, the passing of time made clearer, comprised all in different ways.

Like ma is sometimes moody and sometimes bubbling with excitement, and every time, it seems, when one stops to think about it, the change is occasioned not by immaterial things as I'd always thought, but people.

When lying in bed thinking on such conundrums, Maggie began to appreciate how every soul was influenced by others, how experiences in life affected each one's reactions to others, how the world responded only to the influences of people...

...Like mothers, for instance. There is no categorising their roles in leadership, help, advice, and succour; never more clearly illustrated than when I fled to her, in utter panic when my first 'monthly curse' arrived. Ma simply sat me down and explained what it was, and how I must learn to live my life around both the inconvenience and difficulty of it.

"And the next stage you are going to reach, my girl," Ma then told her, "is boys."

And that was quickly followed by what her ma declared were 'bodily urges rather than surges'."

And sure enough, Ma was to prove herself right again!

~ * ~

Larry Holding was a convict assigned to the family, and over time Maggie developed an increasing fascination for him. He not only gradually lost the gormlessness she had recognised in him on arriving, for day by day she realised how physically attractive he grew. His shoulders became broad, his chest manly and his face handsome.

Ahhh!

So it wasn't long before her urges dictated an exciting need, a fact over which she increasingly took Harriet into her confidence until Harriet herself was becoming excited, not over Larry but over her eagerness to see Maggie's desires bear fruit.

"But you wouldn't let him really do it, Maggie?"

And they would giggle about it.

The day arrived, however, when she whispered firstly to Harriet, then to her ma, and then together to her pa, that she lacked 'surges.'

"Larry and me want to wed," she informed all as her body began developing its telltale bulge.

Baby Ephraim was born in midwinter to sixteen-year old Maggie, and she and Larry married when the parson passed through. A life sentence was mandatory for stealing livestock, and Larry had 'nicked' a horse; so as long as he continued to satisfy his assignor, Ann Newitt, Larry would continue an unpaid 'employee' at Nun-Such.

A year later, just after Tom, Maggie's second child, was born, Harriet married her George Woolley. They set up home on George's grant at nearby Kellevie, half way between the Woolley property Longbottom to its north and Nun-Such to its south.

~ * ~

Two years later Maggie and Larry sat on the Kellevie porch laughing at baby Harry trying to walk. Brothers Ephraim and Tom were in a racing game, charging first this way, then that, little Harry desperately reaching out each time they were close.

It was a trying time economically throughout the colony, depression visiting hardships on people everywhere. Banks that hadn't crashed were denying loans to even those with a proven past. Farmers found themselves with insufficient coin to buy fertilizer or seed for the new season's plantings, let alone pay labour at twenty-five shillings a month to tend crops, harvest and thresh.

Like most, the Newitts had reverted to subsistence farming. Adam lost all his assignees to Britain's new anti-assignment law, and neither could he afford to pay labour.

Larry, no longer assigned and with his Absolute Pardon affirmed, his twenty-years in lieu of 'life' having been served, could find no other work—he and Maggie moved in with George and Harriet to help farm enough for both families to live on.

Maggie fronted Larry one day when all had pulled in belts yet another notch...

"You've been more than usually troubled these last weeks, Larry?"

He took a long time to respond.

"It's not just today's depression, girl—it's the long term. What is there for a man who has nowt but a fine wife, three kids and no prospects? With no land, no skills, letters or numbers, what's the best I can offer you as a future? Or my boys when they grow? All I can do for the rest of my life is labour for a living, and how does a man get ahead on twenty-five-bloody-bob a month?"

She watched the strong man she dearly loved break down and cry.

It's all so unfair. My pa gets fourteen years for stealing shoe-leather, then free land for bringing his family out; George's pa gets seven years for stealing a purse of seven guineas then free land to build up to a lucrative grazing property; George then gets free land before land grants are abandoned; yet my poor man is denied such starts in life because his crime was a horse worth even less than old Will Woolley's seven guineas. It's simply all so damned unfair!

She brought him a glass of water.

"Reason I'm down of late is that I've made a decision I don't like, and one you won't like either. But there's no alternative."

She felt a shiver, not so much from his ominous words but from the look of desperation in his face.

"Several of us lifers on the scrap-heap have had our heads together and agree there is no future here. But in South America, so tars off ships are sayin', they're findin' diamonds and silver in Bolivia and Chile. So we're going."

She dropped the tray and flopped on the bench.

...On that coloured ball in its clever frame! South America is what the man called a place half a world away from here!

"There's a ship in port that's got no crew because the master's run out of money. He will take us there if we work the ship for our passage. He says he can rent out his ship once there, to join us in diggin' for riches. When we've made some money, lass, we'll come home."

...Those years of hopeless shivering and empty bellies back in Long Buckby, the dread of every tomorrow dawning because it could only bring more of the same—just because our breadwinner had gone across the world. I now feel as helpless as Ma felt then. Without Larry, what will life be like for me and my kids?

Yet she realised that her man faced a hopeless future in Van Diemen's Land.

Yet has this bolt from a helpless present any more chance of a successful outcome than all the bolts I've ever heard of?

She sat back, holding in her own tears, promising herself that she would each day hug her Tom, Ephraim, and little Harry ever and ever more tightly.

~ * ~

A month after Larry sailed off on his desperate venture, Maggie realised she was pregnant.

Oh if only I had known this before he went, might it have stayed him?

Yet on further cogitation she realised it could more likely have thrown him into greater dilemma—an extra mouth to feed. And she knew in her heart that if he had then changed his mind, his despair would remain, and she would likely have to re-live his departure.

Then there was drama in the Kellevie house where Maggie, beginning to bulge with her new babe, still lived with her littlies, when George Woolley's father died.

George had idolised his father, as had his brother Liam.

"It seems no time ago Liam told us how excited Pa was about me and Harriet naming our boy after him," George bemoaned.

And a year later Maggie and Harriet's own Ma suddenly died to have them all in a spin.

"A stroke I reckon it was," old Adam declared. "Yesterday she was as fit as a fiddle."

"Pa is shattered," young Adam told Maggie when he brought the news.

She packed up her things and had brother Adam take her and her tots home to Nun-Such.

~ * ~

After the funeral at Sorrell, the Woolleys and Newitts repaired to Kellevie.

"She gave no warnin', Mary," old Adam told Mary Woolley. "She just fell in a faint to leave me all alone. A woman can cope without her man, Mary, but without his woman a man is bloody helpless. What to do now? I never thought I'd be left."

Seldom given thought to any future, has this man. He's ever been a 'now' person, his mind divided solely between the present and himself. And now he is less concerned at poor Ann going so quickly, than on his own selfish situation.

She could only feel how sad it was that Adam could not despair on Ann's behalf at a time like this, rather than his own.

Yet she pushed that thought aside.

"You did more than most, Adam," she sopped, putting her hand on his knee. "Not many lags brought their family out. That was something Ann was ever thankful for. She told me so."

Mary saw no reason to point out to him that he had never deemed it necessary to depend on his own resources, that instead, he simply kept showering problems on himself.

He suffered no labour in chain gangs like Will, never starved like Will, never felt bereft of hope like Will. Dear Will had only years of voiceless suffering, visions of nowt but more hopelessness. For all his penal years, he had no worthwhile future in sight. One could see why they'd risk the bolt. But Adam brought his family out not for their sakes, but his own. He has always depended on someone caring for him, someone to lean on. His dilemma now, with Ann gone, is simply having lost that crutch.

Yet Liam, who had been hovering close listening to their exchange, was not so reticent.

"You're a slow learner, Adam," his said, proffering his pragmatic outlook in earthy tones. "Most accept that even if a load looks a mite heavy, it must be picked up and carried. None can do it for you."

"What will you do now, Adam?" asked Mary, not quite sure herself why she would ask such a question; yet it would be one to turn his mind towards the future.

"Been thinkin' I'll give Nun-Such to the boys. Billy, Ephraim and Adam have between them got it working as well as can be got, the way the country's gone. Ephraim's got a bright head on his shoulders, and he's got ideas on what to do with the place. My heart's not in it, so I'll go into town. Got mates in Sorell, I have. Might just put down roots there, see what turns up."

Mary turned to Maggie. "And you now, dear, will you stay at Nun-Such?"

But Maggie had a surprise for everyone.

"There's something you need to know, Mrs. Woolley—and you too, Pa."

Liam moved behind Maggie's chair, put his hands on her shoulders.

Mary noted out of the corner of her eye that Maggie reached her hands up to rest them on his.

"It's something Ma put to me and Liam a month since..."

Mary waited, and Adam waited.

"Ma said to me six months after Larry's bolt, 'Why don't you and Liam get together?'"

Adam looked shocked. Mary seemed less so, yet certainly surprised

"...And we've today decided that's what we'll do."

All sat silent while the fullness of it spun around their minds.

Mary was the first to smile.

"If your ma is watching now, Maggie, and also your pa, Liam, I reckon they both would have smiles on their faces."

Adam still sat silent, his mouth somewhat agape.

And it was Liam who broke the next silence.

"Maggie is movin' to Longbottom, Ma, if that's all right with you?"

Mary got up and hugged her son, then Maggie, who rose to put her arms around Mary.

"Of course it's all right with me. When I think of all the years of sadness at having no sisters for you boys. Now Longbottom will be young again."

And on the drive home in the gig, she and Liam talked more closely on personal matters than ever, looking at all aspects of the Liam-Maggie relationship: the difference in ages, Liam taking on the responsibility of five children, and even more pertinent, realisation that if Larry should return, especially if that should be after several years had gone, what then would be the situation.

"We want our own children, Ma," Liam insisted.

"Well they're all serious matters, boy. You, a young man of twenty-four, whilst Maggie is what, twenty-nine, thirty?"

He nodded. "That's not a problem for us. For a long time now I've been envious of George with already two sons. And you yourself said how we've missed having girls at Longbottom. Now you can have a daughter in Maggie, and I can not only have two tiny daughters but three rollicking boys, all good lads."

"We'll need another bedroom, boy, with both boys and girls."

"Well, I'm the one with Pa's skills, and I've got his tools. So while I'm building one room I can make it two—so you've got a hide-away if you want a break from the kids sometimes."

"But Larry? That situation doesn't have an easy answer. It could cause great hardship if he comes back, not only for you and Maggie, but the children."

"She sees it that Larry closed a door in leaving. 'Walked out on us' is even the way she termed it. She is bitter about that, Ma, and has already told me she wants to be my wife and mother to my children, even though we can never know if she's been widowed or not..."

Mary held up a hand.

"It's not so much the way either of you think about it now, boy, it's what happens if Larry comes back. Maggie will still be his wife. And the five children she brings here will still be his. He can insist all rejoin him if that should be his want."

"Ma, we've talked over all that and come to the conclusion that not only can we never know what is likely to happen, but that the alternative is we go separate ways with our lives, when what we want is to be together. We've come to read each other pretty well over the years, and no wool has been pulled over our eyes. We look at this from the point of view of 'what are the alternatives?' and neither of us likes any we can see."

Mary smiled again.

"You know, boy? I don't think I've ever heard you with so much to say in a single breath. But it all makes sense; as much good sense as both you and Maggie have shown in discussing it so honestly."

Then she grabbed his arm. "Just pull back on those reins a minute, eh, while I give you a big hug!"

Eighteen

For Hannah Bunker (1833-1922):

> *Ah, Love! could thou and I with Fate conspire*
> *To grasp this sorry Scheme of Things entire,*
> *Would not we shatter it to bits — and then*
> *Re-mould it nearer to the Heart's Desire!*
>   *Rubáiyát of Omar Khayyam — LXXIII*

It feels good to be nine—it makes me nearly ten so no longer a child.

And it's good being in a bigger house with a real upstairs where Caroline and I have not only a whole room to ourselves but a whole bed each. And it's a nice room. Ma had it made over with wallpaper and curtains, and it has its own fireplace with glowing coals to warm everything. I like sitting up with a shawl round my shoulders, to rub holes in the frosty pane. Snowflakes wisp through the trees to make a carpet on the grass. It never looked so pretty at Rokeby. And here the night sounds are different—different in what sense I can't explain, but it's exciting working out what each is. Sometimes the night winds are wild, branches bumping on the shingles to send shivers through me. Pa will hear them too, so he'll know to go up, come daylight, to see if the roof needs mending. And Ma will check her kitchen garden for damage. Pa says the new trees will grow into good windbreaks around her gardens.. Yet many times, night breezes are gentle to make leaves tremble and cause rustles in the swaying corn. And frogs chant their evening prayers to make me purr like a happy kitten.

And watching clouds is fun. I look in them for real creatures and can often see a rabbit frisking, but if the wind is high it can quickly change to one with legs hunched, ready to jump a stile. Ma used to say clouds were drifting fairies with eyes alert for naughty children.

Tuppence has grown, not such fun to lead about now she's grown, however. Pa always told me I would likely have trouble walking her on a leash. "Sheep are not puppies," he would say, but Tuppence was the most wonderful pet in the entire world. I would take her for walks when Nana came to visit. And Pa was right about her not being happy on the leash, of course, as he usually is about everything. It was only later I realised that what I thought were trembles of excitement at whatever adventure we were about, staring into each other's eyes, was rather poor Tuppence cowering in fear.

And when was it? When I was six or seven? Ma and Nana talked about Pa coming out of his time, muttering words like 'absolute pardon' and 'at last he is free'? At night in bed when they thought all us littlies were asleep, Lizzy and Meg would talk about him being convict. But when I then asked him about it, he sternly told me that he knew nowt of what I was talking about, that I was quite mistaken— so that meant Ma and Nana and Lizzy and Meg were all mistaken, too.

And Pa always used to tell us kids that it is not how a person appears that's important—"What is more important than how one appears, my girl," he would say, "is what that person has done in their life. Achievement is what stamps a man." So I began asking that of every visitor until one time Pa cautioned me severely after I'd asked Lizzy's new beau, "Please tell me, Mr. Cullen, what important things have you achieved in your life?"

Grown-ups are sometimes very difficult to understand, especially Pa.

~ * ~

Five years later...

The distant hills shone with tints of mauve in the dusking light as shadows in the valley crept closer. It was a broad valley that stretched to the line of willows along the Wallaby Rivulet that marked the Bunker boundary. During the years since coming to Jerusalem, Sarah had felt content that things were at last taking good shape.

They had a comfortable home now, one to be proud of.

She and Hannah strolled in the herb garden tugging at weeds and plucking pieces of this and that for Hannah's basket. Sarah was free of cooking duties, for it was her birthday; the girls were doing the chores. The family at home was now but five and even at that not for much longer, for Maria was to soon marry. Mark and Sarah would then be left with only Hannah and Caroline. Ed had gone north over the strait, chasing opportunity in the Port Phillip colony; Ruth had married; Lucy had but two months since wed her Daniel, much to Mark's displeasure, Daniel being a trouble-prone lag just out of his time. They had also gone to the Port Phillip colony.

So it was easy times approaching for Sarah, realising she could soon sit back without, for the first time in her life, a sense of guilt.

It had been a sad time when Ed departed, however, at the tender age of seventeen.

It seemed we'd no sooner unpacked after moving, before he was off.

"I stayed to help move," Ed had told them, "but Van Diemen's Land offers a poor future for young'uns these days."

Trade depression had begun shortly after Mark received his pardon. Mark had proved most astute in reading the signs and taking good advice to make the move, and despite the cessation of free land grants, property values now tottered on the brink of collapse. And unemployment escalated to heartbreak proportions. Many once proud families were counting pennies, and more than a goodly proportion of probation convicts turned bushranger, marauding and looting, burning and vandalising. Just across Bass Strait, however, the new colony of Victoria was doing all it could to attract migrants. Fertile land was on offer at 'give-away' prices, and as Victoria had no convict labour, paying jobs were available for all. As Van Diemen's Land sank into deeper depression, Victoria emerged as a vital new land blossoming with development. Young men departed Van Diemen's Land in droves.

Sarah had then felt proud of both her men. Ed was suddenly so much his father's son, straight back, square shoulders, insisting it was Mark's own example of making the hard decisions, him leaving for the sake of his own future. And Mark was as brave.

"Keep your eyes on where you're heading, lad," he told his only son, "yet ever with a sideways glance at what others are about, else you could blunder into traps. The now and hence are the important goals, boy, never the past."

Mark whispered later to Sarah that he gave Ed cash to cover what would later have been his inheritance, to get him started over there.

"You are a mile off, it seems, Ma. What you thinking on?"

Sarah came to the moment with a jolt.

"Your brother, Hannah. Only time I ever saw your father cry, I reckon. Didn't think he could. He's a hard man, as we all know, but he's as hard on himself. It's not easy casting off a life to take on a different one. Especially when it's over many years. I couldn't do it."

"Hard on you, too, Ma."

Hannah for the moment looked older than her fourteen years. She knew what different people her parents were.

Yet they are happy together in their way.

She had always recognised that they had a love for each other, unlike parents of many of her friends. For all their differences, they made a happy home—strict, but happy.

Sarah put her arm about Hannah by way of answer, giving her shoulders a squeeze.

She had ever been conscious of how much her own ma doted on Hannah, was as gentle with Hannah as she was brittle with Mark.

Sarah smiled.

Ma and Mark are alike in many ways, yet each would be horrified to hear me say so.

In some ways they are miles apart, yet in determination they are indeed of a mould. And both astute at reading people. Yet their attitudes to people are different. Mark is intolerant; Ma totally lenient.

"Yer never got a bad word for people, Letty," Sarah's pa used to say.

Yet even with someone Ma is really dotty over, Hannah for instance, she is still tough as far as the child's attitude about people is concerned.

"Don't let her become too confident, Sarah," Old Titia once said. "It does a child good to sense some insecurity, seek dependence, else it never learns to think on others, establish measures. Children who grow up self-important come crashing down later in life for want of a little humility."

And Hannah had grown to establish worthwhile measures, doting on her nana as much as on her father, he whose many sides she recognised.

Of all Sarah and Mark's children it was only Hannah who stood up to him in a measured sense, yet was ever careful to ensure she never caused him loss to his considerable self-respect.

Lucy would blatantly defy him while others, Meg in particular, still totally defers to him. I often need a hand on each rein, knowing how Mark will mull over things in his mind and let them slowly simmer to a climax. I've come to sense his building tensions, recognise the dangers, the best path to tread before the simmer begins to boil when even the airwaves tremble. I can now tell when his bubble is ready, when to jump in to protect whichever daughter before Mark explodes.. All the children have been, and are still, different. Yet some similarities are tossed between them as if with a whisk. All in all, though, a happy, satisfying mix.

~ * ~

Liam quickly became a satisfied man on many fronts.

Maggie made him so.

"The boys are now old enough to help you in the field, Liam, and have the confidence in you to want to follow. And I'm happy at having you, in particular, father them. With all due respects to your brother

George, he is no planner like you. Even his own boys seem to grow up with only the sensible qualities of life that Harriet can impart. I'm far more content having you to guide these three."

It had only been a month after Maggie and the children came to Longbottom, she told him she was pregnant again.

"We'll call him William," was Liam's happy reaction.

And Mary was happy at Longbottom resounding with the laughter of children again.

Ephraim was a bundle of energy, ever in a rush about things. Tom was the quiet one, yet both were thinkers, that she knew appealed to Liam.. And she was excited for Liam having the girls, little though they were. Jemmy, youngest of them, was intrigued by Mary's hair, for she persistently tugged at it as Mary spent countless hours walking the babe, a task she had not had opportunity to do in her now twenty years in the land.

Mary had seldom had time for pleasurable things, Maggie sensed, but now could sit with needle and thread, keep her fingers busy with little girl things that her own life missed out on.

Mary never stopped wondering, however, if Larry might someday return and disrupt what now gave such promise of a happy life for Liam.

And Maggie confided easily in Mary. Without prompting, she had taken to calling her 'Ma,' so it was also, now, an obviously happier life for Maggie too.

At Harriet's house, Maggie had always felt she was intruding. Here, however, Mary clearly stepped back and made sure it was Maggie who was now Longbottom's mistress.

~ * ~

Mark Bunker stood on his porch, eyes drifting beyond his grazing flocks to the tree-line by the creek. The Wallaby Rivulet, his eastern boundary, meandered to the Coal River, while behind the house the land rose gently to a crest of forest. The house was close by the northern line where The Mud-Walls Road cut through a corner of the property. A glade of billowing oaks sheltered it from passing traffic on one side, and straggly gums shaded it from summer sun on the other.

To the south stretched undulating pasture, now a lush green, and all a vista to make a settler proud.

And now the railway was coming.

"Can't come soon enough," he insisted. "Coach drivers seem hell-bent on breaking records, trying to outdo each other in recklessness. Accidents are killing off passengers at an alarming rate."

And he was delighted that the end of convictism was at last a forgone conclusion.

There had yet been no formal announcement, but with so much writing on the wall, it was imminent. Only a week ago *The Guardian* reported that, despite the continuing exodus of people across the strait, convicts comprised only thirty-eight percent of the population when but five years ago, it had been fifty. He smiled.

When I arrived, it was eighty!

Public meetings in Hobart had persistently demanded cessation of transportation, and a petition had already gone off to the Queen. New South Wales had quit it, Norfolk Island's second closure was under way, and Victoria rejected the notion of taking convicts, as had the new colony of South Australia.

So surely its days are numbered in Van Diemen's Land!

'This Land Will Yet Forget' became the cry of abolitionists, a catchword ever in the forefront of Mark's mind. Convictism had always been a nagging cross for him, that lurking in young Ed's resolve to quit the colony had been the desire to pursue a future in a land without the convict stigma, lest maybe one day, should he remain with the family, his own father's past might return to haunt him. Such guilt on Mark's conscience had even furthered his resolve to pursue the This Land Will Yet Forget ideal.

Yet his reverie was broken as he realised it was daughter Meg's gig he had watched dusting up the road, to disappear behind the oak grove. So she would soon reappear on the drive to the house. It worried Mark that Meg insisted on driving around when in her condition. She couldn't have more than a week to go, according to Sarah.

And even less should she have a jolt on the road from the reckless contortions of crazy coaches.

"Should you be out and about so late in your time?" he chided her, once welcoming the young'uns.

Mark shared a particular affinity with Meg, who always seemed to think along a common path with him. So common a path, Sarah believed, that it was nothing short of utter deference to his acquired imperium. But it impressed Mark.

Wasn't it she who insisted I take strong action with Lucy for defying me, marrying that dreadful lag? Marrying a convict was bad enough, let alone one with such an abominable record. And Meg could see that, as clearly as me.

"Solitary confinements and persistent lashings are not what we should happily welcome into the Bunker family," Meg had insisted, knowing full well how much fuel she added to an already raging fire.

"What an embarrassment, Pa, to expect the family to overlook, to have to keep hidden from neighbours and friends who hold us in high regard. And you will be on guard then, Pa, against such a risk with my other sisters?"

Mark had realised how his resolve had faltered over Lucy, that he had obviously been inattentive, left the door ajar enough for the wilful girl to defy him.

Yes, Meg is absolutely right. I must indeed be sure to lay safe and truer paths for Hannah and Caroline.

~ * ~

Maggie chose her moment to touch on a subject she knew would prove prickly.

She waited until after what had become their less regular nightly lovemaking, what with her now seven months along the way with Little William.

"I'm worried about your ma, Liam. Have you noticed she seems more tired?"

She was sure he must have noticed, but it was the only way she could think of, to introduce it.

"I've noticed it for a time. When you and the kids came, she was all a-sparkle again. I was beginning to think that she would never get over Pa dying so young, but when you came, she snapped out of the melancholy. But yes, it's returned."

"'If you open up boxes of worries and talk about them,' my ma used to say, 'they lessen, and sometimes even go away,' so maybe, Liam, we can find some way to help her? I wonder if she is sick inside, or if it's a troubled mind. I do try to make her feel I'm not taking over her home."

"It's not that. She's many times told me how happy she is that you and the kids are here. And I know she's looking forward to seeing me with Little William."

"Harriet said that maybe one of the reasons my pa moved to Sorell, was so he wouldn't have to be kept reminded of Ma. Maybe your ma misses her Will?"

"She does that, all right. They were close, and she's now been four years without him. There is just so much of Longbottom that he built, keeping his memory even more in her mind."

"And she's lost the good appetite she had. I've wondered if it's my cooking. I keep asking her if she has favourite recipes she wants to cook."

"And I've never before known her to stay abed after sunup; so maybe her trouble is a sickness—like Pa's?"

All were questions that neither could answer, yet each was happy they could discuss them. It made the load seem less.

Mary's languor continued. She seemed more prepared, as time went on, to linger abed; and less and less did she walk the babe. And she began not only spending more of her daylight hours on the sofa, but actually complaining of tiredness. And before Maggie and Liam really had a chance to realise that she did indeed suffer from a serious illness, she had taken to her bed over several days, refusing food and accepting Maggie sponging her and dressing her hair.

"Never before have I seen her so," Liam told Maggie, herself, by now, unwell.

Already the local midwife had been warned that the babe was due any time.

"I stood over her bed this morning, Maggie, trying to picture how she must have looked in her youth, cavorting at least in mind if not in body through the green swathes of her cherished Erin. Her hair must have then been like fire, I reckon. Even now, faded with age, it looks radiant against the white pillow."

Next day they both watched over her, Maggie sitting in Mary's rocker while Liam sat bedside, holding his ma's hand.

Mary smiled weakly yet clutched his hand with even a little pressure.

"I know I'm goin' son, yet I'm happy to be joinin' your pa. I'm glad it wasn't too long a wait. He will be happy to see me, I know..."

She paused for difficult breath.

"...and he'll be happy when I tell him about you and Maggie."

But I won't bother you, son, by also saying how happy it will make me if I also find my pa to give a hug to. And Crooked Connor.

Liam felt it was the strain of talking that she passed several minutes in silence. But he waited. He realised that she wanted to say these things.

"Wipe her brow, Liam. It's showing sweat," Maggie whispered.

So he first gave his ma's palm a little squeeze.

"Thought I might make sixty, boy," she then said. "Nearly did. Ann did. She's there in the churchyard, waiting for Adam, close by where I'll be with your pa."

She paused again, so he waited again.

"In one way I'd like to stay longer, see your first little one. First is always a big event for a father..."

She coughed.

"Quiet a minute, Ma, there's no hurry."

She smiled, even as the cough continued.

"Yes there is, son."

With his free hand he stroked the hair. He recalled that even as a tot he used to play with it, even before he learned to talk, its colour always intriguing him.

"I'm glad Maggie is with you, boy," she told him for the thousandth time. "Something nice, there is, about two brothers with two sisters."

And through her mind flashed memories, the watching each of her boys grow, George bottling thoughts up while Liam was more like his pa, letting things out so that there was no later brooding. And it was a big thing he was taking on now, no small feat for a man so young taking on a woman with five children.

She looked forward to telling Will how happy Liam now was.

Hold out your hand, William my love, I'm coming.

And while she looked forward to dying, Liam too was remembering.

"No one in this land," she had always said of her Green Erin, "can imagine the green o' the hills, the glint o' the dales."

She would wax long on the smell of peat bogs.

"Perfume to every soul lucky enough to be Irish," she'd say.

She had always held the strength of character he discovered as a boy. And he would miss her brogue, the cant she never lost. He used often ask why she talked so strange, and the answer never satisfied him.

"It's because I'm Irish, little one." It was an answer as meaningless as his father's when asked about the funny marks on his back.

"It's because I was convict, lad."

And like the question in his mind now—why a woman like her should be taken when still so vibrant. Death was something he could never understand. When his pa was ailing it was the most painful thing Liam had ever had to do, he reckoned, watch such a strong man suffer his way to a slow death. Not often would his pa talk about the colony's early days, yet Liam knew he was on the first ship, arriving on a shore as naked as the savages. And got his lashing for bolting. Among Liam's earliest memories was being piggybacked by his pa, running fingers along the ridges in the flesh beneath the shirt. And all for picking a pocket, nickin' a purse.

"Hard work and hunger summed up our life then, boy," his pa would say.

And only slowly did the boys come to realise as they grew how gruelling must have been the horrors to make men risk such terrible punishment for bolting when the chance of success was next to none.

"Buckley's chance," his pa would say with a laugh.

And now his ma was off to join him.

He gazed down at her again, and it was quite a time before he realised she was already there.

He slowly released her hand, then, to turn and take Maggie's. He helped her to her feet, and they left the room, closing the door.

"You sit, Liam. I'll get the girls to make tea while I see to Ma."

And Maggie struggled off to that unpleasant chore.

They buried Mary with her William in the churchyard at Sorell.

Liam would rather have simply dug a grave on Longbottom, bury her in familiar earth instead of some distant churchyard where family was not on hand to pay homage. But by her William in consecrated ground was where, she had made it clear, she wanted to be.

'William and Mary Woolley' he inscribed the simple cross.

"They'd have wanted it plain," declared Liam, not caring to acknowledge even to himself that the simple inscription had, at that, sorely tested his literary skills.

Nineteen

Hannah Amelia Bunker was now sixteen, same age as her ma when arriving in the colony to so soon marry her Benjamin.

She sat in her room, her own room now, for only she and Caroline remained unmarried and at home. She huddled with a blanket about her knees as coals in the grate cast the warmest of glows, peering through the hole she'd rubbed in the windowpane's mist. She still loved watching winter's snowflakes fluttering like silent feathers seeking a breeze. Snow had ever bemused her, sometimes drifting in wisps, dancing as if unsure of its purpose, yet sometimes driving impatiently, like her father. The similarity ended there, of course, for while her father was the most forceful thing she believed she could ever encounter, there was nothing cold about him. Even when in one of his fierce piques she ever sensed the warmth of him, the realisation that his pique wasn't with her but rather with his own frustration that the world didn't share his opinions, quickly fall into place as expectation demanded.

Ever since little she had understood that much of his stern demeanour was but on the outside, a sort of show, not really of the man inside. She had always thought it strange for someone to be two things at once. Yet at the same time, she sensed that it was never worth testing. Lucy would argue with him, yet he would seem to put it aside only to some time later raise the very matter again with some strong lesson then in tow, with a penalty of some sort for poor Lucy. And with MaryAnn, oldest Briscoe sister, how Pa had taken so long to come around to accepting her unmarried life with her Will who she'd been with several years now, to still be giving him children.

Maybe it is that he still has a wife somewhere, one the world isn't to know about?

But no one asked such questions those days.

She remembered once when her ma remarked on some minor transgression by a convict on the roadside, how her pa had quipped: "A few days in the stocks would help curb his ill manners." It was a reaction natural to him, a fact Hannah ever found strange, him having been a convict. Yet she could see why he never spoke of it, why it was so important to him not to want even to remember it. Many people now said convictism should be forgotten, best not mentioned.

But all in all, Hannah reckoned, her pa was truly a worthy man to emulate.

She pondered on the family as she watched the snowflakes drifting...

Liz was the ever-practical diplomat, ever dependable; Meg shared so many of their pa's characteristics that she earned immediate approbation; Ed, Ruth, Maria, each were like their ma, content to simply tag along, never test the waters by taking sides; Lucy the same except on convictism. She was like their nana in that, remaining aggressively undaunted by her heritage, even proud to be convict; Little Caroline...?

That one still keeps out of Pa's way, hiding behind me like a shadow.

And Ma? Hannah recognised her ma's philosophy on the convict question was that to hide it was tantamount to denying the very people who gave life to the family. Yet in public, if pressed, she respected what convention demanded of a wife, supporting her husband's theory—or at least illustrating tacit support. Indoors she was content to be a bob-each-way girl, that peace reign.

It's sad, though, that I never knew my grandpa. I'd been but a tot when he died. But Nana?—she is another I will ever look up to, whose sayings keep rising in my mind. "When troubles reach their worst, they start to mend" is her favourite adage. Ever full of common sense is that old darling, ever knowing where she is at, seeing every picture of things as clear as if they were spring water.

Her nana was one whose footsteps Hannah would always be proud to walk in.

Only her pa was happy to be the bigot, she reckoned.

A week later, again ensconced in her room but on that occasion with Jane, bosom friends since moving to the district and practically neighbours, she giggled with her friend over two topics, each unwelcome within even their own families when assembled.

On the first, custom of the day precluded family from discussing any member in particular. Propriety demanded that only intimate sharing between father and son on the one hand and mother and daughter on the other were condoned. Sharing the forbidden, however, had ever been bonds between boys on the one hand and girls on the other when privacy afforded opportunity. Hannah and Jane, keyed by their ever-strengthening confidence in each other over the years, observed by now no taboos.

On the second, there was no custom, for the topic was a current one. There no longer raged the divisive battle between those for and against transportation, conducted not in the confines of family intimacy but in open forum, for that battle was already won. What raged instead was the divisive battle between those for and against sweeping the stigma of it under carpets—that, conversely, being conducted not in open forum but in the confines of family intimacy. It was to forever remain a decision of each man or woman's personal attitude—one to remain forever without resolution. Yet that topic, in the case of Hannah and friend Jane, was discussed with considerably less trust than the first.

Yet what dilemma of intrigue was introduced to a fly on the wall, one might ask, when the topics tended to overlap?

"I want Papa to let me go to England to stay with grandparents, Hannah. With the imbalance of sexes in the colony approaching parity for the first time in history, a woman is quickly becoming denied the advantage of choice when it comes to choosing a partner. And in the growing climate of lies, subterfuge and half-truths, how is one to avoid the dreadful discovery of having married a man with tainted blood? So I want to choose myself a gentleman of England rather than run the risk here."

"You seem to overlook the further possibility, Jane, of *not* discovering that you have married a man of 'tainted' blood as you call it. If your fear is so great, imagine the dilemma of living your entire life wondering?"

"Ah!" Jane's hand flew to her mouth.

Hannah in one sense, felt sorry for her friend, burdened with the disadvantage of being born to a worthy family. Her father was extremely wealthy with a string of properties spread throughout the colony. Since arriving, he had travelled twice to England on business and was unofficially categorised as the district's 'Squire' in that his family was by far the most aristocratic in essence.

And on the topic of either men or class, Jane made no attempt to hide her natural expectation that anyone of the convict class fell far below a suitable choice for husband. Her sheltered life in the Bisdee household had precluded her from exposure to the colony's convict elements and her shortsighted view of the reality was a side of her, around which Hannah had ever to carefully manoeuvre.

Hannah's father was, of course, delighted that Hannah and Jane had become friends. It was a further plank in the boardwalk leading to the image he sought for Bunkers. He indeed hoped that much of Jane's class would rub off on Hannah, held absolute faith in the fact that Hannah, conscious of the fact he had been convict, would protect his clean image with her very life.

Her mother, also realising Hannah's knowledge of the truth, had ever cajoled her to be careful of letting the truth slip.

"I would hate to see you revert to lies of course, dear, but then I think you owe it to your father to lie if really backed into a corner."

John Bisdee chaired the Jerusalem chapter of the This Land Will Yet Forget campaign, same as he chaired most committees in the district. He and Mark worked tirelessly together to influence all possible in the community, to, as Sarah jokingly yet confidentially with Hannah referred to it, "sweep the Terrible Truths of convictism under the proverbial carpet."

~ * ~

Two years later...

The 'little William' Maggie had carried emerged on the world as little Emma.

Liam's disappointment was short-lived, however, for Emma won his heart, as do all first-borns. And all the other children accepted their half-sister as readily as they had accepted Liam, he who had by now taken to framing his face in a beard.

"Not just any sort of beard," he joked, for it was soon a mammoth growth, thick, ginger, and bristly such that there was little face left to see.

"Not so many freckles now," he claimed, which the children thought a great joke.

"Shaggy as a ginger sheep it is, Pa," they chided.

Maggie was content that the family had settled into a happy routine on Longbottom. By end of summer not only was the economy showing signs of recovery—especially for her family, for Liam had entered contracts to provide fleece for England's military uniforms—but she was large with what they this time reckoned, the way their luck was shaping, would surely be 'little Will.' Yet there remained the problem of drought.

"If rain don't come soon, Ma,"—as Liam had taken to calling her— "we'll get no better price for mutton than when winter finished."

In the east paddock, the pasture had died, so he'd left the ground to fallow. And the west paddock had turned to hay before the flocks even got to graze it. The dry was so widespread that much of the district erupted in flames for the second summer in a row. Farmers with heavy dependency on crops were in a particularly bad way with yields small and quality poor. Graziers were better off in that hungry sheep still grew wool, yet of what value were skeletal mutton-sheep?

"Losin' a lot up river, they are, and the buggers still dump their carcasses in the creek. You'd think all the bloody puffin' and pantin' we been doin' would have some effect. But they don't bloody listen."

"Like you don't listen, Liam. You dump your carcasses in the creek."

"Only because it's too late once the water's fouled. No use goin' to the trouble of diggin' holes or buildin' pyres when a man can chuck atop those already bloody there, smellin' it all up."

Liam's attitude was typical. A settler's civic pride didn't stretch too far when extra effort didn't pay in coin, Maggie had come to realise.

Yet she continued to love him dearly. He was a good father and husband, so harmony reigned. They were good for each other and had accordingly grown even closer in love as well as in understanding. And the children were happy. Even the littlies spoke up one night over supper, informing the amused parents how much more tolerable their ma was since they'd moved to Longbottom.

Ephraim was a sturdy boy of twelve, lively, forever rushing, anxious to turn any situation into something to enjoy with undue regard to the chaos.

"A typical boy," said Liam, "takes after his grandpa Newitt."

Tom was his brother's opposite, quiet, yet as eager to pull his weight, which made them both Godsends in Liam's book. Eight-year-old Harry was easily led into mischief by Ephraim, and neither of the two Holding girls could do wrong in Liam's eyes.

"They're little yet, still overawed by the beard," Maggie reckoned.

And Emma Woolley was now a near three-year-old bonny bundle of joy.

All were exhausted by the heat, however, and couldn't wait for autumn's cool winds. And its rains.

"All so bloody dry, Ma. Christ knows what the bloody sheep'll eat when the hay's all gone. The dam's but half full, the bloody sun every day suckin' up more than the stock drinks. But what can a man do?"

Maggie arched her back, heaved a sigh. She cared only that little William might come early rather than late. She'd been carrying him more than eight months. He weighed a ton and kicked like a horse.

"And the dam walls a yard around are nowt but bloody mosaics of dried mud, cracks so wide a man could break a bloody leg fallin' into them. And when the rain does come them walls will turn so bloody slippery the stock'll bog to their bloody haunches just tryin' to get a bloody drink..."

Yet several days later he spotted in the heavens the first sign of pending rain. He fondled the copious beard as he gauged the cloud.

"Look, boys, bloody storm comin'. Bloody beauty..."

But his voice trailed off as he studied how the cloud tumbled. Strange indeed, it was, unlike any he'd seen before, so low for so dark, and ringed with a red, not golden, halo, unusual for storm clouds covering a setting sun.

But it's only noon!

Slowly, so very slowly dawned the terrible realisation that they were not storm clouds. Nor was it a setting sun, of course.

Maggie came to join him; she too was intrigued by the eerie glow in the sky.

They watched the black cloud become ever thicker, billowing far too quickly, it seemed, to be real. And in seeming no time it blanketed the sun to make it suddenly dark.

"Dark at high bloody noon for Christ-sake," Liam gasped. "They're not rain clouds," he then half whispered to her. "That's a mountain of bloody ash we're lookin' at, an airborne mountain of hot, burnin' ash that the wind is bringin' this way. Jesus!"

The glow around the clouds began to brighten, soon to spread an eerie, frightening redness across the landscape. Smoke appeared on the north ridge, and the smell of burning crept up their nostrils. Each suddenly realised that a massive bushfire raged beyond the ridge and that when it reached the top, the northerly would gust it straight down on them.

"Holy hell, boys," Liam yelled—"Harry, run, get your sisters. And you two big boys, listen good for there's work to be done bloody quick."

As it happened the girls had heard the excitement and had come running.

"MaryAnn," shouted Liam, noise from the fire and smell of smoke suddenly strong enough now to alert all that a major calamity was on them, "go with your ma, sweetie, you do the heavy work because she's not too able in her state, but get blankets off all the beds. Tom, you go to the barn and bring covers for the rain-barrels before ash fouls the only water we'll have for drinkin' by tomorrow if there's any bloody farm left...

"...Ephraim, you get to the barn too—put halters on the cow and calf, take them and Irish to the dam, right into the bloody water. Take off the hobbles and fix 'em short so they can't get out. Leave Irish free in the dam, he's got sense enough to know we're about what's bloody best. Then get the dogs, herd the sheep down there too. Take Harry and tell him to stay with the dogs that they don't let the sheep out again. Then you come back here, mate. And all at the bloody double, boys."

Maggie's legs began to tremble as MaryAnn led her away from the sight of what she could sense was going to explode with a frightening fury. Yet she quickly shook her head to help her mind return to the tasks at hand, following to the bedrooms.

Liam turned to Tom, who struggled from the barn with barrel covers.

"Come on, mate, none o' yer usual muckin' about. That bloody black cloud is gonna spew hot ash all over us pretty bloody quick."

He took respite from directing traffic to snatch blankets as MaryAnn returned with them, to douse them in the rain barrels, to then wring them out best he could without wasting water.

"Jemmy, stand on this box, eh? When I lift a blanket out, you reckon you can slip this cover on bloody quick? Before the nasty dirt gets in?"

They'd need wet blankets for protection not only in the dam but in fleeing to it. And they'd stay in the dam until the fire had either passed or roasted them alive. Or burned itself out having consumed their all.

A distressed and heaving Maggie, clutching the bigness of her belly, arrived with more blankets.

"Can you see to the baby, Ma? Here, take a wet blanket and get yourself to the dam. When that fire comes over the ridge, I reckon it'll hit the house in less than a half hour. When the boys are back, I'll send them to you. But first we'll need long sleeved coats for all and cloths for our heads. When them ashes start to shower on us they'll be like tiny bloody coals, red-hot ones burnin' our hair, skin, eyes, wherever they land. So keep yerself covered."

A quick look up assured each how urgent their tasks were. Smoke billowed more quickly even than Liam had reckoned. From over the ridge the smell of burning eucalypt smarted in their nostrils. The stench of roasted livestock added frightening realism to their fears. Ephraim trotted past astride a nervous Irish, soothsaying in its ear as they rode, the cows and calf tethered in convoy behind.

"Hurry it up, boy, then get back to help your ma."

Bloody hell, the boy any other time would be at full bloody gallop as if he had but seconds before the world comes to a bloody end.

Never had he seen such a sky. Blackness burgeoned in increasing folds, and Liam swore he could already feel the heat of fire. The north ridge was now in deep shadow, not shadow left by a setting sun but blacked out by tons of swirling, billowing ash about to be sucked into throats and nostrils.

Maggie emerged from the house with bundles of clothing.

"Make for the dam, not too fast in your state, girl, but not too bloody slow either."

"Wouldn't the creek be better? It's got more shelter?"

"All the shelter is trees that will spew us with hot bloody ashes if they burn. And it's likely full of carcasses and snakes, wrigglin' and writhin' their ways from upstream. We're better off in the little water the dam's got, and there we got better chance of controllin' the flock."

Then they stood dumbfounded as fire burst over the ridge: a terrible, frightening conflagration roaring skywards, a wall of blazing terror four or five times the height of any man, suddenly sweeping into their north paddock. Its speed seemed somehow unreal. A whole tree exploded before their eyes as the wall hit it.

With the wind behind it, the wall sped down the slope, each little haystack, so tediously built, gulped up one by one, each becoming added fuel to what was already an inferno.

Jemmy screamed. Maggie looked as if to begin labour on the spot, suddenly realising their helplessness, the power behind the fire, how pregnable their situation.

Liam's predicted half-hour had been wildly optimistic—they now had but seconds.

"Ma, get to the dam. Ephraim should meet you along the way."

He lifted Jemmy from her box.

"You follow your ma. MaryAnn, you carry the baby."

"What of you, Liam?"

"I'll grab food and be a minute behind you all. Now for Christ-sake, go!"

When halfway to the dam she looked back to see him emerge from the cookhouse with a sack. She saw him look up to see how far she had got. Then turning again towards the dam, sensing that little Will was about to begin his entrance to the world at any moment, she saw ahead, Ephraim and Tom running towards her to help.

Liam had grasped bread, apples, and a cheese and now set out after Maggie and the girls. He could see Ephraim and Tom running from the dam.

"Good lads," he shouted despite realising there was no chance they could hear.

He had never felt so impotent, but began running towards them, his mind still whirring.

Maybe with luck it might miss the house.

His pa had insisted that trees close to the house were a risk.

"Better sacrifice shade in the heat than the house in a fire," old Will had said.

The noise was deafening now. The roar of flames and explosions of eucalypt gas thumped in his ears as burning clouds scudded with the wind, bringing fire where it had not been before. Nothing in the northerly's path could survive.

They cowered in the shallow dam, huddling under blankets, Liam continually splashing water over them as ash rained down. Birds dropped from the burning sky by the score, choked for want of clean air and from feathers singed by flying sparks. A kangaroo family raced for the dam, yet when confronted with the horse and cows, dogs, sheep, and shrouded people they veered off in the direction of the creek where they'd no doubt end up yet more carcasses to foul it.

"They'll burn before they can bloody drown, poor buggers."

"Liam, look," shouted Maggie, pointing from under her blanket.

What had been a solid post-and-rail barn, built by his pa, stoutest building on the farm, was a giant firebox, orange flame, black smoke, and sparks competing for airspace. Even as they watched, the entire barn exploded with a mighty roar. The children stared goggle-eyed in shock and fear as blazing timbers hurtled through the air, a million sparks bursting in every direction. Enough reached the dam to cause them all to duck lower, every creature bellowing in pain.

Then the children screamed as one of the dogs took fright, bolted here, then there, quite disorientated, then hurtled off in a frantic charge to nowhere. Liam lunged at Ephraim, who with a great shout, was on his way after it.

"And you fought me like a tiger, mate," Liam later told him.

The noise of the fire was as frightening and intimidating as either the heat or the flames. Maggie could never have believed there could be such a force of nature as they were witness to unless for raging floodwaters. But no surging torrent could equal the terrifying sounds bombarding them. In their panic, many sheep bolted, screaming in almost human cries as fire burned their backs, ashes their feet, as they stampeded from safety, crazed with fear.

The smell of burning wool and flesh invaded every nostril.

For what seemed hours, the family coughed and wheezed as the very air became a grey mist. Eyes burned, and the more Maggie and Liam tried to cover the heads of littlies with wet blankets, the more they struggled to free themselves. Birds continued to fall from the sky, plop-plopping into the dam with tiny splashes. Liam and the older boys moved to settle Irish and the cows near to panic, the still falling ash singeing their hides, burning their eyes even more than it did Liam's beard that she noticed he had to keep dunking in the water. Ephraim wrapped a cloth over the horse's head before mounting him to sit astride, the better to calm him. The remaining dog cowered under Harry's blanket.

"The chickens," wailed Maggie, her cry ending in a choke as she realised it was not only her henhouse she could see ablaze but beyond it, the cookhouse. Kindling stacked by its wall was like a magnet to the flames, and within minutes the wall itself was ablaze. She crouched hand to mouth, huddled against the older girls, tears streaming down all faces as she watched her cookhouse burn. First the roof collapsed in a shower of sparks, then the walls tumbled. The canvas bathhouse alongside offered but token resistance, the bathhouse in which mother Mary had taken such pride.

Liam cradled Maggie's head to his chest while she sobbed, and the children, as desperate for comforting, clung to them.

She coughed and wheezed and felt like retching, her lungs rasping as if scraped with sandstone. All waited in fear until the fire decided it had taken enough.

"I still think the house might be all right," Liam shouted. "I think that might be walls I can see through the smoke."

She prayed that he might be right.

And when the fire eventually moved on to terrorise neighbours in the next valley, to rob them too, of their all, and after having huddled, trembling and wet for what seemed a thousand hours, the bedraggled Woolleys crept slowly up the dam walls, Liam's mosaics of dried mud.

Each picked their way gingerly over the smouldering bracken of Longbottom.

All about them seemed as suddenly released from the noisy, raging inferno, as it had been engulfed by it. The frightening roar had subsided into an uncanny quiet.

Longbottom was an eerie, smelly, smoking, black emptiness.

They looked about, every one crying.

~ * ~

Sarah took the stage to Hobart.

Sister Lizzie's letter said that their ma was suffering what seemed a fit of depression. Lizzie felt that if Sarah were to visit, it might jog their ma out of the hole she seemed to be digging for herself.

"It is so out of character for her," Lizzie explained on arrival. "You know how she is ever the one to hold herself upright, illustrating nowt but utter confidence? Well that is on the wane."

Titia normally lived, those days, in sister Maria's Red Lion Hotel, but Lizzie had brought her to her own home, she having more time to give old Titia constant care.

"Is it in the mind, or physical? I can't recall Ma ever illustrating that there might be something wrong inside. She has always seemed the very tower of strength."

"Indeed. And I feel that is still so. She's simply begun to feel lonely, I reckon."

"Lonely? When living in a pub with people about everywhere?"

"Lonely without Pa."

Their ma was in her room having her afternoon nap. Sarah and Lizzie sat over a cuppa until she appeared in the doorway.

Sarah rose, trying not let surprise show. Her ma looked tired, as if in need of the nap from which she had just woken.

Yet the old face brightened on seeing Sarah.

"I didn't know you were coming, dear."

"There's some shopping I want to do, Ma. Mark dug deep into pockets to let me have a few shillings. But oh, how well you look. That makes me feel even happier for being here."

"I keep well enough, but the years are catching up. The old body is in need of greasing, I reckon. 'Like the un-oiled wheels of a buggy' is what Mrs. Clarke calls her own creaking joints."

Sarah had no idea who was Mrs. Clarke but didn't pursue the point.

"How long since Pa died? Must be quite some years now?"

"Fifteen, dear," Titia quickly replied.

As quick as if she's keeping daily note!

"Well that must make you touching eighty when you look not a day more than sixty. I'd be happy to look as sprightly as you if I live to even seventy."

"Don't talk like that, Sarah. It's bad luck to think of dying."

And was that a flash of the old eye sparkle?

"And what of your family. Mark is well?"

"Like a young puppy off its leash he is, with convictism finishing. He's on the local This Land Will Yet Forget committee. He still reckons that by the time our grandchildren are having their families, that that whole part of our history will have been forgotten."

"Hugh! Pigs might fly!"

Was that another sparkle?

Why don't you start a 'This Land Will *Never* Forget' campaign, Ma? With you likely one of the few First Fleeters still gallivanting around the colony, people would listen. You could start making more realise how the early convicts founded this entire civilisation."

"Huh. If I had somebody to help me stand up on the box in St. Davids Park on Sundays, I might just start thinking on that," she said with a chuckle.

"Pa, if he's looking down, would enjoy it," teased Sarah.

"I might at that, you know."

"Well, work on it. With the depression still leaning hard on all shoulders, it might put a spark back in people's eyes as well as in your own. But I won't tell Mark."

Which brought another chuckle.

"Why don't you suggest to her, Liz," Sarah later said to her sister, "that she move back to The Red Lion, where she has so many friends, to work on something like that?"

<h1 align="center">Twenty</h1>

Adam Newitt, he who had worn his chains later yet more frequently than his Woolley in-law, now gazed at the wizened image that confronted him from his mirror.

It was a visage truly testimony to the etchings of years—wind, sun, heat, cold, ale and worry, each having engraved their unkind signatures.

It truly depicted more that of a seventy-five-year-old than a sixty-five.

But he chuckled.

That's as the world sees me, the cracks and creases by which I'm known.

'Old Rubber Boots' Maggie called him, a name in which he revelled. He enjoyed being seen as one with a history of bouncing back from adversity to continue snapping fingers at authority. It had made the wrinkles worthwhile.

"Never believed in grovellin' to the bastards," he told the image, "else they see coward or dupe in yer. Better to show ya mettle and suffer the bloody arrogance."

For all the character his image displayed, however, one aspect obvious to most still evaded his notice. His face wore no mask to hide inner thoughts. He was of the gullible clan, wore every thought for all to read, which often put him on the back foot, of course, yet never meant disaster, only setback—of which, he was well prepared to admit, there'd been many.

He was a 'now' man, had ever quickly forgotten the past and its lessons and always been largely unconcerned for the future and careless of the present.

'Now' was always the critical moment in his conscious life because tomorrow was too far into the future to be of consequence. He seldom heard those who tried to counsel him, as Ann had ever realised, living life almost as if the good advice he often received had every time fallen on deaf ears and every good example on sightless eyes. Never had he been the family rock for floundering children to grasp, cling to for assurance. That role had always fallen to Ann.

Since she'd gone, he realised she had been the rock of his salvation, too.

He missed her dearly. It was five years ago he buried her in the churchyard at Sorell's St. Georges, yet he'd somehow survived. She had ever reminded him of the terror years in Long Buckby during his absence and that it had been the most traumatically desperate time in her life. Yet she also often reminded him of her gratitude that he arranged for her to flee those traumas in order to rebuild the family here.

He had always mistakenly, however, perceived her gratitude merely as a sop to bolster his morale, ease his guilt. Only too late did he realise that maybe her distress in those crises had been as real as his loneliness now.

Yet Adam being Adam, he tipped a wink at the mirror...

"No," he told the face, still bemused by what Ann had called its 'guilt lines,' "Maggie got it right because after her mum died she told me, 'I recall saying to brother Ephraim at the time, Pa, how you bringin' us here delivered us all from fear and shivering and hunger. And I know Ma was ever thankful.'"

That's it, a far better outlook than sufferin' guilt.

A tear on the face in the mirror staggered a tortuous path down the creases of the face, to hang on its chin, waiting to be wiped away.

Adam felt no remorse for the life he had blundered through. He rather held to the benefits of his great fortune, his sense of bravado that ever shielded him from regrets.

If it comes down to having to hold a bloody opinion, I'd have to reckon every man in the world would admit to having some input in exposing himself to the risks he takes. It was just that in my case, every time in fact, I've had bad luck.

Bad luck seemed endemic in him, he had to admit.

That's it, it ain't fate that delivers misfortune on a man, it's bloody luck. Or in my case, bad luck.

And on that point he grinned again, for he defensively conjured up earlier memories that always softened dour thoughts.

Back in Long Buckby in his days of earliest memory, there had been only one really good thing happen, and that was Phoebe, the only mother he ever knew. He was never sure if she were his real mother, she who experienced pain and suffering simply in order to bring him into the world. He was told as he grew that his pa had been married before wedding Phoebe and that she had been married before wedding his pa. Elder brother John whispered to him, when he was still too young to understand even the rudiments of what parentage was about, that he, John, was unsure if his pa had been his ma's first husband or second. And Adam never asked about the conundrum; he simply grew up believing it highly likely that if this applied to his brother, it must also apply to him, even in reverse—that his mother might or might not be Phoebe. It had all been too complicated to fret over, and it never bothered him enough to seek an answer, for he loved Phoebe dearly. She was a big, fat and happy soul, so growing up was a happy time. There had been precious little to eat, he recalled, and for much of his life he had no shoes and little clothing. All the family shivered each winter, yet he never felt hard done by, for it was normal. And despite there were few comforts, happiness abounded. Lacking pennies to spend on food meant there was ever adventure with his pa and brothers, poaching trout from the squire's stream and trapping game on the common. He could still recall Phoebe's happy chortles when they'd arrive home with such treats, that she could turn on a spunky meal for a change.

Such memories surprised him in their clarity as if he were there again, living all the same emotions and youthful verve. But his wild start had meant troubles. And along with the troubles had come bad luck, the biggest of which was getting nabbed for nickin' shoe leather, simply to earn an extra bob. Twice.

Not as if I'd been nickin' the extra bob—I was still working, still an honest cobbler.

So he was unlucky twice.

And being sent away meant sacrificing all the security of family, that which had always provided the cushion when he tripped.

His grins now were for all the times he wasn't caught, and his image grinned back.

A man needs to bloody grin about things.

He patronised the image with another wink, which it quickly returned.

The trouble with today's young'uns is that they burst into teens with a zest for life, only to hasten too quick into changin' things, like rushin' headlong into marriage with all its responsibilities. And babes quickly follow. And growin' kids quickly bring people down to earth, o' course, so that in no time, troubles surround a man and he makes the mistake of takin' the troubles too much to heart. He tries to bloody best them.

If only he could but laugh, shrug a shoulder and bolt—not that a man can run away from troubles forever, but he can lose himself for a time, get drunk, have a few bloody giggles. Then when he looks about to find they've caught up with 'im, the troubles don't look so overpowering; you've pricked their bloody bubble, you've brought 'em down to a level where a man can smirk. Cos all they do when all's said and done is rap your bloody knuckles so ya back to square one when the bloody trouble ain't a trouble no more. It's all a matter of attitude, mate.

The visage frowned, yet Adam knew that deep down, it agreed.

And somewhere from the distance came a rumble of thunder, a now sound. So he broke off his reverie, exchanged another wink, and moved to close the shutters.

~ * ~

Sarah, Mark, and Hannah were engrossed in conversation upstairs, Hannah curling her ma's hair.

She carefully smoothed a paper patch before lifting the iron from its skillet to press it, to then curl it around a strand of hair. And as the process repeated, paper patch after paper patch, Sarah slowly acquired the visage of the mythical Medusa, each snake a bandaged curl.

"Do you really believe, Mark, that people will forget about convicts, that the only life this colony has ever known will just of a sudden slip from memory just because we stop talking about it?"

"Of course not, Sarah. We know in our hearts that all who have seen it can never dismiss it from our minds, but public opinion can be a powerful influence if sufficient numbers are behind a campaign. Undoubtedly our children's children and their children in turn will find greater opportunity for pride in their civilisation and self respect, if there is no sense of social taint. We must look ahead."

Hannah knew it best not to comment, that her pa's opinions would not be swayed. She continued to smooth, press, curl a paper about another strand of her mother's hair. She in fact felt some pride in her father having the confidence in her, to speak so frankly in her presence.

"The colony is changing," he continued. "It seems no time since we had six or seven men to every woman, yet with so few now arriving and with such an exodus, men flocking across the strait, I see in *The Guardian* that we now have two men for every woman..." He coughed a little, an impish gleam sparking his eye. "....and maybe I should have added, with so many wives presenting their husbands with an abundance of daughters and dearth of sons?"

Hannah giggled. Sarah merely smiled.

"Which brings me to something I have to say to you, Hannah Amelia."

During a pregnant pause while Sarah looked surprised, Hannah waited.

"You are of marriageable age, Hannah—difficult as it might be for Ma and me to realise, our darling girl will turn eighteen soon. And in consideration of yours and Caroline's futures, raising children in the next generation, it is behove on me to refrain from making the mistake on your behalf that I was guilty of on Lucy's. It is imperative, if you are to enjoy a happy future, that you do not enter it bound with the smudge of convictism for your children and your children's children..."

Hannah started, disturbed at the turn of conversation. Which Mark noticed, so hurried on:

"...I have chosen a husband for you, a man most suitable to become part of this family. Already I have spoken to him, and the matter is agreed, my pledge given..."

The hot iron fell from Hannah's hand, burning the carpet, the pungent odour stirring Sarah from her shock, to snatch it up and return it to the skillet.

Bewildered, Hannah stood speechless, hands forward as if for help.

Mark took a hesitant step, extending a hand. He gave every impression of a child stalking a small bird, afraid it might up and fly away before he could get close.

It had ever been important to Mark to always appear reserved, demonstrate dignity, even within family. *Especially within family!* Yet now emotion tore at him, he needed to help her, help her understand that he was doing what was in her best interest.

An eternity seemed to pass.

Hannah tried to speak, yet no sound came. She but slowly shook her disbelieving head.

Mark's composure returned first, and he spoke quietly and so slowly that both women sensed the reality of the moment, cementing their minds to it.

He took her hand, and she didn't pull away.

Sarah, as shocked as Hannah at this turn of events, realised in successive flashes through her mind, both her responsibilities and care as a mother, and as a wife. But she would let a moment pass before interjecting, to see what would follow.

"You are of an age to take the step of marriage, my dear, and you deserve the best chance for happiness," Mark continued. "However, you yet lack the experience to realise early sacrifices must be taken in order to secure the rest of your life. I have chosen a man with a modern outlook on the important matters, not a wealthy man but with sound principles and ethics who I am convinced will make an excellent husband and father. He has assured me that he holds you in the highest esteem and will dedicate his life to making you happy. He—"

"Who, Pa? Who?"

"Mr. William Lewis."

Hannah's shock returned. Yet she remained still lost for words.

"Young Lewis has been in the colony a little more than a year," Mark continued, "from England aboard the ship *Sarah*, an appropriate coincidence I can but believe. So there is no taint of convictism there for you or your children to wear in the future, Hannah."

Hannah's mind reeled, torn between her need not to be railroaded, and that whilst she could see he may have acted in the purest of interest on her behalf, there were areas of doubt he had overlooked. What he related gave her no clear indication of who was her prospective husband.

"There are three William Lewis bachelors in the district to my knowledge. Which, Pa, have you been talking to, given me up to? Can you describe him? Tell me where he lives? And it seems he is aware of me, so please tell me what I need to know so I can place him?"

Sarah now sprang to action, frightened at Hannah's dilemma.

"Mark! You are being most unkind to your daughter. And to me. You have taken a most imperious step that might or might not be best for our Hannah. For pity's sake, Mark, tell us who it is you have promised our daughter to."

Sarah was angry, and it showed.

Mark was on the defensive, an uncustomary role. He was flustered.

"He is in his twenties, ah, rents a room in Green Ponds. He is currently engaged in work to do with road maintenance north to Oatlands."

"Ah. I know the one."

Hannah stamped her foot, dropped the curling paper she had crumpled almost to a pulp, to flop on the bed, her spine extremely straight.

"Father, that William Lewis is as of convict descent as I am. In fact, more so. The belief of me and my friends, and please realise, Pa, that among ourselves we freely talk about this convict thing in respect of people of the district, more than you could imagine, is that the William Lewis you identify, is the son of two convicts. His father was a lag off *Malabar* back in the twenties, and his ma a she-lag off *Brothers* some years later. Your William Lewis, Pa, is even more convict-tainted than me!"

Mark's shock was electric.

Sarah sensed it as it happened as if by instinct bred of anticipating Mark's moods in any crisis. The very air in the room seemed to freeze, the crystals of the chandelier suddenly stilled, the pendulum of the mantle clock stuttered, missed a beat. Certainly the cat in Sarah's lap quit purring, ears twisting in Mark's direction.

Mark responded quickly, too quickly, the women thought, his voice strangely lacking conviction.

"He came free... he told me so."

But Hannah's voice was crisp, brittle...

"I am saying what others believe. You could be victim of one with the same attitude as your own, prepared to lie as you expect your wife and your own daughters to lie to hide what you consider the terrible truth of our heritage..."

From the corner of her eye Hannah caught her ma's frown, warning her to let the confrontation drop. But it was her future that her father toyed with, and she had inherited enough of his bombast to insist on her point...

"How could you, Pa? How could you so gamble with my future? How could you be so wrong? You of all people making such an error of judgement? Inviting yet another convict, it seems, into the family, undoing all you have striven to gain since acquiring this new life?"

Twenty-one

Van Diemen's Land was a changed colony.

After its time of burgeoning growth, poor leadership had not merely whittled away at the budding advantages the people had enjoyed, but lopped robust, fruit-bearing branches.

The population was falling, people fleeing unemployment for the promise of coin in the pocket across Bass Strait. Emigrants from England saw more opportunity in the new colonies of Victoria and South Australia, and with convict transportation in its final days, fewer people arrived in Van Diemen's Land than departed. The result was deep economic recession such that people on city streets had empty pockets, and those on the land, the majority, were reduced to subsistence farming. Bankers lacked incentive to invest in development, nor had they confidence that any man could repay a loan.

On the social front there was also significant change. The community continued divided on the question of hiding The Terrible Truths of their convict heritage, the subject having now emerged from behind closed doors into active campaigns.

The 'This Land Will Yet Forget' movement held that parents should indeed lie to their children about their heritage.

"It is essential that growing generations grow up without the stigma of convictism attached to them. If ignored, the stigma can only die."

In the Goodwin-Bunker family, matriarch Titia, again erect as ever, continued to stand steadfastly in favour of not denying her children's heritage, proudly supported by her children.

With the passage of time, however, the attention of grandchildren was focused less on being part of a community bred of oppression of a prior time, and more on matters of the present and future—so none could realise to what extent the controversy of the social change would engulf young Hannah, for instance, once married and raising her children.

Yet on the frontiers where news of happenings elsewhere seldom penetrated the barriers of illiteracy, families tended to carry on their lives, giving the matter little if any thought. In fact most failed to realise it was happening.

The Maggies, Liams, and their children carried on life without trying to draw lines between family members and neighbours, lines delineating who had scarred backs and who did not. On the Wattle Hill frontier, people also lived with not only isolated problems, but on Longbottom in particular, isolated grief...

~ * ~

"Them gums is pretty shaggy, Pa. Want me to lop 'em?"

Liam looked at Maggie.

She half smiled and shrugged her shoulders. Liam read the unspoken words with a smile.

Eighteen months after the fire, there was regrowth enough for concern should another fireball descend, and Ephraim was drawing it to Liam's attention. The entire family was conscious of the dangers because for days after the fire, Longbottom had been a desert of smoking ash, the heat continuing such they would never forget. The stench of burnt flesh and rotting carcasses filled their nostrils for so long they came to believe they would never lose it. Even Liam's beard had been so singed that he cropped it as close to the skin as pain permitted.

But that had been later, for there were urgent priorities.

The morning after the fire, even before sun-up, they had scuffed through still smouldering ashes, not counting losses, for that achieved nothing, but to find anything still useful.

The carcass of the dog was among the mountain of corpses wedged among rocks in the creek. Two kangaroos were but stinking, bloated hulks black with milling blowflies, that Liam and the boys had to dig away so the loathsome mess could float on down to snag in someone else's stretch of Iron Creek.

All that remained of Longbottom was the blackened house and sour memories. Of the barn, storehouse, cookhouse, and mother Mary's bathhouse, there were nowt but ashes and blackened ironware. No feed for the animals remained, nor hay and chaff reaped and stored so painstakingly to feed the flock through winter, no stores for themselves and no vittles even for the night's supper. The chook-house was gone, the aviary but a pile of charred corpses, and what had been rabbit hutches was a tangle of melted wire. No farm implement survived, no plough nor harrow, tools of any kind, no gear for the horse, and no dray or buggy.

"Not even a pail for milkin' the poor bloody cow, Ma."

Some memories were not only of what commercial assets were now no more than ashes blowing in the wind or scattered by disoriented sheep seeking roots to dig up, but for Liam there other heartaches. Each time rain had since fallen, a little of the hot grief was leeched from him, but much of the icy hatred lingered, even more than the hate he held for the fears put into his family. He had never been quite able to establish what the hate was directed at, for he had to accept that they had not fared as badly as some. At least the house was spared and some stock survived, and the land was still there to regenerate in time. But there had always been around Longbottom a lasting presence of his pa and ma, tools his pa made, outhouses he built, kitchen gardens sown by his ma, the bathhouse. All were unconscious symbols of his birthright, and such monuments were now gone, to leave his home less a part of his heritage, which left bitterness infinitely greater than material loss.

Yet he sighed, grudgingly pushing such conscious thoughts aside.

Me and Maggie have no option but to start building a new future on these ashes of the past.

And a week later, having begged and scrounged food and blankets and fodder for the flocks and railed against God for his retribution against those whose only sacrilege had been careless deference, Maggie delivered into their world of soot and ashes little William Woolley the Third. And a week after little William came the rain, not in gentle showers but day after day of drenching thunderstorms to help rinse Longbottom clean.

Now they were into spring, having stored in their minds the need to keep trees close to the house lopped and paddocks clear of bracken.

The ebullient Ephraim was entrusted to watch, think, and plan, lend his mind to dangers, notice what could prove dangerous in a fire. Tom and Harry were responsible for keeping water barrels topped up with creek water. MaryAnn and Jemmy were old enough to take some responsibility off their ma, who had her hands full tending little Will, who still toddled. The younger girls, Maggie insisted, at seven and five, should take on permanent tasks of housekeeping and laundering. Emma, at three, was relieved of duties 'until further notice' her ma and pa had informed with grins.

But fire did not come the summer just past, and the Woolleys carved several notches in the restoration programme before winter arrived. Yet they continued to struggle against financial loss. Without money or even collateral now on which to borrow, they couldn't feed the flocks. Liam and the boys shot most of the sheep before they starved, while there was yet mutton on the bones for neighbours to eat, those who bartered vegetables or eggs or dried fodder enough to feed the remaining sheep.

The hurt and hunger following the fire left every family in the district scarred in mind if not in body. All survived into winter, however, despite emerging leaner.

So with summer coming up, Ephraim was being mindful of his duties...

"Them gums is pretty shaggy, Pa. Want me to lop 'em? Best if I do 'em before spring growth makes 'em worse."

"Good thinking, lad," Liam responded after the smiles he and Maggie exchanged. "Take the hatchet to 'em. Not too much. We'll still need shade come summer."

But oh, impetuous youth! Spirit and verve bestow fourteen-year-olds fired with more ambition than care, little heed to common sense.

"What a devil-may-careless little sprite," Maggie later bewailed.

"What a mischance of bloody nature," Liam bemoaned.

Maggie had been in the new cookhouse kneading dough while the girls peeled vegetables. Liam, Tom, and Harry were trimming bark to roof the new barn when the snapping branch, followed by dreadful silence, alerted all.

In the tree the bloody boy hung, his lifeless body wedged in a broken fork.

Maggie watched, hands to her trembling mouth as Liam scrambled up there in a flash to quickly realise that any help he could give was too late.

Several thin branches were chopped close to the trunk, she noticed, deliberately chopped as if for impaling.

The boy had worked his way up, standing on the stumps of branches already cut, rather than begin at the top so spear-points were safe above him. And even as Liam eased the lad from where he'd been lanced between the shoulders, he knew. And it was a terrible journey down, knowing Maggie, now big with her eighth due within a month, would insist on inspecting the impossible wound, want to tend it, restore the boy who was already beyond anything they could do, except bury him.

Oh what a happy, wild one he has been, wild and innocent.

They marked out a plot beneath the offending gum and buried Ephraim in its remaining shade. His six brothers and sisters cuddled close, and his ma and pa shed quiet tears, wishing they could read something over him, the better chance of him knowing they would ever hold him in their hearts.

And with chills of winter finally waned, Maggie planted wildflowers on the mound.

Oh, what a wasted young life for a woman's first-born.

Liam took time off from roofing to build a picket fence to keep creatures from nibbling the blooms.

And when the spring arrived, when the cherry trees burst into bloom to swathe the hillside pink, Maggie strolled through her renewed orchard savouring the scent, smiling sadly as apple blossoms drifted like snowflakes to settle on her shoulders and in her hair.

Beyond the garden, gum trees sprouted fresh green, particularly 'Ephraim's tree.'

Oh, where did that fire go? Where the terrible scorched earth now? Except plastered in awful memory?

~ * ~

Once the date for Hannah's marriage was set, Mark suggested Sarah and Hannah go to Hobart for shopping.

"And you come too, Mark," Sarah prompted, "You have worked hard since laying off those hands. The break will do you good."

"Thank you for the thought, Sarah, and yes, I would enjoy a break, but I think the men are not yet ready to be left to their own resources."

Mark had not lain off four of his seven hands, but only one. The other three had been lost to the lure of better wages over the strait and had walked off the job. So in the reallocation of work tasks, he had not only to load extra on to his remaining three, paying them an increased salary, but some on to his own shoulders.

"Fortunately the dogs are by now proficient enough to more easily adapt to changed handlers, otherwise I would have to have taken on another man. So we are at least saved that cost, Sarah. And all in all, my dear, with having now quit three acres of wheat and leaving those fallow, to next season turn them over to grazing, we are in fact better off financially. I'm embarrassed to have to admit that until forced into the changes, I had not worked out the advantages of this system, myself."

"Well I'm sure you know best, Mark. Are you sure we can afford Hannah and me to go shopping?"

"Indeed we can, Sarah. So I will now write a note to sister Maria to let her know you are coming, eh?"

"Yes please, Mark. I will be anxious to see how Ma is keeping since last visit. And I know she will be happy to see Hannah after all these years."

~ * ~

"Hannah to be married?"

Titia, now returned to her domicile at The Red Lion, was surprised when daughter Maria read Mark's letter.

"How old would she be now?"

"When did they leave Rokeby, Ma? And how old was Hannah when they went?"

"Oh, dear. Time passes so quickly these days. It always does as you get older, as you will discover. I'm not sure. But if she is to be married, she is likely seventeen or eighteen."

Sarah and Hannah travelled by day because Mark believed the night coach too dangerous.

"Even then," Hannah explained to old Titia once arrived, "he admonished the drivers at length on their abysmal record, declaring he held them personally responsible for his wife's and daughter's well-being."

Titia laughed. "That sounds very much like your father, dear."

"You will come shopping with us? And come to Jerusalem for my wedding?"

"I am not up to gallivanting around shops, my dear. Nor to the coach journey all the way to Jerusalem and back."

But Maria took time off from her duties to escort them shopping, and Hannah would ever remember the thrills…

So many people and so many stores with wonderful fabrics and bonnets, ribbons, and gloves from haberdashers and milliners of London. But oh, the prices…

"Pa would never forgive the extravagance!"

"Make token selections," Sarah suggested. "Marriage is, after all, a once-in-a-lifetime experience."

At which they paused, but only for the moment before doubling in laughter. Only that morning, Hannah told her nana how her eldest Briscoe sister, MaryAnn, recently took her fourth husband.

But both had been delighted at finding old Titia a happier woman than when Sarah had last seen her. There was certainly less the tired look about her.

And when Titia asked after Hannah's intended husband, how she had met him, the expected questions a woman asks of her favourite grandchild, they told her of Mark's resolve, his choice for Hannah, how Hannah had come to accept her role, one she could not, with family harmony at stake, reject.

"And what of his background? Your William Lewis?"

"Henry, nana. His name is William Henry Lewis, and he is known as Henry. He says nowt of his background and family other than a brother. Whether bound by some commitment to Pa, or if through some personal opinion regarding convictism, he prefers not to discuss what he calls the colony's 'social argument.' He seems as reticent about discussing his origins as about the very subject of convictism. It seems he arrived here with the raindrops, blew in on a gale, or fluttered down in a snowstorm. It will come out one day, I expect."

"How can he really hope to hide it if it is there? I doubt he can."

"It's as if he's torn pages from his book of life and burned them. To all intents, the terrible truths of his heritage, if there be any, never happened."

"Huh. Come the day to answer the impertinent questions children ask, he must explain. Curious children don't settle for subtleties."

And come April, while old Titia could not make the arduous journey, she pictured in mind, her Hannah Bunker marrying her William Henry Lewis.

Twenty-two

"For he's a jolly good fellow..." all sang with gusto, big Fred on the fiddle.

Longbottom resounded to partying.

Harry Holding, although most from Maggie's first marriage considered themselves Woolleys despite there was never a call to declare one way or the other, was celebrating his twelfth birthday. It was a joint party, coinciding near enough with that of little Fred.

Rosy and her two Freds, neighbours a mile over the creek, had become close friends since the fire, both families having lost very near to their all. Rosy was local midwife, Maggie her most regular client. She was a massive woman, her neck lost in rings of fat rising from her shoulders that the happy face sat snug on her bulk without risk of tottering off no matter how much she shook in laughter as she habitually did.

"Good that Rosy lives close," Liam joked to Maggie as each birth neared.

"Yer have 'em regular, but easy," Rosy each time reminded Maggie, ever conscious that little Fred, her own firstborn, had torn her about so much at birth that she could never have another.

"Me first was also me last," she would joke to the mother at every delivery she made, yet Maggie was aware the bravado was more sop to her own disappointment than succour to the new mother. Rosy had delivered little Will following the fire, then Louisa, then more recently, young Alf.

After the fire, Maggie and Rosy had each leaned hard on the other's support, restoring what they could of respective comforts as they shared what remained of old. Many farm chores were beyond the ability of littlies to help, so neighbours lent extra hands all round. And moral support. So if there were perverse side benefits from the fire, their principal one became the cementing of this lasting friendship.

Both women had baked for days before the party, making cream-cakes, cocoa-biscuits, toffees and lemonade. And along with his fiddle, Fred fetched a flagon of his highly respected ale. He also brought, trotting behind their gig, the newest addition to the Woolley family. Old Irish had finally been laid to rest, having contributed mane and tail for mattress stuffing. A foal from Fred's stable was payment for Liam's handiwork in rebuilding Fred's barn. She had by now developed into a fine young filly that three-year-old little Will had immediately taken to calling Pip.

Harry's six brothers and sisters, apart from the new baby Alf, who took little interest in the festivities, and Rosy's little Fred, were due to have been joined by the George Woolley family. George and Harriet had what Liam described a "healthy bloody wagon-load" of six offspring, and when the families had last been together, it was arranged that George and Harriet would come for this party. But they hadn't arrived.

"Maybe the wagon lost a wheel. George never was one to keep his bloody gear in nick."

They waited until mid-afternoon, the children amusing themselves with noisy games, but began the party as the day lengthened.

And when the feasting and games were over, the dark of evening having deepened enough for stars to begin sprinkling the blackness with fairy lights, the women, after clearing up the massive piles of dishes and cook-pots, rested. The men were sprawled languid from the effects of big Fred's ale. A quiet descended.

Maggie whispered to Rosy and Fred that they should bunk in the barn.

"We won't shtay," lisped big Fred. "Gotta get away early tomorrer, off to Forcett. Gotta pick up me new harrow."

Man of the moment Harry complained of a sore throat and tummy.

"Too much lemonade and too much cake, m'lad." Maggie laughed, palm to his forehead that betrayed more than usual warmth. "Just take yourself to bed now. A good sleep will ward off any fever. Pa needs you bright and bubbly for the lambing tomorrow. If he's up to it."

They had a laugh at the sorry state of the menfolk as Rosy took the reins to steer across the stony ford Liam and Fred had built through the creek. And when the Woolleys retired, Maggie brought baby Alf into bed, for he was loudly letting her know his supper was overdue.

All then succumbed to the sleep of the exhausted.

When dawn broke, young Harry's fever had heightened. His throat stung, and an itchy rash had erupted on his neck. Harry seldom felt anything but hale, for he was robust, highly active, and independent.

"Nothing lays me low," he would boast, yet was now content to remain abed, happy for his ma to hover over him. And as the day progressed, excused from the lambing, his fever worsened and the rash spread red and pimply across his chest. Even Maggie's lemonade gave no relief to his sore throat, nor did her concoction of gripe water prove purge enough to help. The boy was seriously ill.

"Take Pip, Tom, get over to aunt Rosy and ask if she has laudanum."

And Tom returned with a bottle and a message.

"When Harry's had his dose, I'm to return it. Little Fred is sick too."

Laudanum wasn't a remedy to mend the sickness, Maggie knew, simply a sedative to ease the soreness. She would keep up gripe water as remedy.

Coming up evening, big Fred arrived with news from the village.

"Sit yer down, and I'll read what the weekly news says."

Liam's pa had had letters, and from time to time got hold of a newspaper to report on events in Hobart Town, but the boys never learned to read. Nor were the Newitts a literary family, so the present generation of Woolleys depended on others for news.

Big Fred read in halting stops and starts, stumbling over difficult words, Maggie and Liam becoming more worried by the minute. The article referred to sicknesses that some thought was caused by stale or fouled drinking water.

But Fred soon conceded that trying to make sense of the decorative language was too difficult, so resorted to simply telling them the gist of what he'd learned.

"A sickness called scarlet fever has hit Hobart, attacking mostly littlies," he told a frightened Maggie and Liam. "In Forcett they reckon this is what ails many local kids. Travellers brung it."

"Around Wattle Hill?"

"Kids from Prosser Plains to Port Arthur. It's cut a swathe through the district like a whetted knife."

Liam grabbed for Maggie, who near fell in a swoon.

"Three children died already," continued big Fred, oblivious to Liam's frantic signalling for him to stop.

"We don't need more such bloody news, Fred. Just tell us what to do."

"Move the sick separate. Nothin' can be shared. Clothin', beddin' and pannikins gotta be washed in carbolic else the sickness can pass to others."

He rose, folding the tract.

"Rosy is already in a state over little Fred."

He laid a parcel on the table.

"I'll leave this soap. It's carbolic I brung from the village. Good luck, mates. Now I gotta get back."

As he mounted, Maggie was already making up the solution.

"Like you when the fire was on us, Liam, already I got goin' through my head so many things we should do straight off. First off, get Pip into the yard so Harry can have the barn. It's already made up for Harriet's..."

She gasped.

"Oh, Liam, this why they didn't come? Could they have it?"

"Fred said all points south, and that includes Kellevie and Bream Creek."

"Brother Ephraim, too?"

"It's every Woolley and Newitt area."

He put an arm around her.

"We don't know if this is Harry's trouble, girl, maybe just belly-ache."

"His rash is worse, and his tongue's got white fuzz. He's got somethin'. We should move him separate."

Sleeping arrangements were two or three to a bed. An ill child would be taken to bed with Maggie and Liam, parental support invariably proving successful sop to infant sickness, yet last night it had done nowt for Harry. All beds were now stripped, blankets soaked in strong carbolic. Liam emptied all ticks so covers could be soaked. He carried Harry to a bed of hay in the barn while Maggie gathered the children's clothing, even what they wore, wrapping them in towels the while, to soak in carbolic. The little house quickly filled with the pungent odour. The washtub was filled with clean rainwater for each child to scrub his or herself with carbolic.

Farm work was forgotten, priority given to clutching at straws of hope.

"I'll tend Harry, Ma. You can't risk bein' near him, with Alf at breast."

He gazed at her sadness. Had she aged in the moment? He knew that inside she was churning, her every nerve taut as a bowstring, her mind frustrated at not knowing which way to aim.

"I can't not be with him, not if he's that sick?"

"Got to be strong, girl, for the safety of the others, especially the baby."

Liam rigged a bed for himself in the barn, neither too close nor too far from Harry. Neither slept. Harry's body burned, and Liam could do nowt to ease the boy's distress. He had never known such helplessness. It reminded him of sitting with his ma when waiting for her to die.

Yet this is but a child!

Nor did Maggie sleep. She left the baby in his cot, hopefully safer alone than exposed to contagion in her bed. She didn't quite understand how contagion worked, knew only that diseases somehow passed from one body to another simply by touching or being close, as if carried on the breath into the very air they all breathed. Her mind flashed back to when she was little, when cholera broke out on the ship. Nothing could be done for the sick then, but to isolate them best they could on a small ship She remembered now with added horror how when any of the convict women then took ill, hope for recovery was straightway abandoned; they were simply kept aside until all that was left was to slide them over the side with a prayer. She dreaded that this scarlet fever might be the same, realising only now how her ma must have then feared.

Right now, however, she could do only what Fred had told them.

Little Will and Louisa were but three and two, couldn't understand all the trauma but sensed the fear. She brought them into her bed and all night listened to breathing, trying to isolate the sounds of each child, waiting in fear of hearing a change, unable to count how often she crept from her bed to check each one, feel brows, measure breathing. And wonder how Harry was faring in the barn.

Is he maybe beginning to mend by now? Am I worrying unduly?

She went outside, calling softly to Liam.

"There's no change," he whispered through the barn wall, hating the lie, for the boy had a temperature that must soon have him bursting into flame.

"Go back to bed, girl, get some sleep."

She couldn't sleep. She woke the baby, lifting him from his cot, something she would never do in the normal course, to put him to her breast. She needed the comfort of his suckling. And come morning neither Maggie in her bed with the littlies nor Liam in his barn with the tortured boy had slept. For both, the night's fears had lasted a year.

Liam tried lifting Harry's head to pour cool water down his throat but the lad gagged. Liam could see how the rash had not only reddened but spread further about his body; the boy's frantic scratching had broken the skin in many places. He was greatly distressed, and Liam could do nowt but bathe him constantly, leaving him only for minutes to let out the cows.

Tom can feed them later. Maybe at fourteen Tom is old enough to be safe. Fred didn't say aught but that it attacks littlies.

He planned extra chores to keep the girls busy. He then checked on Maggie, who reported no change other than the children's sense of trauma. And fear.

"They seem to fear even the septic air," she said.

She had already organised the older girls to tend the chickens, birds and rabbits.

Come mid-day Tom reported a dust cloud on the road, and Liam walked out to turn away whoever was coming. It was no time for visitors.

It was George with his wagonload of his young Woolleys, waving hellos.

Liam grabbed the bridle, urging the horse to a halt.

"George, you're a bloody day late, but don't bring the kids close."

"Oh, Jesus, Liam. Not you, too?"

"We got the sickness. Young Harry's bad."

George slumped his shoulders, a tear straggling down his face.

"We buried our Will last night..."

Liam froze in shock.

"What, from the scarlet fever?"

"Yes, mate, and today young George is bad. I brung the others to leave with you."

"Leave the kids on the wagon, George, I'll fetch lemonade. You must take 'em back. But come in first, Maggie's worried about how you fared."

George climbed down, and the brothers embraced.

But Maggie already knew they were there because they could now see her watching, hand to mouth, wondering the course of their conversation.

"Oh, George," she lamented when told, "you poor dear—and darling Harriet. How long was he sick? What were the symptoms? What..."

Liam stayed her.

"We don't mean to seem selfish, George, but..."

Maggie burst into tears. "You must go, George. It's no safer here."

So George, distraught, watered his horse and turned for home.

And that night there was drama in the house and drama in the barn.

Maggie lay awake, feeling as one might expect of someone who hadn't slept in forty hours. With Harriet's little Will having died with the disease, the fears now took on a whole new, terribly realistic horror.

One of the girls, was that a gasp in her breathing? Or maybe she was just turning over?

Maggie listened. A little cough? Was it a groan? She leapt up, hurried to the bed. Little Emma was awake.

"My throat hurts, Ma."

Oh dear God!

She snatched up the child, fear washing over her in wave after turbulent wave.

Little Emma, Liam's first-born, but five years old—surely not.

She dare not take the child back to her bed where the two littlies lay, so pulled pillows to the floor and snuggled Emma to her bosom there, cooing and cuddling, blowing on the forehead to cool it.

Meanwhile in the barn, Liam's blood boiled in silent rage as Harry died.

Maggie, unknowing, far away in the house, lay worrying.

She put Emma aside with soothing words while she lit a candle behind a screen to shield its glow from other beds. She soaked a cloth and bathed Emma's forehead, dreading that they might have to move her to the barn. Tomorrow she would take baby Alf, with his cot, to the cookhouse, isolate him from all.

Surely a tiny baby must be the most vulnerable.

The nimbus of light from behind the screen wavered and flickered as the breeze toyed with the flame, casting ominous shadows. Yet it was enough she could see to bathe the little forehead again, whisper more encouragement.

"Oh, the senselessness of it all," she called aloud in desperation.

Ephraim in his tree—and now maybe Harry—and sweet Emma?

The shadows on the wall writhed in weird contortions, and she wondered should she look in them for omens. She had never had time for things occult yet now felt resolved to embrace anything to help her babies. And eventually, still awake and worrying, she became conscious of the outline of the window in the wall, a hint of daylight easing its way through night's blackness. But there was something else now, a sound, a strange sound intruding on the vagueness of her tired mind. She listened again; it was outside the house and it wasn't a regular sound, one she wouldn't have expected to hear, it was...

She bounded from the bed with a cry. What she could hear burst on her like a punctured wound. It was the sound of digging.

They buried Harry alongside his brother. Liam tore hoarding from the barn to make the coffin as he had done for Ephraim.

And for how many more, they wondered?

They grieved their Harry in silence, brothers and sisters holding breaths in fear they might be next. Liam burned Harry's bedding and made up fresh for Emma. Sweet Emma, his dearest baby, his firstborn, and "as lovely as a bubbling brook in sunlight" he had said to Maggie one time as they watched her in the paddock, humming to herself as she threaded bush daisies on a string.

He had just installed her in the deadly barn when a voice called.

A stoic Rosy stood outside with a bundle of fresh clouts for the baby.

"Make sure he's always in clean clouts, Maggie," she instructed with a hint of midwife authority. "Never rig him up in nowt but what's fresh cleaned. These I always keep handy for women in labour."

"You walk all the way over?"

Maggie tried to fathom what it was Rosy was taking care didn't show. Everything about the way she spoke suggested subterfuge.

"Yes, love. Walkin' is good for me."

"How's little Fred?"

Which shattered the pretence. Stoicism dissolved in the instant.

"We just buried 'im. These are his old clouts I brung for yer."

Maggie sat the sobbing Rosie on the bench by the cookhouse and pointed to the flowered new mound under Ephraim's tree.

"Harry?"

Maggie nodded, and they cried together.

Maggie called to MaryAnn. "Get me and Aunt Rosy a cuppa, darlin'?"

The child wiped back her own frightened tears and turned to the cookhouse, leaving the stricken mothers to console each other with silence.

Scarlet fever was no subtle plague, they'd discovered; it declared itself with savage brutality.

Rosy proved her friendship, the woman who had just buried her first, last, and only born. She declared herself a 'temporary Woolley' and moved in, that Maggie's workload of worry was less burdensome and so she could get some rest. Rosy sat with the disoriented children, each now afraid of every night noise, of dark, of candlelight, of being alone. Maggie came to Liam in the barn to watch over little Emma, who all too quickly took on the symptoms that Harry had them conscious of. And within days, little Will, three years old, was also brought to the barn, crying in his fear.

When the evening sun cast horizontal beams through cracks in the barn wall, Maggie looked longingly at Liam slumped into a corner as if cowering from even his own presence, sinking in the quicksands of a futile life. She wanted to do more to help him than she knew how. To see him like that made her ache. She loved him more every day now, this husband and father who suffered so, his exhaustion painful to see. His face even in eventual sleep showed nowt but sadness. Yet behind it she knew, surged the inner energy and determination that only a father with babes in danger can summon.

And when, later, it was his turn to study her, he anguished in similar sympathy for his woman. He sat stroking her brow until she dissolved in sleep. Yet he couldn't arrest her dreams, the nightmares that beset her in which, in the most recurring, she was trapped in raging white-water, tumbling over and over in a black abyss of helplessness, or was it a tunnel of hopelessness? She was in a torrent, hurtling through the dark of it, bobbing hither and thither like a cork sucked into a vortex, an ever-closing spiral. Childish hands reached out as she passed, fingers grasping. And there were rocks with clawing fingers, others with jagged teeth to snap at her to keep her from her bairns. She felt no conscious pain, yet blood spurted from holes in her chest and slashes the rocks made in her flailing arms as she tried desperately to grasp the fingers, save the children, or at least hold to something, anything to halt the charge that hurried her beyond their pleading cries. She knew she must forever flail and tumble in the torrent, leaving them helpless, failing her motherly duties for all eternity.

And when sweet, pleading little Emma died, Liam savagely ripped more hoarding from the barn walls, heedless anger surging inside. She too, they interred under Ephraim's tree, none able to read a parting message to give her comfort on her journey.

In her sadness Maggie swore that they must somehow find a way for at least the sons left them to learn to read so they need never suffer the pain of feeling that helpless.

But little Will cast off the fever. One time when they looked to see if a rash had developed, he gave them a smile, a tinge of roses touching the freckled cheeks. They hugged him and cried.

They then hugged Rosy, she who had helped when another might have hidden herself away in her own grief.

Fifteen children died in the Wattle Hill district that spring, and Maggie one day told Liam how back in England when she was little, the dawns were often so grey and dank, the days so wet and cold, the Newitt table so bare, that their bellies seemed forever hungry, and when neighbours were ever too miserable with their own sorry lots to care, that life was a misery that none of them as children looked forward to.

"Yet in this country," she had then added, "even when all about us erupts into heartbreak and horror, each day's dawn glows brightly, spring and summers are dependably warm, earth and neighbours each freely give physical and spiritual sustenance enough to compensate for the ravages."

"At least," she now said with a sigh, "even if the sadness is never quite forgot, it will slowly ease, mend like the most hurtful wound. And each tomorrow's brighter dawn will make living with the scars somehow sufferable."

Twenty-three

Eighteen months after her marriage, Hannah sat in a rocker cogitating on where life had brought her, her firstborn Edith Sarah bouncing on a knee.

Reasonable, I reckon.

She had, since the day of saying "I do" to Henry, searched for a word to sum up her level of satisfaction with life. And to sum up what she thought of Henry. And sum up what pleasures she could expect in future.

At their first meeting she had sat across the table from the man chosen as life's companion, to lead her along whatever path he chose, sire her children, guide their futures according to the inner forces that directed his ethics, morals, common sense, and worldliness. Henry Lewis did not impress as a model suitor nor even illustrate the values that had won her father's admiration. He was twenty years old, not tall, in fact stockily short; he was not bad looking when all said and done, features angular and pale, wide and rather frightened greenish eyes looking rather insipid against his pallor of freckled skin, hair thin and wispy, promising to recede early in life.

Passably handsome, a reasonable personality, one could likely sum up.

'Reasonable' also summed up his countenance, she then realised.

Yet it's far too generous in respect of his overall bearing, business acumen, and strength of character. And certainly charm as a lover.

Despite courtship and intimacy in arranged marriages tended to be strained, they had arrived at an understanding reasonable enough, with some resignation from either side. Hannah had listened when her ma advised how marriage for a woman, viewed in the light of common sense, meant more than the initial excitement that romance invited.

"Romance quickly dissolves once children arrive," Sarah had summed up. "Take my word for it."

So Hannah had sought and encouraged areas of compatibility, shared amusement at what Henry referred to as Mark's 'grandiose posturing.'

And it's fortunate his farm is not far from Mud Walls Road, for whilst we have the privacy to compose our lives, we are close enough that I don't feel distanced.

They farmed hops and maize and ran a few sheep—a physical atmosphere happily familiar for her—so the main thrust of readjustment was directed at finding her way with him. And abetted by her prosaic nature, she soon realised the marriage could provide opportunity to grasp a tangible purpose, become the foundation of a path in life.

Not the glowing path young girls dream about of course, but reasonable.

And Henry saw opportunity to begin life anew, she reckoned, maybe even found it a release from a self-effacing strain touching the heritage he remained so close about. And certainly her pa had been right declaring Henry was not a wealthy man, for he was far from it. He struggled. And to Hannah's mind he had not made such a fist of his career as had her father despite being more prepared to roll up shirtsleeves to attack dirty work.

Henry rather keeps rueing the dearth of the economy and his bad luck, eyeing with envy those free of family ties, able to rush across the strait to the Victorian goldfields where fortune waits.

Soon after their marriage, news had exploded throughout Van Diemen's Land of the massive gold strike in the fortunate new colony across the strait, of fabulous riches made by the few.

"He's off to Ballarat" was the cry of so many suffering in the depression, that the already burgeoning exodus from Van Diemen's Land became a stampede to fire Henry's hopes. But with his recent marriage and a baby quickly due, obligations kept him from joining his contemporaries.

"At least," he had admitted to Hannah, "with so many having left, your pa reckons the depression will lapse the quicker. Fewer unemployed means a greater share of what the colony has left for those who stay. So maybe next year will be better?"

~ * ~

"Musta been the fires in '50, Maggie."

Adam Newitt laughed as little Will dashed by, ginger hair streaming in the wind, face speckled in freckles as if shaken on from a pepper pot. Mud streaked his face, wiped from the backs of hands, eyes darting this way then that, a sign he was already planning his next heroic act.

"I always reckoned Ephraim was my wildest, Pa, but Will is a hell-raiser. Every time he moves, he raises dust."

"His wildness is like a bushfire, girl, charges at a gallop without aim. And with his grandma Woolley's hair, his face is also the colour of one."

"And more'n a touch of grandpa Newitt inside him, too, I reckon."

They sat in the arbour Liam had built under Ephraim's tree, where all could relax by the little mounds.

"So Ephraim and Harry and little Emma can still enjoy our company," Maggie had explained to the littlies.

"We were sure, Adam," said Liam, "that he was then on his way to join Harry and Emma, and he's not stopped still since. Ever on the bloody burst he is, as if makin' up for that lost time. Physique like a broom handle he's got so I don't know where he stores the bloody energy..."

William the Third was on his way to being six.

"...and in as tearin' a hurry to get there as he is to get where he's bound every time he bloody moves. As if he's goin' to run out of time before he gets there. Only plan he makes for his many schemes is to do them quick."

Even as they laughed, the lad was off again, dogs yapping after him.

"Full of the bloody mysteries of the spirit world he is, Pa, a phase I hope. Sam tells him stories about the convicts and blacks, stories to get him all fired up about pointing the bone, casting spells."

"How's the new man makin' out?"

"No complaints," Liam replied, "but a strange cuss, distant, little to say."

Liam had taken on a roustabout. Without the hands Ephraim and Harry had contributed, he now had only Tom to help. Old Sam Schofield was known as a good worker. He had chanced by one day looking for work.

"But his wife has a fear of plague, Pa, won't bring her children to live any place the plague has touched, so she lives in Sorell. Sam is there now, visits every Sunday."

Adam, also living in the town, knew her by sight.

"Frowsy woman, like a duck, I've ever thought, with her straggle of kids following behind as if on a string."

"He's strange, too, Pa," Maggie insisted, "strange stance, little body with shoulders hunched over. Good with kids, though. Sad, I reckon he is, away from his own family."

"The boy's never seen someone as expressionless, Adam. Told his ma Sam looks like the gargoyles on Sorell's courthouse. But he warmed to Sam when he found what a great teller of tales he is, tales of ghosts and goblins."

"And Abo spirits," Maggie added.

"No niggers left now, boy," Sam had told young Will. "All killed off back in your grandpa's day, they were—my pa's day, that was. I saw it. Young fella like you, I was then. But they had it comin', burnin' farms, spearin' sheep."

Sam's yarns on Aboriginal spirits were best though, little Will reckoned, because nigger spirits had magic powers to cast spells. The boy ever came away from Sam's stories full of the excitement such mystery could generate. He would look around corners as he readied for bed, wonder where the spirits of Longbottom's past Abos might lurk, then lie abed dreaming up the fantastic things he could do if he were an Abo spirit.

He followed Sam about whilst ever the hunger was being fed. And when he'd taken aboard more than he could store without releasing some of the bubble, he hovered around Liam like a bee around pollen. The thought of passing on his newfound knowledge to little Alf was time wasted; little Alf being but two was not up to marvelling at such meaty stuff. And the intricacies of the spirit world were far beyond the comprehension of sisters, and his ma's mind was ever on a thousand other things, which left only his pa with a worthy ear. He would tag after Liam, pitch in to help on chores he would otherwise avoid, so long as within earshot.

"Did you know, Pa, the Abos reckoned there are spirits in the trees, in rivers and mountains, and when the trees burn up in a bushfire, when the rivers turn to flood, it's the spirits takin' revenge? All bad things like fires and fevers happen to kin of poor bloody lags, because it was the bloody lags wot took to their kin back then. So we all gotta watch it, mind the spirits don't breathe on us like they did on Harry and Emma, like..."

"Whoa, boy, whoa. You're takin' off like in your chasin' games, no pausin' for breath. Or thought. If this is what old Sam is puttin' in your head, then I should have a word with Samuel bloody Schofield."

"It's true, Pa, when a willy-willy raises dust to choke Ma's chickens..."

"Hold it, boy, just hold it, you hear?"

Will clamped up. He sensed when his pa felt pushed into a corner.

"Got an imagination like I never realised, Ma," Liam said as they sat in the arbour once the children were abed.

"Then talk with Sam."

"The boy learnin' what really went on, don't reck me. It can only be good if he grows up knowin' how things really were. But Sam needs more care in the tellin', separate facts from what we can but reckon Abos had in their bloody heads."

"Rosy and Fred talk around that. Seems Fred's Pa was strong on putting the Abos down."

"I reckon it's the only thing my pa and ma ever argued on. He was all for kickin' them off the land to make it safe for me and George. Had some run-ins with 'em in the early days, it seems. But Ma always took their side."

"Well, I don't know. When we came, that war was over."

"Only wars now, girl, are fires and floods."

"And plagues."

~ * ~

A year later...

In the parlour of Hobart's *Birmingham Arms*, Sarah's sister Maria's third hotel, it having belonged to her husband when she married again, Mark sat over a tankard of ale. *The Guardian* lay open before him, and his concentration was divided between it and Titia and Sarah by the window, heads together, whispering.

What connivance is afoot there, I wonder?

Many years living in a household of daughters had taught him to always first assume a defensive role when women chose to closet themselves in confidential chitchat. Maria had, until a few minutes ago, been sitting with them, nattering away in sub-tones as women do, but had been called away. So maybe the two left were whispering now about Maria, or else any gossip women who could get together only occasionally seemed to find irresistible. Maybe it was innocent enough that his defensive guard could be relaxed?

Yet when one of the pair is my mother-in-law, it is not only possible, but in fact probable, that it could be me they are discussing; and that certainly would not be innocent. A man can never be sure when the hairs on the back of his neck start bristling.

"The newspaper has an interesting article on suppression, ladies. Would you like to hear it?"

They broke off whispering and turned, Titia looking a mite more tired than when he had last seen her.

But then she should expect to. She is no chicken, and her life's been hard. Yet she's still sharp of mind, enough to create unease in such a circumstance.

What he didn't realise was that right now she was acutely aware that he would not so deliberately have drawn their attention to something unless it be of unequivocal support for some theory he approved of.

"If it gives you pleasure, Mark, then by all means read it."

"It is a short poem, well constructed and speaks for many I am sure."

"I'm sure it speaks for you, Mark."

He read:

> *We are infants now no longer,*
> *Brighter prospects glimmer faint;*
> *'Tis not parental to inflict us,*
> *With the loathed fettered taint.*

"There now, do you not agree that it sums up the popular feeling?"

"Once troubles reach their worst, they start to mend, I believe, Mark. And many colony troubles are mending, I agree. And yes, my memory tells me fetters were always loathsome. Does yours?"

Mark Ashby Bunker couldn't help but smile inside. None of his children would dare be so bold, even Hannah. He couldn't help but admire the old lady's spirit. She was of the few yet alive of the first convicts, those of the First Fleet, trodden her tortuous path of life near ninety years, yet still strode it defiantly, seeming never to stumble on the rough bits, always able to glide over the roughage with an enviable air of confidence.

"Thank you for the reminder, Ma. You know I admit to a terrible memory on some things."

And the mischievous smile of one met the puckish gleam of the other.

"When you two are finished your sparring, I want Ma to finish what she was telling me, Mark. Seems our Lucy's been having a hard time of it."

Mark was stung.. He had ever been sensitive about Lucy departing in strained circumstances after marrying her convict. It had ever smacked of disappointment for him as a father, a hurtful hint of possible failure. And it was a penalty of illiteracy that in separation of kin, families often lost contact. His daughters had never had the benefit of tuition, and Lucy's lag certainly had none. So he and Sarah had heard little of Lucy since she left.

"What is it that you know, Ma? Is Lucy returned?"

"No, but she had someone write. A letter came here to the hotel, to Maria. Seems her man, the Daniel fellow, drowned somehow, leaving her with three littlies. And she has married again."

"Well I'm sorry the fellow drowned. And it is sad Lucy was left destitute with littlies..." Mark glanced at Sarah, who was already watching with a wry smile. All that so smacked of her particular history.

"We know the situation, don't we, Sarah? Did she send an address, Ma?"

"I should expect so."

"I shall ask Maria and write to Lucy. We can compose a letter, eh Sarah? Whoever wrote this can read it to her."

"Then while at it, Mark, could you please write a note to Hannah from me, to say how happy I am that she named her second little one after me? Giving it both her name and mine brings Hannah and me the closer."

Hannah had named her second daughter Hannah Letitia. And old Titia was particularly pleased that Hannah had already intimated that the child would always be called simply 'Titia.'

Mark and Sarah were taking a holiday unhindered by children. Bound in apron strings and housebound with parental obligations for years, they were now free, with last daughter Caroline recently married and off their hands, to take 'selfish' breaks as Mark termed them. Thirty-four years married and raising fourteen children, apart from little Benjie who drowned before Mark arrived on Sarah's scene, had kept them busy. Now life was simpler.

Yet Sarah missed home.

"Please do it soon, Mark, unless you have reason to stay. I want only to buy trinkets for the grandchildren."

Mark smiled, and old Titia looked surprised.

"Hotel life is fine for those more used to it than me," Sarah explained, "but despite it's my own sister's inn and we're treated as family, it's unsettling being tied to timetables. I miss my own routine."

Sarah also recognised that another benchmark was reached. Titia and Mark had this time got along admirably; not that either had changed, she reckoned, nor mellowed, rather that old Titia was astute enough to avoid letting his superior airs irk her. They coped whilst ever harmony reigned, and the time to part was never discussed. It invariably happened, however, neither earlier than any could wish, nor any later, for each had an uncanny knack of sensing when harmony had maybe run its course.

~ * ~

Pip strained and struggled until a lather of stress foamed around her mouth.

"All off except Ma. Tom, you take Pip to the top, easy now."

Liam, Maggie with her seven-month bulge, and the children were en-route to Sorell to see old Adam. Winter rains and snow had left the rutted road a slippery mire. Liam in gumboots and the kids happy in bare feet, as usual, jumped into the mud to plod their way. Old Adam now lived in The Gordon Highlander where he could enjoy daily ales with mates. Occasionally he would stay a few days with Harriet and George, or with sons still at Nun-Such, or at Longbottom.

Once arrived, no sooner were the children outdoors playing than Maggie and Liam noticed that young Will instead sat in conversation with his grandpa. The lad was thrashing arms about, talking twenty to the dozen.

Guessing the content of the story, they moved closer.

Adam was beginning to giggle, which wrinkled his face like a winter apple too long in the barrel.

"What you feed him on, girl? Got the bloody verbal shits he has."

"Liam had a word with Sam about filling the boy's head like this, Pa. We hoped maybe he was over it."

But the boy gave Adam no time to answer.

"It's the spirits, gramps, all Abo spirits can do mischief for the living, like it's brung bad luck on the Woolleys cos of wot happened way back..."

Liam shut him up. "You got it all mixed up, boy, that's not the way of it."

But the lad knew; sure as any precocious boy would vouch to.

"Then what caused the big fire when I was born, eh? Did Ma drop a lamp in the barn? Someone must've lit it, so if not you, it must've been the spirits. An' what snapped the branch under Ephraim? An' who gave the fever to Harry and Emma? An' Irish died because the spirits was unhappy with us, and I reckon Pip'll bring us bad luck, too…"

Liam shut him up with a clout.

"You, me and old Sam will have a good bloody talk on it when we get home. Now there'll not be another word on it until then. You hear good?"

The boy nodded in disappointment as Maggie led him out the door to join the other kids.

"Jesus, Adam, he gets so fired up. Be glad when he's grown I will, when he's got more sense than to pay heed to such rubbish. And he's leadin' baby Alf along the same bloody path."

Liam, now over the heat of it, afforded himself the luxury of a giggle.

"He's sowin' seeds of wildness already for baby Alf. Just the other day Maggie caught him leadin' Pip from the barn on a rope, and atop Pip, bareback and gripping the mane for all he's worth, is the bloody three-year-old. Christ knows how Will got him up there, but there's little Alf showin' nowt but dog-like devotion, blind utter faith in his scallywag brother."

Neither, of course, could envisage the dramatic future that was in store for both William Woolley the Third, and his now tiny brother Alf Woolley.

Twenty-four

Meanwhile, in Jerusalem...

"Changes take some keeping up with, Mark—end of convictism, change of colony name, business looking up. So much is happening all at once after years of things just getting worse."

Mark pulled on his greatcoat and wrapped his scarf tightly.

"If the government could effect one more change, of controlling the winter chills, Sarah, then the future would look perfect indeed."

She sat with her crochet.

"Please move that sconce a little closer, Mark, this is a difficult colour."

Then when he did, she stared at the flame, so steady it could have been a painting.

"Just look at the flame on this candle, Mark, straight as Ma's backbone."

He smiled. Being alone in the house was a situation they were getting used to after a lifetime of children. Both were nearing sixty and learning to live alone.

They had recently journeyed to Hobart for the jubilee celebrations, fifty years since the colony was founded, or 'foundered' as the jokesters told it. And it coincided with the cessation of convictism.

It had been a long time since Mark had permitted his memory to even think about his journey on *Lady Castlereagh*, yet now on such an occasion, he thought back to his assignment to Charles Cox and his life of subservience, to find, to his surprise, that with convictism now abandoned, his memory of it was on the path to oblivion; he could now happily look on his past, admit, at least to himself, that he did not fear the memory nor resent the stain as much.

He smiled at the realisation, felt it a sort of cleansing, a yoke lifted, a freeing of spirit.

Yes, this stigma can become banished from the minds of people over time. It can be expunged that they sense the same freedom.

It was a satisfying sensation indeed, even smug. The years of constant endeavour suppressing the taint at last seemed worthwhile.

My grandchildren will be the better for it, I am now doubly sure.

"And you know something else, my dear, something I believe is the most significant declaration of all on the end of transportation, of convictism?"

"What is that?"

"What I read to you in the newspaper last week, that despite hundreds of people have been hanged for various crimes during these fifty years, not even one native born Vandemonian has been capitally convicted. Every man and woman to mount the gallows came either as convict or as immigrant. Our children are guiltless of serious crime, Sarah, despite parents of most were felons. I find amazingly significant the fact that every convict parent, felon enough to be despatched in chains from his native land, has raised a moral generation in his name."

She smiled.

Was that a slight tightening of the waistline that I noticed, the chest expanding a fraction, the chin tilting even a little higher?

Mark looked to the grandfather clock and moved towards the door.

"I must be off. It will be an interesting meeting at the Bisdee house."

"This the meeting on the name change?"

"Yes. And the movement is spreading. A significant nail, it is, in the coffin of what the old Van Diemen's Land name conjures up in most minds. We expect that John Bisdee will by now have received confirmation on it."

And he departed.

~ * ~

Sarah smiled when he gently closed the door.

Tasmania. It is a nice name. But can it really help erase the convict stigma?

But she was happy that all the decisions concerning it were in the hands of others. She was no campaigner; she was simply happy to carry on her domestic life without becoming embroiled in controversial affairs.

And she didn't in the least mind being left alone on occasions. She had, in fact, come to enjoy such times after years of wondering where time for endless chores was to be found. And whilst Mark was considerably easier to live with now that the colony was going the way his mind had travelled over the years, it was pleasant to simply sit, let the mind waste time, enjoy the freedom that all the things coming about instilled in one.

So many things we have achieved in life, when one takes time to consider. And with people now saying the depression is easing, it is amazing how clear that becomes given time to ponder it. Yes! Already peddler carts are up and down the roads again with treats, from San Francisco many of them, with the American clipper service started, it being so much closer than England. Wonderful things now, like crackers and loaf-sugar and hams and cheeses, not to mention beautiful satins and silks.

And Mark had read to her not so long ago of learned men in Hobart making palates of artificial teeth for people left with too few of their own.

Marvellous things are happening all right.

She was gradually coming to see what Mark meant when he spoke of changing standards.

Yes, the children's world will certainly be different. And it continues to surprise me how, again now given the time to ponder it, I am still discovering previously unrecognised things about Mark.

One would think that after all these years there wouldn't be things I'd not noticed. Or had I always noticed such things without realising?

She laid down her needlework and pondered that factor more deeply. It came as quite a surprise to her that this might not be illustrating a new Mark but that there were some qualities of which she had never been conscious. Were they the same qualities and that she was now simply seeing in a different light?

There was a depth in him she had ever been conscious of yet one she tended to simply feel rather than understand. It had drawn her to him like a magnet, she now realised, yet in the opposite direction. She held a love for him, had always done. Not the romantic love one dreamed about in excited youth...

No, for let's face it, I was a woman of twenty-nine who had bred six children when I married Mark. No, it was not a love born of romance but undoubtedly of togetherness and respect, a sharing of the common goals.

She picked up her sewing to make a fresh start, only to put it down again...

And Hannah's Henry; what a conundrum that man is...

She had understood Mark's viewpoint at the time, yet was far, even now, from understanding who was the William Henry Lewis that Hannah married. He continued quite the enigma. If he were not the came-free man Mark considered him, having now talked with him on many occasions, even probed with due care, she was no closer to knowing the truth.

Nor is Hannah it seems.

And if in fact Mark had been misled at that time, she could now understand how. Even someone as astute as Mark, she believed, could come away from talking deeply with Henry on a matter, thoroughly convinced in respect of something you later felt you should have had doubts about.

...That time when I watched him through the window when he first called on Hannah...

She now smiled at the memory of peeping through the curtain with all the furtiveness of a town gossip.

...Henry sat so quietly in his saddle as if, having arrived, he had no intention of alighting. His quiet, his reticence, the way he simply sat there, was quite disconcerting. Even his horse seemed to hang its head as if contemplating the flies settling about its ears and eyes. And it was not until a swallow darted by Henry's face, unaware it intruded on his embarrassment or whatever was his reason for waiting, that Henry stirred himself. I would love to know what had been in his mind, on what relative to the purpose of his being here, he cogitated on so intently.

And his name—or more to the point, his name and his brother's name...

She had met Henry's brother at the wedding, a few years older, three years or four, maybe. Hannah's husband was baptised William Henry, and his brother was introduced as 'William Charles known as Charles.' Sarah had always been of the impression that giving brothers the same name was a Jewish custom, yet when posing that to Hannah, she had simply shrugged.

"Oh, I don't know, Ma," she had said, "but I doubt it. Henry gives every indication he is Christian Anglican. He was happy enough to wed in St. James and that Edie be baptised there. Question on the matter was never raised."

"But surely you have asked him?"

"No, Ma, nor will I. He has strong convictions respecting convictism, his own background included. He states simply that he believes anything past has no bearing on the present or the future in respect of personal standing, so there is no purpose in discussing the past. And I learned from my own father not to persist on such matters. When there is strong feeling one way or another it is best left fallow. And I have observed in you, Ma, that you think the same when it comes to your own husband."

Sarah had had to agree, so pressed Hannah no further.

Yet she continued intrigued that Hannah's friend Jane was convinced of Henry being the son of a convict assigned to her father years ago...

According to Jane, her father had recommended his once assigned and by then pardoned convict for a land grant at nearby Kempton, but could that be the same family that later, but before we came to Jerusalem, acquired the allotment adjoining the Bisdee property, the same now farmed by Hannah's Henry?

If so, it is certainly likely that Henry is that man's son.

If that theory is correct, then Henry is indeed the son of two convicts. Yet he convinced Mark that he and his brother arrived as free men.

It all is so confusing.

But then, Sarah postulated, did it really matter?

Epilogue

It was to matter indeed, as the ensuing years would illustrate...

Hannah Lewis on the one hand, witnesses her daughter Jane, ignorant of the stigma attached to her family, marry Alf Woolley.

Maggie Woolley on the other hand, witnessing the same marriage, wonders how her Alf will handle the situation, he professing so much ethnic pride in being of Australia's founding convicts.

All unfolds in the third of the trio on Old Titia's family.

In what had been the old tainted colony of Van Diemen's Land, yet with now its glisteningly pristine name of Tasmania, *The Terrible Truths* concludes the saga when the Bunker-Lewis line merges with the Woolley-Newitt line.

Grand matriarch Titia lives long enough to see both the end of convictism and her Van Diemen's Land change its name, to die only months after it, at ninety. She was not only one of the handful of souls to see the entire history of Australia's convictism from its first dark day to its enlightened last, but lived long enough to be the colony's last surviving First Fleeter!!!

Sarah and Mark each live to grand ages as do many of their children, well into the twentieth century...

MaryAnn Briscoe-Parott-Cockerell-Foy-Carroll-Tathill dies at Stanley in 1896, aged eighty-six, after bearing fourteen children to her five husbands.

Eliza Briscoe-Evans dies in 1908, aged ninety.

Margaret Bunker-Briggs dies at Jerusalem (now Colebrook) in 1890 aged sixty-seven, after having thirteen children.

Lucy Bunker-Molyneux-Stonehouse dies at Warrnambool, Victoria in 1912, aged eighty-three, after nine children (plus three step-children) to two husbands.

Hannah plays a significant role in *The Terrible Truths*, living through a baffling marital situation, also to the age of ninety, in 1922.

Sarah's only Bunker son, Edward, dies in Kangaroo Ground, Victoria, at age fifty-one.

Other than little Benjamin Briscoe who drowned in infancy, death dates of their other eight children are not known.

~ * ~

The Terrible Truths, final link in the family chain, takes readers through the agonising of families having to lie to their children that the real truths of their heritage can never be realised.

The Woolleys play a significant role in Tasmania's future, Alf and Jane not only bearing seventeen children but being significant players in Anchor Tin Mine becoming the biggest in the world. Hannah and her Charles Lewis feature significantly throughout the work (what happened to Henry Lewis may never be truly known, some say—but there are evocative theories!). Hannah ends her days in what was to become one of Tasmania's most elegant National Trust homes.

The Terrible Truths is a tale to clearly illustrate how over continuing generations, a family can indeed carve progressive niches along its journey from chains to riches, as they play significant roles in developing one of the world's most unique cultures.

Bibliography...

(coded with abbreviations)

AJCP: Australian Joint Copying Project
AONSW: Archives Office of NSW
AOT: Archives Office of Tasmania
COT: *Cyclopaedia of Tasmania Vol.1*
CRO: County Records Office (England)
CS: *The Convict Ships 1787-1868* Chas Bateson, Libr.Aust.Hist.1988
CU: *Convicts Unbound* Marjorie Tipping, Penguin 1988
EHS: *Early Hawkesbury Settlers* Bobbie Handy, Kangaroo Press 1985
EPH: *The English Prison Hulks* W.Branch Johnson, Christ.Johnson 1957
FG: *The Forgotten Generation of Norfolk Island and Van Diemen's Land* Reg Wright, Libr.Aust.Hist.1988
FOA: *Founders of Australia* Mollie Gillen, Libr.Aust.Hist.1989
FS: *The Fatal Shore* Robert Hughes, Collins Harvill 1988
HTG: *Hobart Town Gazette*
HOT: *History of Tasmania* Vol.1 John West A&R 1971
HRA: Historical Records of Australia Vol.1
IGI: International Genealogical Index
KAB: *Knopwood, A Biography* Geoffrey Stephens (self pub.) 1990
LOV: *Life in Old Van Diemen's Land* Joan Goodrick, Thos. Nelson 1977
NSADG: *Notorious Strumpets and Dangerous Girls, Convict Women in Van Diemen's Land 1803-1829* Phillip Tardif, A&R 1990
PEM: *Pemulwuy* Eric Willmot, Bantam 1991
PNI: *Profiles of Norfolk Islanders* Irene Schaffer & Thelma McKay Vol 2 self publ 1992
PRO: Public Records Office London

TCS: *Tasmania from Colony to Statehood* W.A.Townley, StDavids Park Publ. 1991

Note: BDM (birth, death & marriage) references for family members are not in the following lists. All those that survive can be found in state archives of NSW, Victoria, or Tasmania, some of them on-line.

References...

Chapter 1

1 - trials, **CU** - Woolley p325, Morris p296, Gibson p275

2 - conditions on Hulks, **EPH** — see index *Portland* Hulk, Portsmouth

Chapter 3

1 - why Port Phillip settlement, **CU** pp44-8

2 - HMS *Calcutta* had been the old *Warley Castle*, refitted as a man-o-war

3 - Hobart's instructions to King, **CU** p49

4 - 'Colony Wives' - Ann Innett and King, **WBB** p187, **FG** p10, Ann Yates (Yeates) and Collins, **CU** pp49, 122, 329

5 - agreed food rations, **CU** p54

6 - WmSteel, **CU** p313, WmAppleton p250

7 - WmBuckley, **CU** pp259-60

8 - David Gibson **CU** pp275-7

9 - Collins and Hannah Power, **CU** pp20, 57, 122, 137, 329

10 - Knopwood: **KAB** paints the Reverend's character, traits and history with the expedition. *To Plough Van Diemen's Land* keeps all refs and events true to that biography.

11 - 'amusing incidents,' **CU** Chap.10 "A Long Sea Voyage" pp53-62

12 - events at PortPhillip, **CU** (refer index). Of 308 convicts shipped, 8 die on voyage, 15 at Port Phillip, bolters fail to return, **CU** p331. Ninety-nine men left on the beach at Sorrento, p109

13 - *Calcutta* returns to war. Sunk by French in Bay of Biscay, **CU** ii, iii

14 - Today, the fifteen graves on the ridge beyond the beach are the only memorial of the Port Phillip settlement. The site regularly hosts re-enactments, staged by descendants of the HMS *Calcutta* shipment.

Chapters 4-5

1 - events at HobartTown, **CU** (refer index).

2 - baptisms, marriages, burials, **KAB** p49

3 - penalty for bolting, **CU** p134.

4 - most brutal flogging was to MnePts RobertAndrews and JamesRay, nine hundred lashes each. Collins report to King that two floggers used simultaneously, one right-handed, one left-handed. Both men collapsed before the floggings complete, recuperated and received the rest, **CU** p91

5 - Bligh and the settlers, **FG** p119-26

6 - VDL conditions and events in formative years, **CU** pp111-24, **FG** pp83-94

Chapter 6

1 - Goodwin family to Hobart, **FG** (refer index 'Goodwin')

2 - *...55 settlers, 11 delinquints (sic), 37 women and 78 children* **AONSW** 4/1168B p117

3 - BenBriscoe trial, **M'sex Qtr Sessions** 28th Apr 1802 trial #307

4 - BenBriscoe lashed, **CU** p258

5 - Five Derwent districts, **FG** pp107-14, 117-8

Chapter 7

1 - Woolley pardon, no record survives

2 - WmWoolley sheep from Geils, **CU** p325

3 - 'BrownBess' musket from War of Independence used by First Fleet marines and NSW Corps, derived its name from its forty-two-inch brown barrel, muzzle-loaded using powder horn and plunger. Flintlock fired with range of eighty yards.

4 - Briscoe pardon, no record survives

Chapter 8

1 - David Collins' funeral, **LOV** p26

Chapter 9

1 - Bushrangers in VDL, **LOV** p59-60

2 - *Calcutta* reunion, **CU** p183

3 - David Gibson story, **CU** pp275-7

4 - WmWoolley's outwork, **CU** p325

5 - Augustus Morris, **CU** pp190, 296, William Stocker pp313-4

6 - Guvn'r Davey's ineptitude, **LOV** p26-7

7 - Feb1812 Geils appointed acting Lt.Governor until arrival of Davey in Feb1813, **CU** pp128, 150, 171, **HOT**

Chapter 10

1 - Mark Bunker trial, Cal of Prisoners, Midsummer QtrSess'1817. Trial transcript publ. *The Huntingdon, Bedford and Cambridge Gazette* 2nd Aug 1817

2 - Mark Bunker to *Justitia* Hulk Woolwich 1st Sep1817, **CRO** Beds QGV 10/1.

3 - Mark Ashby Bunker - Bastardy Recognizance charge 17th Jan 1814 by Hannah Johnson, **CRO** Beds ref.QSR 1814/4. Eliz Burgess takes him to court 5thOct1816 on similar charge, **CRO** Beds ref.QSR 1816/157. He m. Eliz Burgess at St.Peter & St.Paul Cranfield Beds 21stOct1816, **IGI** Beds 1992. They had a son who was never baptised. A MarkAshby Bunker m. Mary Balls at neighbouring Wootton Beds 11thAug1844, **IGI** Beds

4 - *Lady Castlereagh*, **CS** pp69, 342, 356, 382

5 - Conditions on hulks, **EPH**pp5, "*...in two years 176 out of 632 died...*", **EPH** pp10-7

Chapter 11

1 - *Canada* Fourth journey, **CS** pp194, 340, 382

2 - *Elizabeth Henrietta,* **NSADG** #313 p244

3 - no record of Mary's assignment survives, nor pardon.

4 - No record of WmWoolley assignees survive.

5 - assignment system changed from time to time, **FS** pp282-322 - Mark Bunker assigned to Cox, **AOT** LSD 1/87 pp30-5

7 — Gov. Davey's ineptitude - Sorell replaces him and sets about restoring order, **LOV** pp26-7, 59-676

Chapter 12

1 - Temp. church of St.Davids had been situate in what has since become St.Davids Park. Rev.Knopwood held first service in the new church, later to become Cathedral 25thApril 1819, **KAB** p116

Chapter 13

1 - Mary and William m. St.Davids Hobart, **AOT** Hobart 1818 #221

2 - WmWoolley 30acresPitt Water, 6 in wheat, 1 in potatoes, 13 in pasture, 200 sheep, 1 wife, a child and 2 govt servants, **AOT** Oct1819 Land & Stock Muster

3 - ten bushrangers hanged, **KAB** p124

4 - Davie Gibson, **CU** pp275-7

5 - Augustus Morris dies, **CU** p296

6 - VDL sovereign colony 3rdDec1825 under GeoArthur, **KAB** p138

7 - Arthur martinet and tyrant, **FS** pp381-3

8 - war against aborigines, **FS** pp414-24 - war against bushrangers, **FS** pp233

Chapter 14

1 - Adam Newitt bap.13thAug1794, **CRO** Nthmtn T.RS/PCB-6/86

2 - Adam's trial - *The Northampton Mercury* Sat 3rd March 1827 reports Adam Newitt shoemaker committed for trial Northants Lent Assizes along with WmClarke 38 and ThosHall 70. Hall acquitted, Clarke sentenced three months in county gaol. AdamNewitt to be transported 14 years

3 - *Asia V* indent, **AOT** CON 22/2, CSO 217/5237 p249 ML4

4 - Adam's prison record, **AOT** CON 31/29 #152

5 - Arthur's grading of convicts, **FG** pp385-6

6 - Adam's application for family, **AOT** CON 280 reel 245 doc #363

7 - Sarah applies for reg'n of property in her own name, **AOT** LSD 1/1 p368

8 - *Hydery* arrives Hobart 10thAug1832, **AOT** CON 171. Shipping indent #174

9 - depression strikes colony, **HOT, LOV** p87

10 - JasGoodwin grant, **AOT** CSO 1/57 #1198.

11 - Sarah's additional grant, **LSD** 1/87 p30-5 NS282

Chapters 15-16

1 - Nun-Such from *The Kings and Queens of England* AlanPalmer, Mandarin Publ. HongKong p80 also from *London Through the Ages* Harold Bagust, Thornhill Press Cheltenham Glost. 1982

2 - Guvn'r Arthur's sacking, **LOV** pp30-2, **KAB** pp188-9

3 - demise of VDL aborigines, *Hobarton Mercury* in 1854 published: *To what melancholy state have the Aboriginal tribes of this island been reduced, may be imagined from the fact that out of the hundreds who, twenty years since, trod proudly their native soil, only five men, eleven women and two boys remain to lament their premature termination of their race. Notwithstanding the care and attention paid by the Government to this miserable remnant of a once dreaded race, their confinement to one locality, so adverse to their peculiarly erratic habits, has tended in a great measure to annihilate them. In a few short years the Aborigines of Van Diemen's Land will exist only in history.* On 8thMay 1876 Truganini, last surviving full-blood Tasmanian Aborigine died in Hobart, **LOV** p58

4 - MaryAnnBriscoe at 16, m. Wm J.Parrott 31stJan1825. Widowed, defacto m. with Wm Jas Cockerell (*Calcutta* at 8 yrs of age, free settler's child), has 8 children by him. Her next defacto m. Chas Froy. She m. Thos Carroll at Launceston 8thJun 1846. Widowed, she m. StanRobt Tathill 13th May1864

5 - Lydia Hines, **NSADG** pp488-90

Chapters 17-18

1 - depression strikes colony, **HOT**, **LOV** p87

2 - Adam's pardon, **AOT**.CON Records

3 - end of assignment 1843, **FS** p523

4 - Wm Buckley story, **CU** p92

5 - convict statistics, **AOT** Con.

6 - Mark Bunker pardon, **AOT** CON 31/1

Chapters 19-21

1 - bushfires burn southeast, **LOV** p184

2 - Who is WmLewis? Several records (**AOT** CON) of the nineteen WmLewis' in the district at the time have given researchers to date no clear lead as to which WmLewis Hannah married. Most likely options are a): two WmLewis' arrived Sydney aboard *Sarah* from Plymouth 10thDec 1849, one aged 23 the other 27 (**AONSW** shipping arrivals

reel #2). However, the record cites both literate whilst Hannah's WmL signed birth records of first three children with 'X'. Several WmL's travelled to VDL from both PtPhillip and Sydney about this time. b): Convict WmLewis arr. Hobart *Malabar* Oct 1821 and freed 1828. He m. Mary Thomas convict *Brothers* at GreenPonds (Jerusalem district) 1829 to have son Wm bn. 1830. This WmLewis convict was assigned to JnoBisdee. A map of land holdings 1842 shows land adjacent to the Bisdee property in name of W.Lewis.

3 - economy of VDL, including the apt quotation **LOV** pp88-9, 112

4 - PhoebeFennell-Newitt, bn PhoebeMakin, **PRO** Northants, LongBuckby Parish

5 - deaths but no burials are on record for the children interred under Ephraim's tree

Chapters 22-23-24

1 - Scarlet Fever in southeast, **LOV** pp129-30

2 - Mark's poem from the newspaper, **LOV** p205

3 - end of convictism VDL, **LOV** p19, 205-8

4 - Tasmania proclaimed 1856, **LOV** pp210, **HOT**

Meet *Kev Richardson*

Following a career in business management at international level, Kev attained a degree in journalism to then sweat as far up the River Nile as one can get, canoe down the Amazon, flash countless rolls of film from atop the Eiffel Tower, the heights above Yosemite, the Victoria Falls *et al*, scream *"Ole"* at a Chihuahua bullfight, ride elephant trails in Thai jungles, wallow in the incredible history of Rapa Nui's Maoi - and as convention almost demands, was mugged in Bogota. His articles on travel to exotic lands have featured in travel and airline magazines around the world.

Meanwhile, being a sixth generation descendant from Australia's First Fleet with an obsessive interest in his country's founding history, he was consequently disappointed at generations of suppression in the education of Australians at the lack of truth in what really happened. Years of fact-finding with the help of other dedicated researchers revealed all and Kev vowed to set the history books aright by bringing the unsavoury truths of convictism to light. He is well qualified to do so for as a student of First Fleet history he has presented his subject on many occasions in press, radio and television interviews. He is a Past President of 'The First Fleet Fellowship' and a Past Secretary of 'The

Descendants of Convicts Inc.'. During Australia's 1988 Bicentenary he officiated in Founding celebrations in Sydney, Melbourne, Hobart and Norfolk Island and for his work during that Bicentenary, was created Honorary Life Member of 'The Regiment of Redcoat Descendants'.

Kev now devotes his life to writing on not only his country's convict history, but general fiction with an Australian flavour. He recognises the growing trend towards digital reading so follows the world's top authors in publishing his works both as traditional paperbacks and eBooks.

His *Gurrewa* (two books in the series) and *Brogan* (4 books in the series to date), all released by *Wings-Press* (http://www.wingsepress. com/), are followed by *Letitia Munro, To Plough Van Diemen's Land* and *The Terrible Truths*, the latter three being more works on his country's convict beginnings. Synopses of all can be read on www.key-richardson.com. More works are in the pipeline.

These days Kev travels less, having retired from his home on Australia's Gold Coast, left his grown family and friends to write from experiences and adventures during his exciting travels, happily ensconced in the foothills of the Golden Triangle in amazing Thailand's exotic north.

Other Works From The Pen Of
Kev Richardson

Gurrewa - June 2006 – onvicts found a new nation (Finalist in the Independent eBook Awards 2002)

Brogan*- May 2007* - A tale of life on Australia's desert edge

Brogan's Bust - November 2007 - Brogan is embroiled in intrigue and adventure

Brogan's Bella - March 2008) - Isabella and Brogan are victims in a deadly hijack

Adam–Son of Gurrewa - July 2008) – A tale of discovery in New South Wales

Letitia Munro - October 2008 – A tale of Australia's first white settlement

The Terrible Truths - December 2008 – Changing social attitudes haunt the children of Australia' first convicts.

Brogan Abroad - June 2010 - Smuggling sex-flesh here...caught up in revolution there!

Letter to Our Readers

Enjoy this book?

You can make a difference.

As an independent publisher, Wings ePress, Inc. does not have the financial clout of the large New York publishers. We can't afford large magazine spreads or subway posters to tell people about our quality books.

But we do have something much more effective and powerful than ads. We have a large base of loyal readers.

Honest reviews help bring the attention of new readers to our books.

If you enjoyed this book, we would appreciate it if you would spend a few minutes posting a review on the site where you purchased this book or on the Wings ePress, Inc. webpages at:

https://wingsepress.com/

Thank You

Visit Our Website

For The Full Inventory
Of Quality Books:

Wings ePress.Inc
https://wingsepress.com/

Quality trade paperbacks and downloads
in multiple formats,
in genres ranging from light romantic comedy
to general fiction and horror.
Wings has something for every reader's taste.
Visit the website, then bookmark it.
We add new titles each month!

Wings ePress Inc.
3000 N. Rock Road
Newton, KS 67114